T0023950

PENGUIN BOOKS

DISSOLUTION

After a career as an attorney, C. J. Sansom now writes full time. *Dissolution,* which P. D. James picked as one of her five favorite mysteries in *The Wall Street Journal; Dark Fire,* winner of the CWA Ellis Peters Historical Dagger Award; *Sovereign;* and *Revelation,* a *USA Today* Best Book of the Year for 2009, are all available from Penguin. *Heartstone,* the fifth book in the Shardlake series, is now available from Viking. Sansom is also the author of the international bestseller *Winter in Madrid,* a novel set in the aftermath of the Spanish Civil War, also available from Penguin. A number one bestseller, his books have been sold in twenty-five countries. Sansom lives in Brighton, England.

C. J. SANSOM

Dissolution

§

PENGUIN BOOKS

PENGUIN BOOKS

Published by the Penguin Group

Penguin Group (USA) Inc., 375 Hudson Street, New York, New York 10014, U.S.A.

Penguin Group (Canada), 90 Eglinton Avenue East, Suite 700, Toronto, Ontario, Canada M4P 2Y3
(a division of Pearson Penguin Canada Inc.)

Penguin Books Ltd, 80 Strand, London WC2R 0RL, England

Penguin Ireland, 25 St Stephen's Green, Dublin 2, Ireland (a division of Penguin Books Ltd)

Penguin Group (Australia), 250 Camberwell Road, Camberwell, Victoria 3124, Australia
(a division of Pearson Australia Group Pty Ltd)

Penguin Books India Pvt Ltd, 11 Community Centre, Panchsheel Park, New Delhi – 110 017, India

Penguin Group (NZ), 67 Apollo Drive, Rosedale, North Shore 0632, New Zealand
(a division of Pearson New Zealand Ltd)

Penguin Books (South Africa) (Pty) Ltd, 24 Sturdee Avenue, Rosebank,
Johannesburg 2196, South Africa

Penguin Books Ltd, Registered Offices:
80 Strand, London WC2R 0RL, England

First published in the United States of America by Viking Penguin,
a member of Penguin Group (USA) Inc. 2003
Published in Penguin Books 2004

THE LIBRARY OF CONGRESS HAS CATALOGED THE HARDCOVER EDITION AS FOLLOWS:

Sansom, C. J.

Dissolution : a novel of Tudor England / C. J. Sansom.

p.   cm.

ISBN 0-670-03203-4 (hc.)

ISBN 978-0-14-200430-2 (pbk.)

1. Great Britain—History—Henry VIII, 1509-1547—Fiction.   2. Monasticism and religious orders—
Fiction.   3. Benedictine monasteries—Fiction.   4. Monks—Fiction.   I. Title.

PR6119.A57D57 2003

823'.92—dc21   2003050152

Printed in the United States of America
Set in Poliphilus MT

To the writers' group:
Jan, Luke, Mary, Mike B, Mike H, Roz, William
and especially Tony, our inspiration. The crucible.

And to Caroline

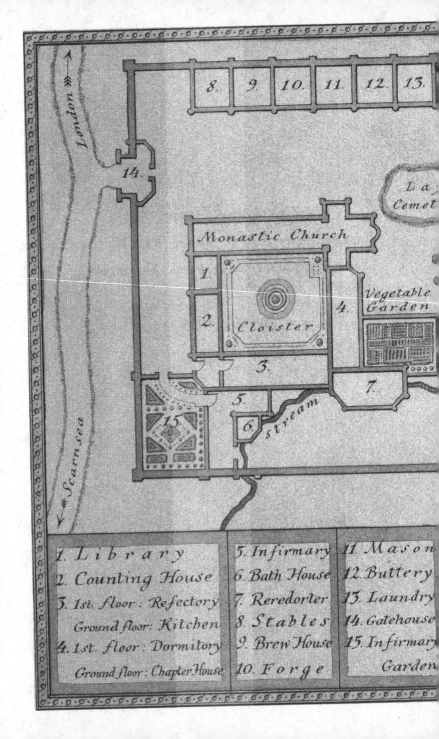

8. 9. 10. 11. 12. 13.

14.

London

Scarnsea

Monastic Church

La,
Cemet

1

2

Cloister

4

Vegetable
Garden

3

5

6

stream

7

15

1. Library
2. Counting House
3. 1st. floor: Refectory
   Ground floor: Kitchen
4. 1st. floor: Dormitory
   Ground floor: Chapter House

5. Infirmary
6. Bath House
7. Reredorter
8. Stables
9. Brew House
10. Forge

11. Mason
12. Buttery
13. Laundry
14. Gatehouse
15. Infirmary
    Garden

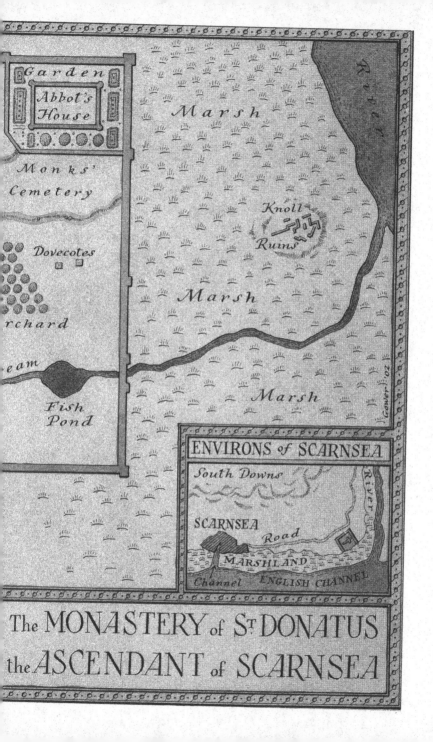

Garden

Abbot's
House

Monks'
Cemetery

Dovecotes

rchard

eam

Fish
Pond

Marsh

River

Marsh

Knoll
Ruins

Marsh

J. Gower 02

ENVIRONS of SCARNSEA

South Downs

SCARNSEA

Road

River

MARSHLAND

Channel

ENGLISH CHANNEL

The MONASTERY of St DONATUS
the ASCENDANT of SCARNSEA

Senior Obedentiaries (Officials) of
the Monastery of St Donatus the Ascendant
at Scarnsea, Sussex, 1537

ABBOT FABIAN
Abbot of the monastery, elected for life by the brethren.

BROTHER EDWIG
Bursar. Responsible for all aspects of monastery finance.

BROTHER GABRIEL
Sacrist and precentor; responsible for the maintenance and decoration of the monastic church, and for its music.

BROTHER GUY
Infirmarian. Responsible for the monks' health. Licensed to prescribe medicines.

BROTHER HUGH
Chamberlain. Responsible for household matters within the monastery.

BROTHER JUDE
Pittancer. Responsible for payment of monastery bills, wages to monks and servants, and distribution of the charitable doles.

BROTHER MORTIMUS
Prior, second in command to Abbot Fabian; responsible for the discipline and welfare of the monks. Also novice master.

Chapter One

I WAS DOWN IN SURREY, on business for Lord Cromwell's office, when the summons came. The lands of a dissolved monastery had been awarded to a Member of Parliament whose support he needed, and the title deeds to some woodlands had disappeared. Tracing them had not proved difficult and afterwards I had accepted the MP's invitation to stay a few days with his family. I had been enjoying the brief rest, watching the last of the leaves fall, before returning to London and my practice. Sir Stephen had a fine new brick house of pleasing proportions and I had offered to draw it for him; but I had only made a couple of preliminary sketches when the rider arrived.

The young man had ridden through the night from Whitehall and arrived at dawn. I recognized him as one of Lord Cromwell's private messengers and broke the chief minister's seal on the letter with foreboding. It was from Secretary Grey and said Lord Cromwell required to see me, immediately, at Westminster.

Once the prospect of meeting my patron and talking with him, seeing him at the seat of power he now occupied, would have thrilled me, but this last year I had started to become weary; weary of politics and the law, men's trickery and the endless tangle of their ways. And it distressed me that Lord Cromwell's name, even more than that of the king, now evoked fear everywhere. It was said in London that the beggar gangs would melt away at the very word of his approach. This was not the world we young reformers had sought to create when we sat talking at those endless dinners in each other's houses. We had once believed with Erasmus that faith and charity would be enough to settle religious differences between men; but by that early winter of 1537 it had come to rebellion, an ever-increasing number of executions and greedy scrabblings for the lands of the monks.

There had been little rain that autumn and the roads were still good, so that although my disability means I cannot ride fast it was only mid-afternoon when I reached Southwark. My good old horse, Chancery, was unsettled by the noise and smells after a month in the country and so was I. As I approached London Bridge I averted my eyes from the arch, where the heads of those executed for treason stood on their long poles, the gulls circling and pecking. I have ever been of a fastidious disposition and do not enjoy even the bear baiting.

The great bridge was thronged with people as usual; many of the merchant classes were in mourning black for Queen Jane, who had died of childbed fever two weeks before. Tradesfolk cried their wares from the shops on the ground floors of the buildings, built so closely upon it they looked as though they might topple into the river at any moment. On the upper storeys women were hauling in their washing, for clouds were now darkening the sky from the west. Gossiping and calling to each other, they put me in mind, in my melancholy humour, of crows cawing in a great tree.

I sighed, reminding myself I had duties to perform. It was largely due to Lord Cromwell's patronage that at thirty-five I had a thriving legal practice and a fine new house. And work for him was work for Reform, worthy in the eyes of God; so then I still believed. And this must be important, for normally work from him came through Grey; I had not seen the chief secretary and vicar general, as he now was, for two years. I shook the reins and steered Chancery through the throng of travellers and traders, cutpurses and would-be courtiers, into the great stew of London.

✝

As I PASSED DOWN Ludgate Hill, I noticed a stall brimming with apples and pears and, feeling hungry, dismounted to buy some. As I stood feeding an apple to Chancery, I noticed down a side street a crowd of perhaps thirty standing outside a tavern, murmuring excitedly.

I wondered whether this was another apprentice moonstruck from a half-understood reading of the new translation of the Bible and turned prophet. If so, he had better beware the constable.

There were one or two better-dressed people on the fringe of the crowd and I recognized William Pepper, a Court of Augmentations lawyer, standing with a young man wearing a gaudy slashed doublet. Curious, I led Chancery down the cobbles towards them, avoiding the piss-filled sewer channel. Pepper turned as I reached him.

'Why, Shardlake! I have missed the sight of you scuttling about the courts this term. Where have you been?' He turned to his companion. 'Allow me to introduce Jonathan Mintling, newly qualified from the Inns and yet another happy recruit to Augmentations. Jonathan, I present Master Matthew Shardlake, the sharpest hunchback in the courts of England.'

I bowed to the young man, ignoring Pepper's ill-mannered reference to my condition. I had bested him at the bar not long before and lawyers' tongues are ever ready to seek revenge.

'What is passing here?' I asked.

Pepper laughed. 'There is a woman within, said to have a bird from the Indies that can converse as freely as an Englishman. She is going to bring it out.'

The street sloped downwards to the tavern so that despite my lack of inches I had a good enough view. A fat old woman in a greasy dress appeared in the doorway, holding an iron pole set on three legs. Balanced on a crosspiece was the strangest bird I had ever seen. Larger than the biggest crow, it had a short beak ending in a fearsome hook, and red and gold plumage so bright that against the dirty grey of the street it almost dazzled the eye. The crowd moved closer.

'Keep back,' the old woman called in shrill tones. 'I have brought Tabitha out, but she will not speak if you jostle round her.'

'Let's hear it talk!' someone called out.

'I want paying for my trouble!' the beldame shouted boldly. 'If you all throw a farthing at her feet, Tabitha will speak!'

'I wonder what trickery this is,' Pepper scoffed, but joined others in hurling coins at the foot of the pole. The old woman scooped them up from the mud, then turned to the bird. 'Tabitha,' she called out, 'say, "God save King Harry! A Mass for poor Queen Jane!"'

The creature seemed to ignore her, shifting on its scaly feet and eyeing the crowd with a glassy stare. Then suddenly it called out, in a voice very like the woman's own, 'God save King Harry! Mass for Queen Jane!' Those at the front took an involuntary step back, and there was a flurry of arms as people crossed themselves. Pepper whistled.

'What do you say to that, Shardlake?'

'I don't know. Trickery somewhere.'

'Again,' one of the bolder spirits called out. 'More!'

'Tabitha! Say, "Death to the pope! Death to the Bishop of Rome!"'

'Death to the pope! Bishop of Rome! God save King Harry!' The creature spread its wings, causing people to gasp with alarm. I saw that they had been cut cruelly short halfway down their length; it would never fly again. The bird buried its hooked beak in its breast and began preening itself.

'Come to the steps of St Paul's tomorrow,' the crone shouted, 'and hear more! Tell everyone you know that Tabitha, the talking bird from the Indies, will be there at twelve. Brought from Peru-land, where hundreds of these birds sit conversing in a great nest city in the trees!' And with that, pausing only to scoop up a couple of coins she had missed earlier, the old woman picked up the perch and disappeared inside, the bird fluttering its broken wings wildly to keep its balance.

The crowd dispersed, muttering excitedly. I led Chancery back up the lane, Pepper and his friend by my side.

Pepper's usual arrogance was humbled. 'I have heard of many wonders from this Peru the Spaniards have conquered. I have always thought you cannot believe half the fables that come from the Indies – but that – by Our Lady!'

'It is a trick,' I said. 'Did you not see the bird's eyes? There was no intelligence in them. And the way it stopped talking to preen itself.'

'But it spoke, sir,' Mintling said. 'We heard it.'

'One can speak without understanding. What if the bird just responds to the crone's words by repeating them, as a dog comes to its master's call? I have heard of jays doing such things.'

We had reached the top of the lane and paused. Pepper grinned.

'Well, 'tis true that the people in church respond to the priests' Latin mummings without understanding them.'

I shrugged. Such sentiments about the Latin Mass were not yet orthodox, and I was not going to be drawn into religious debate.

I bowed. 'Well, I fear I must leave you. I have an appointment with Lord Cromwell at Westminster.'

The boy looked impressed, and Pepper tried not to, as I mounted Chancery and headed back into the crowd, smiling wryly. Lawyers are the greatest gossips God ever placed in the world, and it would do business no harm to have Pepper mentioning it about the courts that I had had a personal audience with the chief secretary. But my pleasure did not last, for as I passed down Fleet Street fat drops began to splash in the dusty road, and by the time I passed under Temple Bar a heavy rain was falling, driven into my face by a sharp wind. I turned up the hood of my coat and held it tightly as I rode into the storm.

✠

BY THE TIME I reached Westminster Palace the rain had become torrential, gusting against me in sheets. The few horsemen who passed were, like me, hunched inside their coats, and we exclaimed to each other at the drenching we were getting.

The king had abandoned Westminster for his great new palace at Whitehall some years before, and nowadays Westminster was used mainly to house the courts. Pepper's Court of Augmentations was a new addition, set up to deal with the assets of the small religious houses dissolved the year before. Lord Cromwell and his burgeoning retinue of officials had their offices there too, so it was a crowded place.

Usually the courtyard was thronged with black-clad lawyers debating over parchments and state officials arguing or plotting in quiet corners. But today the rain had driven all indoors and it was almost empty. Only a few bedraggled, poorly dressed men stood huddled, soaked, in the doorway of Augmentations: ex-monks from the dissolved houses, come to plead for the lay parishes the Act had promised them. The official on duty must be away somewhere — perhaps it was Master Mintling. One proud-faced old man was still dressed in the habit of a Cistercian, rain dripping from his cowl. Wearing that apparel around Lord Cromwell's offices would do him little good.

Ex-monks usually had a hangdog air, but this group were looking with horrified expressions over to where some carriers were unloading two large wagons and stacking the contents against the walls, cursing at the water dripping into their eyes and mouths. At first glance I thought they were bringing wood for the officials' fires, but when I brought Chancery to a halt I saw they were unloading glass-fronted caskets, wooden and plaster statues, and great wooden crosses, richly carved and decorated. These must be the relics and images from the dissolved monasteries, whose worship all of us who believed in Reform sought to end. Brought from their places of honour and piled up in the rain, they were at last stripped of power. I suppressed a stab of pity and nodded grimly at the little group of monks before steering Chancery through the inner arch.

✝

IN THE STABLES I dried myself as best I could on a towel the ostler gave me, then entered the palace. I showed Lord Cromwell's letter to a guard, who led me from the public area into the labyrinth of inner corridors, his brightly polished pike held aloft.

He took me through a large door where two more guards stood, and I found myself in a long, narrow hall, brightly lit with candles.

Once it had been a banqueting hall, but now it was filled from end to end with rows of desks at which black-clad clerks sat sifting mountains of correspondence. A senior clerk, a short plump man with fingers black from years of ink, bustled across to me.

'Master Shardlake? You are early.' I wondered how he knew me and then realized he would have been told to expect a hunchback.

'The weather was kind – until just now.' I looked down at my soaked hose.

'The vicar general told me to bring you in as soon as you arrived.'

He led me on down the hall, past the rustling clerks, the wind created by our passage making their candles flicker. I realized just how extensive was the web of control that my master had created. The church commissioners and the local magistracy, each with their own network of informers, were under orders to report all rumours of discontent or treason; each was investigated with the full rigour of the law, its penalties harsher every year. There had already been one rebellion against the religious changes; another might topple the realm.

The clerk halted before a large door at the end of the hall. He bade me stop, then knocked and entered, bowing low.

'Master Shardlake, my lord.'

✝

IN CONTRAST to the antechamber, Lord Cromwell's room was gloomy, only one small sconce of candles by the desk lit against the dark afternoon. While most men in high office would have had their walls adorned with the richest tapestries, his were lined from floor to ceiling with cupboards divided into hundreds of drawers. Tables and chests stood everywhere, covered with reports and lists. A great log fire roared in a wide grate.

At first I could not see him. Then I made out his stocky form, standing by a table at the far end of the room. He was holding up a casket and studying the contents with a contemptuous frown, his wide, narrow-lipped mouth downturned above his lantern chin. His jaw held thus made me think of a great trap that at any moment might open and swallow one whole with a casual gulp. He glanced round at me and, with one of those mercurial changes of expression that came so easily to him, smiled affably and raised a hand in welcome. I bowed as low as I could, wincing, for I was stiff after my long ride.

'Matthew, come over here.' The deep, harsh voice was welcoming. 'You did well at Croydon; I am glad that Black Grange tangle is resolved.'

'Thank you, my lord.' As I approached, I noticed the shirt beneath his fur-trimmed robe was black. He caught my glance.

'You've heard the queen is dead?'

'Yes, my lord. I am sorry.' I knew that after Anne Boleyn's execution Lord Cromwell had hitched his fortunes to those of Jane Seymour's family.

He grunted. 'The king is distracted.'

I looked down at the table. To my surprise it was piled high with caskets of various sizes. All seemed to be of gold and silver; many were studded with jewels. Through ancient spotted glass I could see pieces of cloth and bone lying on velvet cushions. I looked at the casket he still held, and saw it contained a child's skull. He held it up in both hands and shook it, so that some teeth that had come loose rattled inside. The vicar general smiled grimly.

'These will interest you. Relics brought specially to my attention.' He set the casket on the table and pointed to a Latin inscription on the front. 'Look at that.'

'*Barbara sanctissima*,' I read. I peered at the skull. A few hairs still clung to the pate.

'The skull of St Barbara,' Cromwell said, slapping the casket with his palm. 'A young virgin murdered by her pagan father in Roman times. From the Cluniac Priory of Leeds. A most holy relic.' He bent and picked up a silver casket set with what looked like opals. 'And here – the skull of St Barbara, from Boxgrove nunnery in Lancashire.' He gave a harsh laugh. 'They say there are two-headed dragons in the Indies. Well, we have two-headed saints.'

'By Jesu.' I peered in at the skulls. 'I wonder who they were?'

He gave another bark of laughter and clapped me soundly on the arm. 'Ha, that's my Matthew, always after an answer for everything. It's that probing wit I need now. My Augmentations man in York says the gold casket is of Roman design. But it will be melted down in the Tower furnace like all the others and the skulls will go to the dunghill. Men should not worship bones.'

'So many of them.' I looked through the window, where the rain still beat down in torrents, sweeping the courtyard as the men continued unloading. Lord Cromwell crossed the room and stood looking out. I reflected that though he was now a peer, entitled to wear scarlet, he still dressed in the same style as I, the black gown and flat black cap of legal and clerical officials. The cap was silk velvet, though; the gown lined with beaver. I noticed his long brown hair had become flecked with grey.

'I must have those things taken in,' he said. 'I need them dry. Next time I burn a papist traitor, I want to use some of that wood.' He turned and smiled grimly at me. 'Then people will see that using the heretic's own images as fuel does not make him scream any the less, let alone make God strike out the fire.' His expression changed again, became sombre. 'Now come, sit down. We have business.' He sat behind his desk, motioning me brusquely to a chair facing him. I winced at a spasm from my back.

'You seem tired, Matthew.' He studied me with his large brown eyes. Like his face, their expression constantly changed and now they were cold.

'A little. It was a long ride.' I glanced over his desk. It was covered in papers, some with the royal seal glinting in the candlelight. A couple of small gold caskets appeared to be in use as paperweights.

'You did well to find the deeds to that woodland,' he said. 'Without them the matter could have dragged on in Chancery for years.'

'The monastery's ex-bursar had them. He took them when the house was dissolved. Apparently the local villagers wanted to claim the woods as common lands. Sir Richard suspected a local rival, but I started with the bursar as he would last have had the deeds.'

'Good. That was logical.'

'I tracked him to the village church where he had been made rector. He admitted it soon enough and gave them up.'

'The villagers paid the ex-monk, no doubt. Did you have him in charge of the justice?'

'He took no payment. I think he only wanted to help the villagers, their land is poor. I thought it better to make no stir.'

Lord Cromwell's face hardened and he leaned back in his chair. 'He had committed a criminal act, Matthew. You should have had him in charge, as an example to others. I hope you are not becoming soft. In these times I need hard men in my service, Matthew, hard men.' His face was suddenly full of the anger I had seen in him even when we first met ten years before. 'This is not Thomas More's Utopia, a nation of innocent savages waiting only for God's word to complete their happiness. This is a violent realm, stewed in the corruption of a decadent church.'

'I know.'

'The papists will use every means to prevent us from building the Christian commonwealth, and so by God's blood I will use every means to overcome them.'

'I am sorry if my judgement erred.'

'Some say you *are* soft, Matthew,' he said quietly. 'Lacking in fire and godly zeal, even perhaps in loyalty.'

Lord Cromwell had the trick of staring fixedly at you, unblinking, until you felt compelled to drop your gaze. You would look up again to find those hard brown eyes still boring into you. I felt my heart pound. I had tried to keep my doubts, my weariness, to myself; surely I had told nobody.

'My lord, I am as against papacy as I have always been.' As I said the words I could not help thinking of all those who must have made that answer before him, under interrogation about their loyalties. A stab of fear lanced through me, and I took deep breaths to calm myself, hoping he would not notice. After a moment he nodded slowly.

'I have a task for you, one suited to your talents. The future of Reform may depend on it.'

He leaned forward and picked up a little casket, holding it up. Within, at the centre of an intricately carved silver column, lay a glass phial containing a red powder.

'This,' he said quietly, 'is the blood of St Pantaleon, skinned alive by pagans. From Devon. On his saint's day, it was said, the blood liquefied. Hundreds came every year to watch the miracle, crawling on their hands and knees and paying for the privilege. But look.' He turned the casket round. 'See that little hole in the back? There was another hole in the wall where this was set, and a monk with a pipette would push little drops of coloured water inside the phial. And lo – the holy blood, or rather burnt umber, liquefies.'

I leaned forward, tracing the hole with my finger. 'I have heard of such deceits.'

'That is what monasticism is. Deceit, idolatry, greed, and secret loyalty to the bishop of Rome.' He turned the relic over in his hands, tiny red flakes trickling down. 'The monasteries are a canker in the heart of the realm and I will have it ripped out.'

'A start has been made. The smaller houses are down.'

'That barely scratched the surface. But they brought in some money, enough to whet the king's appetite to take the large ones where the real wealth is. Two hundred of them, owning a sixth of the country's wealth.'

'Is it truly as much as that?'

He nodded. 'Oh yes. But after the rebellion last winter, with twenty thousand rebels camped on the Don demanding their monasteries back, I have to proceed carefully. The king won't have any more forced surrenders, and he's right. What I need, Matthew, are *voluntary* surrenders.'

'But surely they'd never——'

He smiled wryly. 'There's more than one way to kill a pig. Now listen carefully, this information is secret.' He leaned forward, speaking quietly and intently.

'When I had the monasteries inspected two years ago, I made sure everything that might damage them was carefully recorded.' He nodded at the drawers lining the walls. 'It's all in there; sodomy, fornication, treasonable preaching. Assets secretly sold away. And I have more and more informers in the monasteries too.' He smiled grimly. 'I could have had a dozen abbots executed at Tyburn, but I have bided my time, kept up the pressure, issued strict new injunctions they have to follow. I have them terrified of me.' He smiled again, then suddenly tossed the relic in the air, catching it and setting it down among his papers.

'I have persuaded the king to let me pick a dozen houses on which I can bring particular pressures to bear. In the last two weeks I have sent out picked men, to offer the abbots the alternatives of voluntary surrender, with pensions for all and fat ones for the abbots, or prosecution. Lewes, with its treasonable preaching; Titchfield, where the prior has sent some choice information about his brethren; Peterborough. Once I've pressed a few into voluntary surrender, the others will realize the game is up and go quietly. I've been following the negotiations closely and everything was going well. Until yesterday.' He picked up a letter from his desk. 'Have you ever heard of the monastery of Scarnsea?'

'No, my lord.'

'No reason you should have. It's a Benedictine house, in an old silted-up Channel port on the Kent–Sussex border. There's a history of vice there and according to the local Justice of the Peace, who is one of us, the abbot is selling land off cheap. I sent Robin Singleton down there last week to see what he could stir up.'

'I know Singleton,' I said. 'I've been against him in the courts. A forceful man.' I hesitated. 'Not the best lawyer, perhaps.'

'No, it was his forcefulness I wanted. There was little concrete evidence, and I wanted to see what he could browbeat out of them. I gave him a canon lawyer to assist him, an old Cambridge reformer called Lawrence Goodhaps.' He fished among his papers, and passed a letter across to me. 'This arrived from Goodhaps yesterday morning.'

The letter was scrawled in a crabbed hand, on a sheet of paper torn from a ledger.

My Lord,

I write in haste and send this letter by a boy of the town as I dare trust none in this place. My master Singleton is foully murdered in the heart of the monastery, in a most terrible manner. He was found this morning in the kitchen, in a lake of blood, his head cut clean off. Some great enemy of Your Lordship must have done this, but all here deny it. The church has been desecrated and the Great Relic of the Penitent Thief with its bloody nails is vanished away. I have told Justice Copynger and we have adjured the abbot to keep silence. We fear the consequences if this be noised abroad.

Please send help my lord and tell me what I should do.

Lawrence Goodhaps

'A commissioner murdered?'

'So it appears. The old man seems to be in terror.'

'But if it was a monk, that would only ensure ruin for the monastery.'

Cromwell nodded. 'I know. It's some maniac, some cloistered madman who hates us more than he fears us. But can you see the implications? I seek the surrender of these monasteries as a precedent. English laws and English ways are based on precedent.'

'And this is a precedent of another sort.'

'Precisely. The king's authority struck down — literally. Old Goodhaps did the right thing to order this kept quiet. If the story got abroad, think of the notions it would give to fanatics and lunatics in every religious house in the land.'

'Does the king know?'

He stared hard at me again. 'If I tell him, there will be an explosion. He would probably send soldiers in and hang the abbot from his steeple. And that would be the end of my strategy. I need this resolved quickly and secretly.'

I could see where this was heading. I shifted in my seat, for my back pained me.

'I want you down there, Matthew, at once. I am granting you full powers as commissioner under my authority as vicar general. Power to give any order, obtain any access.'

'Would not this be a task better suited to an experienced commissioner, my lord? I have never had official dealings with the monks.'

'You were educated by them. You know their ways. My commissioners are formidable men, but they're not known for finesse and this needs delicate handling. You can trust Justice Copynger. I've never met him but we've corresponded, he is a strong reformer. But no one else in the town is to know. Fortunately Singleton had no family, so we won't be pestered by relatives.'

I took a deep breath. 'What do we know of this monastery?'

He opened a large book. I recognized a copy of the *Comperta*, the report of the monastic visitations two years before, whose riper parts had been read to Parliament.

'It is a large Norman foundation, well endowed with lands and fine buildings. There are only thirty monks and no less than sixty servants – they do themselves well, typical Benedictines. According to the visitor the church is scandalously over-decorated, full of plaster saints, and they have – or had – what is alleged to be a relic of the Penitent Thief crucified with Our Lord. A hand nailed to a piece of wood – part of his cross, they say. Apparently people would come long distances; it was supposed to cure cripples.' He glanced involuntarily at my twisted back, as people do when cripples are mentioned.

'Presumably the relic Goodhaps referred to.'

'Yes. My visitors found a nest of sodomites at Scarnsea, as happens often enough in those filthy dog-holes. The old prior, who was the chief offender, was removed. Sodomy is punishable by death under the new Act, it's a good pressure point. I wanted Singleton to see how things stood in that regard as well as investigating the land sales Copynger wrote to me about.'

I thought a moment. 'Wheels within wheels. Complicated.'

Lord Cromwell nodded. 'It is. That's why I need a clever man. I have had your commission sent to your house, with the relevant parts of the *Comperta*. I want you to set off first thing tomorrow. That letter is three days old already and it may take you another three to travel down there. The Weald can be a quagmire this time of year.'

'It has been a dry autumn till today. It might be done in two.'

'Good. Take no servants; tell no one except Mark Poer. He still shares your house?'

'Yes. He has been looking after my affairs in my absence.'

'I want him to accompany you. He has a sharp brain, I'm told, and it may be good to have a pair of strong arms at your side.'

'But, my lord, there may be danger. And, to be frank, Mark has no great religious zeal – he will not understand all that is at stake.'

'He does not need to. So long as he is loyal and does what you tell him. And it may help young Master Poer work his passage back to employment in the courts, after that scandal.'

'Mark was a fool. He should have known someone of his rank must not become involved with a knight's daughter.' I sighed. 'But he is young.'

Lord Cromwell grunted. 'If the king had learned what he did, he'd have had him whipped. And it showed a poor gratitude towards you, for finding him work.'

'It was a family obligation, my lord; an important one.'

'If he acquits himself well on this mission I may ask Rich to allow him back to his clerk's post – the one I found him at your request,' he added pointedly.

'Thank you, my lord.'

'Now I have to go to Hampton Court; I must try to persuade the king to attend to business. Matthew, make sure no word gets out, censor letters from the monastery.'

He rose and, coming round the desk, put his arm round my shoulder as I got to my feet. It was a recognized sign of favour.

'Find the culprit quickly, but above all quietly.' He smiled, then reached over and handed me a tiny golden box. Inside was another phial, a tiny circular one containing a gobbet of thick pale liquid that slopped against the glass. 'What do you think of this, by the way? You might be able to work out how it's done. I can't.'

'What is it?'

'It's stood in Bilston Nunnery four hundred years. Said to be the milk of the Virgin Mary.'

I exclaimed with disgust. Cromwell laughed.

'What amazes me is how they imagined anyone would *get* milk from the Virgin Mary. But look, it must have been replaced recently to stay liquid like that; I was expecting to see a hole in the back like that other, but it seems quite sealed in. What do you think? See, use this.' He passed me a jeweller's glass and I examined the box, peering for a tiny hole, but I could see nothing. I pushed and prodded for a secret hinge, then shook my head.

'I can't fathom it. It appears completely sealed.'

'Pity. I wanted to show it to the king, it would amuse him.' He walked me to the door and opened it, his arm still round me so that the clerks should see I was favoured. But as I left the chamber my eye fell again on the two grinning skulls, the candlelight playing about their ancient eye sockets. My master's arm still round me as it was, I had to suppress a shiver.

Chapter Two

MERCIFULLY THE RAIN had stopped when I left Westminster. I rode home slowly as dusk fell. Lord Cromwell's words had frightened me. I realized I had grown used to being in favour; the thought of being cast out chilled me, but more than that I was frightened by his questions about my loyalty. I must take care what I said around the courts.

Earlier that year I had bought a spacious new house in Chancery Lane, the broad avenue bearing the name of His Majesty's court and of my horse. It was a fine stone property with fully glassed windows, and had cost a great deal. Joan Woode, my housekeeper, opened the door. A kindly, bustling widow, she had been with me some years and greeted me warmly. She liked to mother me, which I did not find unwelcome even if sometimes she exceeded her place.

I was hungry, and though it was early I told her to prepare supper, before going through to the parlour. I was proud of the room, whose panelling I had had painted with a classical woodland scene at some expense. Logs burned in the fireplace and beside it, on a stool, sat Mark. He made a strange sight. He had taken off his shirt, baring a white muscular chest, and was sewing buttons of agate embossed with an elaborate design onto the neck. A dozen needles, each trailing a length of white thread, were stuck into his codpiece, one of the exaggerated ones then in fashion. I had to check myself from laughing.

He smiled his habitual broad grin, showing good teeth a little too large for his mouth.

'Sir. I heard you arrive. A messenger from Lord Cromwell brought a package and said you were back. Forgive me not rising, but I would hate one of these needles to slip.' Despite his grin, his eyes were guarded; if I had seen Cromwell, his disgrace was likely to have been mentioned.

I grunted. I noticed his brown hair was cut short; King Henry, following the close cutting of his own hair to hide his growing baldness, had ordered all at court to wear cropped hair and it had become the fashion. The new style became Mark well enough, though I had decided to keep mine long as it better suited my angular cast of features.

'Could Joan not do your sewing?'

'She was busy preparing for your arrival.'

I picked up a volume from the table. 'You have been reading my Machiavelli, I see.'

'You said I might, for a pastime.'

I dropped into my cushioned armchair with a sigh. 'And how do you like him?'

'Not well. He counsels his prince to practise cruelty and deception.'

'He believes these things are necessary to rule well, and that the calls to virtue of the classical writers ignore life's realities. "If a ruler who wants to act honourably is surrounded by unscrupulous men his downfall is inevitable."'

He bit off a piece of thread. 'It is a bitter saying.'

'Machiavelli was a bitter man. He wrote his book after being tortured by the Medici prince to whom it was addressed. You had better not tell people you have read it if you go back to Westminster. It is not approved of there.'

He looked up at the hint. 'I may go back? Has Lord Cromwell—'

'Perhaps. We will talk more at dinner. I am tired and would rest a little.' I heaved myself out of the chair and went out. It would do Mark no harm to stew a little.

JOAN HAD BEEN BUSY; there was a good fire in my room and my feather bed had been made up. A candle had been lit and set on the desk beside my most prized possession, a copy of the newly licensed English Bible. It soothed me to see it there, lit up, the focus of the room, drawing the eye. I opened it and ran my fingers across the Gothic print, whose glossy surface shone in the candlelight. Next to it lay a large packet of papers. I took my dagger and cut the seal, the hard wax cracking into red shards and falling onto the desk. Inside was a letter of commission in Cromwell's own vigorous hand, a bound volume of the *Comperta* and documents relating to the Scarnsea visitation.

I stood a moment, looking through the diamond-paned window into my garden with its walled lawn, peaceful in the gloom. I wanted to be here, in the warmth and comfort of home, as winter came on. I sighed and lay down on the bed, feeling my tired back muscles twitch as they slowly relaxed. I had another long ride tomorrow, and those were becoming more difficult and painful every year.

☩

MY DISABILITY had come upon me when I was three; I began to stoop forward and to the right, and no brace could correct it. By the age of five I was a true hunchback, as I have remained to this day. I was always jealous of the boys and girls around the farm, who ran and played, while I could manage nothing more than a crab-like scuttle they mocked me for. Sometimes I would cry out to God at the injustice of it.

My father farmed a good acreage of sheep and arable land near Lichfield. It was a great sorrow to him that I could never work the farm, for I was his only surviving child. I felt it all the more because he never reproached me for my infirmity; he simply said quietly one day that when he grew too old to work the farm himself he would appoint a steward, who perhaps could work for me when he was gone.

I was sixteen when the steward arrived. I remember biting back a flood of resentment when William Poer appeared in the house one summer's day, a big, dark-haired man with a ruddy open face and strong hands which enveloped mine in a horny grip. I was introduced to his wife, a pale pretty creature, and to Mark, then a sturdy, tousle-headed toddler who clung to her skirts and stared at me with a dirty thumb in his mouth.

By then it had already been decided that I was to go to London to study at the Inns of Court. It was the coming thing, if one wished financial independence for a son and he had a modicum of brains, to send him to law. My father said that not only was there money to be made, but legal skills would one day help me in supervising the steward's running of the farm. He thought I would return to Lichfield, but I never did.

I arrived in London in 1518, the year after Martin Luther posted his challenge to the pope on the door of Wittenberg Castle church. I remember how hard it was at first to get used to the noise, the crowds – above all, the constant stench – of the capital. But in my classes and lodgings I soon found good company. Those were already days of controversy, the common lawyers arguing against the spreading use of the Church courts. I sided with those who said the king's courts were being robbed of their prerogative – for if men dispute the meaning of a contract, or slander each other, what business is that of an archdeacon? This was no mere cynical desire for business; the Church had become like a great octopus, spreading its tentacles into every area of the nation's life, all for profit and without authority in Scripture. I read Erasmus, and began to see my callow thraldom to the Church of my youth in a new light. I had reasons of my own to be bitter against the monks especially, and now I saw that they were good ones.

I completed my schools and began to make contacts and find business. I discovered an unexpected gift for disputation in court, which stood me in good stead with the more honest judges. And in the late 1520s, just as the king's problems with the papacy over the annulment of his marriage to Catherine of Aragon began to make a public stir, I was introduced to Thomas Cromwell, a fellow lawyer then rising high in the service of Cardinal Wolsey.

I met him through an informal debating society of reformers, which used to meet in a London inn – secretly, for many of the books we read were forbidden. He began to put some work from departments of state my way. And so I was set on my future path, riding behind Cromwell as he rose to supplant Wolsey and became the king's secretary, commissioner general, vicar general, all the time keeping the full extent of his religious radicalism from his sovereign.

He began to seek my assistance with legal matters affecting those who enjoyed his patronage – for he was building a great network – and I became established as one of 'Cromwell's men'. So when, four years ago, my father wrote to ask if I could find William Poer's son a post in one of the expanding departments of state my master controlled, it was something I was able to do.

Mark timed his arrival for April 1533, to see the coronation of Queen Anne Boleyn. He much enjoyed that great celebration for the woman we were later taught to believe was a witch and fornicator. He was sixteen then, the same age I was when I had come south; not tall but broadly built, with wide blue eyes in a smooth angelic face that reminded me of his mother's, although there was a watchful intelligence in his pale blue eyes that was his distinctively.

I confess when he first arrived in my house I wanted him out of it again as soon as possible. I had no wish to act *in loco parentis* for this boy, who I had no doubt would soon be slamming doors and sending papers to the floor, and whose face and form stirred all the feelings of regret I associated with home. I had imaginings of my poor father wishing Mark were his son instead of me.

But somehow my wish to be rid of him eased. He was not the country boor I had expected; on the contrary he had a quiet, respectful demeanour and the rudiments of good manners. When he made some mistake of dress or table etiquette, as he did in the early days, he showed a self-mocking humour. He was reported as conscientious in the junior clerking posts I obtained for him, first at the Exchequer and then at Augmentations. I let him come and go as he pleased and if he visited the taverns and bawd houses with his fellow clerks he was never noisy or drunken at home.

Despite myself I grew fond of him, and took to using his agile mind as a sounding board for some of the more puzzling points of law or fact I dealt with. If he had a fault it was laziness, but a few sharp words could usually rouse him. I went from resenting that my father might have wished him for a son to wishing he might have been my own. I was not sure now that I would ever have a son, for poor Kate had died in the plague of 1534. I still wore a death's head mourning ring for her, presumptuously, for had she lived Kate would certainly have married another.

✝

AN HOUR LATER Joan called me down to supper. There was a fine capon on the table, with carrots and turnips. Mark was sitting quietly at his place, in his shirt again and a jerkin of fine brown wool. I noticed the jerkin was adorned with more of the agate buttons. I said grace and cut a limb from the chicken.

'Well,' I began, 'it seems Lord Cromwell may have you back at Augmentations. First he wants you to aid me with a task he has set me, and then we shall see.'

Six months before Mark had had a dalliance with a lady-in-waiting to Queen Jane. The girl was only sixteen, too young and silly to be at court but pushed there by ambitious relatives. In the end she brought them disgrace, for she took to wandering all over the precincts of Whitehall and Westminster until she found herself in Westminster Hall, among the clerks and lawyers. There the little wanton met Mark, and ended by rutting with him in an empty office. Afterwards she repented and blurted everything out to the other ladies, from where in due course the story reached the chamberlain. The girl was packed off home and Mark found himself turned out of a hot sheet into hot water, interrogated by high officials of the royal household; he had been astonished and frightened. Though angry with him, I sympathized with his fear as well; he was very young after all. I had petitioned Lord Cromwell to intervene, knowing he had an indulgent approach towards that type of misdemeanour at least.

'Thank you, sir,' he said. 'I am truly sorry for what happened.'

'You are lucky. People of our station don't often get a second chance. Not after something like that.'

'I know. But — she was bold, sir.' He smiled weakly. 'I am but flesh.'

'She was a mere silly girl. You could have got her with child.'

'If that had happened I would have married her if our degree had permitted. I am not without honour, sir.'

I put a piece of chicken in my mouth and waved my knife at him. This was an old argument. 'No, but you are a light-brained fool. The difference in degree is everything. Come, Mark, you have been in government service four years. You know how things work. We are commoners and must keep our place. People of low birth like Cromwell and Rich have risen high in the king's service, but only because he chooses to have them there. He could remove them in a moment. If the chamberlain had told the king instead of Lord Cromwell you could have found yourself in the Tower, after a whipping that would have scarred you for life. I feared that might happen, you know.' Indeed the affair had given me several sleepless nights, though I never told him that.

He looked cast down. I washed my hands in the fingerbowl.

'Well, this time it may blow over,' I said more gently. 'What of business? Have you prepared the deeds for the Fetter Lane conveyance?'

'Yes, sir.'

'I will look at them after dinner. I have other papers to study as well.' I put down my napkin and looked at him seriously. 'Tomorrow we have to go down to the south coast.'

I explained our mission, though saying nothing of its political importance. Mark's eyes widened as I told him of the murder; already the thoughtless excitement of youth was returning.

'This could be dangerous,' I warned him. 'We have no idea what is happening down there; we must be prepared for anything.'

'You seem worried, sir.'

'It's a heavy responsibility. And, frankly, just now I would rather stay here than travel down to Sussex. It is desolate down there beyond the Weald.' I sighed. 'But like Isaiah we must go down and fight for Zion.'

'If you succeed Lord Cromwell will reward you well.'

'Yes. And it would keep me in favour.'

He looked up in surprise at my words, and I decided it would be wise to change the subject. 'You have never been to a monastery, have you?'

'No.'

'You went to the grammar school, you didn't have the doubtful privilege of the cathedral school. The monks scarcely knew enough Latin to follow the ancient tomes they taught from. It's as well for me I had some native wit, or I would be as illiterate as Joan.'

'Are the monasteries truly as corrupt as it is said?' Mark asked.

'You've seen the Black Book, the extracts from the visitations, which is being hawked around.'

'So has most of London.'

'Yes, people love tales of naughty monks.' I broke off as Joan came in with a custard.

'But yes, they are corrupt,' I continued once she had gone. 'The rule of St Benedict – which I have read – prescribes a life devoted to prayer and work, separate from the world and with only the barest essentials of life. Yet mostly these monks live in great buildings attended by servants, living off fat revenues from their lands, scabbed with every sort of vice.'

'They say the Carthusian monks lived austerely and sang joyful hymns when they were taken to be disembowelled at Tyburn.'

'Oh, a few orders live straitly. But don't forget the Carthusians died because they refused to recognize the king as head of the Church.

They all want the pope back. And now it seems one of them has turned to murder.' I sighed. 'I am sorry you must be involved in this.'

'Men of honour should not be afraid of danger.'

'One should always be afraid of danger. Are you still attending those swordsmanship classes?'

'Yes. Master Green says I progress very well.'

'Good. There are sturdy beggars everywhere on the quieter roads.'

He was silent a moment, looking at me thoughtfully. 'Sir, I am grateful I may get my post back at Augmentations, but I wish it were not such a sewer. Half the lands go to Richard Rich and his cronies.'

'You exaggerate. It is a new institution; you must expect those in charge to benefit those who have given them loyalty. It is how good lordship works. Mark, you dream of ideal worlds. And you should be careful what you say. Have you been reading More's *Utopia* again? Cromwell quoted that at me today.'

'*Utopia* gives you hope for man's condition. The Italian makes you despair.'

I pointed at his jerkin. 'Well, if you want to be like the Utopians, you should exchange those fine clothes for a plain shift of sackcloth. What is the design on those buttons, by the way?'

He removed his jerkin and passed it across. Each button had a tiny engraving of a man with a sword, his arm round a woman, a stag beside them. It was finely done.

'I picked them up cheaply in St Martin's market. The agate is fake.'

'So I see. But what does it signify? Oh, I know, fidelity, because of the stag.' I passed the jerkin back. 'This fashion for symbolic designs that people have to puzzle out, it tires me. There are enough real mysteries in the world.'

'But you paint, sir.'

'If ever I find time I do. But I try in my poor way to show people directly and clearly, like Master Holbein. Art should resolve the mysteries of our being, not occlude them further.'

'Did you not wear such conceits in your youth?'

'There was not such a fashion for it. Once or twice perhaps.' A phrase from the Bible came to me. I quoted it a little sadly. '"When I was a child, I thought as a child: but when I became a man I put aside childish things." Well, I must go up, I have much reading to do.' I rose stiffly and he came round to help me up.

'I can manage,' I said irritably, wincing as a spasm of pain went through my back. 'Wake me at first light. Get Joan to have a good breakfast ready.'

I took a candle and mounted the stairs. Puzzles more complex than designs on buttons lay ahead, and any help that study of the honest English printed word could give, I needed.

Chapter Three

WE LEFT AT DAYBREAK the following morning; the second of November, All Souls' Day. After an evening's reading I had slept well and felt in a better mood; I began to feel a sense of excitement. Once I had been a pupil of the monks; then I had become the enemy of all they stood for. Now I was in a position to delve into the heart of their mysteries and corruption.

I chivvied and cajoled a sleepy Mark through his breakfast and out into the open air. Overnight the weather had changed; a dry, bitterly cold wind from the east had set in, freezing the muddy ruts in the road. It brought tears to our eyes as we set out, swathed in our warmest furs, thick gloves on our hands and the hoods of our riding coats drawn tight round our faces. From my belt hung my dagger, usually worn only for ornamentation but sharpened this morning on the kitchen whetstone. Mark wore his sword, a two-foot blade of London steel with a razor's edge bought with his own savings for his swordsmanship classes.

He made a cradle of his hands to help me mount Chancery, for I find it hard to swing myself into the saddle. He mounted Redshanks, his sturdy roan, and we set off, the horses laden with heavy panniers containing clothes and my papers. Mark still looked half-asleep. He pushed back his hood and scratched at his unkempt hair, wincing at the wind that ruffled it.

'By God's son, it's cold.'

'You've had too much soft living in warm offices,' I said. 'Your blood needs thickening.'

'Do you think it will snow, sir?'

'I hope not. Snow could hold us up for days.'

We rode through a London that was just awakening and onto London Bridge. Glancing downriver past the fierce bulk of the Tower, I saw a great ocean-going carrack moored by the Isle of Dogs, its heavy prow and high masts a misty shape where grey river met grey sky. I pointed it out to Mark.

'I wonder where that has come from.'

'Men voyage nowadays to lands our fathers never dreamt of.'

'And bring back wonders.' I thought of the strange bird. 'New wonders and maybe new deceits.' We rode on across the bridge. At the far end a smashed skull lay by the piers. Picked clean by the birds, it had fallen from its pole and the pieces would lie there till souvenir hunters, or witches looking for charms, fetched them away. The St Barbaras in Cromwell's chamber, and now this relic of earthly justice. I thought uneasily on omens, then chided myself for superstition.

✝

FOR SOME WAY south of London the road was good enough, passing through the fields that fed the capital, now brown and bare. The sky had settled to a still milky white and the weather held. At noon we stopped for dinner near Eltham, then shortly afterwards we crested the North Downs and saw laid out before us the ancient forest of the Weald, bare treetops dotted with the occasional evergreen stretching to the misty horizon.

The road became narrower, set beneath steep wooded banks half-choked with fallen leaves, little trackways leading off to remote hamlets. Only the occasional carter passed us. By late afternoon we reached the little market town of Tonbridge and turned south. We kept a sharp lookout for robbers, but all we saw was a herd of deer foraging in a lane; as we rounded a corner the silly creatures clambered up the bank and disappeared into the forest.

Dusk was falling when we heard the tolling of a church bell

through the trees. Turning another bend, we found ourselves in the single street of a hamlet, a poor place of thatched wattle houses but with a fine Norman church and, next to it, an inn. All the windows of the church were filled with candles, a rich glow filtering through the stained glass. The bell tolled, on and on.

'The All Souls' service,' Mark observed.

'Yes, the whole village will be in church praying for the relief of their dead in purgatory.'

We rode slowly down the street, little blond children peeping suspiciously from doorways. Few adults were about. The sound of Mass being chanted reached us from the open doors of the church.

In those days All Souls' Day was one of the greatest events in the calendar. In every church parishioners met to hear Masses and say prayers to help the passage through purgatory of kin and friends. Already the ceremony was stripped of royal authority, and soon it would be forbidden. Some said it was cruel to deprive people of comfort and remembrance. But it is surely a gentler thing to know that one's kin are, according to God's will, either in heaven or hell, than to believe they are in purgatory, a place of torment and pain they must endure perhaps for centuries.

We dismounted stiffly at the inn, tying our horses to the rail. The building was a larger version of the others; mud and wattle with the plaster falling away in places and a high thatched roof reaching down to the first-floor windows.

Inside a fire burned in a circular grate in the middle of the floor in the old manner, as much smoke filling the room as escaped through the round chimney above. Through the gloom a few bearded ancients peered curiously at us from their dice. A fat man in an apron approached, keen eyes taking in our expensive furs. I asked for a room and a meal, which he offered us for sixpence. Struggling to follow his thick, guttural accent, I beat him down to a groat. Having confirmed the way to Scarnsea and ordered warm ale, I took a seat by the fire while Mark went out to supervise the stabling of the horses.

I was glad when he rejoined me, for I was tired of being stared at by the clutch of old men. I had nodded to them but they turned their heads away.

'They're a hard-eyed bunch,' Mark whispered.

'They won't see many travellers. And no doubt they believe hunchbacks bring bad luck. Oh come, it's what most people think. I've seen men cross themselves at my approach often enough, for all my fine clothes.'

We ordered supper and were served a greasy mutton stew with heavy ale. The sheep, Mark grumbled, was long dead. In the course of the meal a group of villagers arrived, in their best clothes, the Hallowtide services apparently over. They sat together, talking in sombre voices. Occasionally they glanced over at us, and we had more nosy looks and hostile faces.

I noticed that three men in a far corner also seemed to be ignored by the villagers. They were rough looking, with ragged clothes and unkempt beards. I saw them examining us; not staring openly like the villagers but with sidelong looks.

'See that tall fellow?' Mark whispered. 'I'd swear that's the rags of a monk's robe.'

The largest man, an ugly giant with a broken nose, wore a ragged shift of thick black wool and I saw that indeed it had a Benedictine cowl at the back. The innkeeper, who alone had been civil to us, appeared to refill our glasses.

'Tell me,' I asked quietly, 'who are those three?'

He grunted. 'Abbey-lubbers from the priory dissolved last year. You know how it is, sir. The king says the little houses of prayer must go, and the monks are given places elsewhere, but the servants are put out on the road. Those fellows have been begging about here this last twelvemonth — there's no labour for them. See that skinny fellow, he's had his ears cropped already. Be careful of them.'

I glanced round and saw that one of them, a tall thin fellow with wild yellow hair, had no ears, only holes with scar tissue around, the penalty for forgery. Doubtless he had been involved in some local enterprise of clipping coins and using the gold to make poor fakes.

'You allow them here,' I said.

He grunted. 'It's not their fault they were thrown out. Them and hundreds more.' Then, feeling perhaps he had said too much, the innkeeper hurried away.

'I think this might be a good time to retire,' I said, taking a candle from the table. Mark nodded, and we downed the last of our ale and headed for the stairs. As we passed the abbey servants my coat accidentally brushed the big man's robe.

'You'll have bad luck now, Edwin,' one of the others said loudly. 'You'll need to touch a dwarf to bring your luck back.'

They cackled with laughter. I felt Mark turn and laid my arm on his.

'No,' I whispered. 'No trouble here. Go up!' I half-pushed him up a rickety wooden staircase to where our bags were set out on truckle beds in a room under the thatch, whose population of rats could be heard scurrying away as we entered. We sat down and pulled off our boots.

Mark was angry. 'Why should we suffer the insults of these hinds?'

'We are in hostile country. The Weald people are still papists, the priest in that church probably tells them to pray for the death of the king and the pope's return every Sunday.'

'I thought you hadn't been in these parts before.' Mark stretched out his feet to the broad iron chimney pipe, which ran up through the centre of the room to the roof, providing the only warmth.

'Careful of chilblains. I haven't, but Lord Cromwell's intelligencers send back reports from every shire since the rebellion. I have copies in my bag.'

He turned to me. 'Do you not find it wearying sometimes? Always having to think when one talks to a stranger, lest something slips an enemy could turn to treason. It did not used to be like this.'

'This is the worst time. Things will improve.'

'When the monasteries are down?'

'Yes. Because Reform will finally be safe. And because then Lord Cromwell will have enough money to make the realm secure from invasion and do much for the people. He has great plans.'

'By the time the Augmentations men have had their cut, will there be enough left even to buy those churls downstairs new cloaks?'

'There will, Mark.' I spoke earnestly. 'The large monasteries have untold wealth. And what do they give to the poor, despite their duty of charity? I used to see the destitute crowding round the gates on dole days at Lichfield, children in rags pushing and kicking for the few farthings handed through the bars in the gate. I felt ashamed going into school on those days. Such a school as it was. Well, now there'll be proper schools in every parish, paid for by the king's Exchequer.'

He said nothing, only raised his eyebrows quizzically.

'God's death, Mark,' I snapped, suddenly irritated by his scepticism. 'Take your feet away from that chimney. They stink worse than that sheep.'

He clambered into bed and lay looking up at the thatched vault of the roof. 'I pray you are right, sir. But Augmentations has made me doubt men's charity.'

'There is godly leaven in the unregenerate lump. It works its way, slowly. And Lord Cromwell is part of it, for all his hardness. Have faith,' I added gently. Yet even as I spoke I remembered Lord Cromwell's grim pleasure as he talked of burning a priest with his own images, saw him again shaking the casket containing the child's skull.

'Faith will move mountains?' Mark said after a moment.

'God's nails,' I snapped, 'in my day it was the young who were idealistic and the old cynical. I'm too tired to argue further. Goodnight.' I began to undress; hesitantly, for I do not like people to see my disability. But Mark, sensitively, turned his back as we took off our clothes and donned our nightshifts. Wearily, I climbed into my sagging bed and pinched out the candle.

I said my prayers. But for a long time I lay awake in the darkness, listening to Mark's even breathing and the renewed scrabblings of the rats in the thatch as they crept back to the centre of the room, near the chimney where it was warmest.

✠

I HAD MADE light of it, as I always did, but the looks the villagers gave my hump, and the abbey-lubber's remark, had sent a familiar stab of pain through me. It had settled miserably in my guts, crushing my earlier enthusiasm. All my life I had tried to shrug off such insults, though when I was younger I often felt like raging and screaming. I had seen enough cripples whose minds had been made as twisted as their bodies by the weight of insult and mockery they suffered; glowering at the world from beneath knitted brows and turning to swear foul abuse at the children who called after them in the streets. It was better to try and ignore it, get on with such life as God allowed.

I remembered one occasion, though, when that had been impossible. It was a moment that had defined my life. I was fifteen, a pupil at the cathedral school in Lichfield. As a senior scholar it was my duty to attend and sometimes serve at Sunday Mass. That seemed a wonderful thing after a long week at my books, struggling with the Greek and Latin poorly taught by Brother Andrew, a fat cathedral monk with a fondness for the bottle.

The cathedral would be brightly lit, candles flickering before the altar, the statues and the gloriously painted rood screen. I preferred those days when I did not serve the priest but sat with the congregation. Beyond the screen the priest would intone Mass in the Latin I was coming to understand, his words echoing as the congregation made their responses.

Now that the old Mass is long gone it is hard to convey the sense of mystery it communicated: the incense, the rising Latin cadences, then the ringing of the censing bell as the bread and wine were elevated and, everyone believed, transformed into the actual flesh and blood of Jesus Christ in the priest's mouth.

In the last year my head had become increasingly filled with godly fervour. Watching the faces of the congregation, quiet and respectful, I had come to see the Church as a great community binding the living and the dead, transforming people if only for a few hours into the obedient flock of the Great Shepherd. I felt called to serve this flock; and as a priest I could be a guide to my fellows, earn their respect.

Brother Andrew soon disabused me of that when, trembling with the import of what I had to say, I sought an interview with him in his little office behind the schoolroom. It was the end of the day and he was red-eyed as he studied a parchment on his desk, his black habit stained with ink and food. Haltingly I told him I believed I had a vocation and I wished to be considered as a trainee for ordination.

I expected him to question me about my faith, but he only raised a pudgy hand dismissively.

'Boy,' he said, 'you can never be a priest. Do you not realize that? You should not be taking up my time with this.' His white eyebrows creased together in annoyance. He had not shaved; white stubble stood out like frost on his fat red chaps.

'I don't understand, Brother. Why not?'

He sighed, filling my face with his alcoholic breath. 'Master Shardlake, you know from the Book of Genesis that God made us in his own image, do you not?'

'Of course, Brother.'

'To serve his Church you must conform to that image. Anyone with a visible affliction, even a withered limb, let alone a great crooked humpback like yours, can never be a priest. How could you show yourself as an intercessor between ordinary sinful humanity and the majesty of God, when your form is so much less than theirs?'

I felt as though suddenly encased in ice. 'That cannot be right. That is cruel.'

Brother Andrew's face went puce. 'Boy,' he shouted, 'do you question the teachings of Holy Church, time out of mind? You that come here asking to be ordained as a priest! What sort of priest, a Lollard heretic?'

I looked at him sitting in his dirty food-stained robe, his stubbly face red and frowning. 'So I should look like *you*, should I?' I burst out before I had time to think.

With a roar he got up, landing me a great clout on the ear. 'You little crookback churl, get out!'

I ran from the room, my head singing. He was too fat to pursue (he died of a great seizure the next year) and I fled from the cathedral and limped home through the darkening lanes, bereft. In sight of home I sat on a stile, watching a spring sunset whose green fecundity seemed to mock me. I felt that if the Church would not have me I had nowhere to go, I was alone.

And then, as I sat there in the dusk, Christ spoke to me. That is what happened, so there is no other way to put it. I heard a voice inside my head, it came from inside me but was not mine. 'You are not alone,' it said and suddenly a great warmth, a sense of love and peace, infused my being. I do not know how long I sat there, breathing deeply, but that moment transformed my life. Christ himself had comforted me against the words of the Church that was supposed to be his. I had never heard that voice before, and though I hoped, as I knelt praying that night and in later weeks and years, that I would hear it again, I never have. But perhaps once in a lifetime is all we are given. Many are not given even that.

†

WE LEFT AT first light, before the village woke. I was still in sombre mood and we said little. There had been a hard frost, turning the road and trees white, but mercifully there was still no snow as we made our way out of the village, back into the narrow lane between the high tree-lined banks.

We rode all morning and into the early afternoon, until at last the woodland thinned and we came to a country of tilled fields with, a little way ahead, the slope of the South Downs. We followed a pathway up the hillside, where stringy looking sheep grazed. At the top we saw, below us, the sea, rolling in slow grey waves. To our right a tidal river cut through the low hills, reaching the sea through a great swathe of marshland. Bordering the marsh was a small town, and a mile off stood a great complex of buildings in ancient yellow stone, dominated by a great Norman church almost as large as a cathedral and surrounded by a high enclosing wall.

'The monastery of Scarnsea,' I said.

'"The Lord has brought us safe through our tribulations,"' Mark quoted.

'I think we have more of those ahead,' I replied. We led the tired horses down the hill, just as a light snow began to blow in from the sea.

Chapter Four

WE GUIDED THE HORSES carefully down the hill to where a
road led into the town. They were nervous, shying away from
the snowflakes brushing their faces. Happily, the snow stopped as we
arrived.

'Shall we call on the Justice?' Mark asked.

'No, we must reach the monastery today; if the snow starts again
we could have to stay the night here.'

We made our way down Scarnsea's cobbled main street, where
the top storeys of ancient houses overhung the road, keeping to one
side to avoid the emptying of pisspots. We noticed that the plaster and
timbers of many houses were decayed, and the shops seemed poor
places. The few people about gave us incurious glances.

We reached the town square. On three sides more dilapidated-
looking houses stood, but the fourth consisted of a wide stone wharf.
Once no doubt it had fronted the sea, but now it faced the mud and
reeds of the marsh, sullen and desolate under the grey sky and giving
off a mingled smell of salt and rot. A canal, large enough only for a
small boat, had been cut through the mud and stretched in a long
ribbon to the sea, a steely band a mile off. Out on the marsh we saw
a train of donkeys roped together while a group of men shored up the
canal bank with stones from panniers on the animals' backs.

There had evidently been recent entertainment, for on the far side
of the square a little knot of women stood conversing by the town
stocks, round which lay a mess of rotten fruit and vegetables. Sitting
on a stool with her feet clamped in the stocks was a plump middle-
aged woman of the poorer sort, her clothing a mess of burst eggs and

pears. She wore a triangular cap with 'S' for 'scold' daubed on it. She looked cheerful enough now, as she took a cup of ale from one of the women, but her face was bruised and swollen and her blackened eyes half-shut. Seeing us, she raised her tankard and essayed a grin. A little group of giggling children ran into the square, carrying old rotten cabbages, but one of the women waved them off.

'Go away,' she called in an accent as thick and guttural as the villagers' had been. 'Goodwife Thomas has learnt her lesson and will give her husband peace. She'll be let out in an hour. Enough!'

The children retreated, calling insults from a safe distance.

'They have mild enough ways down here, it seems,' Mark observed. I nodded. In the London stocks it is common enough for sharp stones to be thrown, taking out teeth and eyes.

We rode out of town towards the monastery. The road ran alongside the reeds and stagnant pools of the marsh. I marvelled that there were pathways through such a foul mire, but there must be or the men and animals we had seen could not have found their way.

'Scarnsea was once a prosperous seaport,' I observed. 'That marshland has built up from silt and sand in a hundred years or so. No wonder the town is poor now; that canal would barely take a fishing boat.'

'How do they live?'

'Fishing and farming. Smuggling too, I daresay, from France. They'll still have to pay their rents and dues to the monastery to keep those lazy drones of monks. Scarnsea port was given as a prize to one of William the Conqueror's knights, who granted land to the Benedictines and had the monastery built. Paid for with English taxes, of course.'

A peal of bells sounded from the direction of the monastery, loud in the still air.

'They've seen us coming,' Mark said with a laugh.

'They'd need good eyes. Unless it's one of their miracles. God's wounds, those bells are loud.'

The tolling continued as we approached the walls, the noise

reverberating through my skull. I was tired and my back had pained me increasingly as the day wore on, so that now I rode slumped over Chancery's broad back. I pulled myself upright; I needed to establish a presence at the monastery from the start. Only now did I appreciate the full extent of the place. The walls, faced with flints set in plaster, were twelve feet high. The enclosure reached back from the road to the very edge of the marsh. A little way along there was a large Norman gatehouse, and as we watched a cart laden with barrels and led by two big shire horses rattled out onto the road. We reined in our horses, and it rumbled past us towards the town, the driver touching his cap to us.

'Beer,' I noted.

'Empty barrels?' Mark asked.

'No, full ones. The monastery brewhouse has a monopoly in supplying the town's beer. They can set the price. It's in the founding charter.'

'So if anyone gets drunk, it's on holy beer?'

'It's common enough. The Norman founders kept the monks comfortable in return for prayers for their souls in perpetuity. Everyone was happy, except those who paid for it all. Thank God, those bells have stopped.' I took a deep breath. 'Now, come. Don't say anything, take your lead from me.'

We rode up to the gatehouse, a solid affair faced with carvings of heraldic beasts. The gates were closed. Looking up, I glimpsed a face peering down from the window of the gatekeeper's house on the first floor, quickly withdrawn. I dismounted and banged on a small side gate set in the wall. After a few moments it opened to reveal a tall, burly man with a head as bald as an egg, wearing a greasy leather apron. He glared at us.

'Wod'ya want?'

'I am the king's commissioner. Kindly take us to the abbot.' I spoke coldly.

He looked at us suspiciously. 'We're expecting nobody. This is an enclosed monastery. You got papers?'

I reached into my robe and thrust my papers at him. 'The Monastery of St Donatus the Ascendant of Scarnsea is a Benedictine house. It is not an enclosed order, people may come and go at the abbot's pleasure. Or perhaps we are at the wrong monastery,' I added sarcastically. The churl gave me a sharp look as he glanced at the papers – it was clear he could not read – before handing them back.

'You've made them richer by a couple of smears, fellow. What's your name?'

'Bugge,' he muttered. 'I'll have ye taken to Master Abbot, sirs.' He stood aside and we led the horses through, finding ourselves in a broad space under the pillars supporting the gatehouse.

'Please wait.'

I nodded, and he stomped off and left us.

I passed under the pillars and looked into the courtyard. Ahead stood the great monastery church, solidly built of white stone now yellow with age. Like all the other buildings it was of French limestone, built in the Norman way with wide windows, quite unlike the contemporary style of high narrow windows and arches reaching to the heavens. Big as it was, three hundred feet long and with twin towers a hundred feet high, the church gave an impression of squat power, rooted to the earth.

To the left, against the far wall, stood the usual outbuildings – stables, mason's workshop, brewery. The courtyard was full of the sort of activity familiar to me from Lichfield: tradesmen and servants bustling to and fro and talking business with monks in the shaved heads and black habits of the Benedictines; habits of fine wool, I noticed, with good leather shoes showing underneath. The ground was packed earth, littered with straw. Big lurcher dogs ran everywhere barking and pissing against the walls. As with all those places, the atmosphere of the outer court was of a business rather than an enclosed refuge from the world.

To the right of the church the inner wall separated off the claustral buildings, where the monks lived and prayed. Against the far wall stood a separate, one-storey building with a fine herb garden before it, plants staked out and carefully labelled. That, I guessed, would be the infirmary.

'Well, Mark,' I asked quietly, 'what do you think of a monastic house?'

He kicked out at one of the big dogs, which had approached us with raised hackles. It backed off a little, to stand barking angrily. 'I had not expected anything so large. It looks as if it could support two hundred men in a siege.'

'Well done. It was built to provide for a hundred monks and a hundred servants. Now everything – buildings, lands, local monopolies – supports just thirty monks and sixty servants, according to the *Comperta*, on the fat of the land.'

'They've noticed us, sir,' he murmured, and indeed the cur's continued barking had drawn eyes from all over the courtyard – unwelcoming eyes, quickly averted as people whispered to each other. A tall, thin monk, leaning on a crutch by the church wall, was staring fixedly at us. His white habit with its long scapular in front contrasted with the plain black of the Benedictines.

'A Carthusian, unless I'm mistaken,' I said.

'I thought the Carthusian houses were all closed, with half the monks executed for treason.'

'They were. What's he doing here?'

There was a cough at my elbow. The gatekeeper had returned with a stocky monk of around forty. The fringe round his tonsure was brown streaked with grey and he had a hard, strong-featured, ruddy face, whose lines were softened with the sags and pouches of good living. A badge of office showing a key was sewn onto the breast of his habit. Behind him stood a nervous-looking red-haired boy in a novice's grey robe.

'All right, Bugge,' the newcomer said in the harsh clear accent of the Scots, 'back to your duties.' The gatekeeper reluctantly turned away.

'I am the prior, Brother Mortimus of Kelso.'

'Where is the abbot?'

'I fear he is out just now. I am his second in command, responsible for the daily administration of St Donatus." He gave us a keen stare. 'You have come in response to Dr Goodhaps's message? We have had no messenger to tell us you were coming, I fear there are no rooms ready.' I took a step back, for a ripe odour came from him. I knew from my own education by the monks how rigidly they clung to the old notion that washing was unhealthy, bathing only half a dozen times a year.

'Lord Cromwell sent us at once. I am Master Matthew Shardlake, appointed commissioner to investigate the events reported in Dr Goodhaps's letter.'

He bowed. 'I welcome ye to St Donatus Monastery. I apologize for our gatekeeper's manners, but the injunctions require us to keep as separate as possible from the world.'

'Our business is urgent, sir,' I said sharply. 'Kindly tell us, is Robin Singleton truly dead?'

The prior's face set and he crossed himself. 'He is. Struck down most foully by an unknown assailant. A terrible thing.'

'Then we must see the abbot at once.'

'I will take ye to his house. He should be back shortly. I pray ye may cast light on what has happened here. Bloodshed on consecrated ground, and worse.' He shook his head and then, with a complete change of manner, turned and snapped at the boy, who was staring at us with wide eyes. 'Whelplay, the horses! Stable them!'

He seemed scarcely more than a child, thin and frail-looking, looking more like sixteen than the eighteen necessary to qualify for the novitiate. I removed the pannier containing my papers, handing it to Mark, and the boy led the animals away. After a few paces he turned and looked back at us, and in so doing he slipped in a mess of dog turds and went over backwards, landing on the earth with a crash. The horses stirred anxiously and there was a ripple of laughter round the courtyard. Prior Mortimus's face reddened with anger. He crossed to the boy, who was pulling himself to his feet, and pushed him over to land again in the dog mess, bringing more laughter.

'God's wounds, Whelplay, you are an oaf,' the prior shouted. 'Would ye have the king's commissioner's horses running loose in the courtyard?'

'No, Master Prior,' the boy replied in a trembling voice. 'I beg pardon.'

I stepped forward, taking Chancery's reins with one hand and offering my other arm to help the boy up, avoiding the dog shit on his robe.

'The horses will panic with all this disturbance,' I said mildly. 'Do not distress yourself, lad; such accidents happen to everyone.' I handed him the reins and with a glance at the prior's face, which had gone red with anger, he led the animals away. I turned back to the prior. 'Now, sir, if you would lead the way.'

The Scotsman glared at me. His face was puce now. 'With respect, sir, I am responsible for discipline in this house. The king has ordered many changes in our life here, and our younger brethren especially need to be taught obedience.'

'You have problems in getting the brethren to obey Lord Cromwell's new injunctions?'

'No, sir, I do not. So long as I am allowed to use discipline.'

'For slipping in a dog's mess?' I said mildly. 'Would it not be better to discipline those dogs, keep them out of the yard?'

The prior looked ready to argue, then suddenly let out a harsh bark of laughter.

'You're right, sir, but the abbot won't have the dogs shut up. He likes them kept fit for when he goes hunting.' As he spoke I watched the colour of his face fading from purple to its previous red. I reflected that he must be a man of unusually high choler.

'Hunting. I wonder what St Benedict would have said to that?'

'The abbot has his own rules,' the prior said meaningfully.

He led us past the row of outbuildings. Ahead I saw a fine two-storey house set in a rose garden, a well-built gentleman's residence which would not have looked out of place in Chancery Lane. We passed the stables and through the open doors I saw the boy leading Chancery into a stall. He turned, giving me a strange, intent look. We passed the brewery and the forge, whose red glow looked inviting in the cold. Next to it was a large outhouse with blocks of stone, carved and ornamented, visible through the open doors. Outside a trestle table was drawn up, on which plans had been laid out, and a grey-bearded man in a mason's apron stood with arms folded beside two monks who were arguing intently.

'It c-cannot be done, Brother,' the older monk said firmly. He was a short, plump man of around forty, with a fringe of curly black hair beneath his tonsure, a round pale face and hard little dark eyes. Fat little fingers waved over the plans. 'If we use Caen stone it w-will exhaust your entire annual budget for the next three years.'

'It can't be done cheaper,' the mason said. 'Not if it's done properly.'

'It must be done properly,' the other monk said emphatically in a deep, rich voice. 'Otherwise the whole symmetry of the church is destroyed, the eye would immediately be led to the different facing. If you can't agree, Master Bursar, I must take it to the abbot.'

'Take it then, it'll do you no good.' He broke off as he saw us, looked at us sharply with his black button eyes, then bent his face to the plans. The other monk studied us. He was tall and strongly built, in early middle age and with a deeply lined, handsome face and untidy yellow hair sticking out beneath his tonsure like a twist of straw. His eyes were large, a clear pale blue. He cast a lingering look at Mark, who returned his gaze coldly, then bowed to the prior as we passed, receiving a curt nod in return.

'Interesting,' I murmured to Mark. 'You'd think there was no threat hanging over this place. They're talking of renovating the church as though it would all go on for ever.'

'Did you see the look that tall monk gave me?'

'Yes. That was interesting too.'

We were passing the far wall of the church, nearly at the house, when a white-robed figure stepped from behind a buttress into our path. It was the Carthusian we had seen in the courtyard. The prior stepped quickly in front of him.

'Brother Jerome,' he called harshly, 'no trouble now! Back to your prayers!'

The Carthusian stepped round the prior, ignoring him except for a quick glance of contempt. I saw that he dragged his right leg and needed his crutch, held firmly under his right armpit, to move at all. His left arm hung limply at his side, misshapen, the hand held at a strange angle. He was a stringy man of about sixty, the straggling hair around his tonsure whiter than his stained and threadbare robes. The eyes in his thin pale face burned with the sort of ferocious intensity that seems bent on penetrating the soul. He stepped up to me, moving with surprising deftness to avoid the prior's outstretched arm.

'You are Lord Cromwell's man?' The voice was cracked and tremulous.

'I am, sir.'

'Know then that those who draw the sword shall die by the sword.'

'Matthew twenty-six, verse fifty-two,' I replied. 'What do you mean?' I thought of what had taken place here. 'Is that a confession?'

He laughed contemptuously. 'No, crookback, it is God's word, and it is true.' Prior Mortimus grabbed the Carthusian's good arm none too gently. He shook it off and hobbled away.

'Please ignore him.' The prior's face had gone pale this time; broken purple veins stood out on his cheeks. 'He is unhinged,' he added, setting his lips tight.

'Who is he? What is a Carthusian monk doing here?'

'He is a pensioner. We took him in as a favour to his cousin, who owns land nearby. Out of charity for his condition.'

'Which house is he from?'

The prior hesitated. 'The London house. He is known as Jerome of London.'

I stared. 'Where Prior Houghton and half the monks refused to take the oath of allegiance and were executed?'

'Brother Jerome took the oath. Eventually. After Master Cromwell applied certain pressures.' He gave me a hard stare. 'You understand?'

'He was racked?'

'With most dire pains. Giving in unhinged him. He deserved it for his disloyalty though, did he not? And this is how he repays our charity. He'll hear more about this.'

'What did he mean just now?'

'Jesu knows. I told you, the man's insane.' He turned away, and we followed him through a wooden gate into the abbot's garden, where a few livid winter roses stood out among the bare thorny branches. I glanced back, but the crippled monk had disappeared. The memory of those burning eyes made me shiver.

Chapter Five

A FAT MAN in the blue robe of a servant answered the prior's knock. He eyed us worriedly.

'Urgent visitors for his lordship, from the vicar general. Is he here?'

The servant bowed deeply. 'That terrible killing.' He crossed himself fervently. 'We had no warning of your coming, sirs. Abbot Fabian is not back, though he is expected any time. But pray come in.'

He ushered us into a wide hall, the panels brightly painted with hunting scenes.

'Perhaps you would wait in the reception room,' the prior suggested.

'Where is Dr Goodhaps?'

'In his room upstairs.'

'Then we will see him first.'

The prior nodded to the servant, who led us up a broad staircase to the upper floor. The prior halted before a closed door and knocked loudly. There was a squeal from within, then we heard a key turn and the door opened a crack. A thin face topped with untidy white hair peered out anxiously.

'Prior Mortimus,' the old man said in a squeaky voice, 'why clout the door like that? You startled me.'

A sardonic smile flickered briefly across Mortimus's face. 'Did I? Forgive me. Ye're safe now, good Doctor, Lord Cromwell has sent an emissary, a new commissioner.'

'Dr Goodhaps?' I asked. 'Commissioner Matthew Shardlake. I have been sent in reply to your letter. I come from Lord Cromwell.'

The old man stared a moment, then opened the door, admitting us to a bedroom. It was well appointed, with a curtained four-poster bed, fat cushions on the floor and a window overlooking the busy courtyard. A pile of books lay on the floor, a tray containing a pitcher of wine and pewter cups balanced on top. A log fire burned in the grate and Mark and I made for it at once, for we were both chilled to the bone. I turned to the prior, who stood in the doorway, eyeing us watchfully.

'Thank you, Brother. Perhaps you could inform me when the abbot returns.' He bowed and closed the door behind him.

'Lock the door, in Our Saviour's name,' the old man squeaked, wringing his hands. He made a sorry sight with his white hair disarrayed and his black cleric's robe creased and stained. From his breath I gathered that he had already sampled the wine.

'The letter arrived? Thank the Lord! I feared it would be intercepted. How many of you are there?'

'Only we two. May I sit?' I asked, lowering myself carefully onto the cushions. As they took my weight the relief to my back was wonderful. Master Goodhaps noticed my disability for the first time, then looked at Mark, who was unbuckling his heavy sword.

'The boy, he's a swordsman? He can protect us?'

'If need be. Are we likely to need protecting?'

'In this place, sir, after what happened – we are surrounded by enemies, Master Shardlake—'

I saw he was terrified, and smiled reassuringly. A nervous witness, like a nervous horse, needs to be soothed along.

'Calm yourself, sir. Now, we are tired and would be grateful for a little of that wine while you tell us exactly what has happened here.'

'Oh sir, by Our Lady, the blood . . .'

I raised my hand. 'Start at the beginning, from your arrival.'

He poured us wine and sat down on the bed, running his fingers through his shock of white hair.

'I did not want to come here,' he sighed. 'I have laboured hard in the vineyard at Cambridge, working for Reform since the start, and I am too old for assignments like this. But Robin Singleton was my student once, and he asked me to help him try for the surrender of this pestiferous house. He needed a canon lawyer, you see. I could not refuse a summons from the vicar general,' he added resentfully.

'That is difficult,' I agreed. 'So you arrived here what, a week ago?'

'Yes. It was a hard ride.'

'How did the negotiations proceed?'

'Badly, sir, as I knew they would. Singleton went blustering in, saying this was a decayed and sinful house and they would be well advised to take the pensions he offered and surrender. But Abbot Fabian wasn't interested; he loves his life here too much. Playing the country squire, lording it over the stewards and reeves. He's only the local ship chandler's son, you know.' Goodhaps drained his cup and poured himself another. I could not blame the helpless old noddle, all alone here, for seeking succour in his pitcher.

'He's clever, Abbot Fabian. He knew there would be no more forced closures, not after the northern rebellion. The commissioner told me to find something in my legal books to threaten him with. I told him he was wasting his time, but Robin Singleton was never any good as a scholar; he made his way by bluster. God rest him,' he added, though as a good reformer he did not cross himself.

'What you say is true enough,' I agreed, 'unless one can find other breaches of the law. Sodomy was spoken of, I hear, and theft. Capital offences both.'

Goodhaps sighed. 'For once Lord Cromwell has the wrong notion. The local Justice is a good reformer but his reports of land sales at undervalue don't hold water. There is no evidence of anything improper in the accounts.'

'And the talk of vice?'

'Nothing. The abbot insists they have all reformed since the visitation. The last prior encouraged those vile practices, but he was removed together with a couple of the worst offenders, and that Scots brute put in.'

I emptied my cup, but forbore to ask for more. I was bone-tired, and the wine and the warmth from the fire made me want to lie down and sleep, but I needed a clear head for some hours yet.

'How do you find the brothers?'

He shrugged. 'Like them all. Lazy and content. They play cards and hunt – you'll have seen the place is crawling with dogs – and skimp the services, but they observe the injunctions, have sermons in English, and don't have bawdy women walking around the place. That red-faced prior's a disciplinarian. He makes himself out a supporter of Lord Cromwell's injunctions, but I trust none of them. The senior monks are a smooth, clever lot but under the surface they're all full of the old heresies. They keep that to themselves, though. Except that Carthusian cripple, of course, and he's not part of the community.'

'Ah yes, Brother Jerome. We encountered him.'

'Do you not know who he is?'

'No.'

'A relative of Queen Jane, God rest her. He refused the oath, but to have him executed like the other Carthusians would have been an embarrassment. They tortured him into swearing, and then hid him away down here as a pensioner – another relative is a big landowner hereabouts. I would have thought Lord Cromwell's office would have known he was here.'

I inclined my head. 'Papers get lost, I suppose, even in his office.'

'The other monks don't like him because he insults them, calls them soft and lazy. He's not allowed to leave the precincts.'

'No doubt Commissioner Singleton spoke to many of the monks to see what he could uncover. Some of those involved in the sodomy scandal would still be here?'

'The tall one with wild fair hair perhaps?' Mark interjected.

Goodhaps shrugged. 'Oh, him. Brother Gabriel, the sacrist. Yes, he was one. Looks quite normal, doesn't he? Big and tall. He has a wild look about him sometimes, though. Commissioner Singleton pressed them, but they all say they are as pure as angels nowadays. He got me to do some interviews, question some of them about the detail of their lives – though I'm a scholar, I'm not trained for that sort of thing.'

'I gather Commissioner Singleton did not make himself popular? I knew him, by the way. He had a fierce manner.'

'Yes, his brusque ways never made him friends, not that he cared.'

'Tell me how he died.'

The old man hunched his shoulders and seemed to shrink into himself.

'He had given up trying to pressurize the monks. He set me to listing all the ways a monastery may break the canon law – scraping the bottom of the barrel. He spent most of his time looking through the accounts and the archives. He was getting anxious, he needed something for Lord Cromwell. I didn't see him much the last couple of days, he was busy going through the bursar's accounts.'

'What was he looking for?'

'Any trouble he could find. As I said, he was scraping the bottom of the barrel. But he has some experience of these new Italian accounts, where everything goes in twice.'

'Yes, double-entry. He knew his accounts then, if not much law?'

'Yes.' He sighed. 'That last night we had supper on our own as usual. Singleton appeared in a more cheerful mood. He said he was going to his room to look at some new book he'd prised out of the bursar. The bursar himself was away that night – the night it happened.'

'Would the bursar be a fat little man with black eyes? We saw someone like that in the courtyard, arguing about money.'

'That's him. Brother Edwig. Arguing with the sacrist about his building schemes, I daresay. I like Brother Edwig, he's a practical man. Doesn't like spending money. We could do with someone like him in my college. When it comes to the day-to-day running of the monastery, Prior Mortimus and Brother Edwig have control between them and they run tight ships.' He took another draught of wine.

'What happened next?'

'I worked for an hour, then said my prayers and went to bed.'

'And slept?'

'Yes. I woke suddenly at about five. There was a commotion outside, then a great bang on the door — just like the prior made just now.' He shuddered. 'The abbot and a dozen monks were outside. The abbot looked shocked, startled out of his wits. He told me the commissioner was dead, someone had killed him, I must come at once.

'I dressed and went down with them. It was all so confused, everyone was babbling about locked doors and blood, and I heard someone say it was God's vengeance. They found torches and we went through the monks' quarters to the kitchens. It was so cold, all those endless dark passageways, monks and servants standing around in little huddles looking scared. And then they opened the door to the kitchen. Dear God.' To my surprise, he quickly crossed himself.

'There was this smell of —' he gave a fractured laugh — 'a butcher's shop. The room was full of candles, they'd put them on the long tables, the food cupboards, everywhere. I stood in something, and the prior pulled me to one side. When I lifted my foot it was sticky. There was a great pool of dark liquid on the floor, I didn't know what it was.

'Then I saw Robin Singleton lying in the middle of it on his stomach, his robe all smeared. I knew there was something wrong, but my eyes could make no sense of it at first. Then I realized he had *no head*. I stared round and then I saw it, his head, lying under the butter churn glaring up at me. It was only then I realized the pool was blood.' He closed his eyes. 'Dear God, I was so frightened.' He opened them again, emptied his cup and reached once more for the bottle, but I covered it with my hand.

'Enough for now, Dr Goodhaps,' I said gently. 'Go on.'

Tears came into his eyes. 'I thought they'd killed him, I thought it was an execution and I was next. I looked at their faces, looked to see which one was carrying an axe. They all looked so grim. That

Carthusian was there, smiling horribly, and he called out "Vengeance is mine, saieth the Lord."'

'He said that, did he?'

'Yes. The abbot snapped, "Be quiet," at him, and came over to me. "Master Goodhaps," he said, ' "you must tell us what to do," and then I realized they were all as frightened as I.'

'Might I say something?' Mark ventured. I nodded.

'That Carthusian couldn't have struck someone's head off. It would take strength and balance.'

'Yes, it would,' I nodded. 'You're quite right.' I returned to the old man. 'What did you say to the abbot?'

'He said we should consult the civil authorities, but I knew Master Cromwell should be told first. I knew there would be political implications. The abbot said that the gatekeeper, old Bugge, had reported meeting Singleton on his night rounds not an hour before. He told Bugge he was on his way to meet one of the monks.'

'At that time? Did he say whom?'

'No. Singleton sent him away with a flea in his ear apparently.'

'I see. What then?'

'I ordered all the monks to strict silence. I said no letters should leave this place without my approval, and sent my letter out via the village postboy.'

'You did well, Master Goodhaps, your thinking was quite right.'

'Thank you.' He wiped his eyes with his sleeve. 'I was sore afraid, sir. I came back here and here I have stayed. I am sorry, Master Shardlake, this has unmanned me. I should have made enquiries, but – I am only a scholar.'

'Well, we are here now. Tell me, who found the body?'

'The infirmarian, Brother Guy. That dark monk.' He shuddered. 'He said there was an old brother sick in the infirmary and he came to get some milk from the kitchen. He has a key. He unlocked the outer door then went up the little hall to the kitchen. When he opened the door and stepped into the pool of blood he raised the alarm.'

'So the kitchen is normally locked at night?'

He nodded. 'Yes, to stop the monks and servants helping them-selves. The monks think of nothing but stuffing their bellies, you'll see how fat most of them are.'

'So the murderer had a key. Like the meeting the gatekeeper reported, that points to someone from inside the monastery. But you said in your letter that the church was desecrated, a relic stolen?'

'Yes. We were all still standing in the kitchen when one of the monks brought news that—' he swallowed, 'that a cock had been sacrificed on the church altar. Later they found the relic of the Penitent Thief stolen too. The monks are saying some outsider came in to desecrate the church and steal the relic, encountered the commissioner on one of his late wanderings, and killed him.'

'But how would an outsider have entered the kitchen?'

He shrugged. 'Bribed a servant to make a copy of the key perhaps? That's what the abbot thinks, though the cook is the only servant with a key.'

'What about the relic? Was it valuable?'

'That horrible thing! A hand nailed to a piece of wood. It was in a big gold casket set with stones: they were real emeralds, I believe. It is believed to cure broken or twisted bones, but it's just another fake to gull the foolish.' For a moment his voice rose with a reformer's ardour. 'The monks are more upset about the relic than about Singleton's murder.'

'What do you think?' I asked. 'Who do you think could have done this?'

'I don't know what to think. The monks talk of Devil-worship-pers breaking in to steal the relic. But they hate us, you can feel it in the very air. Sir, now you are here, may I go home?'

'Not just yet. Soon, perhaps.'

'At least I will have you and the boy here.'

There was a knock at the door, and the servant poked his head in.

'The abbot has returned, sir.'

'Very well. Mark, help me up. I am stiff.' He aided me to my feet and I brushed myself down.

'Thank you, Dr Goodhaps, we may talk again later. By the way, what happened to the account books the commissioner was studying?'

'The bursar took them back.' The old man shook his white poll. 'How did it come to this? All I wanted to see was reform of the Church; how has it come to a world where these things happen? Rebellion, treason, murder. Sometimes I wonder if there is a way through it all.'

'There is a way at least through the mysteries men make,' I said firmly. 'That I believe. Come on, Mark. Let us go and meet the good lord abbot.'

Chapter Six

THE SERVANT LED US down the staircase again and showed us into a wide room whose walls were hung with colourful Flemish tapestries, old but very fine. The windows looked over a large cemetery dotted with trees, where a couple of servants were raking away the last of the leaves.

'My lord abbot is changing out of his riding clothes. He will be with you shortly.' He bowed himself out, and we stood warming our rears at the fire.

The room was dominated by a large desk covered with a clutter of papers and parchments, a cushioned chair behind it and stools in front. The great seal of the abbey lay on a block of sealing wax in a brass tray, next to a flagon of wine and some silver cups. Behind the desk, bookshelves lined the wall.

'I didn't realize abbots lived so well,' Mark observed.

'Oh yes, they have their own separate households. Originally the abbot lived among the brethren, but when the Crown started to tax their households centuries ago they hit on the device of giving the abbot his own revenues, legally separate. Now they all live in fine state, leaving most of the daily supervision to the priors.'

'Why doesn't the king change the law, so the abbots can be taxed?'

I shrugged. 'In the past kings needed the abbots' support in the House of Lords. Now – well, it won't matter for much longer.'

'So that Scottish brute actually runs the place from day to day?'

I went behind the desk and examined the bookshelves, noting a printed set of English statutes. 'One of nature's bullies, isn't he? He seemed to enjoy mistreating that novice.'

'The boy looked ill.'

'Yes. I am curious to know why a novice has been set to menial servants' work.'

'I thought monks were supposed to spend part of their time in manual labour.'

'That is part of St Benedict's rule. But no monk in a Benedictine house has done honest toil for hundreds of years. Servants do the work. Not only cooking and stabling, but tending the fires, making the monks' beds, sometimes helping them dress and who knows what else.'

I picked up the seal and studied it by the light from the fire. It was of tempered steel. I showed Mark the engraving of St Donatus, in Roman clothing, bending over another man lying on a pannier whose arm was stretched up to him in appeal. It was beautifully done, the folds of the robes rendered in detail.

'St Donatus bringing the dead man back to life. I looked it up in my *Saints' Lives* before we left.'

'He could raise the dead? Like Christ with Lazarus?'

'Donatus, we are told, came upon a dead man being carried to his grave. Another man was berating the widow, saying the deceased owed him money. The blessed Donatus told the dead man to get up and settle his accounts. He sat up and convinced everyone that he had paid his debt. Then he lay down dead again. Money, money, it's always money with these people.'

There were footsteps outside and the door opened to admit a tall, broad man in his fifties. Beneath his black Benedictine habit could be seen hose of wool velvet and silver-buckled shoes. His face was ruddy, with a Roman beak of a nose set in square features. His thick brown hair was long and his tonsure, a little shaven circle, the barest concession to the Rule. He came forward with a smile.

'I am Abbot Fabian.' The manner was patrician, the voice richly aristocratic, but I caught a note of anxiety underneath. 'Welcome to Scarnsea. *Pax vobiscum*.'

'Master Matthew Shardlake, the vicar general's commissioner.' I did not give the formal reply of 'and with you', for I was not to be drawn into Latin mummery.

The abbot nodded slowly. His deep-set blue eyes quickly swept my bent figure up and down, then widened a little when he saw I was holding the seal.

'Sir, I beg you, be careful. That seal has to be impressed on all legal documents. It never leaves this room. Strictly, only I should handle it.'

'As the king's commissioner I have access to everything here, my lord.'

'Of course, sir, of course.' His eyes followed my hands as I laid the seal back on his desk. 'You must be hungry after your long journey; shall I order some food?'

'Later, thank you.'

'I regret keeping you waiting, but I had business with the reeve of our Ryeover estates. There is still much to do with the harvest accounts. Some wine, perhaps?'

'A very little.'

He poured me some, then turned to Mark. 'Might I ask who this is?'

'Mark Poer, my clerk and assistant.'

He raised his eyebrows. 'Master Shardlake, we have very serious matters to discuss. Might I suggest that would be better done in confidence? The boy can go to the quarters I have prepared.'

'I think not, my lord. The vicar general himself requested me to bring Master Poer. He shall stay unless I wish him to leave. Would you care to see my commission now?'

Mark gave the abbot a grin.

He reddened and inclined his head. 'As you wish.'

I passed the document into his beringed hand. 'I have spoken with Dr Goodhaps,' I said as he broke the seal. His expression became strained and his nose seemed to tilt upwards as though the smell of Cromwell himself rose from the paper. I looked out at the garden, where the servants were making a fire of the leaves, sending a thin white finger of smoke into the grey sky. The light was starting to fade.

The abbot pondered a moment, then laid the commission on his desk. He leaned forward, clasping his hands.

'This murder is the most terrible thing that has ever happened here. Accompanied by the desecration of our church, it has left me — shocked.'

I nodded. 'It has shocked Lord Cromwell too. He does not want it noised abroad. You have kept silence?'

'Totally, sir. The monks and servants have been told if a word is breathed outside these walls they will answer to the vicar general's office.'

'Good. Please ensure all correspondence arriving here is shown to me. And no letters are to go out without my approving them. Now, I gather Commissioner Singleton's visit was not welcome to you.'

He sighed again. 'What can I say? Two weeks ago I had a letter from Lord Cromwell's office saying he was sending a commissioner to discuss unspecified matters. When Commissioner Singleton arrived, he astonished me by saying he wished me to surrender this monastery to the king.' He looked me in the eye, and now there was defiance as well as anxiety in his gaze. 'He stressed he sought a voluntary surrender and he seemed keen to have it, alternating promises of money with vague threats about misconduct — quite without foundation, I must add. The Instrument of Surrender he wanted me to sign was extraordinary, containing admissions that our life here has consisted of pretended religion, following dumb Roman ceremonies.' An injured note entered his voice. 'Our ceremonies faithfully follow the vicar general's own injunctions, and every brother has sworn the oath renouncing the pope's authority.'

'Of course,' I said. 'Otherwise there would have been consequences.' I noticed he wore a pilgrim badge prominently on his habit; he had been to the shrine of Our Lady at Walsingham. But then, of course, so had the king in days past.

He took a deep breath. 'Commissioner Singleton and I had a number of discussions, centring on the fact that the vicar general has no legal right to order my monks and me to make over the house to them. A fact which Dr Goodhaps, a canon lawyer, could not dispute.'

I did not answer him, for he was right. 'Perhaps we could turn to the circumstances of the murder,' I said. 'That is the more pressing matter.'

He nodded sombrely. 'Four days ago Commissioner Singleton and I had another long and, I fear, fruitless discussion in the afternoon. I did not see him again that day. He had rooms in this house, but Dr Goodhaps and he had taken to dining separately. I went to bed as usual. Then at five in the morning I was woken by Brother Guy, my infirmarian, bursting into my room. He told me that on visiting the kitchen he had found Commissioner Singleton's body lying in a great pool of blood. He had been decapitated.' The abbot's face twisted with distaste and he shook his head. 'The shedding of blood on consecrated ground is an abomination, sir. And then there was what was found in the church, by the altar, when the monks went in to Matins.' He paused, a deep furrow appearing between his brows, and I saw he was genuinely upset.

'And what was that?'

'More blood. The blood of a black cockerel that lay with its head also off, before the altar. I fear we are dealing with witchcraft, Master Shardlake.'

'And you have lost a relic, I believe?'

The abbot bit his lip. 'The Great Relic of Scarnsea. It is rare and holy, the hand of the Penitent Thief who suffered with Christ, nailed to a fragment of his Cross. Brother Gabriel found it gone later that morning.'

'I understand it is valuable. A gold casket set with emeralds?'

'Yes. But I am more concerned with the contents. The thought of something of such holy power in the hands of some witch—'

'It was not witchcraft that beheaded the king's commissioner.'

'Some of the brethren wonder about that. There are no implements in the kitchen that could strike a man's head off. It is hardly an easy thing to do.'

I leaned forward, placing a hand on my knee. It was to ease my back, but it looked challenging. 'Your relations with Commissioner Singleton were not good. You say he used to take supper in his room?'

Abbot Fabian spread his hands. 'He was afforded every courtesy as an emissary of the vicar general. It was his preference not to share my dinner table. But please,' he raised his voice slightly, 'let me repeat, I abhor his death as an abomination. Indeed I would like to give his poor remains Christian burial. Their continued presence here makes my monks uneasy, they fear his ghost. But Dr Goodhaps insisted the body be kept for inspection.'

'A sensible suggestion. Its examination will be my first task.'

He eyed me carefully. 'Are you to investigate this crime alone, without involving the civil authorities?'

'Yes, and speedily. But I expect your full co-operation and assistance.'

He spread his hands wide. 'Of course. But, frankly, I do not know where you would begin. It seems an impossible task for one man. Especially if, as I am sure, the culprit came from the town.'

'Why do you say that? I have been told the gatekeeper encountered Commissioner Singleton during the night. He said he was on his way to meet someone. And that a key is needed to open the kitchen door.'

He leaned forward earnestly. 'Sir, this is a house of God, devoted to the worship of Christ.' He bowed his head at the mention of Our Lord's name. 'Nothing like this has happened in the four hundred years it has stood. But in the sinful world outside — some lunatic or, worse, someone dabbling in witchcraft could have entered the grounds with desecration in mind. The spoliation of the altar makes that obvious to me. I think Commissioner Singleton surprised the intruder, or intruders, on his way to this assignation of his. As for the key, the commissioner had one. He had requested it from Prior Mortimus that afternoon.'

'I see. Have you any idea whom he might have been meeting?'

'I wish I had. But that information died with him. Sir, I do not know what violent madmen there may have been in the town lately, but certainly there are rogues enough; half the people are involved in smuggling wool to France.'

'I will raise that tomorrow when I visit the town's Justice, Master Copynger.'

'He is to be involved?' The abbot's eyes narrowed. Plainly that did not please him.

'He and no one else. Tell me, how long have you been abbot here?'

'Fourteen years. Fourteen peaceful years, till now.'

'But there were problems two years ago, were there not? The visitation?'

He reddened. 'Yes. There had been some – backsliding. The old prior – there were corrupt practices, it happens even in the holiest of places.'

'Corrupt and illegal.'

'The old prior was removed, defrocked. The prior is, of course, responsible for the monks' welfare and discipline under me. He was a crafty villain and kept his ill deeds well concealed. But now we have godly discipline again under Prior Mortimus. Commissioner Singleton did not deny that.'

I nodded. 'Now, there are sixty servants here?'

'We have a large complex of buildings to maintain.'

'And – what – thirty monks?'

'Sir, I cannot believe that one of my servants, let alone a monk devoted to the service of God, could have done this thing.'

'All must be suspect at the start, my lord. After all, Commissioner Singleton was here to negotiate the surrender of the monastery. And for all that the pensions His Majesty is graciously offering are generous,

I imagine some may take very unkindly to the prospect of the end of their life here.'

'The monks were not told of his purpose. They know only that the commissioner was an emissary of the vicar general. I had Prior Mortimus put it about there was a problem with the title to one of the estates. At Commissioner Singleton's specific request. Only my senior officials, the senior obedentiaries, knew his purpose.'

'Who are they exactly?'

'As well as Prior Mortimus there are Gabriel, the sacrist; Brother Edwig, our bursar; and Brother Guy, the infirmarian. They are the most senior and have all been here for years, save for Brother Guy who came last year. Since the murder there have been all sorts of rumours about why the commissioner was here, but I have kept to the story about a title dispute.'

'Good. We shall hold to that arrangement for the present. Although the question of surrender is one I may wish to return to.'

The abbot paused, choosing his next words carefully.

'Sir, even in these terrible circumstances I must insist on my rights. The Act dissolving the smaller houses said specifically that the greater monasteries were in good order. There is no legal basis to demand a surrender, unless the house has been guilty of some gross breach of the injunctions, which we have not. I do not know why the vicar general should want possession of this monastery. I have heard rumours that others are being asked to surrender, but I must say to you as I said to Master Singleton: I call on the protection the law affords me.' He leaned back, his face red and his lips set, cornered but defiant.

'I see you have a collection of statutes,' I observed.

'I studied law at Cambridge many years ago. You are a lawyer, sir, you know that observance of law is the basis of our society.'

'So it is, but the law changes. New Acts have come, and others will follow.'

He looked at me without expression. He knew as well as I that there would be no more Acts dissolving monasteries by force while the country remained unsettled.

I broke the silence. 'Now, my lord, I would be grateful if you could arrange for me to inspect poor Singleton's body, which as you say is overdue for Christian burial. I will want someone to show me over the monastery, too, but perhaps that would be better done tomorrow. Dusk draws on.'

'Certainly. The body is in a place I think you will agree is both safe and fitting, in the custody of the infirmarian. I will arrange for you to be escorted to him. Please let me state clearly that I will do all I can to help you, though I fear you have a hopeless task.'

'I am grateful.'

'And, now, I have a guest room prepared for you upstairs.'

'Thank you, but I think I would prefer to be nearer the locus of the deed. You have guest rooms in your infirmary?'

'Well, yes — but surely the king's representative should lodge with the abbot?'

'The infirmary would be better,' I said firmly. 'And I will need a complete set of keys to all the buildings within the precincts.'

He smiled in disbelief. 'But — have you any idea how many keys there are here, how many doors?'

'Oh, many, I should think. Surely there must be complete sets.'

'I have one. And the prior and the gatekeeper. But they are all in constant use.'

'I shall need a set, my lord. Please arrange it.' I stood up, trying not to exclaim at a spasm from my back. Mark followed. Abbot Fabian looked thoroughly discomfited as he too rose, smoothing down his robe. 'I will see you are taken to the infirmarian.'

We followed him into the hall, where he bowed and bustled away. I blew out my cheeks.

'Will he give you the keys?' Mark asked.

'Oh, I think so. He's afraid of Cromwell. God's death, he knows his law. If he's of lowly origin as Goodhaps said, being abbot of a this great place must mean everything to him.'

'His accent was that of a man of breeding.'

'Accents can be adopted. Many put a great deal of effort into it. Lord Cromwell's voice has little of Putney left in it. Yours has little of the farm, come to that.'

'He wasn't pleased we are not staying here.'

'No, and old Goodhaps will be disappointed. But I can't help that; I don't want to be isolated here under the abbot's eye, I need to be near the heart of the place.'

✝

AFTER A FEW MINUTES Prior Mortimus appeared, bearing an enormous bunch of keys on a ring. There were over thirty, some huge ornamented affairs, centuries old. He handed them to me with a tight smile.

'I beg you not to lose them, sir. They are the only spare set the house possesses.'

I passed them to Mark. 'Carry these, would you? So there *is* a spare set?'

He avoided replying. 'I have been asked to take you to the infirmary. Brother Guy is expecting you.'

He led us out of the house and back past the workshops, closed and shuttered for it was now dark. The night was moonless and colder than ever. In my tired state the chill seemed to penetrate my bones. We passed the church, from which chanting could be heard. It was a beautiful, elaborate polyphony, accompanied by organ music; quite unlike the off-key warbling I knew from Lichfield.

'Who is your precentor?' I asked.

'Brother Gabriel, our sacrist, is master of music as well. He is a man of many talents.' I caught a sardonic note in the prior's voice.

'Is it not a little late for Vespers?'

'Only a little. Yesterday was All Souls, the monks were standing in church all day.'

I shook my head. 'Everywhere the monasteries follow their own timetable, an easier one than that St Benedict set.'

He nodded seriously. 'And Lord Cromwell is right to say the monks should be kept up to the mark. So far as is in my power, I see that they are.'

We followed the cloister wall separating off the monks' quarters and entered the big herb garden I had seen earlier. Close to, the infirmary was bigger than I had thought. The prior turned the iron ring in the stout door, and we followed him in.

The long infirmary hall stretched before us, its rows of beds on each side widely spaced and mostly empty. It reminded me how shrunken in numbers the Benedictines had become; only at the height of their numbers before the Great Pestilence would the community have needed so large an infirmary. Only three beds were occupied, all by old men in nightshirts. In the first a fat, red-cheeked monk sat up eating dried fruits; he peered at us curiously. The man in the next bed did not look towards us and I saw he was blind, his eyes milky white with cataracts. In the third bed a very old man, his thin face a mass of wrinkles, lay muttering, half-conscious. A figure in a white coif and blue servant's robe stood leaning over him, gently wiping his brow with a cloth. I saw to my surprise that it was a woman.

At a table at the far end, by the little altar, half a dozen monks sat playing cards, their arms bandaged after being bled. They looked up at us with wary eyes. The woman turned and I saw that she was young, in her early twenties. She was tall, with a fine, full figure and a strong square face with high cheekbones. She was not beautiful, but striking. She came across, studying us with intelligent dark-blue eyes before dropping her gaze submissively at the last moment.

'The king's new commissioner, for Brother Guy,' the prior said peremptorily. 'They're to lodge here, they'll need a room prepared.' For an instant, a look of dislike passed between him and the girl. Then she nodded and curtsied. 'Yes, Brother.'

She walked away, disappearing through a door by the altar. She had a poised and confident bearing, quite unlike a young maidservant's normal scuttle.

'A woman within the precincts,' I said. 'That is against the injunctions.'

'We have a dispensation, like many houses, to employ women assistants in the infirmary. The gentle hand of a woman skilled in medicine – though I don't think ye'd get much gentleness from the hands of that malapert. She has manners above her station, the infirmarian's too soft with her.'

'Brother Guy?'

'Brother Guy of Malton – of Malton but not *from* Malton, as ye'll see.'

The girl returned. 'I will take you to the dispensary, sirs.' She spoke with the local accent; her voice was soft and husky.

'I'll leave ye, then.' The prior bowed and left.

The girl was appraising Mark's costume; he had decked himself out in his finest for the journey and under his fur-trimmed coat he wore a blue jacket over a yellow tunic from which, at the bottom, his codpiece poked out. Her eyes moved to his face; many women looked at Mark, but this one's expression was different: I caught an unexpected sadness in her eyes. Mark gave her a winning smile, and she reddened.

I waved my hand. 'Please lead the way.'

We followed her into a dark, narrow passage with doors leading off. One stood open and glancing in I saw another old monk, sitting up in bed.

'Alice, is that you?' he asked querulously as we passed.

'Yes, Brother Paul,' she said gently. 'I will be with you in a moment.'

'The shaking came again.'

'I will bring you some warm wine.'

He smiled, reassured, and the girl led us on, halting before another door. 'This is Brother Guy's dispensary, sirs.'

My hose brushed against a stone pitcher outside the door. To my surprise it felt warm, and I bent for a closer look. The pitchers were filled with a thick, dark liquid. I sniffed, then jumped up quickly and gave the girl a shocked stare.

'What is that?'

'Blood, sir. Only blood. The infirmarian is giving the monks their winter bleeding. We keep the blood, it helps the herbs grow.'

'I never heard of such a thing. I thought monks were forbidden from shedding blood in any way, even infirmarians. Does not a barber-surgeon come to bleed people?'

'Brother Guy is exempt as a qualified physician, sir. He says keeping the blood is a common enough practice where he comes from. He asks would you wait a few minutes, he has just begun to bleed Brother Timothy and must supervise the process.'

'Very well. Thank you. Your name is Alice?'

'Alice Fewterer, sir.'

'Then tell your master we will wait, Alice. We would not have his patient bleed to death.'

She bowed and went off, wooden heels clacking on the stone flags.

'A well-made girl,' Mark observed.

'So she is. A strange job for a woman, this. I think your codpiece amused her, as well it might.'

'I don't like bleeding,' he said, changing the subject. 'The only time I had it done it left me weak as a kitten for days. But they say it balances the humours.'

'Well, God made me of a melancholy humour and I don't believe bleeding will change that. Now, let's see what we have here.' I unclipped the great bunch of keys from my belt, peering at them in the dim light of a wall lantern until I came to one marked 'Inf.' I tried it and the door swung open.

'Shouldn't we wait, sir?' Mark asked.

'We have no time for niceties.' I took the lantern from the wall. 'It's a chance to learn something about the man who found the body.'

The room was small, whitewashed and very neat, full of a rich spicy odour. A lying couch for the patients was covered with a clean white cloth. Bundles of herbs hung from hooks alongside surgeons' knives. There was a complex astrological chart on one wall, while opposite was a large cross in the Spanish style, dark wood with blood dripping from the five wounds of an alabaster-white Christ. Under a high window, on the infirmarian's desk, papers were neatly ordered in little piles and weighted down with pretty stones. I glanced at notes of prescriptions and diagnoses written in English and Latin.

I made my way along the shelves looking at the jars and bottles, all carefully labelled in Latin script. I lifted the lid from a large bowl to find his leeches, the black slimy creatures wriggling in the unexpected light. It was all as one would expect to find: dried marigolds for fever, vinegar for deep cuts, powdered mice for earache.

At the end of the top shelf were three books. One was a printed volume of Galen, another Paracelsus, both in French. The third, with a beautifully decorated leather cover, was handwritten in a strange language of spiky curls.

'Look at this, Mark.'

He peered over my shoulder at the book. 'Some medical code?'

'I don't know.'

I had had an ear open for footsteps, but had heard nothing and jumped at the sound of a polite cough behind us.

'Please do not drop that book, sir,' a strangely accented voice said. 'It is of great value to me if no-one else. It is an Arabic medical book, it is not on the king's forbidden list.'

We spun round. A tall monk of about fifty, with a thin, austere face, was looking at us calmly from deep-set eyes. To my surprise, his face was brown as an oak plank. I had seen brown men occasionally in London, by the docks, but had never found such a being staring me in the eye.

'I would be most thankful if you could give me the book,' he said in his soft, lisping voice, respectfully but firmly. 'It was given to my father by the last emir of Granada.'

I handed it to him and he bowed gracefully.

'You are Master Shardlake and Master Poer?'

'Indeed. Brother Guy of Malton?'

'I am. You have a key to my room? Normally only my assistant Alice comes in here unless I am present, lest someone mess with the herbs and potions. The wrong dose of some of these powders could kill, you see.' His eyes flickered over the shelves. I found myself reddening.

'I have been careful to touch nothing, sir.'

He bowed. 'Quite so. And how may I assist His Majesty's representative?'

'We wish to take accommodation here. You have guest rooms?'

'Certainly. Alice is preparing a room now. But most of this corridor is taken up with aged monks. They often require attention in the night and you may find yourself disturbed. Most guests prefer the abbot's house.'

'We would rather stay here.'

'As you wish. And may I help in any other way?' His tone was perfectly respectful, but somehow his questions made me feel like a foolish patient asked to check off symptoms. However strange his appearance, this was a man of presence.

'I gather you have charge of the body of the late commissioner?'

'I have. It is in a crypt in the lay cemetery.'

'We would like to view it.'

'Most certainly. In the meantime perhaps you may wish to wash and rest after your long journey. Will you be dining with the abbot later?'

'No, we will eat with the monks in the refectory, I think. But first I think we will take an hour's rest. That book,' I added, 'you are a Moor by birth?'

'I am from Málaga, now in Castile but when I was born part of the emirate of Granada. When Granada fell to Spain in 1492 my parents converted to Christianity, but life was not easy. In due course we made our way to France; we found life easier at Louvain, it is an international town. Arabic was, of course, their language.' He smiled gently, but his coal-black eyes stayed sharp.

'You studied medicine at Louvain?' I was astonished, for it was the most prestigious school in Europe. 'Surely you should be serving at the court of a noble or a king, not in a remote monastery.'

'Indeed so; but as a Spanish Moor I have certain disadvantages. Over the years I have bounced from post to post in France and England, like one of your King Henry's tennis balls.' He smiled again. 'I was at Malton in Yorkshire five years; I kept the name when I came here two years ago. And if rumour speaks true, I may be on the move again soon.'

I remembered he was one of the officials who knew of Singleton's purpose. He nodded reflectively at my silence.

'So. I will take you to your room, and I will return in an hour so you can inspect Commissioner Singleton's body. The poor man should be given Christian burial.' He crossed himself, sighing. 'It will be hard enough for the soul of a murdered man to find rest, unconfessed and without the last sacrament at his end. Pray God none of us should ever meet such a fate.'

Chapter Seven

OUR ROOM IN THE INFIRMARY was small but comfortable, wood-panelled and with new, sweet-scented rushes on the floor. It was warmed by a fire, before which chairs had been set. The girl Alice was there when Brother Guy showed us in, laying towels beside a pitcher of warm water. Her face and bare arms had a healthy flush from the fire.

'I thought you might like to wash, sirs,' she said deferentially.

I smiled at her. 'That is most kind.'

'I need something to get me warm,' Mark said, giving her a grin. She lowered her head and Brother Guy gave Mark a stern look.

'Thank you, Alice,' he said. 'That will be enough.' The girl bowed and left.

'I hope the room is comfortable. I have sent word to the abbot you will be dining in the refectory.'

'This room will do very well. Thank you for your trouble.'

'If you have any needs, Alice will attend to them.' He gave Mark another sharp look. 'But please bear in mind that she has many duties with the aged and sick monks. And that she is a woman alone here, apart from some old kitchen maids. She is under my protection, such as it is.'

Mark coloured. I bowed to the infirmarian. 'We will remember that, sir.'

'Thank you, Master Shardlake. Then I will leave you.'

'Black old moldwarp,' Mark grumbled when the door closed. 'It was only a look — and she was pleased to get it.'

'He is responsible for her welfare,' I said shortly.

Mark looked at the bed. It was one of those with a high bed for the master and a narrow space underneath where a servant's wooden bunk slid in and out on wheels. He pulled out the lower tier and looked gloomily at the hard board covered with a thin straw mattress, before removing his coat and sitting down.

I went over to the ewer and splashed some warm water on my face, letting it drip down my neck. I felt exhausted; my head was spinning with the kaleidoscope of faces and impressions of the last few hours. I groaned. 'Thank God we're alone at last.' I sat down in the chair. 'Christ's wounds, I'm sore.'

Mark looked up at me with concern. 'Does your back pain you?'

I sighed. 'It will be better after a night's rest.'

'Are you sure, sir?' He hesitated. 'There are cloths there, we could make a hot poultice . . . I could apply it for you.'

'No!' I snapped. 'Will you be told, I'll be all right!' I hated anyone looking at my deformed back; only my physician was allowed to do that and then only when it was especially painful. My skin crawled at the thought of Mark's eyes on it, his pity and perhaps disgust, for why should someone formed as he was not feel disgust? I pulled myself to my feet and went over to the window, looking out over the dark, empty quadrangle. After a few moments I turned round; Mark was looking up at me, resentfulness mixed with anxiety in his face. I raised a hand apologetically.

'I am sorry, I should not have shouted.'

'I meant no ill.'

'I know. I am tired and worried, that is all.'

'Worried?'

'Lord Cromwell wants a result quickly and I wonder if I will be able to get one. I had hoped for – I don't know, some fanatic among the monks who had already been locked up, at least some clear pointer to the culprit. Goodhaps is no help; he's so scared he'd leap at his own shadow. And these monkish officials do not seem likely to be easily overawed. On top of that we seem to have a mad Carthusian stirring up trouble, and talk of a break-in by practitioners of dark arts from the town. Jesu, it's a tangle. And that abbot knew his law, I can see why Singleton found him difficult.'

'You can only do what it is in your power to do, sir.'

'Lord Cromwell would not see things that way.' I lay down on the bed, staring at the ceiling. Usually when I began grappling with a new case I would enjoy a sense of pleasurable excitement, but here I could see no thread to guide me through what seemed an enormous labyrinth.

'This is a gloomy place,' Mark said. 'All those dark stone corridors, all those arches. Each one could hide an assassin.'

'Yes, I remember when I was at school how endless and frightening all the echoing corridors seemed if one was sent on an errand. All the doors one was not allowed to open.' I tried to be encouraging: 'But now I have a commission affording me every access. It's a place like every other, and we'll soon find our way around.' There was no reply and the sound of deep breathing told me Mark had fallen asleep. I smiled wryly, closed my eyes for a moment, and the next thing I knew there was a loud knock on the door and an exclamation from Mark as he was jolted awake. I got to my feet, surprisingly refreshed by my unintended sleep, my mind alert once more. I opened the door. Brother Guy stood outside, his candle casting the strangest shadows across his dark troubled face, his eyes serious.

'Are you ready to view the body, sir?'

'Ay, as ready as we'll ever be.' I reached for my coat.

✞

IN THE INFIRMARY hall the girl brought a lamp for Brother Guy. He donned a thick robe over his habit and led us along a dim, high-ceilinged corridor with vaulted ceilings.

'It is quickest to cross the cloister yard,' he said, opening a door into the cold air.

The yard, enclosed on three sides by the buildings where the monks lived and on the fourth by the church, made an unexpectedly pretty picture. Lights flickered at the many windows.

Surrounding the yard was the cloister walk, a covered area supported by elaborate arches. Long ago that would have been where the monks studied, in carrels lining the walk and open to cold and wind; but in these softer times it was a place for walking and talking. Against one pillar stood the lavatorium, an elaborate stone bowl used for washing hands, where a little fountain made a gentle tinkling sound. The soft glow from the stained-glass windows of the church made coloured patterns on the ground. I noticed strange little motes dancing in the light, and was puzzled for a moment before realizing it had started to snow again. The flags of the cloister yard were already speckled with white. Brother Guy led us across.

'You found the body, I believe?' I asked.

'Yes. Alice and I were up tending Brother August, who had a fever and was in much distress. I wanted to give him some warm milk and went to the kitchen to fetch some.'

'And that door is normally kept locked.'

'Of course. Otherwise the servants, and I regret also the monks, would help themselves to food whenever they wanted. I have a key because I often need things urgently.'

'This was at five o'clock?'

'The clock had struck a little before.'

'Had Matins begun?'

'No, Matins is sung late here. Usually towards six.'

'St Benedict's rule prescribes midnight.'

He smiled gently. 'St Benedict wrote his rule for Italians, sir, not people who have to live through English winters. The office is sung and God hears it. We cut through the chapter house now.'

He opened another door and we found ourselves in a large chamber, its walls richly painted with biblical scenes. Stools and cushioned chairs were dotted around, and there was a long table before a roaring fire. The room was warm and musty with body odour. About twenty monks sat around; some were talking, some reading, and half a dozen were playing cards at a table. Each monk had a pretty little crystal glass by his elbow, filled with green liquid from a large bottle of French liqueur that stood on the card-players' table. I looked round for the Carthusian, but there was no white habit among the black; the straggle-haired sodomite Brother Gabriel and Mortimus the sharp-eyed bursar were also absent.

A thin-faced young monk with a wispy beard had just lost a game, judging by his annoyed expression.

'That's a shilling you owe us, Brother,' a tall, cadaverous monk said cheerfully.

'You'll have to wait. I will need an advance from the chamberlain.'

'No more advances, Brother Athelstan!' A plump old brother sitting nearby, his face disfigured by a warty growth on one cheek, wagged a finger at him. 'Brother Edwig says you've had so many advances you're getting your wages before you've earned them—' He broke off, and the monks hastily rose to their feet and bowed to me. One, a young fellow so obese even his shaven head was lined and puckered with fat, knocked his glass to the floor.

'Septimus, you dolt!' His neighbour prodded him sharply with his elbow, and he stared round with the vague glance of the simple-minded. The monk with the disfigured face stepped forward, bowing again obsequiously.

'I am Brother Jude, sir, the pittancer.'

'Master Matthew Shardlake, the king's commissioner. I see you are enjoying a convivial evening.'

'A little relaxation before Vespers. Would you care for some of this fine liqueur, Commissioner? It is from one of our French sister houses.'

I shook my head. 'I still have work to do,' I said severely. 'In the earlier days of your order, the day's end would have been taken up with the Great Silence.'

Brother Jude hesitated. 'That was long ago, sir, in the days before the Great Pestilence. Since then the world has fallen further towards its end.'

'I think the English world does very well under King Henry.'

'No, no—' he said hastily. 'I did not mean—'

The tall thin monk from the card table joined us. 'Forgive Brother Jude, sir, he speaks without thinking. I am Brother Hugh, the chamberlain. We know we need correction, Commissioner, and we welcome it.' He glared at his colleague.

'Good. That will make my work easier. Come, Brother Guy. We have a corpse to inspect.'

The fat young monk stepped forward hesitantly. 'Forgive me slipping, good sire. My leg pains me, I have an ulcer.' He gave us a woebegone look. Brother Guy put a hand on his shoulder.

'If you would follow my diet, Septimus, your poor legs would not have to bear such weight. No wonder they protest.'

'I am weak flesh, Brother, I need my meat.'

'Sometimes I think it a pity the Lateran Council ever lifted the prohibition on meat. Now excuse us, Septimus, we are on our way to the crypt. You will be pleased to hear Commissioner Singleton may be laid to rest soon.'

'Thanks be to God. I am afraid to go near the cemetery. An unburied body, an unshriven man—'

'Yes, yes. Go now, it is almost time for Vespers.' Brother Guy gently moved him aside and led us through another door, out into the night again. An expanse of flat ground lay ahead, dotted with headstones. Ghostly white shapes stood out here and there, which I recognized as family crypts. Brother Guy raised the hood of his habit against the snow, which was coming down thickly now.

'You must forgive Brother Septimus,' he said. 'He is a poor silly creature.'

'No wonder his leg gives trouble,' Mark observed. 'Carrying all that weight.'

'The monks stand for hours at a time in a cold church every day, Master Mark, a good covering of fat is not unhealthy. But the standing brings on varicose ulcers. It is not so easy a life. And poor Septimus has not the wit to cease from gorging.'

I shivered. 'This is not the weather to stand talking.'

Holding his lamp high, Brother Guy led us between the head, stones. I asked him whether, when he came to the kitchen that morning, the door had been locked.

'Yes,' he replied. 'I went in through the door from the cloister yard, which is always locked at night, then up the short passage leading to the kitchen. The kitchen itself is not locked because the only way is via the passage. I opened the door and at once I slipped in something and almost went over. I put my lamp down, then saw that headless body.'

'Dr Goodhaps said he slipped too. So the blood was liquid?'

The infirmarian considered. 'Yes, it had not started to congeal.'

'So the deed had not been done long?'

'No, it cannot have been.'

'And you saw no one on your way to the kitchen?'

'No.'

I was pleased to find my brain working again, my mind racing along. 'Whoever killed Singleton would himself have been covered in blood. He would have had bloody clothes, left bloody footsteps.'

'I saw none. But I confess it was not in my mind to look, I was shocked. Later, of course, when the house was roused, there were bloody footprints everywhere from those who had entered the kitchen.'

I thought a moment. 'And the killer may then have gone to the church, desecrated the altar and stolen the relic. Did you, did anyone, notice any traces of blood on the way across the cloister to the church, or inside the church?'

Brother Guy gave me a sombre look. 'There was blood spilt about the church. We assumed it came from that sacrificed cock. As for the cloister, it started to rain before dawn and went on all day. It would have washed away any traces.'

'And after you found the body, what did you do?'

'I went straight to the abbot, of course. Now, here we are.'

He had led us to the largest of the crypts, a one-storey building in the ubiquitous yellow limestone, set on a little rise. It had a stout wooden door, wide enough for a coffin to be carried in.

I blinked a snowflake from my eyelashes. 'Well, let us get this over with.' He produced a key and I took a deep breath, breathing a silent prayer that God might strengthen my weak stomach.

✝

WE HAD TO STOOP to enter the low, whitewashed chamber. The ossuary was bitterly cold, the wind slicing in through a small barred window. The air held the faint, sickly tang all tombs possess. In the dim light of Brother Guy's lamp I saw the walls were lined with stone sarcophagi, figures representing the dead carved atop the lids, hands clasped in poses of supplication. Most of the men wore the full armour of past centuries.

Brother Guy put his lamp down and folded his arms, tucking his hands inside the long sleeves of his habit for warmth. 'The Fitzhugh crypt,' he said. 'The family were the original founders of the monastery and were buried here till the last of them died in the civil wars of the last century.'

The silence was suddenly broken by a jangling metallic crash. I jumped involuntarily and so did Brother Guy, his eyes wide in his dark face. I turned to see Mark bent over, picking the abbot's bunch of keys from the flagstones.

'I'm sorry, sir,' he muttered. 'I thought they were securely tied.'

'God's death!' I snapped. 'Oaf!' My legs were shaking.

There was a large metal sconce filled with fat candles in the centre of the room. Brother Guy lit them from his lamp and a yellow glow filled the chamber as he led us across to a sarcophagus with a bare stone lid, without inscription.

'"This tomb is the only one without a permanent occupant and will never have one now. The last male heir perished at Bosworth with King Richard III."' He smiled sadly. '"*Sic transit gloria mundi*."'

'And Singleton is laid there?' I asked.

He nodded. 'He's been there four days, but the cold should have kept him fresh.'

I took another deep breath. 'Then let us have the lid off. Mark, help him.'

Mark and Brother Guy strained to slide the heavy stone lid onto the neighbouring tomb. It resisted their efforts at first, then slid off in a rush. At once the chamber was filled with a sickening smell. Mark stepped back a pace, his nose wrinkling with distaste. 'Not so fresh,' he murmured.

Brother Guy peered in, crossing himself. I stepped forward, gripping the edge of the sarcophagus.

The body was wrapped in a white woollen cloth; only the calves and feet were visible, alabaster white, the toenails long and yellow. At the other end of the blanket a little watery blood had run out from the neck, and there was a pool of darker blood under the head, which had been set upright beside the body. I looked into the face of Robin Singleton, whom once I had outstared across the courtroom.

He had been a thin man in his thirties, with black hair and a long nose. I saw there was a dark stubble on the white cheeks and felt my stomach turn at the sight of this head set upon a bloody piece of stone instead of a neck. The mouth was almost closed, the tips of the teeth showing under the lips. The dark-blue eyes were wide open, filmy in death. I saw a tiny black insect walk from under one eyelid across the orb and under the opposite lid. Swallowing, I turned and stepped over to the little barred window, taking a deep breath of cold night air. As I fought down bile, I forced another part of my mind to order what I had seen. I heard Mark come to my side.

'Are you all right, sir?'

'Of course.' Turning, I saw Brother Guy standing with arms folded, quite composed, looking at me thoughtfully. Mark himself was a little pale, but crossed back to look again at that dreadful head.

'Well, Mark, what would you say about the manner of that man's death?' I called.

He shook his head. 'It is as we knew, his head was struck from his shoulders.'

'I didn't think he died from an ague. But can we tell anything more from what is there? I would take a guess that the assailant was of at least medium height, to start with.'

Brother Guy looked at me curiously. 'How can you say that?'

'Well, firstly, Singleton was quite a tall man.'

'It's hard to tell without a head,' Mark said.

'I met him in court. I remember I had the disadvantage of having to twist my neck to look up at him.' I made myself go over and look at the head again. 'And see how the neck is cut straight across. It sits perfectly upright on the stone. If he and his attacker were both standing when he was attacked, which seems most likely, a shorter man would have had to strike upwards at an angle, and the neck would not have been cut straight through.'

Brother Guy nodded. 'That is true. By Our Lady, sir, you have the eye of a physician.'

'Thank you. Though I would not wish to spend my days looking on such sights. But I have seen a head severed before. I remember the –' I sought a word – 'the mechanics.' I met the infirmarian's curious gaze, digging my fingernails into my palms as I remembered a day I wished dearly to forget. 'And, talking of such matters, observe how clean the blow is, the head sheared off with one strike. That is difficult to achieve even if someone is lying down with his neck on a block.'

Mark looked again at the head lying on its side, and nodded once more. 'Aye. Axes are difficult to handle. I was told they had to hack away at Thomas More's neck. But what if he was bending down? To pick something up from the floor? Or perhaps he was made to bend down?'

I thought a moment. 'Yes. Good point. But if he was bent over as he died the body would have been bent when it was found. Brother Guy will remember.' I looked at him enquiringly.

'He lay straight,' the infirmarian said thoughtfully. 'The difficulty of striking off someone's head like that has been in all our minds. You couldn't do it with a kitchen implement, even the biggest knife. That is why some of the brothers fear witchcraft.'

'But what weapon *could* slice the head off a man standing upright?' I asked. 'I'd guess not an axe, the blade is too thick. You'd need a very sharp cutting edge, like a sword. In fact I can't think of anything that would do it but a sword. What do you say, Mark? You're the swordsman here.'

'I think you are right.' He gave a nervous laugh. 'Only royalty and the nobility have the right to be executed with a sword.'

'Precisely because a sharp sword blade ensures a swift end.'

'Like Anne Boleyn,' Mark said.

Brother Guy crossed himself. 'The witch queen,' he said quietly.

'That is what brought it to mind,' I said softly. 'The one beheading I have seen. Just like Anne Boleyn.'

Chapter Eight

WE WAITED OUTSIDE while Brother Guy locked the crypt. The snow was heavier now, thick flakes swirling down. Already the ground was white.

'We were lucky to miss this on the road,' Mark said.

'We'll have problems getting back if this goes on. We may have to return by sea.'

Brother Guy joined us. He gave me a serious look. 'Sir, we would like to bury poor Commissioner Singleton tomorrow. It would make the community easier – and allow his soul to find rest.'

'Where will you bury him? Here? He had no family.'

'In the lay cemetery. If you permit.'

I nodded. 'Very well. I have seen enough, the sight is etched in my mind all too clearly.'

'You deduced much, sir.'

'Educated guesswork only.' Standing close to Brother Guy I noticed a faint odour, like sandalwood. He certainly smelt better than his brethren.

'I will tell the abbot arrangements can be made for the funeral,' he said with relief.

The church bell boomed out, making me start. 'I have never heard such a loud peal. I noticed it earlier.'

'The bells are really too large for the tower. But they have an interesting history. They originally hung in the ancient cathedral of Toulouse.'

'Why move them here?'

'They came a roundabout way. The cathedral was destroyed in

an Arab raid eight hundred years ago and the bells taken as a trophy. They were found at Salamanca in Spain when that city was reconquered for Christ, and donated to Scarnsea when the monastery was founded.'

'I still think you would be better served with smaller bells.'

'We have become used to them.'

'I doubt I will.'

He smiled, a quick sad flicker. 'You must blame my Arab ancestors.'

We reached the cloister just as the monks were leaving the church in procession. The sight made an impression that comes clearly to mind all these years later: almost thirty black-robed Benedictines walking in double file across the old stone cloister, cowls raised and arms folded in their wide sleeves to give protection against the snow, which fell in a silent curtain, coating them as they walked, the whole scene illuminated from the church windows. It was a beautiful scene and despite myself I was moved.

✞

BROTHER GUY took us back to our room, promising to collect us shortly and take us to the refectory. We shook the snow from our coats, then Mark wheeled out his little bed and lowered himself onto it.

'How do you think a swordsman could have killed Singleton, sir? Waited for him and struck him from behind?'

I began unpacking my pannier, sorting papers and books. 'Possibly. But what was Singleton doing in the kitchen at four in the morning?'

'Perhaps he had arranged to meet the monk there, the one he told the gatekeeper about?'

'Yes, that is the most likely explanation. Someone arranged to meet Singleton in the kitchen, perhaps with a promise of information, and killed him. Executed him, more like. The whole thing has the flavour of an execution. Surely it would have been far easier just to knife him in the back.'

'He looked a hard man,' Mark said. 'Though it was difficult to tell, his head stuck on the floor of that tomb.' He laughed, a touch shrilly, and I realized he too had been affected by the sight.

'Robin Singleton was a type of lawyer I detest. He had little law and that ill-digested. He made his way by bullying and bluff, supplemented with gold slipped into the right hand at the right time. But he did not deserve to be killed in that terrible way.'

'I had forgotten you were at the execution of Queen Anne Boleyn last year, sir,' Mark said.

'I wish I could.'

'At least it served to give you some ideas.'

I nodded sadly, then gave him a wry smile. 'I remember a teacher we had when I first went to the Inns of Court, Serjeant Hampton. He taught us evidence. He had a saying. "In any investigation, what are the most relevant circumstances? *None*," he would bark in reply. "*All* the circumstances are relevant, *everything* must be examined from *every* angle!"'

'Don't say that, sir. We could be here for ever.' He stretched himself out with a groan. 'I could sleep for twelve hours, even on this old board.'

'Well, we can't sleep, not yet. I want to meet the community at supper. If we're to get anywhere, we must know these people. Come, there's no rest for those called to Lord Cromwell's service.' I kicked at the wheeled extension, sending him sliding back under my bed with a yell.

✝

BROTHER GUY led us to the refectory, along dark corridors and up a staircase. It was an impressive chamber, a high ceiling supported by thick pillars with wide vaulting arches. Despite its size, it was lent a comfortable air by the tapestries lining the walls and the thick rattan matting on the floor. A large, beautifully carved lectern stood in one corner. Sconces filled with fat candles cast a warm glow over two tables set with fine plate and cutlery. One, with half a dozen places, stood before the fire and the other, much longer, table was further off. Kitchen servants bustled about, setting out jugs of wine and silver tureens, rich odours escaping from under their lids. I studied the cutlery at the table nearest the fire.

'Silver,' I remarked to Brother Guy. 'And the plates too.'

'That is the obedentiaries' table, where the monastery office holders sit. The ordinary monks have pewter.'

'The common people have wood,' I observed, as Abbot Fabian came bustling in. The servants stopped their work to bow, receiving benevolent nods in return. 'And the abbot dines off gold plate, no doubt,' I muttered to Mark.

The abbot came over to us, smiling tightly.

'I had not been told you wished to dine in the refectory. I have had roast beef prepared in my kitchens.'

'Thank you, but we will take supper here.'

'As you wish.' The abbot sighed. 'I suggested Dr Goodhaps might join you, but he adamantly refuses to leave my house.'

'Did Brother Guy tell you I have given authority for Commissioner Singleton to be buried?'

'He did. I will make the announcement before dinner. It is my turn to give the reading. In English, in accordance with the injunctions,' he added solemnly.

'Good.'

There was a bustle at the door, and the monks began filing in. The two officials we had seen earlier, the fair-haired sacrist Brother Gabriel and Edwig, the dark-haired bursar, walked side by side to the obedentiaries' table, not speaking. They made an odd pair; one tall and fair, his head slightly bowed, the other striding confidently along. They were joined by the prior, the two officials I had met at the chapter house and Brother Guy. The other monks stood at the long table. I noticed the old Carthusian among them; he gave me a venomous look. The abbot leaned across.

'I hear Brother Jerome caused offence earlier. I apologize. But his vows mean he takes his meals in silence.'

'I understand he is lodged here at the request of a member of the Seymour family.'

'Our neighbour, Sir Edward Wentworth. But the request originally came from Lord Cromwell's office.' He gave me a sidelong look. 'He wanted Jerome kept somewhere quiet, out of the way. As a distant relative of Queen Jane he was something of an embarrassment.'

I nodded. 'How long has he been here?'

The abbot looked at Jerome's frowning face. 'Eighteen long months.'

I cast my eye over the assembled monks, who gave me uneasy glances as though I were a strange beast set among them. I noticed they were mainly middle-aged or elderly, few young faces and only three in novices' habits. One old monk, his head trembling with palsy, crossed himself quickly as he studied me.

My eye was drawn to a figure standing uncertainly by the door. I recognized the novice who had taken our horses earlier; he stood shifting uneasily from foot to foot, holding something behind his back. Prior Mortimus looked up from his table.

'Simon Whelplay!' he snapped. 'Your penance is not over, you will have no dinner tonight. Take your place in that corner.'

The boy bowed his head and crossed to a corner of the room, furthest from the fire. He brought his hands round and I saw he held a fool's pointed cap, with the letter 'M' stencilled on it. Reddening, he put it on. The other monks barely glanced at him.

'M?' I asked.

'For *maleficium*,' the abbot said. 'He has broken the rules, I am afraid. Please, sit.'

Mark and I took places beside Brother Guy, while the abbot went to the lectern. I saw a bible was placed there and was pleased to see it was the English Bible, not the Latin Vulgate with its mistranslations and invented gospels.

'Brethren,' Abbot Fabian announced sonorously, 'we have all been greatly shocked by recent events. I am pleased to welcome the vicar general's representative, Commissioner Shardlake, who has come to investigate the matter. He will be speaking to many of you, and you are to afford him all the help Lord Cromwell's representative deserves.' I eyed him sharply; those words carried a double meaning.

'Master Shardlake has given authority for Master Singleton to be buried, and the funeral service will take place after Matins, the day after tomorrow.' There was a relieved murmur along the tables. 'And now, our reading is from Revelation, Chapter 7: "And after those things I saw four angels standing on the four corners of the earth . . ."'

I was surprised he chose Revelation, for it was a text favoured much by reformists of the hot gospeller sort, keen to tell the world they had fathomed its mysteries and violent symbols. The passage dealt with the Lord's roll-call of the saved at the Day of Judgement. It seemed like a challenge to me, identifying the community with the righteous.

'"And he said unto me, these are they which came out of great tribulation, and have washed their robes, and made them white in the blood of the Lamb."'

'Amen,' he concluded sonorously, then closed the bible and walked solemnly out of the refectory; doubtless his roast beef was waiting in his dining room. It was the signal for a babble of chatter to break out as half a dozen servants entered and began serving soup. It was a thick vegetable broth, richly spiced and delicious. I had not eaten since breakfast and concentrated on my bowl for a minute before glancing over at Whelplay, still as a statue in the shadows. Through the window beside him I saw the snow still tumbling down. I turned to the prior, who was sitting opposite me.

'The novice is not to have any of this fine soup?'

'Not for another four days. He's to stand there through the meal as part of his penance. He must learn. D'ye think me too severe, sir?'

'How old is he? He does not look eighteen.'

'He's nearly twenty, though you wouldn't think it from his scrawny looks. His novitiate was extended, he had problems mastering the Latin, though he has musical skills. He assists Brother Gabriel. Simon Whelplay needs to learn obedience. He is being punished, among other things, for avoiding the services in English. When I set people a penance I give them a good lesson that'll stick in their minds and those of others.'

'Quite r-right, Brother Prior.' The bursar spoke up, nodding vigorously. He smiled at me; a cold smile, making a brief slash across his chubby face. 'I am Brother Edwig, Commissioner, the bursar.' He set his silver spoon down in his plate, which he had quickly emptied.

'So you have responsibility for distributing the monastery's funds?'

'And c-c-collecting them in, and ensuring expenditure does not outstrip revenue,' he added. His stammer could not occlude the self-satisfaction in his voice.

'I believe I passed you in the yard earlier, discussing some – building works, was it? – with one of your brethren.' I glanced at the tall, fair-haired monk who had cast that lascivious look at Mark earlier. He sat almost opposite him now, and had been giving him covert glances whilst avoiding his eye. He caught mine, though, and leaned over to introduce himself.

'Gabriel of Ashford, Commissioner. I am the sacrist, and also the precentor; I have charge of the church and library as well as the music. We have to combine the offices, our numbers are not what they were.'

'No. A hundred years ago you would have had, what, twice as many monks? And the church is in need of repair?'

'Indeed it is, sir.' Brother Gabriel leaned eagerly towards me, nearly causing Brother Guy to spill his soup. 'Have you seen our church?'

'Not yet. I plan to visit it tomorrow.'

'We have the finest Norman church on the south coast. Over four hundred years old. It compares to the best Benedictine houses in Normandy. But there is a bad crack running down from the roof. We need repairs, and they should be done with Caen stone again, to match the interior . . .'

'Brother Gabriel,' the prior interjected sharply, 'Master Shardlake has more serious things to do than admire the architecture. It may be too rich for his taste,' he added meaningfully.

'But surely the New Learning does not frown on architectural beauty?'

'Only when the congregation is encouraged to worship the building rather than God,' I said. 'For that would be idolatry.'

'I meant nothing of that sort,' the sacrist replied earnestly. 'Only that in any great building the eye should be led to rest on exact proportions, unity of line . . .'

Brother Edwig gave a sarcastic grimace. 'What my brother means is that to satisfy his aesthetic notions the monastery should b-bankrupt itself importing great blocks of limestone from France. I would be interested to know how he p-p-plans to ferry them across the marsh.'

'Does the monastery not have ample reserves?' I asked. 'I read the revenues from its lands run to £800 a year. And rents are rising all the time now, as the poor know to their cost.'

As I spoke the servants returned, setting out plates on which big carp lay steaming, and tureens of vegetables. I noticed a woman among them, a hook-nosed old crone, and reflected that Alice must be lonely if she had only such as this for female company. I turned back to the bursar. He gave a quick frown.

'Land has had to be sold recently, f-f-for various reasons. And the amount Brother Gabriel asks for is more than the whole repairs budget for five years. Take one of these fine carp, sir. Caught in our own stewpond this morning.'

'But surely money could be borrowed against the annual surpluses you must have?'

'Thank you, sir. Precisely my argument,' Brother Gabriel said.

The bursar's frown deepened. He put down his spoon, waving his chubby little hands.

'P-prudent accounting does not allow for a great hole in the revenues for years to come, sir, interest p-payments eating away at them like m-mice. The abbot's policy is a b-balanced b-b-b—' His face reddened as, in his excitement, he lost control of his stutter.

'Budget,' the prior concluded for him with a sour grin. He passed me a carp and plunged his knife into his own fish, slicing into it with enthusiasm. Brother Gabriel gave him a glare and took a sip of the good white wine.

I shrugged. 'It is a matter between you, of course.'

Brother Edwig set down his cup. 'I ap-pologize if I became heated. It is an old argument between the sacrist and me.' He gave his slash of a smile again, showing even white teeth. I nodded gravely in acknowledgement, then turned my gaze to the window, where the snow still whirled down. It was settling thickly now. There was a draught from the window and, although my front was warm where it faced the fire, my back was cold. Next to the window the novice gave a cough. His bowed head under its cap was in shadow, but I noticed his legs trembling under his habit.

The silence was broken by a sudden harsh voice.

'Fools! There will be no new building. Do you not know that the world has at last rolled down to its end? The Antichrist is here!' The Carthusian had half-risen from his bench. 'A thousand years of devotion to God, in all these houses of prayer, is ended. Soon there will be nothing, empty buildings and silence, silence for the Devil to fill with his roaring!' His voice rose to a shout as he fixed everyone in turn with bitter looks. The monks averted their eyes. Turning in his place, Brother Jerome lost his balance and fell sprawling across the bench, his face contorted with pain.

Prior Mortimus rose, slamming his hand on the table. 'God's death! Brother Jerome, you will leave this table and keep to your cell till the abbot decides what is to be done with you. Take him out!'

His neighbours lifted the Carthusian under the arms, hauled him quickly to his feet and hustled him from the refectory. As the door closed behind them, an exhalation of held breaths sounded across the room. Prior Mortimus turned to me.

'Once again, my apologies on behalf of the community.' There was a mumble of assent along the tables. 'I only ask you to excuse the man on the grounds that he is mad.'

'Who does he think is the Antichrist, I wonder? Me? No, Lord Cromwell more likely, or perhaps His Majesty the King?'

'No, sir, no.' There was an anxious murmur along the obeden-tiaries' table. Prior Mortimus set his thin lips.

'If I had my way, Jerome would be turned out of doors tomorrow to cry his madness in the streets till he was put in the Tower, or more likely the Bedlam, for that's where he belongs. The abbot only keeps him because he needs the favour of his cousin Sir Edward. You know of Jerome's connection with the late queen?' I nodded. 'But this is too much. He must go.'

I raised a hand, shaking my head. 'I take no official note of a madman's babble.' I felt a palpable sense of relief along the table at my words. I lowered my voice again, so only the obedentiaries could hear. 'I would have Brother Jerome kept here, I may wish to question him. Tell me, did he treat Master Singleton to such discourse as I have had?'

'Yes,' the prior replied bluntly. 'When he first arrived Brother Jerome accosted him in the yard and called him perjurer and liar. Commissioner Singleton gave as good as he got, calling him a Roman whoreson.'

'Perjurer and liar. That's more specific than the general abuse he's given me. I wonder what he meant?'

'God alone knows what madmen ever mean.'

Brother Guy leaned forward. 'He may be mad, Commissioner, but he would never have been capable of killing Commissioner Singleton. I have treated him. His left arm was wrenched out of its socket on the rack, the ligaments shredded. His right leg is scarcely better and his balance is gone, as you saw. He can scarcely carry himself, yet alone wield a weapon to sever a man's head. I have treated the effects of official torture before, in France,' he added in quieter tones, 'but never before in England. I am told it is a new thing.'

'The law permits it in times of extreme threat to the State,' I replied, stung. I saw Mark's eyes on me and read disappointment, sadness. 'Regrettable though it always is,' I added with a sigh. 'But to return to poor Singleton. Brother Jerome may have been too infirm to kill, but he could have had an accomplice.'

'No, sir, never, no.' It was a chorus along the table. I read only fear in the officials' faces, anxiety not to be associated with murder and treason and their terrible penalties. But men, I reflected, are adept at concealing their true thoughts. Brother Gabriel leaned forward again, his thin face furrowed with anxiety.

'Sir, no one here shares Brother Jerome's beliefs. He is a blight on us. We wish only to carry on our life of prayer in peace, loyal to the king and in obedience to the forms of worship he dictates.'

'There at least my brother speaks for all,' the bursar added loudly. 'I say "Amen" to that.' A chorus of 'Amens' followed along the table.

I nodded in acknowledgement. 'But Commissioner Singleton is still dead. So who do you think killed him? Brother Bursar? Brother Prior?'

'It was p-people from the world outside,' Brother Edwig said. 'He was on his way to meet someone and he disturbed them. Witches, Devil-worshippers. They broke in to desecrate our church and steal our relic, came across poor Singleton and killed him. The person he was to meet, whoever he was, no doubt took fright at the tumult.'

'Master Shardlake hazarded the killing may have been done with a sword,' Brother Guy added. 'And such people would be unlikely to carry weapons lest they be discovered.'

I turned to Brother Gabriel. He sighed deeply, running his fingers through the straggly locks below his tonsure. 'The loss of the hand of the Penitent Thief — it is a tragedy, that most holy relic of Our Lord's Calvary — I shudder to think what abominable uses the thief may be putting it to now.' His face looked drawn. I remembered the skulls in Lord Cromwell's room and realized again the power of relics.

'Are there known practitioners of witchcraft hereabouts?' I asked.

The prior shook his head. 'A couple of wise women in the town, but they're just old crones who mutter incantations over the herbs they peddle.'

'Who knows what evils the Devil works in the sinful world?' Brother Gabriel said quietly. 'We are protected from him in this holy life, as well as men can be, but outside—' He shivered.

'Then there are the servants,' I added. 'All sixty of them.'

'Only a dozen living in,' the prior said. 'And the premises are well locked at night, patrolled by Master Bugge and his assistant under my supervision.'

'Those who live in are mostly old, loyal servants,' Brother Gabriel added. 'Why would one of them kill an important visitor?'

'Why would a monk or a villager? Well, we shall see. Tomorrow I wish to question some of you.' I looked down a row of discomfited faces.

The servants came in to remove our plates, replacing them with pudding bowls. There was silence until they left. The bursar took a spoon to the sugary confection in his bowl. 'Ah, wet suckets,' he said. 'Welcome and warming on a cold night.'

There was a sudden loud crash from the corner of the room. Everyone jumped and turned to where the novice had collapsed in a heap on the floor. Brother Guy rose with an exclamation of disgust, his habit billowing round him as he ran to where Simon Whelplay lay still on the rush matting. I stood up and joined him, as did Brother Gabriel and then, with an angry expression, the prior. The boy was as white as a sheet. As Brother Guy gently lifted his head, he moaned and his eyes flickered open.

'It's all right,' Brother Guy said gently. 'You fainted. Have you hurt yourself?'

'My head. I banged my head. I am sorry—' Tears glistened suddenly in the corners of his eyes, his thin chest shook and he began to weep most piteously. Prior Mortimus snorted. I was surprised at the anger that appeared then in Brother Guy's dark eyes.

'No wonder the boy weeps, Master Prior! When was he last properly fed? He is naught but skin and bone.'

'He has had bread and water. You are well aware, Brother Infirmarian, that is a penance sanctioned by St Benedict's rule . . .'

Brother Gabriel turned on him furiously. 'The saint did not intend God's servants to be starved to death! You have been working Simon like a dog in the stables, then making him stand in the cold for hours on end.' The novice's crying turned to a violent fit of coughing, his pale face suddenly puce as he struggled for breath. The infirmarian cocked a sharp ear to the wheezing sounds from his chest.

'His lungs are full of bile. I want him in the infirmary now!'

The prior snorted again. 'Is it my fault he's as weak as water? I gave him work to toughen him up. It's what he needs—'

Brother Gabriel's voice rang round the refectory. 'Does Brother Guy have your authority to take Simon to the infirmary, or do I go to Abbot Fabian?'

'Take the churl!' the prior snapped. He strode back to the table. 'Softness! Softness and weakness. They'll be the end of us all!' He glowered defiantly around the refectory as Brother Gabriel and the infirmarian supported the weeping, coughing novice from the room. Brother Edwig cleared his throat.

'Brother Prior, I think we may say g-grace and rise now. It is nearly time for C-Compline.'

Prior Mortimus said a perfunctory grace, and the monks rose, those at the long table waiting until the obedientiaries had filed out. As we went through the door, Brother Edwig leaned over to me, his voice unctuous.

'Master Shardlake, I am sorry your meal should have been disturbed t-twice. Very r-r-regrettable. I must ask you to forgive us.'

'Not at all, Brother. The more I see of the life of Scarnsea, the more my investigations are illuminated. Speaking of which, I would be grateful if you could make yourself available tomorrow, with all your recent account books. There are some matters arising from Commissioner Singleton's investigations I would like to raise with you.' I confess I enjoyed the disconcerted look that came into the bursar's face. I nodded and passed on to where Mark stood, looking from a window. The snow still fell, covering every surface with white, deadening all sound and blurring sight as hunched, cowled figures began to make their way across the cloister yard to the church, and Compline, the day's last service. The bells began to toll once more.

Chapter Nine

WHEN WE REGAINED our room Mark lay down once more on his cot. But though I was as tired as he, I needed to organize my impressions of all that had happened at the meal. I dashed water from the pitcher over my face, then went to sit by the fire. Very faintly, through the window, I heard the sound of chanting.

'Listen,' I said, 'the monks at Compline. Praying to God to watch over their souls at the day's end. Well, what do you think of this holy community of Scarnsea?'

He groaned. 'I am too tired to think.'

'Come on, it's your first day inside a monastery. What do you make of it?'

Reluctantly, he heaved himself up on his elbows and his face assumed a thoughtful impression. The first faint lines in his smooth features were emphasized by the shadows the candles cast. One day, I thought, they would deepen into real lines and furrows as they had in mine.

'It appears a world of contradictions. On the one hand their life seems a world apart. Those black habits they wear, all their prayers. Brother Gabriel said they are separate from the sinful world. Yet did you see how he looked at me again, the dog? And they live so well. Warm fires, tapestries, food as good as any I have eaten. Playing cards like men in any tavern.'

'Yes. St Benedict would be as disgusted as Lord Cromwell by their rich living. Abbot Fabian disporting himself like a lord – and he is a lord, of course, he sits in the House like most of the abbots.'

'I think the prior dislikes him.'

'Prior Mortimus paints himself a reformist sympathizer, an opponent of easy living. He certainly believes in giving those under him a hard time. And enjoys it, I would say.'

'He reminds me of one or two of my schoolmasters.'

'Schoolmasters do not drive their charges to collapse. Most parents would have something to say about the treatment he gave that boy. There is no separate novice master, apparently; there are not enough vocations. The novices are wholly under the prior's power.'

'The infirmarian tried to help. He seems a good man, for all he looks like he's been toasted on a spit.'

I nodded. 'And Brother Gabriel helped too. He threatened the prior with the abbot. I can't imagine Abbot Fabian being over-concerned with the novices' welfare, but if the prior's taste for brutality sometimes goes too far, he would have to keep it in check to avoid scandal. Well, we've met them all now; the five who knew why Singleton was here. Abbot Fabian, Prior Mortimus, Brother Gabriel, Brother Guy. And the bursar, of course—'

'B-b-brother Edwig.' Mark imitated his stutter.

I smiled. 'He's a man of power here for all he trips at his words.'

'He seemed a slimy toad to me.'

'Yes, I took a dislike to him, I must say. But one must not be deceived by impressions. The greatest fraudster I ever met had the most chivalrous demeanour a man could possess. And the bursar was away the night Singleton was killed.'

'But why would any of them kill Singleton? Surely it gives Lord Cromwell stronger grounds for closure?'

'What if the motive was more personal? What if Singleton had found something out? He had been here several days. What if he was about to expose someone for some serious crime?'

'Dr Goodhaps said he was investigating the accounts books the day he was killed.'

I nodded. 'Yes, that's why I want to see them. But I come back to the manner of his death. If someone wanted to silence him, a knife in the ribs would have been so much easier. And why desecrate the church?'

Mark shook his head. 'I wonder where the murderer hid the sword, if it *was* a sword. And the relic. And his clothes, they would have been bloody.'

'There must be a thousand hiding places in this great warren.' I thought a moment. 'On the other hand, most of the buildings are in constant use.'

'The outhouses we saw? The stonemason's and brewery and so on?'

'Them most of all. We must keep our eyes open as we get to know this place, look out for likely spots.'

Mark sighed. 'The killer might have buried his clothes and the sword. But we won't be able to go looking for mounds of fresh earth if this snow lasts.'

'No. Well, I shall start tomorrow by questioning the sacrist and the bursar, those two brotherly foes. And I would like you to talk to the girl Alice.'

'Brother Guy warned me from her.'

'I said talk to her. Do no more than talk, I don't want trouble with Brother Guy. You've a way with the women. She seems intelligent and probably knows as many secrets about this place as anybody.'

He stirred uneasily. 'I would not wish her to think I – liked her – if it was only to wring information from her.'

'Getting information is our duty here. There's no need to give her wrong ideas. If she reveals anything that helps us I'll see she's rewarded. She should be found another place. A woman like that shouldn't be mouldering away among these monks.'

Mark smiled at me. 'I think you like her too, sir. Did you note her bright eyes?'

'She is out of the common run of women,' I said non-committally.

'It still seems a shame to be cozening information from her.'

'You must get used to cozening things from people, Mark, if you are to work in the service of the law or the State.'

'Yes, sir.' He sounded unconvinced. 'It's just – I would not like to place her in any danger.'

'Nor would I. But we could all be in danger.'

He was silent a moment. 'Could the abbot be right about witchcraft? That would fit with the desecration of the church.'

I shook my head. 'The more I consider it, the more I think this killing was planned. The desecration may even have been carried out to throw enquirers off the scent. The abbot, of course, would much prefer for it to have been done by an outsider.'

'No Christian would desecrate a church in such a way, papist or reformer.'

'No. The whole thing is an abomination.' I sighed and closed my eyes, feeling my face sag with tiredness. I could think no more today. I opened them again to find Mark looking at me keenly.

'You said Commissioner Singleton's body reminded you of Queen Anne Boleyn's beheading.'

I nodded. 'That memory still sickens me.'

'Everyone was surprised how suddenly she fell last year. Though she was much disliked.'

'Yes. The Midnight Crow.'

'They say the head tried to speak after it was cut off.'

I held up a hand. 'I can't talk about it, Mark. I was there as an official of state. Come, you are right. We should sleep.'

He looked disappointed, but said nothing more, banking up the fire with logs. We clambered into bed. From where I lay I could see through the window that the snow still fell, the flakes outlined against a lit window some way off. Some of the monks were up late, but then the days when the brethren retired before dark in winter, to be up for prayer again at midnight, were long gone.

Despite my tiredness I tossed and turned, my mind still active. I thought especially of the girl Alice. Everyone was potentially in danger in this place, but a woman alone was always more at risk than most.

I liked the spark of character I had seen in her. It reminded me of Kate.

✝

DESPITE MY WILL to sleep, I found my tired mind going back three years. Kate Wyndham was the daughter of a London cloth merchant accused of false accounting by his partner, in a case brought in the Church court on the basis that a contract was equivalent to an oath before God. In fact his partner was related to an archdeacon who had influence with the judge, and I managed to get the case transferred to King's Bench, where it was thrown out. The grateful merchant, a widower, invited me to dinner and there I met his only daughter.

Kate was lucky; her father believed in educating women beyond what they needed for the kitchen accounts, and she had a lively mind. She had a sweet, heart-shaped face, too, and rich brown hair falling round her shoulders. She was the first woman I had ever met with whom I could talk as an equal. She liked nothing better than to discuss the doings of the law, the court, even the Church – for her father's experience had turned them both into ardent reformers. Those evenings talking with her and her father at their house, and later the afternoons with Kate alone when she accompanied me on long walks into the countryside, were the best times of my life.

I knew she saw me as only a friend – it became a joke between us that I conversed with her as freely as with another man – yet I began to wonder if it might not blossom into something more. I had been in love before but always held from pressing my suit, fearing my twisted form could only bring rejection and I would be better waiting till I had built a fortune that I could offer as a compensating attraction. But I could give Kate other things she would value: good conversation, companionship, a circle of congenial friends.

I wonder to this day what might have happened had I shown my real feelings earlier, but I left it too late. One evening I called at her house unannounced and found her sitting with Piers Stackville, the son of a business associate of her father's. I was unworried at first, for although handsome as Satan, Stackville was a young man of few accomplishments beyond a laboriously mannered chivalrousness. But I saw her blush and simper at his crass remarks; my Kate transformed into a silly girl. From then on she could talk of nothing but what Piers had said or done, with sighs and smiles that cut me to the heart.

In the end I told her of my feelings. It was clumsily and stupidly done, I fumbled and faltered at my words. The worst thing was her utter surprise.

'Matthew, I thought you wanted only to befriend me, I have never heard one word of love from you. You appear to have kept much hidden.'

I asked her if it was too late.

'If you had asked me even six months before – perhaps,' she said sadly.

'I know my form is not such as to stir passion.'

'You do yourself disservice!' she said with unexpected heat. 'You have a fine manly face and good courtesy, you make too much of your bent back, as though you were the only man that had one. You have too much self-pity, Matthew, too much pride.'

'Then—'

She shook her head, tears in her eyes. 'It is too late. I love Piers. He is to ask Father for my hand.'

I said roughly that he was not good enough, she would pine away from boredom, but she replied hotly that soon she would have children and a good house to look after and was that not a woman's proper role, appointed by God? I was crushed and took my leave.

I never saw her again. A week later the sweating sickness hit the City like a hurricane. Hundreds began shivering and sweating, took to their beds and died within two days. It struck high and low and it took both Kate and her father. I remember their funeral, which I had arranged as the old man's executor, the wooden boxes slowly lowered into the earth. Looking at Piers Stackville over the coffin, his ravaged face told me he had loved Kate no less than I. He nodded to me in silent acknowledgement and I nodded back with a small, sad smile. I thanked God that at least I had released myself from the false doctrine of purgatory, which would have had Kate enduring its pains. I knew that her pure soul must be saved, at rest with Christ.

Tears come to my eyes as I write these words. They came to me that first night at Scarnsea, too. I let them fall silently, keeping myself from sobbing lest I waken Mark to an embarrassing scene. They cleansed me, and I slept.

✝

BUT THE NIGHTMARE returned that night. I had not dreamed of Queen Anne's killing for months, but seeing Singleton's body brought all back. Again I stood on Tower Green on a bright spring morning, one of the huge crowd standing round the straw-covered scaffold. I was at the front of the crowd; Lord Cromwell had ordered all those under his patronage to attend and identify themselves with the queen's fall. He himself stood nearby, at the front of the crowd. He had risen as one of Anne Boleyn's party; now he had prepared the indictment for adultery that brought her down. He stood frowning sternly, the embodiment of angry justice.

Straw was laid thickly around the block, and the executioner brought from France stood in his sinister black hood, arms folded. I looked for the sword he had brought to ensure a merciful end, at the queen's own request, but could not see it. I stood with my head deferentially lowered, for some of the greatest men in the land were there: Lord Chancellor Audley, Sir Richard Rich, the Earl of Suffolk.

We stood like statues, no one talking at the front, though there was a buzz of conversation from the crowd behind. There is an apple tree on Tower Green. It was in full blossom and a blackbird sat singing on a high branch, careless of the crowd. I watched it, envying the creature its freedom.

There was a stirring, and the queen appeared. She was flanked by ladies-in-waiting, a surpliced chaplain and the red-coated guards. She looked thin and haggard, bony shoulders hunched inside her white cloak, her hair tied up in a coif. As she approached the block she kept looking back, as though a messenger might arrive with a reprieve from the king. After nine years at the heart of the court she should have known better; this great orchestrated spectacle would not be stopped. As she came close, huge brown eyes surrounded by dark rings darted wildly round the scaffold and I think, like me, she was looking for the sword.

In my dream there are none of the long preliminaries; no long prayers, no speech from the scaffold by Queen Anne beseeching all to pray for the life of the king. In my dream she kneels down at once, facing the crowd, and starts to pray. I hear again her thin harsh cries, over and over, 'Jesu, receive my soul! Lord God, have pity on my soul!' Then the executioner bends and produces the great sword from where it had lain hidden in the straw. 'So that's where it was,' I think, then flinch and cry out as it swings through the air faster than the eye can follow and the queen's head flies up and outwards in a great spray of blood. Again I feel a rush of nausea and close my eyes as a great murmur comes from the crowd, broken by the odd 'hurrah'. I open them again at the prescribed words, 'So perish all the king's enemies,' barely intelligible in the executioner's French accent. The straw and his clothes are drenched with the blood that still pumps from the corpse, and he holds up the queen's dripping head.

The papists say that at that moment the candles in Dover church lit spontaneously, and there were other such silly legends around the country, but I can attest for myself that the eyes in the queen's severed head did move, roving madly round the crowd, the lips working as though trying to speak. Someone shrieked in the crowd behind me and I heard a susurration as the crowd, all in their best puffed-sleeved clothing, crossed themselves. In truth it was less than thirty seconds, not the half an hour people said later, before the movement stopped. But in my nightmare I relived each of those seconds, praying for those ghastly eyes to be still. Then the executioner tossed the head into an arrow box, which served as coffin, and as it landed with a thud I woke with a cry to the sound of someone knocking at the door.

I lay breathing heavily, my sweat congealing in the bitter cold.

The knocking came again, then Alice's voice called urgently, 'Master Shardlake! Commissioner!'

It was dead of night, the fire burned low and the room was icy. Mark groaned and stirred in his pallet.

'What is it?' I called, my heart still pounding after the nightmare, my voice shaky.

'Brother Guy asks you to come, sir.'

'Wait a moment!' I heaved myself out of bed and lit a candle from the embers of the fire. Mark rose too, blinking and tousle-haired.

'What's happening?'

'I don't know. Stay here.' I threw on my hose and opened the door. The girl stood outside, a white apron over her dress.

'I beg your pardon, sir, but Simon Whelplay is very sick and must speak to you. Brother Guy said I should wake you.'

'Very well.' I followed her down the freezing corridor. A little way along a door stood open. I heard voices: Brother Guy's and another that whimpered in distress. Looking in, I saw the novice lying on a truckle bed. His face shone with sweat and he muttered feverishly, his breath wheezing and rasping. Brother Guy sat by the bed, mopping his brow with a cloth that he dipped in a bowl.

'What ails him?' I could not keep the nervousness from my voice, for the sweating sickness made people writhe and gasp so.

The infirmarian looked at me, his face serious. 'It is a congestion of the lungs. No wonder, standing about in the cold with no food. He has a dangerous temperature. But he keeps asking to speak with you. He will not rest till he has done so.'

I approached the bed, reluctant to go too close lest he breathe the humours of his fever on me. The boy fixed red-rimmed eyes on me. 'Commissioner, sir,' he croaked. 'You are sent here to do justice?'

'Yes, I am here to investigate Commissioner Singleton's death.'

'He is not the first to be killed,' he gasped. 'Not the first. I know.'

'What do you mean? Who else has died?'

A series of racking coughs shook his thin frame, phlegm gurgling in his chest. He lay back, exhausted. His eyes fell on Alice.

'Poor, good girl. I warned her of the danger here . . .' He began to cry, retching sobs turning into another fit of coughing that looked ready to shake his thin frame apart. I turned to Alice.

'What does he mean?' I asked sharply. 'What has he warned you of?'

Her face was clouded with puzzlement. 'I don't understand, sir. He has never warned me of anything. I have barely spoken to him before today.'

I looked at Brother Guy. He seemed equally puzzled. He studied the boy anxiously.

'He is very ill, Commissioner. He should be left to rest now.'

'No, Brother, I must question him some more. Have you any idea what he meant there?'

'No, sir. I know no more than Alice.'

I moved closer to the bed and bent over the boy.

'Master Whelplay, tell me what you mean. Alice says you have given her no warning—'

'Alice is good,' he croaked. 'Dulce and gentle. She must be warned—' He began coughing again, and Brother Guy stepped firmly between us.

'I must ask you to leave him now, Commissioner. I thought talking to you might ease him, but he is delirious. I must give him a potion to make him sleep.'

'Please, sir,' Alice added, 'for charity. You can see how ill he is.'

I drew away from the boy, who seemed to have collapsed into an exhausted stupor. 'How ill is he?' I asked.

The infirmarian set his lips. 'Either the fever will break soon, or it will kill him. He should not have been treated so,' he added angrily. 'I have made a complaint to the abbot; he will be coming to see the lad in the morning. Prior Mortimus has gone too far this time.'

'I must find out what he meant. I will come again tomorrow and I want to be told at once if his condition worsens.'

'Of course. Now pray excuse me, sir, I must prepare some herbs—'

I nodded, and he left. I smiled at Alice, trying to seem reassuring.

'A strange business,' I said. 'You have no idea what he meant? First he said he had warned you, then that he must do so.'

'He has said nothing to me, sir. When we brought him in he slept a little, then as his fever rose he started asking for you.'

'What could he mean by saying Singleton was not the first?'

'On my oath, sir, I do not know.' There was anxiety in her voice. I turned to her and spoke gently.

'Do you feel you could be in danger from any source, Alice?'

'No, sir.' Her face reddened and I was surprised at the degree of anger and contempt that came into her face. 'I have had approaches from certain monks from time to time, but I deal with them with the aid of Brother Guy's protection and my own wits. That is a nuisance, not a danger.'

I nodded, struck once more by the strength of her personality.

'You are unhappy here?' I asked quietly.

She shrugged. 'It is a post. And I have a good master.'

'Alice, if I can help you or there is anything you want to tell me, please come to me. I would not like to think of you in danger.'

'Thank you, sir. I am grateful.' Her tone was guarded; she had no reason to trust me any more than the monks. But perhaps she would unwind to Mark. She turned back to her patient, who had begun tossing in his fever, threatening to throw off the bedclothes.

'Goodnight then, Alice.'

She was still trying to settle the novice, and did not look up. 'Goodnight, sir.'

I made my way back up the freezing corridor. Stopping at a window, I saw the snow had ceased at last. It lay deep and unbroken, glowing white under a full moon. Looking out on that wasteland broken by the black shapes of the ancient buildings, I felt as trapped and isolated in Scarnsea as though I stood in the moon's own empty caverns.

Chapter Ten

WHEN I WOKE I did not at first know where I was. Daylight of unaccustomed brightness cast a leached white light over an unfamiliar room. Then I remembered all and slowly sat up. Mark, who had fallen asleep again by the time I returned from my talk with the novice, had already risen; he had banked up the fire and stood in his hose, shaving at a ewer of steaming water. Through the window bright sunlight was reflected from the snow that lay thick everywhere, dotted here and there with birds' footprints.

'Good morning, sir,' he said, squinting at his features in an old brass mirror.

'What time is it?'

'Past nine. The infirmarian says breakfast is waiting in his kitchen. He knew we would be tired and let us sleep.'

I threw off the clothes. 'We haven't time to waste sleeping! Hurry, finish that and get into your shirt.' I started pulling on my clothes.

'Will you not shave?'

'They can take me unshaven.' The burden of work to be done filled my mind. 'Hurry now. I want to see this place properly and talk to the obedentiaries. You must find an opportunity to talk to Mistress Alice. Then take a walk around the place, look for likely hiding places for that sword. We have to cover the ground as fast as we can, we have a new problem now.' As I laced up my hose, I told him of my visit to Whelplay the night before.

'Someone else killed? Jesu. This skein gets more tangled by the hour.'

'I know. And we have little time to untangle it. Come.'

We went down the corridor to Brother Guy's infirmary. He was at his desk, squinting at his Arabic book.

'Ah, you are awake,' he said in his soft accent. He closed the text reluctantly and led us to a little room, where more herbs hung from hooks. Inviting us to sit at the table, he set bread and cheese and a jug of weak beer before us.

'How is your patient?' I asked as we ate.

'A little easier this morning, thank God. The fever has broken and he is in a deep sleep. The abbot is coming to visit him later.'

'Tell me, what is Novice Whelplay's history?'

'He is the son of a small farmer towards Tonbridge. Brother Guy smiled sadly. 'He is one of those too soft by nature for this harsh world, too easily bruised. Such souls often gravitate here, I think it is where God intends them to be.'

'A soft refuge from the world, then?'

'Those like Brother Simon serve God and the world with their prayers. Is that not better for all than the life of mockery and ill-treatment such people often have outside? And in the circumstances he could hardly be said to have found a refuge.'

I looked at him seriously. 'No, he found mockery and ill-treatment here too. When we have eaten, Brother Guy, I would like you to take me to the kitchen where you found the body. I fear we have had a late start.'

'Of course. But I should not leave my patients for too long—'

'Half an hour should be enough.' I took a last swig of beer and rose, wrapping my cloak around me. 'Master Poer will stay here in the infirmary this morning, I have allowed him a morning's rest. After you, Brother.'

We went through the hall, where Alice was again attending to the old monk. He was as ancient as any man I had ever seen, and lay breathing slowly and with effort. He could not have been a greater contrast to his plump neighbour, who sat up in bed playing a card game. The blind patient was asleep in a chair.

The infirmarian opened the front door, stepping back as nearly a foot of snow banked up against the door fell over the threshold.

'We should have overshoes,' he said, 'or we shall get foot-rot walking in this.' He excused himself and left me looking out, my breath steaming before me. Under a blue sky the air was as still and cold as any I remember. The snow was that light, fluffy sort that comes in the hardest weather, the devil to walk through. I had brought my staff, for with my poor balance I could easily go over. Brother Guy returned carrying stout leather overshoes.

'I must have these issued to the monks with outside duties,' he said. We laced them up and stepped up to our calves in the snow, Brother Guy's features standing out darker than ever against the whiteness. The door to the kitchens was only a short distance away, and I saw the main building had a common wall with the infirmary. I asked if there was a connecting door.

'There was a passage,' he said. 'It was closed off at the time of the Black Death, to minimize the spread of infection, and has never been reopened. A sensible measure.'

'Last night when I saw that boy I feared he had the sweating sickness. I have seen it, it is terrible. But of course it is produced by the foul airs of the towns.'

'Mercifully I have seen little plague. Mostly I have to deal with the consequences of too much standing at prayer in a cold church. And of old age, of course.'

'You have another patient there who seems poorly. The ancient.'

'Yes. Brother Francis. He is ninety-four. So old he is become a child again and now he has an ague. I think he may be near the end of his pilgrimage at last.'

'What is wrong with the fat fellow?'

'Varicose ulcers like Brother Septimus, but worse. I have drained them, and now he is enjoying some rest.' He smiled gently. 'I may have a task getting him up again. People do not like to leave the infirmary. Brother Andrew has become a fixture, his blindness came on him late and he fears to go outside. His confidence has gone.'

'Have you many old monks under your care?'

'A dozen. The brothers tend to be long-lived. I have four past eighty.'

'They have not the strains or hardships of most people.'

'Or perhaps their devotions strengthen the body as well as the soul. But here we are.'

He led me through a stout oak door. As he had described the night before, a short passage led into the kitchen itself. The door was open and I heard voices and the clattering of plates. A rich smell of baking drifted out as we proceeded up the passage. Inside, half a dozen servants were preparing a meal. The kitchen was large, and seemed clean and well organized.

'So, Brother, when you came in that night, where was the body?'

The infirmarian paced out a few steps, the servants watching curiously.

'Just here, by the big table. The body lay on its front, legs pointing to the door. The head had come to rest there.' He pointed to an iron vat marked 'Butter'. I followed his gaze, as did the servants. One crossed himself.

'So he had just come through the door when he was struck,' I mused. There was a big cupboard by the spot where he had fallen; the assailant could have hidden at the side and then, when Singleton passed, leaped out and struck him down. I paced out the steps and swung my staff in the air, making a servant jump back in alarm. 'Yes, there's room for a big swing. I'd guess that's how it was done.'

'With a sharp blade and a strong hand, yes, you could do it,' Brother Guy said pensively.

'If you were skilled, used to swinging a large sword about.' I looked around the servants. 'Who is head cook here?'

A bearded man in a stained apron stepped forward, bowing. 'Ralph Spenlay, sir.'

'You are in charge here, Master Spenlay, and you have a key to the kitchens?'

'Yes, Commissioner.'

'And the door to the courtyard is the only way in and out?'

'It is.'

'Is the door to the kitchen itself locked?'

'No need. The courtyard door is the only way in.'

'Who else has keys?'

'The infirmarian, sir, and the abbot and prior. And Master Bugge the watchman, of course, for his night patrols. No one else. I live in; I open up in the morning and close at night. If anyone wants a key they come to me. People will steal the viands, you see. No matter that it's for the monks' table. Why, I've seen Brother Gabriel hanging about the corridor some mornings, looking as though he was waiting for our backs to be turned before snatching something. And he an official—'

'What happens if you are ill, or away, when someone wants access?'

'They'd have to ask Master Bugge or the prior.' He smiled. 'Not that people like to bother either, if they don't have to.'

'Thank you, Master Spenlay, that is very helpful.' I reached out and took a little custard from a bowl. The cook looked put out.

'Very nice. I will trouble you no further, Brother Guy. I will see the bursar next, if you could point me to his counting house.'

✠

HE GAVE ME directions and I plodded off, the snow creaking under my overshoes. The precinct was much quieter today, people and dogs keeping indoors. The more I thought, the more I considered only an expert swordsman would have had the confidence to step out behind Singleton and strike off his head. I could not imagine any of the people I had seen managing it. The abbot was a big man, and so was Brother Gabriel, but swordsmanship was a craft for gentlemen, not monks. Thinking of Gabriel, I remembered the cook's words. They puzzled me; the sacrist had not struck me as the kind of man to hang around a kitchen to steal food.

I looked around the snowy courtyard. The road to London would be impassable now; it was not pleasant to reflect that Mark and I were more or less trapped here, with a murderer. I realized that unconsciously I had been walking in the centre of the courtyard, as far as possible from shadowy doorways. I shivered. It was strange walking alone through this white silence under the high walls and it was with a sense of relief that I saw Bugge by the gate, shovelling a path through the snow with the help of another servant.

As I approached the gatekeeper looked up, red-faced with effort. His companion, a stocky young man with a face disfigured by warty growths, smiled nervously and bowed. Both had been working hard, and gave off a vile stink.

'Good morning, sir,' Bugge said. His tone was unctuous; doubt-less he had been ordered to treat me with respect.

'Cruel weather.'

'Indeed it is, sir. Winter is come early again.'

'Now we are met, I would like to ask about your night-time routine.'

He nodded, leaning on his shovel. 'The whole precinct is patrolled twice every night, at nine and three-thirty. Either me or David here makes a complete round, checking every door.'

'And the gates? Are they locked at night?'

'Every night at nine. And opened at nine in the morning, after Prime. Not a dog could get in here when the gates are shut.'

'Not a cat,' the boy added. His eyes were sharp; he might be ugly but he was no fool.

'Cats can climb,' I suggested. 'And so can people.'

A touch of truculence appeared in the gatekeeper's face. 'Not a twelve-foot wall, they can't. You've seen it, sir, it's sheer; no one could scale it.'

'The wall is secure all round the monastery?'

'Except at the back. It's crumbled in places there, but it gives straight onto the marsh. No one would go wading through that, especially at night. People have taken a wrong step and disappeared over their heads in the mud —' he lifted a hand and pushed it down — 'glug.'

'If no one can get in, why do you patrol?'

He leaned close. I recoiled from his stench, but he seemed not to mind. 'People are sinful, sir, even here.' His manner became confiden, tial. 'Things were very lax in the days of the old prior. When Prior Mortimus came, he ordered the night patrols, anyone out of bed reported straight to him. And that's what I do. Without fear or favour.' He smiled happily.

'What about the night of Commissioner Singleton's murder? Did you see anything that might indicate someone might have broken in?'

He shook his head. 'No, sir, I'll swear all was as it should have been between three,thirty and four,thirty, I made that round myself. I tried the courtyard door to the kitchen as usual and it was locked. I saw the commissioner, though.' He nodded self,importantly.

'Yes, I heard you did. Where?'

'On my round. I was passing through the cloister when I saw something moving and called out. It was the commissioner, fully dressed.'

'What was he about at that hour?'

'He said he had a meeting, sir.' He smiled, enjoying the attention. 'He said if I met any of the brethren and they said they were on their way to see him, I was to let them pass.'

'So he *was* on his way to meet someone!'

'I would say so. He was near enough the kitchens, as well.'

'What time was this?'

'I'd say about a quarter past four. I was near the end of my round then.'

I nodded at the great bulk behind us. 'Is the church locked at night?'

'No sir, never. But I went round it as usual before checking the cloister, and all was normal. Then I was back in my house at half, past four. Prior Mortimus has given me a little clock,' he said proudly, 'and I always check the time. I slept a little, leaving David on watch, then I was woken by the great hue and cry at five.'

'So Commissioner Singleton was on his way to meet one of the monks. It does seem then that the great crime committed here a week ago was the work of a monk.'

He hesitated. 'I say no one broke in, that's all I know. It's impossible.'

'Not impossible, but unlikely, I agree.' I nodded. 'Thank you, Master Bugge, you have been most helpful.' I set my staff before me and turned away, leaving them once more to their labours.

✝

I RETRACED MY STEPS to where a green door marked the counting house. Entering without knocking, I found myself in a room that reminded me of my own world: whitewashed walls lined with shelves of ledgers, any bare patches covered with lists and bills. Two monks sat working at desks. One, counting out coins, was elderly and rheumy-eyed. The other, frowning over a ledger, was the young bearded monk who had lost at cards the night before. Behind them stood a chest with the largest lock I had ever seen; the abbey's funds, no doubt.

The two monks jumped to their feet at my entry. 'Good morning,' I said. My breath made a mist in the air, for the room was unheated. 'I seek Brother Edwig.'

The young monk glanced at an inner door. 'Brother Edwig is with the abbot—'

'In there? I'll join them.' I passed to the inner door, ignoring a hand half-raised in protest. Opening it, I found myself facing a staircase. It led to a little landing, where a window gave a view out over the white landscape. Opposite, voices could be heard behind a door. I paused outside, but could not make out what it was they were saying. I opened the door and went in.

Abbot Fabian was speaking to Brother Edwig in peevish tones. 'We should ask more. It doesn't befit our status to let it go for less than three hundred . . .'

'I need the money in my coffers *now*, Lord Abbot. If he'll p-pay cash for the land, we should t-take it!' Despite his stutter, there was a steely note in the bursar's voice. Abbot Fabian looked round, disconcerted.

'Oh, Master Shardlake—'

'Sir, this is a private conversation,' the bursar said, his face filled with sudden anger.

'I am afraid there is no such thing where I am concerned. If I knocked and waited at every door, who knows what I might miss?'

Brother Edwig controlled himself, fluttering his hands, once more the fussy bureaucrat. 'N-no, of course, forgive me. We w-were discussing the monastery finances, some lands we must sell to meet the costs of the building w-works, a mat-mat—' His face reddened again as he struggled for words.

'A matter of no concern to your investigation,' the abbot finished with a smile.

'Brother bursar, there is a relevant issue I *would* discuss.' I took a seat at an oak desk with many drawers, the only furniture in the little room apart from yet more shelves of ledgers.

'I am at your service, sir, of course.'

'Dr Goodhaps tells me that on the day he died Commissioner Singleton was working on an account book he had obtained from your office. And that afterwards it disappeared.'

'It did not d-disappear, sir. It was returned to the counting house.'

'Perhaps you could tell me what it was.'

He thought a moment. 'I cannot remember. The inf-firmary accounts, I believe. We keep accounts for all the different departments – sacristy, infirmary and so on, and a central set for the whole monastery.'

'Presumably if Commissioner Singleton took account books from you, you would keep a record.'

'I m-most certainly would.' He frowned petulantly. 'But more than once he took books without telling me or my assistant, and we had to spend the day hunting for something he had taken.'

'So there is no actual record of all he took?'

The bursar spread his arms. 'How c-could there be, w-when he helped himself? I am s-sorry—'

I nodded. 'All is in order now, in the counting house?'

'Thank the Lord.'

I stood up. 'Very well. Please have all the account books for the last twelve months brought to my room in the infirmary. Oh, and those from the departments as well.'

'*All* the books?' The bursar could not have looked more aghast had I ordered him to remove his habit and parade naked in the snow. 'That would be very disruptive, it would bring the work of the counting house to a halt—'

'It will only be for one night. Maybe two.'

He seemed set to argue further, but Abbot Fabian interjected.

'We must co-operate, Edwig. The books will be brought to you as soon as they can be fetched, Commissioner.'

'I am obliged. Now, my lord Abbot, last night I visited that unfortunate novice. Young Whelplay.'

The abbot nodded seriously. 'Yes. Brother Edwig and I will be visiting him later.'

'I have the m-month's dole accounts to check,' the bursar muttered.

'Nevertheless, as my most senior official after Prior Mortimus, you must accompany me.' He sighed. 'As a complaint has been made by Brother Guy—'

'A serious complaint,' I said. 'It appears the boy might have died—'

Abbot Fabian raised a hand. 'Rest assured, I shall investigate the matter fully.'

'Might I ask, my lord, what exactly is the boy supposed to have done, to earn such punishment?'

The abbot's shoulders set with tension. 'To be frank, Master Shardlake—'

'Yes, frankness, please—'

'The boy does not like the new ways. The preaching in English. He is much devoted to the Latin Mass, and the chant. He fears the chant will be put in English—'

'An unusual concern for one so young.'

'He is very musical, he assists Brother Gabriel with his service books. He is gifted, but has opinions beyond his station. He spoke out in Chapter, although as a novice he should not—'

'Not treasonable words, I hope, like Brother Jerome?'

'None of my monks, sir, no one, would speak treasonable words,' the abbot said earnestly. 'And Brother Jerome is not part of our community.'

'Very well. So Simon Whelplay was set to work in the stables, put on bread and water. That seems harsh.'

The abbot reddened. 'It was not his only failing.'

I thought a moment. 'He assists Brother Gabriel, you said. I understand Brother Gabriel has a certain history?'

The abbot fiddled nervously with the sleeve of his habit. 'Simon Whelplay did speak in confession of – certain carnal lusts. Towards Brother Gabriel. But sins of thought, sir, only thought. Brother Gabriel did not even know. He has been pure since the – the trouble two years ago. Prior Mortimus keeps a close eye, a very close eye, on such matters.'

'You have no novice master, do you? Too few vocations.'

'Numbers in all the houses have been falling for generations, since the Great Pestilence,' the abbot said in tones of gentle reasonableness. 'But with a revived religious life under the king's guidance, perhaps now our houses will be revitalized, more will choose the life—'

I wondered if he could really believe that, be so blind to the signs. The pleading note in his voice made me realize he could; he really thought the monasteries could survive. I glanced at the bursar; he had taken a paper from his desk and was studying it, divorcing himself from the conversation.

'Who knows what the future may bring?' I turned to the door. 'I am obliged to you, gentlemen. Now I must brave the elements again, to see the church – and Brother Gabriel.' I left the abbot looking after me anxiously, while the bursar examined his double-entries.

✝

AS I CROSSED the cloister yard an uncomfortable ache told me I needed to visit the privy. Brother Gabriel had pointed it out to me the night before; there was a quick way via the back of the infirmary across a yard to the reredorter, where the privy was housed.

I went through the infirmary hall again and out into the yard. It was enclosed on three sides and I saw a little stream had been culverted, running under a small bath house attached to the infirmary and on under the reredorter, so it could drain both. I had to admire the ingenuity of the monastic builders. Few houses, even in London, had such arrangements and I sometimes thought with foreboding of what would happen when the twenty-foot cesspit in my garden eventually filled up.

Chickens ran squawking round the yard, from which most of the snow had already been swept. A couple of pigs peered over the walls of a makeshift sty. Alice was feeding them, pouring a bucket of slops over the wall into their trough. I went over to her. My bodily need could wait a little.

'You have many duties, I see. Pigs as well as patients.'

She smiled dutifully. 'Yes, sir. A maid's work is never done.'

I looked over the sty, wondering whether something could be concealed among the straw and mud, but of course the brown hairy creatures would have rooted anything out. They might eat a bloody robe, but not a sword or a relic. I looked out over the yard. 'I see only hens. Have you no cockerel?'

She shook her head. 'No, sir. Poor Jonas is gone. It was he who was killed at the altar. He was a fine bird, his strutting antics used to make me laugh.'

'Yes, they are comical creatures. Like little kings marching and preening among their subjects.'

She smiled. 'That is how he was. His wicked little eyes would look at me with challenge as I approached. He would flap his wings angrily and shriek, but it was all for show. A step too close and he would turn and run.' To my surprise her large blue eyes filled with tears and she bowed her head. Evidently she had a warm heart as well as a stout one.

'That desecration was a wicked thing altogether,' I said.

'Poor Jonas.' She shook herself and took a deep breath.

'Tell me, Alice, when did you notice him gone?'

'The morning the murder was discovered.'

I glanced round the yard. 'There's no way in here, is there, save from the infirmary or the reredorter?'

'No, sir.'

I nodded. Another indication the killer had come from inside the monastery and knew the layout. A griping in my guts warned me not to tarry. Reluctantly, I excused myself and hurried off to the reredorter.

✝

I HAD NEVER been in a monks' privy. At school in Lichfield there were many jokes about what the monks got up to in there, but the privy at Scarnsea was ordinary enough. The stone walls of the long chamber were undecorated and the room was dim, for the only windows were high up. Along one wall lay a long bench with a row of circular holes, and at the far end there were three private cubicles for the obedentiaries' use. I made my way towards them, passing a couple of monks seated on the communal row. The young monk from the counting house was there. The monk next to him stood up and bowed to me awkwardly as he adjusted his habit before turning to his neighbour.

'Are you going to be there all morning, Athelstan?'

'Leave me be. I have the colic.'

I went into a cubicle, bolted the door and took a seat with relief. When I had finished I sat listening to the stream tinkling far below. I thought again of Alice. If the monastery closed she would be without a place. I wondered what I might do for her; perhaps I could help her find something in the town. It saddened me that such a woman had ended up in a place like this, but likely as not her family were poor. How sad she had been at the loss of a bird. I had been tempted to take her arm and comfort her. I shook my head at my weakness. And after what I had told Mark, too.

Something snapped me out of my reflections, made me jerk my head upright and still my breathing. Someone was outside the cubicle, moving quietly, but I had heard the soft footfall, leather on stone. My heart pounded, and I was glad now of the sense of danger that had kept me away from the doorways. I tied up my hose and rose soundlessly, reaching for my dagger. I leaned over and put my ear against the door. I could hear breathing on the other side; someone was standing right against the door.

I bit my lip. That young monk would probably be gone by now; I could be alone in the reredorter save for the man outside. I confess the thought that Singleton's assassin might be waiting for me as he had waited for him unnerved me.

The cubicle door opened outwards. With infinite care I slid back the bolt, then stepped back and kicked it open with all the force I could muster. There was a startled yell from outside as the door flew open to reveal Brother Athelstan. He had jumped back and stood waving his arms in the air to keep his balance. With a wash of relief, I saw his hands were empty. As I advanced on him with my dagger held high, his eyes widened like saucers.

'What were you doing?' I snapped. 'I heard you outside!'

He gulped, his prominent Adam's apple jerking up and down.

'I meant no harm, sir! I was about to knock, I swear!'

He was as white as a sheet. I lowered my weapon. 'Why? What do you want?'

He glanced anxiously towards the door to the dormitory. 'I needed to talk to you secretly, sir. When I saw you come in I waited till we were alone.'

'What is it?'

'Not here, please,' he said urgently. 'Someone may disturb us. Please, sir, can you meet me at the brewhouse shortly? It is next to the stables. There is no one there this morning.'

I studied him. He looked on the point of collapse.

'Very well. But I shall bring my assistant.'

'Yes, sir, of course—' Brother Athelstan broke off as the tall thin form of Brother Jude appeared from the dormitory. He scurried away. The pittancer, doubtless taking a break from calculating what rich meals the monks should have, gave me an odd look. He bowed and entered a cubicle, and I heard the bolt slide home with a bang. As I stood there, I realized I had started to tremble. I was shaking like an aspen leaf from head to foot.

Chapter Eleven

I PULLED MYSELF TOGETHER with some deep breaths and hurried back to the infirmary. Mark was in the breakfast room; Alice had returned and was washing dishes, talking to him as he sat at the table. Her manner seemed cheerful and relaxed, without the reserve she had shown with me, and I felt a pang of jealousy.

'Are you allowed time off?' he was asking her.

'Half a day a week. If we are quiet, sometimes Brother Guy lets me take a whole day.'

They looked round as I bustled in. 'Mark, I must speak with you.'

He followed me to our room, and I told him how Brother Athelstan had waylaid me.

'Come with me now. Bring your sword. He doesn't look dangerous, he's a weasely fellow, but we cannot be too careful.'

We returned to the main courtyard, where Bugge and his assistant still laboured in the snow, and passed the stables. I glanced through the open door; a stablehand was piling up hay, watched by the horses, their breath steaming thickly in the freezing air. It was no work for a sickly boy like Whelplay.

I pushed open the brewhouse door. Here it was warm. Through a door to one side a slow fire burned; a stairway led to the drying house above. The main chamber, full of barrels and vats, was empty. I jumped as something fluttered above me and, looking up, saw hens roosting among the rafters.

'Brother Athelstan,' I called in a loud whisper. There was a thud somewhere behind us and Mark's hand went to his sword as the monk's skinny form appeared from behind a barrel. He bowed.

'Commissioner. Thank you for coming.'

'I hope it was something important for you to disturb me in the privy. Are we alone here?'

'Yes, sir. The brewer is away, waiting for the hops to dry.'

'Don't those hens spoil the beer? Their mess is everywhere.'

He smiled uneasily, fingering his little beard. 'The brewer says it adds bite to the flavour.'

'I doubt the townsfolk think so,' Mark observed.

Brother Athelstan came closer, looking at me keenly. 'Sir, you know the part in Lord Cromwell's injunctions that says any monk with a complaint may go directly to the vicar general's officials, rather than his abbot?'

'I do. Have you a complaint?'

'Information, rather.' He took a deep breath. 'I know Lord Cromwell seeks information on ill-doings in the religious houses. I have heard, sir, his informants are rewarded.'

'If their information is valuable.' I studied him. In my work I had to deal often with informers, and there were never more of that noisome breed abroad than in those years. Could it have been Athelstan whom Singleton was going to meet that night? But this young man, I guessed, had never played the role before. He was keen for reward, but afraid.

'I thought – I thought any information about ill-doings here must help you find Commissioner Singleton's killer.'

'What have you to tell me?'

'The senior monks, sir, the obedentiaries. They do not like Lord Cromwell's new injunctions. The sermons in English, the stricter rules of life. I have heard them talking together, sir, in the chapter house. Sitting muttering together before meetings of the community.'

'And what have you heard?'

'I have heard them say the injunctions are an imposition by people who do not know or care for the life. The abbot, Brother Guy,

Brother Gabriel and my master Brother Edwig, they all think the same.'

'And Prior Mortimus.'

Athelstan shrugged. 'He swims with the tide.'

'He is not the only one. Brother Athelstan, have you heard any of the obedentiaries say that the pope should be brought back, or speaking against the royal divorce or Lord Cromwell?'

He hesitated. 'No. But I – I could say I had, sir, if it would help you.'

I laughed. 'And people would believe you, as you shuffle your feet and cast down your eyes. I do not think so.'

He fingered his beard again. 'If there is any other way I can be of use to you, sir,' he mumbled, 'or to Lord Cromwell, I would be happy to be his man.'

'Why is that, Brother Athelstan? Are you discontented here?'

His face darkened. It was a weak face and an unhappy one.

'I work in the counting house for Brother Edwig. He is a hard master.'

'Why? What does he do?'

'He works you like a dog. If so much as a penny is out, he makes your life a misery, makes you audit all your accounts over again. I committed a small offence and now he keeps me in the counting house night and day. He has gone out for a while, otherwise I would never have dared spend so long away.'

'And so,' I said, 'because your master punishes your mistakes, you would put Brother Gabriel and others in trouble with Lord Cromwell in the hope he will make your life easier?'

He looked puzzled. 'But does not he wish monks to inform, sir? I seek only to help him.'

I sighed. 'I am here to investigate Commissioner Singleton's death, Brother. If you have any information relevant to that, I would hear from you. Otherwise you are wasting my time.'

'I am sorry.'

'You may leave us.' He seemed about to say something more, then thought better of it and hastily left the shed. I kicked one of the barrels, then laughed angrily.

'God, what a creature! Well, that takes us nowhere.'

'Informers. More trouble than they're worth.' Mark jumped aside with an oath as one of the chickens above dropped its mess on his tunic.

'Yes, they're like those hens, they don't care where their shit lands.' I paced up and down the brewhouse. 'Jesu, that knave scared me when I heard him outside my cubicle door. I thought it was the assassin come after me.'

He looked at me seriously. 'I confess I do not like being alone here. One jumps at every shadow. Perhaps we should stay together, sir.'

I shook my head. 'No, there's too much to do. Go back to the infirmary. You seem to be getting on well with Alice.'

He gave a self-satisfied smile. 'She is telling me all about her life.'

'Very well. I am off to visit Brother Gabriel. Perhaps he may tell me about his. I don't suppose you've had time yet to explore the place?'

'No, sir.'

'Well, see you do. Get some overshoes from Brother Guy.' I gave him a serious look. 'But take care.'

†

I PAUSED OUTSIDE the church. Watching one of the kitchen servants plod wearily though the snow, his cheap woollen hose soaking wet, I was grateful for Brother Guy's overshoes. No overshoes for servants, though. That would be expensive; Brother Edwig would have a seizure.

I studied the church front. Around the great wooden doors, twenty feet high, the stonework was richly carved with gargoyles and monsters to frighten off evil spirits, their faces worn after four centuries but still vivid. The monastery church, like the great cathedrals, was there to impress the laity: a magnificent simulacrum of heaven. A promise of prayers for a loved one in purgatory, or a miraculous cure from a relic, would carry a hundred times more weight in that setting. I hauled open the door and squeezed inside, into echoing space.

All around, the great vaulted arches of the nave rose nearly a hundred feet, supported by pillars brightly painted in red and black. Blue and yellow tiles covered the floor. The eye was led to the high stone rood screen halfway down the nave, richly painted with figures of the saints. On top of the screen, lit by candles, stood the statues of John the Baptist, the Virgin and Our Lord. A great window at the far end of the church, built to catch the morning light from the east, was painted in geometric designs of yellow and orange. It flooded the nave with a gentle umber light, peaceful and numinous, softening the kaleidoscope of colours. The builders knew how to create atmosphere, no doubt of that.

I walked slowly up the nave. The walls were lined with painted statues of saints and little reliquaries, where strange objects peeped out from beds of satin, candles burning before them. A servant moved slowly around, replacing those that had burned down. I paused to glance into the side chapels, each with its own statues and little candlelit altar. It occurred to me that these side chapels, filled with railed-off altars, statues and biers, might be good places to hide things.

In several of the side chapels monks stood intoning private Masses. Local people of wealth, terrified of the pains of purgatory awaiting them, would have left great portions of their assets away from wives and children to the monks, for Masses to be said until the Last Judgement came. How many days' remission from purgatory was a Mass here worth, I wondered; sometimes a hundred were promised, sometimes a thousand. While those without means were left to suffer for however long God appointed, of course. Pick-penny purgatory, we reformers called it. The Latin chanting stirred an impatient anger in me.

At the rood screen I stopped and looked up. My breath, still a fog, for the church was scarcely warmer than outside, dissipated into the yellow-tinted air. On either side a flight of stairs set into the wall gave access to the top of the screen. At that level, I saw, a narrow railed parapet ran the length of the church. Above the parapet the walls arched gradually inward to the great vault of the roof. To the left I noticed a great crack, stained round with damp, running from the roof almost to ground level. I remembered that Norman churches and cathedrals were not in fact the solid edifices they appeared; the walls might be twenty feet thick, but between the expensive stone blocks making up the interior and exterior walls there was usually an infill of rubble.

Where the abscission ran down the wall the stone blocks, and the plaster between them, were discoloured and there was a little heap of powdery plaster on the floor beneath. I saw that above the parapet a series of statues were set in niches at intervals; they showed the same figure of St Donatus leaning over the dead man that was on the monastery seal.

Where the crack ran through one of the niches the statue had been removed and lay, discoloured-looking, on the parapet. An extraordinary cat's cradle of pulleys and ropes had been set up there; the ropes were secured to the wall behind the parapet and ran out over the void, before disappearing upward into the darkness of the bell tower, where presumably they were secured at their other end.

Dangling from the ropes was a wooden basket, big enough to hold two men. Presumably the cat's cradle allowed the basket to be moved inwards and outwards and had allowed the removal of the statue. It was an ingenious arrangement but a dangerous one; scaffolding was surely needed to effect proper repairs. But the bursar was right to say a full repair programme would be enormously expensive. Otherwise, though, as frost and water did their work, the crack could only widen, eventually threatening the whole structure. The imagination reeled at the thought of the great building falling on one's head.

Apart from the susurration of prayers from the side chapels, the church was silent. Then I caught a faint murmur of voices, and followed the sound to where a little door stood ajar, candlelight flickering within. I recognized the deep voice of Brother Gabriel.

'I've every right to ask after him,' he was saying in angry tones.

'If ye're always round the infirmary, people will be talking again,' the prior replied in his harsh voice. A moment later he emerged, his ruddy face set hard. He started a little when he saw me.

'I was looking for the sacrist. I thought he might show me the church.'

The prior nodded at the open door. 'Ye'll find Brother Gabriel in there, sir. He'll be glad to be taken from his desk in this cold. Good morning.' He bowed quickly and passed on, his footsteps echoing loudly away.

The sacrist sat behind a table strewn with sheets of music in a little book-filled office. A statue of the Virgin leaned drunkenly against one wall, her nose broken off, giving the bitterly cold, windowless room a depressing air. Brother Gabriel sat at a table, a heavy cloak over his black habit. His lined face was anxious; in some ways it was a strong face, long and bony, but the mouth was pulled down tightly at the corners and there were deep bags beneath his eyes. At the sight of me he rose, forcing his mouth into a smile.

'Commissioner. Master Shardlake. How may I help you?'

'I thought you might show me the church, Brother Sacrist, and the scene of the desecration.'

'If you wish, sir.' His tone was reluctant, but he stood and led me back into the body of the church.

'You are responsible for the music, Brother, as well as the upkeep of the church?'

'Yes, and our library. I can show you that too if you wish.'

'Thank you. I understand Novice Whelplay used to help you with the music.'

'Before he was sent to freeze in the stables,' Brother Gabriel said bitterly. Collecting himself, he continued in a milder tone. 'He is very talented, though rather over-enthusiastic.' He turned anxious eyes on me. 'Forgive me, but you are lodging in the infirmary. Do you know how it goes with him?'

'Brother Guy believes he should recover.'

'Thank God. Poor silly lad.' He crossed himself.

As he led me on a circuit of the church he became a little more cheerful, talking animatedly about the history of this or that statue, the architecture of the building and the workmanship of the stained-glass windows. He appeared to find a refuge from his anxieties in words; it seemed not to strike him that as a reformer I might not approve of the things he was showing me. My impression of a naive, unworldly man was reinforced. But such people could be fanatical, and I noticed again that he was a big man, strongly built. He had long delicate fingers, but also thick strong wrists that could easily wield a sword.

'Have you always been a monk?' I asked him.

'I was professed at nineteen. I have known no other life. Nor would I wish to.'

He paused before a large niche containing an empty stone pedestal, on which a black cloth had been laid. Against it was heaped an enormous pile of sticks, crutches and other supports used by cripples; I saw a heavy neck-brace such as crookback children wear to try and straighten them; I had worn one myself, though it did no good.

Brother Gabriel sighed. 'This is where the hand of the Penitent Thief stood. It is a terrible loss; it has cured many unfortunate people.' He gave the inevitable glance at my back as he spoke, then looked away and gestured at the pile.

'All those things were left by people cured by the Penitent Thief's intervention over the years. They no longer needed them and left them behind in gratitude.'

'How long had the relic been here?'

'It came from France with the monks who founded St Donatus's in 1087. It had been in France for centuries, and at Rome for centuries before that.'

'The casket was valuable, I believe. Gold set with emeralds.'

'People used to be glad to pay to touch it, you know. They were disappointed when the injunctions forbade relics to be shown for lucre.'

'It is quite large, I imagine?'

He nodded. 'There is an illustration in the library, if you would care to see.'

'I would. Thank you. Tell me, who found the relic missing?'

'I did. I found the desecrated altar too.'

'Pray tell me what happened.' I sat down on a projecting buttress. My back was much better, but I did not wish to stand around for too long.

'I rose towards five as usual, and came to prepare the church for Nocturns. There are only a few candles lit before the statues at night, so when first I came into the church with my assistant, Brother Andrew, we noticed nothing amiss. We went into the choir; Andrew lit the candles at the stalls and I set the books open at that morning's prayers. As he was lighting the candles Brother Andrew saw a trail of blood on the floor, and called out. The trail led –' he gave a shuddering sigh ' – into the presbytery. There, on the table before the high altar, was a black cock, its throat cut. God have mercy on us, black bloodstained feathers lying on the very altar, a candle lit on either side in satanic mockery.' He crossed himself again.

'Would you show me the place, Brother?'

He hesitated. 'The church has been reconsecrated, but I do not believe it is fitting to relive those events before the altar itself.'

'Nevertheless, I must ask—'

With reluctant steps he led me through a door in the rood screen, into the choir stalls. I remembered Goodhaps's remark that the monks seemed more upset by the desecration than by Singleton's death.

The choir held two rows of wooden pews, black with age and richly carved, facing each other across a tiled space. Brother Gabriel pointed to the floor. 'That's where the blood was. The trail led in here.' I followed him through to the presbytery, where the high altar stood, covered with a white cloth, before a beautifully carved altar screen decorated with gold leaf. The air was full of incense. He pointed to two ornate silver candlesticks flanking the centre of the altar table, where the paten and chalice would be laid for Mass.

'It was there.'

I believe the Mass should be a simple ceremony in good English, so men can reflect on their relationship with God, rather than be distracted by magnificent surroundings and ornate Latin. Perhaps because of that, or perhaps because of what had happened there, looking at the richly decorated altar in the dim candlelight I had a sudden sense of evil, so strong that I shuddered. Not a sense of some ordinary crime, nor some furtive little sins, but of evil itself in this business. Beside me, the sacrist's face was bleak with sorrow. 'I have been a monk for twenty years,' he said. 'In the darkest, coldest days of winter I have stood watching the altar at Matins, and whatever weight there has been on my soul it has lifted with the first ray of light coming through the east window. It fills one with the promise of light, the promise of God. But now I will never be able to contemplate the altar without that scene coming into my mind. It was the Devil's work.'

'Well, Brother,' I said quietly, 'there was a human perpetrator, and I must find him.' I led the way back to the choir, where I took a seat in one of the pews, indicating Brother Gabriel should sit beside me.

'When you saw this outrage, Brother Sacrist, what did you do?'

'I said we must fetch the prior. But just then the door from the night stairs was thrown open and one of the monks ran in to tell us the commissioner had been found murdered. We all left the church together.'

'And saw the relic was gone?'

'No. That was later. Around eleven I passed the shrine and saw it was empty. But it must have been done at the same time, surely.'

'Perhaps. Now you too would have come in from the night stairs linking the monks' dormitory to the church. Is that door kept locked?'

'Of course. I unlocked it.'

'So whoever desecrated the church would have had to come in by the main door, which is unlocked?'

Yes. It is our principle that servants and visitors as well as monks should be able to enter the church when they please.'

'And you arrived just after five. You are sure?'

'I have been performing the routine for the last eight years.'

'So the intruder was working in semi-darkness, spreading the fowl's blood and – probably – stealing the relic. Both the desecration and Singleton's murder were carried out between a quarter past four, when Bugge met the commissioner, and five, when you entered the church. Whoever it was worked quickly. That implies they knew the layout of the church.'

He gave me a keen look. 'Yes. It does.'

'And townsfolk do not attend Mass at monastery churches. When outsiders attend special festivals or come to pray to the relics, they are not allowed beyond the rood screen?'

'No. Only monks may come into the choir and before the altar.'

'So, only a monk would know these routines and the layout of the church. Or a servant who worked here – like that man peregrinating the church lighting the candles.'

He looked at me seriously. 'Geoffrey Walters is seventy years old and deaf. The church servants have all been here for years. I know them well and none of them could conceivably have done this.'

'That leaves us with one of the monks, then. Abbot Fabian, and your friend the bursar, would have it that an outsider was responsible. I have to disagree.'

'I think an outsider may be possible,' he said hesitantly.

'Go on.'

'On rising some mornings this autumn I have seen lights out on the marsh; my chamber in the dormitory overlooks it. I think the smugglers are active again.'

'The abbot talked of smugglers. But I thought that marsh was dangerous.'

'It is. But there are paths known to the smugglers running by the little island of higher ground, where the ruins of the founders' church stands, out to the river. Boats can be loaded with contraband wool for France. The abbot complains to the town authorities now and again, but they're not interested. Some of the officials no doubt profit from the trade.'

'So someone who knew those paths could have got in and out of the monastery that night?'

'Possibly. The wall down there is in poor shape.'

'Did you mention seeing lights to the abbot?'

'No. As I said, he has given up complaining. I have been too sore in my mind to think clearly, but now—' An eager look came into his face. 'Perhaps that is the answer. Those men are criminals and one sin can lead to another, even to blasphemy—'

'Of course it would suit the community to lay the blame elsewhere.'

He turned to me, his face set. 'Master Shardlake, it may be you see our prayers, our devotion to the relics of the saints, as foolish ceremonies performed by men who live easily while the world outside groans and suffers.'

I inclined my head non-committally.

He spoke with a sudden intentness. 'Our life of prayer and worship is an effort to approach Christ, to come nearer to his light and further from this sinful world. Every prayer, every Mass is an attempt to come closer to him, every statue and ritual and piece of stained glass is a reminder of his glory, a distraction from the world's wickedness.'

'I see you believe so, Brother.'

'I know we live easier than we should, our comfortable clothes and food are not what St Benedict intended. But our purpose is the same.'

'To seek communion with God?'

He turned, looking at me intently. 'It is not easy. People who say it is are wrong. Sinful mankind is full of wicked impulses, planted by the Devil. Do not think monks are immune, sir. Sometimes I believe the more we aspire to approach God, the more the Devil stirs himself to tempt our minds to wickedness. And the more we have to strive against him.'

'And can you think of anyone who might have had his mind tempted to murder?' I asked quietly. 'Remember I speak with the authority of the vicar general, and through him the Supreme Head of the Church, the king.'

He looked me directly in the eye. 'I can think of no one in our community who might do such a thing. If I could, I would have informed the abbot. I told you, I believe an outsider was responsible.'

I nodded. 'But there has been talk of other grave sins here, has there not? The scandal under the last prior. And small sins may lead to larger ones.'

His face reddened. 'It is a large step from – those things – to what was done last week. And those acts were in the past.' He stood abruptly and moved to stand a few paces off.

I got up and stood beside him. His face was set and his brow had a sheen of sweat despite the cold.

'Not all in the past, Brother. The abbot tells me Simon Whelplay's penance was in part because of certain feelings he nurtured towards another monk. Yourself.'

He turned, suddenly animated. 'He is a child! I was not responsible for the sins he contemplated in his poor mind. I did not even know till he confessed to Prior Mortimus, or I would have put a stop to it. And yes, I have lain with other men, but I have confessed and repented and sinned no more in that way. There, Commissioner, you have plumbed my history. I know the vicar general's office loves such tales.'

'I seek only the truth. I would not trouble your soul merely for a pastime.'

He seemed about to say something more, then paused and took a deep breath. 'Do you wish to see the library now?'

'Yes, please.'

We returned down the nave. 'By the way,' I said after we had walked some distance in silence, 'I saw the great crack in the side of the church. That is indeed a large job. The prior will not approve the expenditure?'

'No. Brother Edwig says any programme of repairs must be limited to the revenues available each year. That will barely suffice to prevent the damage from spreading.'

'I see.' In that case, I thought, why were Brother Edwig and the abbot talking of needing capital from land sales?

'These men of accounts always believe that what is cheapest is best,' I continued philosophically, 'and prink and save till all falls about them.'

'Brother Edwig thinks saving money is a holy duty,' he said bitterly.

'Neither he nor the prior appears much given to charity.'

He gave me a sharp look, but said nothing more as he led me from the church.

✠

OUTSIDE, my eyes watered in the cold white light. The sun was high now and gave brightness if not warmth. More paths had been cleared through the snow and people were going about their business again, black habits criss-crossing the white expanse.

The library building, next to the church, was surprisingly large. Light streamed in from high windows, illuminating shelves crammed with books. The desks were empty, save for a novice scratching his head over a heavy tome, and an old monk in a corner laboriously copying a manuscript.

'Not many at study,' I observed.

'The library is often empty,' Brother Gabriel said regretfully. 'If someone has to consult a book, he usually takes it to his cell.' He went over to the old monk. 'How are you progressing, Stephen?'

The old man squinted up at us. 'Slowly, Brother Gabriel.' I

glanced at his work; he was copying an early bible, the letters and the painted figures beside the text worked in intricate detail, the colours standing out brightly on the thick parchment, only slightly faded after centuries. The monk's copy, though, was a poor affair, the letters scratchy and uneven, the colours gaudy. Brother Gabriel patted him on the shoulder. '*Nec aspera terrent*, Brother,' he said, before turning to me. 'I will show you the illustration of Barabbas's hand.'

The sacrist led me up winding stairs to the upper floor. Here were more books, innumerable shelves stacked with ancient volumes. Thick dust lay everywhere.

'Our collection. Some of our books are copies of Greek and Roman works made in the days when copying was an art. Even fifty years ago those desks downstairs would have been filled with brothers copying books. But since printing came in no one wants illustrated works, they are happy with these cheap books with their ugly, square letters all squashed together.'

'Printed books may be less beautiful, but now God's word can be brought to all.'

'But can it be understood by all?' he replied with animation. 'And without illustration and art to stimulate our awe and reverence?' He took an old volume from the shelves and opened it, coughing amidst the dust it raised. Little painted creatures danced impishly among lines of Greek text.

'Reputedly a copy of Aristotle's lost work *On Comedy*,' he said. 'A fake, of course, thirteenth-century Italian, but beautiful nonetheless.' He closed it, turning to an enormous volume that shared a shelf with a number of rolled-up plans. He pulled them out and I took one to assist him. I was surprised when he grabbed it back.

'No! Don't take it!'

I raised my eyebrows. His face reddened.

'I am sorry – I – I would not have you get dust on your clothes, sir.'

'What are those?'

'Old plans of the monastery. The mason consults them sometimes.' He withdrew the volume beneath. It was so large he had difficulty in heaving it over to a desk. He turned the pages carefully.

'This is an illustrated history of the monastery's treasures, set down two hundred years ago.' I saw coloured pictures of the statues I had seen in the church, and other items like the lectern in the refectory, each drawing annotated with measurements and a Latin commentary. The centre pages were taken up with a coloured illustration of a large square casket set with jewels. Inside a glass panel, on a purple cushion, lay a piece of dark wood. A human hand was fixed there by a broad-headed nail driven through the palm; withered and ancient, every sinew and tendon visible. From the measurements the box was two feet square and a foot deep.

'So those are the emeralds,' I said. 'They are large. The casket could have been stolen for its precious jewels and gold?'

'Yes. Though any Christian doing such a thing would lose their immortal soul.'

'I always thought the thieves crucified with Christ had their hands tied to the cross rather than being nailed to it, so that their suffering should be prolonged. So it is shown in religious paintings.'

He sighed. 'No one really knows. The gospels say Our Lord died first, but he had been tortured beforehand.'

'The misleading power of paintings and statues,' I said. 'And there is a paradox here, is there not?'

'What do you mean, sir?'

'That hand belonged to a thief. Now his relic, which people paid to view until that was forbidden as usury, is itself stolen.'

'It may be a paradox,' Brother Gabriel replied quietly, 'but to us it is a tragedy.'

'Could one man carry it?'

'Two men bear it in the Easter procession. A strong man could carry it, perhaps, but not far.'

'To the marsh, perhaps?'

He nodded. 'Perhaps.'

'Then I think it is time I had a look out there, if you would show me the way.'

'Certainly. There is a gate in the rear wall.'

'Thank you, Brother Gabriel. Your library is fascinating.'

He led me back outside and pointed to the cemetery. 'Follow the path through there, past the orchard and the fish pond, and you will see the gate. The snow will be thick.'

'I have my overshoes. Well, no doubt we shall meet again at supper. You will be able to meet my young assistant again then.' I smiled disingenuously. The sacrist blushed and lowered his head.

'Ah – yes, indeed—'

'Well, Brother, I thank you for your help and your frankness. Good day.' I nodded and left him. When I glanced back he was walking slowly back towards the church, head bowed.

Chapter Twelve

I PASSED THE WORKSHOPS and turned through a little gate into the lay cemetery. In daylight it seemed smaller. The headstones of locals who had paid for a place here, or visitors who had died within the walls, lay half-buried in the snow. There were three other large stone family tombs similar to the Fitzhugh crypt we had visited the night before. At the far end rows of fruit trees raised bare arms to the sky.

These crypts, I reflected, would make good hiding places. I ploughed my way towards the nearest, unhitching the abbot's key ring from my belt. I fumbled among the keys with cold, stiff fingers until I found one of the right size that fitted.

I tried each crypt in turn, but there was nothing hidden among the white marble tombs. The stone floors were dusty and there was no sign any of them had been visited for years. One belonged to a prominent Hastings family whose name I remembered as another ancient line wiped out in the civil wars. And yet those buried here would be remembered, I reflected, recalling the monks reciting their private Masses; remembered as names memorized and chanted to the empty air every day. I shook my head and turned back towards the orchard, where starveling crows cawed in the skeleton trees; I was glad of my staff as I stumbled among the gravestones.

A wicket gate led me into the orchard and I picked my way between the snow-laden trees. Everything was still and silent. Out here in the open, I felt that at last I had space to think.

It was strange to be inside a monastery again after so many years. When I was a pupil at Lichfield I had been a mere cripple-boy, of no account. Here I had the powers of a commissioner of Lord Cromwell, greater powers than any outsider had ever had over a religious house. Yet now as then I felt isolated, alone, disliked. The different element here was their fear of me, but I had to handle my authority carefully, for when men are frightened they close up like clams.

My talk with Brother Gabriel had depressed me. He lived in the past, a world of painted books, ancient chants, plaster statues. I guessed it was a world in which he sought refuge from continuing temptations. I recalled his anguished expression when I confronted him with his history. There were many I encountered in my career, blustering liars and deceitful rogues, whom I confess it was a pleasure to question, watching their faces fall and their eyes swivel as I unpicked some edifice of lies. But to harry unsavoury sins from a man like Brother Gabriel, who had a certain fragile dignity it was all too easy to undermine, that was no thing to enjoy. After all, I knew only too well what it was like to be a despised outsider.

I remembered how sometimes the taunts of the other children when I could not play their games had led me to plead with my father to take me away from the cathedral school and educate me at home. He had replied that if I was allowed to retreat from the world I would never rejoin it. He was a stern man, not given to sympathy and less so after my mother died when I was ten. Perhaps he was right, yet that morning I wondered whether I was better off if worldly success had led me to such a place as this. It seemed to do nothing but bring back bad memories.

I passed a row of dovecotes, beyond which a large pond surrounded by reeds could be seen. It was a stewpond, dug out for the keeping and breeding of fish. The little stream flowed into it before running through a small culvert under the rear wall a little way off. There was a heavy wooden gate nearby. Monasteries, I recalled, were always built by a stream to carry away waste. The early monks were clever plumbers; there was probably some arrangement to divert the waste to prevent it befouling the fish pond. I stood looking out over the scene, leaning on my staff, chiding myself for my gloomy thoughts. I was here to investigate a murder, not mewl over past sorrows.

I had made some progress, though not much. It seemed unlikely to me that this crime had been committed by an outsider. But although the five senior officials all had knowledge of Singleton's purpose, I could not see any of them becoming so overcome with wild hatred that they would kill him and place St Donatus's future in even greater danger. Yet they were all hard men to read, and about Gabriel at least there was something tormented and desperate.

I turned over the idea that Singleton had been killed because he had found something out about one of the monks. That seemed more likely, yet I could not square it with the dramatic manner of his murder. I sighed. I wondered if I would end by having to interview every monk and servant in the monastery, and my heart sank at the thought of how long that might take. The sooner I was away from this wretched pile and its dangers the happier I would be; and Lord Cromwell needed a solution. But as Mark had said, I could only do what was possible. I must plod on, as lawyers do. And next I must check whether outsiders could gain access from this marsh. 'All the circumstances,' I muttered as I ploughed on through the snow. 'All the circumstances.'

I reached the pond and looked in. It was covered with a thin skin of ice, but the sun was almost overhead now and I made out the dim shapes of large carp flickering through the reedy water.

As I straightened up something else caught my eye, a faint yellowish glint at the bottom. Puzzled, I leaned forward again. At first I could not locate what I had seen among the reeds and wondered whether it had been a trick of the light, but then I saw it again. I knelt down, my hands smarting at the touch of the snow, and peered in. There was something, a patch of yellow at the bottom. The casket was gold, and many expensive swords have gilt handles. It was worth investigating. I shivered. I did not fancy confronting those icy depths now, but I would come back later with Mark. I rose, brushed the snow from my clothes, then gathered my coat around me and headed for the gate.

I saw that in a couple of places the wall had crumbled and been patched up, crudely and unevenly. Unhooking the bunch of keys from my belt, I found one that fitted the heavy, ancient lock. The gate creaked open and I stepped out onto a narrow path. It ran alongside the wall, the land dropping away at the edge a final few inches to the marsh. I had not realized it came so close. In places the path was broken where the mire had advanced right up to the wall, undermining it so it had had to be rebuilt. It was even more crudely patched outside. In places an agile man could climb that uneven surface. 'Damn it to hell,' I muttered, for now I could not eliminate even that possibility.

I looked out over the marsh. Covered with snow, broken by thick clusters of reeds and frozen stagnant pools, it stretched for half a mile to the broad band of the river, the blue sky reflected in its unfrozen waters. Beyond the river the ground rose slowly again to a woodland horizon. Everything was still, a pair of seabirds on the river the only sign of life. As I watched they rose into the air, calling their sad cries to the cold heavens.

Halfway between the river and where I stood was a large knoll, an island in the marsh. It was topped with a jumble of low ruins. That must be the place Brother Gabriel had mentioned, where the monks had first settled. Curious, and holding my staff carefully, I set one foot down from the path. To my surprise, the ground under the snow was firm. I let down my other leg and took a step forward. Again I felt firm ground. But it was only a skin of frozen, matted grass, and suddenly my foot crunched through, squelching into miry softness. I let out a cry, dropping my staff. My leg was being sucked slowly into what felt like thick mud; I felt slime and icy water come over the top of my overshoe and trickle down my shin.

I flailed my arms wildly to keep my balance; I had a horror of tipping over and landing face down in the mud. My left leg was still on firm ground and I pulled back with all my strength, terrified that leg too would crunch through a skin of solid ground into some nameless depth. But the ground there held and, sweating with exertion and fear, I was able, painfully slowly, to pull out the other leg, black with mud. A sucking, gurgling sound and a cesspit odour came from the mire. I stepped back and sat with a thump on the path, my heart pounding. My staff lay where it had fallen on the marsh, but I did not think of trying to rescue it. Looking down at my leg encased in stinking mud, I cursed myself for a fool. Lord Cromwell's face would have been worth seeing had he learned that his carefully chosen commissioner had braved the mysteries and dangers of Scarnsea only to fall in a bog and drown.

'You are a noddle,' I said aloud.

I heard a sound behind me, and turned sharply. The gate in the wall was open and Brother Edwig was standing there, a warm coat over his habit, staring at me in amazement.

'Master Sh-Shardlake, are you all right?' He gazed around the bare landscape, and I realized he had heard me talking to myself.

'Yes, Brother Edwig.' I climbed to my feet, realizing I did not cut an impressive figure, bespattered with mud as I was. 'I have had a slight accident. I nearly fell in.'

He shook his head. 'You should not go in there, sir. It is very dangerous.'

'So I see. But what are you doing out here, Brother? Is there no work in the counting house?'

'I have been v-v-visiting the sick novice with the abbot. I wanted to c-clear my head. Sometimes I come out here for a walk.'

I looked at him curiously. He was not someone I could easily imagine tramping through snowy orchards for exercise.

'I like to come out here and l-look out towards the r-r-river. It is c-calming.'

'So long as one minds one's footing?'

'Er – yes. C-can I help you back, sir? You are c-covered with mud.'

I was starting to shiver. 'I can manage. But yes, I should go back.'

We returned through the gate and plodded back to the monastery. I went as fast as I could, my sodden leg like a block of ice.

'How is the novice?'

He shook his head. 'He appears to be r/recovering, but one can never tell with these chesty agues. I had one m/myself last winter; it kept me out of the c/counting house two weeks.' He shook his head.

'And what is your opinion of Simon Whelplay's treatment by the prior?'

He shook his head again, impatiently. 'It is d/difficult. We must have discipline.'

'But should one not temper the wind to the shorn lamb?'

'P/people need certainty, they n/need to know that if they do wrong they will be p/punished.' He looked at me. 'Do you not th/ think so, sir?'

'Some people find it harder to learn than others. I was told not to go in that bog, but I did.'

'But that was a mistake, sir, not a sin. And if one finds it hard to learn, all the more reason to give a firm lesson, surely. And that boy is weakly, he could have taken an ague in any case.' His tone was stern.

I raised my eyebrows. 'You appear to view the world in black and white, Brother.'

He looked puzzled. 'Of course, sir. Black and white. Sin and virtue. God and the Devil. The rules are laid down and we must follow them.'

'Now the rules are laid down by the king, not the pope.'

He looked at me seriously. 'Yes, sir, and we must follow those.'

I reflected that that was not what Brother Athelstan had reported him and the others as saying. 'I understand, Brother Bursar, that you were away on the night Commissioner Singleton was killed?'

'Y/yes. We have some estates over at W/Winchelsea. I was not happy with the steward's accounts, I rode over to make a spot check. I was away three nights.'

'What did you uncover?'

'I thought he'd b-been cheating us. But it was just a matter of errors. I've sacked him, though. If people can't keep proper ac-counts they're no good to me.'

'Did you go alone?'

'I took one of my assistants, old Brother William, whom you saw in the counting house.' He looked at me shrewdly. 'And I was at the steward's house the night Commissioner S-Singleton was killed. G-God rest him,' he added piously.

'You have many duties then,' I said. 'But at least you have assistants to help you. The old man and the boy.'

He gave me a sharp look. 'Yes, though the boy's more trouble than he's worth.'

'Is he?'

'No head for figures, n-none at all. I have s-set him to looking out the books you requested, they should b-be with you soon.' He almost slipped, and I caught his arm.

'Thank you, sir. By Our Lady, this snow!'

✝

FOR THE REST of the journey he concentrated on where he was putting his feet, and we said little more till we reached the monastery precinct. We parted in the courtyard; Brother Edwig returned to his counting house and I turned my steps back towards the infirmary. I needed some dinner. I thought about the bursar; a jack-in-office, obsessed with his financial responsibilities probably to the exclusion of all else. But devoted to the monastery too. Would he be prepared to countenance dishonesty to protect it, or would that mean crossing the line between white and black? He was an unsympathetic man, but as I had said to Mark the night before, that did not make him a murderer any more than the sympathy I felt for Brother Gabriel made him innocent. I sighed. It was hard to be objective among these people.

As I opened the infirmary door, all seemed quiet. The hall was deserted. The sick old man lay quietly in his bed, the blind monk was asleep in his chair and the fat monk's bed was empty; perhaps Brother Guy had persuaded him it was time to leave. A fire crackled welcomingly in the grate and I went to warm myself for a moment.

As I stood watching steam rise from my wet hose, I heard sounds from within; confused, fractured noises, cries and shouts and the crash of pottery breaking. The sounds came closer. I stared in astonishment as the door to the sick rooms burst open and a tangle of struggling figures fell into the hall: Alice, Mark, Brother Guy, and at the centre a thin figure in a white nightshift, who as I watched threw the others off and staggered away. I recognized Simon Whelplay, but he was a very different figure now from the half-dead wraith I had seen the night before. His face was puce, his eyes wide and staring and there was a froth of spittle at the corner of his mouth. He seemed to be trying to speak but could only gasp and retch.

'God's blood, what's happening?' I called out to Mark.

'He's gone stark mad, sir!'

'Spread out! Catch him!' Brother Guy shouted. His face was grim as he nodded to Alice, who moved to one side, spreading her arms. Mark and Brother Guy followed her example and they closed in on the novice, who had come to a halt and stood staring wildly around. The blind monk had woken and sat twisting his head anxiously around, his mouth agape. 'What is it?' he asked tremulously. 'Brother Guy?'

Then a dreadful thing happened. It seemed to me that Whelplay caught sight of me and at once bent his trunk forward in imitation of my twisted gait. Not only that, but he stretched forth his arms and began waving them to and fro, seeming to waggle his fingers mockingly. It is a mannerism I have when I am excited, so those who have seen me in court have told me. But how could Whelplay know such a thing? I was taken back again to those schooldays I had been reflecting on, when cruel children would imitate my movements, and I confess that as I watched the novice staggering about, bent and gesticulating, the hair rose on my neck.

I was brought to my senses by a shout from Mark. 'Help us! Catch him, sir, for pity's sake, or he'll get out!' My heart thumping, I too spread my arms and approached the novice. I looked into his eyes as I came closer and they were terrible to see, the pupils twice the normal size, staring wildly, without recognition even as he performed his mocking stagger. Brother Gabriel's talk of satanic forces came back to me and I thought with a jolt of sudden terror that the boy was possessed.

As the four of us closed on him he made a sudden lurch to the side and disappeared through a half-open door.

'He's in the bath house!' Brother Guy called. 'There's no way out of there. Be careful, the floor is slippery.' He ran in, Alice just after him. Mark and I stared at each other then followed him inside.

The bath house was dim, only a faint milky light coming through a high window half-choked with snow. It was a small, square room with a tiled floor and a sunken bath in the middle, perhaps four feet deep. Brushes and scraping knives stood in one corner, and there was a pervasive musty smell of unwashed skin. I heard running water and looking down saw that the stream actually ran through a culvert in the bottom of the bath. Simon Whelplay stood in the far corner, still crouched over, trembling in his white nightshift. I stood by the door while Brother Guy approached him from one side, Mark and Alice from the other. Alice stretched out an arm to him.

'Come, Simon, it's Alice. We won't harm you.' I had to admire her dauntlessness; not many women would have approached such a frightful apparition so calmly.

The novice turned, his face twisted into an agonized expression, almost unrecognizable. He stared at her unseeingly for a moment, then his eyes turned to Mark beside her. He pointed a skinny finger and shouted in a cracked, hoarse voice quite unlike his own, 'Keep away! You are the Devil's man in your bright raiment! I see them now, the devils swarming through the air as thick as motes, they are everywhere, even here!' He covered his eyes with his hands, then staggered and suddenly fell forward into the bath. I heard his arm break with a crack as it hit the tiles. He lay still, his body sprawled across the culvert. Freezing water washed around him.

Brother Guy lowered himself into the bath. We stood on the edge as he turned the novice face up. His eyes had rolled back into his head, making a ghastly contrast with his still livid face. The infirmarian felt his neck and then let out a sigh. He looked up at us. 'He is dead.'

He rose and crossed himself. Alice let out a wail, then collapsed against Mark's chest, bursting into a frenzy of choking sobs.

Chapter Thirteen

MARK AND BROTHER GUY carefully lifted Simon's body out of the bath and carried it back into the infirmary hall. Brother Guy took the shoulders, and a pale-faced Mark the bare white feet. I followed behind with Alice, who after her brief outburst of sobbing had regained her usual composed demeanour.

'What is happening?' The blind monk was on his feet, waving his hands before him, his face piteous with fear. 'Brother Guy? Alice?'

'It is all right, Brother,' Alice said soothingly. 'There has been an accident, but all is safe now.' I wondered again at her control.

The body was laid in Brother Guy's infirmary, under the Spanish crucifix. He covered it with a sheet, his face set hard.

I took a deep breath. My mind was still reeling, and not just with shock at the novice's death. What had passed just before had shaken me to my bones. The echoes of childhood torments have great power, even when not brought to mind in such an inexplicable and horrifying way.

'Brother Guy,' I said, 'I never met that boy before yesterday, yet when he saw me he appeared to – to mock me, imitating my bent posture and – certain gestures I sometimes make in court, waving my hands. It seemed to me l-like something devilish.' I cursed myself, I was stammering like the bursar.

He gave me a long, searching look. 'I can think of a reason for that. I hope I am wrong.'

'What do you mean? Speak plainly.' I heard myself snap peevishly.

'I need to consider,' he replied as sharply. 'But first, Commissioner, Abbot Fabian should be told.'

'Very well.' I grasped the corner of his table; my legs had begun to shake uncontrollably. 'We will wait in your kitchen.'

Alice led Mark and me back to the little room where we had breakfasted.

'Are you all right, sir?' Mark asked anxiously. 'You are trembling.'

'Yes, yes.'

'I have an infusion of herbs that eases the body at times of shock,' Alice said. 'Valerian and aconite. I could heat some if you wish.'

'Thank you.' She remained composed, but there was a strange, almost bruised-looking sheen on her cheeks. I forced a smile. 'The scene affected you too, I saw. It was understandable. One feared the Devil himself was present in that poor creature.'

I was surprised by the anger that flashed into her face. 'I fear no devils, sir, unless it be such human monsters as tormented that poor boy. His life was destroyed before it began, and for such we should always weep.' She paused, realizing she had gone too far for a servant. 'I will fetch the infusion,' she said quickly, and hurried out.

I raised my eyebrows at Mark. 'Outspoken.'

'She has a hard life.'

I fingered my mourning ring. 'So have many in this vale of tears.' I glanced at him. He's smitten, I thought.

'I spoke with her as you asked.'

'Tell me,' I said encouragingly. I needed a distraction from the memory of what had just passed.

'She has been here eighteen months. She comes from Scarnsea, her father died young and she was brought up by her mother, who was a wise woman, a dispenser of herbs.'

'So that's where she gets her knowledge.'

'She was to be married, but her swain died in an accident felling trees. There's little work in the town, but she found a place as assistant to an apothecary in Esher, someone her mother knew.'

'So she's travelled. I thought she was no village mouse.'

'She knows the country round here well. I was talking to her about that marsh. She says there are paths through if you know where to find them. I asked her if she would show us and she said she might.'

'That could be useful.' I told him what Brother Gabriel had said about the smugglers, of my own visit there and my accident. I displayed my muddy leg. 'If there are paths, any guide had better be careful. God's wounds, this is a day of shocks.' My hand lying on the table was trembling; I seemed unable to stop it. Mark, too, was still pale. There was silence for a moment, a silence I was suddenly desperate to fill.

'You seem to have had a long talk. How does Alice come to be here?'

'The apothecary died, he was an old man. After that she came back to Scarnsea, but her mother died too shortly after. Her cottage was on a copyhold and the landowner took it back. She was left alone. She didn't know what to do, then someone said the infirmarian was looking for a lay assistant. No one in the town wanted to work for him – they call him the black goblin – but she had no choice.'

'I have the impression she does not much admire our holy brethren.'

'She said some of them are lascivious men, forever sidling up and trying to touch her. She is the only young woman in the place. The prior himself has been a problem apparently.'

I raised an eyebrow. 'God's wounds, she did speak freely.'

'She is angry, sir. The prior made a nuisance of himself when she first came.'

'Yes, I noticed she disliked him. Fie, the man's a hypocrite, punishing other people's sins and chasing the women servants himself. Does the abbot know?'

'She told Brother Guy and he made the prior stop. The abbot seldom intervenes; he supports the prior's strong discipline and leaves him to do much as he will. Apparently all the monks are terrified of him, and those who were guilty of sodomy before are too terrified of him to follow their base hearts.'

'And we've seen the results of that discipline.'

Mark passed a hand over his brow. 'Yes, we have,' he agreed sombrely.

I thought a moment. 'Disloyal of Mistress Alice, to speak so to the commissioner's assistant. Is she of reformist persuasion?'

'I don't think so. But she does not see why she should keep the secrets of those who have pestered her. She has strong feelings, sir, but fine ones. She is no malapert. She spoke warmly of Brother Guy. He has taught her much and protected her from those who trouble her. And she is fond of the harmless old men she looks after.'

I looked at him thoughtfully. 'Don't form too much of an attachment to the girl,' I said quietly. 'Lord Cromwell wants the surrender of this monastery, and we may end up putting her out of house and home again.'

He frowned. 'That would be cruel. And she's not a girl, she's twenty-two, a woman. Could not something be done for her?'

'I could try.' I mused a moment. 'So the infirmarian protects her. I wonder whether she would protect him in turn.'

'You mean Brother Guy may have secrets?'

'I don't know.' I stood up and walked to the window. 'My head spins.'

'You said the novice appeared to be imitating you,' Mark said hesitantly.

'Did it not seem like that to you?'

'I don't see how he could have known—'

I gulped. 'How I wave my arms around when speaking in court? No, neither do I.' I stood looking out of the window, biting my thumbnail, until I saw Brother Guy reappear, striding along with the abbot and prior beside him. The three figures passed quickly by the window, kicking up little clouds of snow. A few moments later we heard voices from the room where the body lay. There were more footsteps, and the three monks entered the little kitchen. I sat studying each in turn. Brother Guy's brown features were expressionless. Prior Mortimus's face was red, filled with anger but I saw fear too. The abbot seemed to have shrunk into himself; the big man looked somehow smaller, greyer.

'Commissioner,' he said quietly, 'I am sorry you had to witness such a terrible scene.'

I took a deep breath. I felt more like curling up in a corner somewhere than trying to exercise authority over these wretched people, but I had no choice.

'Yes,' I said. 'I come to the infirmary looking for peace and quiet while I carry out my investigations, and I am confronted with a novice frozen and starved till first he catches a fever that almost kills him, then goes stark mad and falls to his death.'

'He was possessed!' The prior spoke in hard, clipped tones, the sarcasm gone. 'He allowed his mind to become so polluted that the Devil possessed it in his hour of weakness. I confessed him, I put him to penance to mortify him, but I was too late. See the Devil's power.' He set his lips and glared at me. 'It is everywhere, and all arguments between Christians distract us from it!'

'The boy spoke of seeing devils in the air as thick as motes,' I said. 'Do you think he saw true?'

'Come, sir, even the most ardent reformers do not dispute the world is filled with the Devil's agents. Is it not said Luther himself once threw a bible at a demon in his room?'

'But sometimes such visions can come from brain fever.' I looked at Brother Guy, who nodded.

'Indeed they can,' the abbot agreed. 'The Church has known that for hundreds of years. We must have a full investigation.'

'Ah, there's nothing to investigate,' the prior burst out angrily. 'Simon Whelplay opened his soul to the Devil, a demon took him and made him throw himself into that bath, kill himself like the Gadarene swine going over the cliff. His soul's in hell now, for all I tried to save it.'

'I do not think the fall killed him,' Brother Guy said.

Everyone looked at him in surprise. 'How can ye tell that?' the prior asked contemptuously.

'Because he did not strike his head,' the infirmarian replied quietly.

'Then how—'

'I do not know yet.'

'In any event,' I said sharply, looking at the prior, 'he appears to have been driven into a seriously weakened state by excess of discipline.'

The prior looked at me boldly. 'Sir, the vicar general wants order brought back to the monasteries. He is right, the former laxity placed souls in peril. If I failed with Simon Whelplay it is because I was not severe *enough*; or perhaps his heart was already too cankered. But I say with Lord Cromwell, only by stern discipline shall the orders be reformed. I do not regret what I did.'

'What do you say, my lord Abbot?'

'It is possible your severity went too far in this case, Mortimus. Brother Guy, you and I and Prior Mortimus will meet to consider matters further. A committee of investigation. Yes, a committee.' The word seemed to reassure him.

Brother Guy sighed deeply. 'First I should examine his poor remains.'

'Yes,' the abbot said. 'Do that.' His confidence seemed to be returning as he turned back to me. 'Master Shardlake, I must tell you that Brother Gabriel has been to see me. He remembers seeing lights out on the marsh in the days before Commissioner Singleton was killed. It seems to me our local smugglers may have been responsible for the murder. They are godless people: if you break the law's commandments, it is but a further step to breaking those of God.'

'Yes, I have been out to look at the marsh. It is something I shall raise with the Justice tomorrow; it is one line of enquiry.'

'I think it is the answer.'

I made no reply. The abbot went on. 'For the moment, it might be best simply to tell the brethren that Simon died as a result of his illness. If you agree, Commissioner.'

I thought a moment. I did not wish to spread more panic abroad. 'Very well.'

'I will have to write to his family. I will tell them the same—'

'Yes, better than to tell them the prior is sure their son is roasting in hell,' I snapped, suddenly disgusted by them both. Prior Mortimus opened his mouth to argue further, but the abbot interjected.

'Come, Mortimus, we must go. We must arrange for another grave to be dug.' He bowed and took his leave, the prior following with a last challenging stare at me.

'Brother Guy,' Mark said, 'what do you think killed that boy?'

'I am going to find out. I will have to open him.' He shook his head. 'It is never an easy thing to do with one you have known. But it must be done now, while he is fresh.' He bowed his head and closed his eyes a moment in prayer, then took a deep breath. 'If you will excuse me.'

I nodded, and the infirmarian left, his footsteps padding slowly towards the dispensary. Mark and I sat in silence for a few moments. The colour was starting to return to his cheeks, but he was still paler than I had ever seen him. I still felt as though stunned, although at least my shaking had stopped. Alice appeared, bearing a cup of steaming liquid.

'I have prepared your infusion, sir.'

'Thank you.'

'And the two clerks from the counting house are in the hall, with a great pile of books.'

'What? Ah, yes. Mark, would you see they are taken to our room?'

'Yes, sir.' As he opened the door I heard a sound of sawing from the direction of the dispensary. He shut it again, and I closed my eyes with relief. I took a sip of the liquid Alice had brought. It had a heavy, musky taste.

'It is good for shocks, sir, it settles the humours.'

'It is comforting. Thank you.'

She stood with her hands clasped before her. 'Sir, I would apologize for my words earlier. I spoke out of turn.'

'No matter. We were all troubled.'

She hesitated. 'You must think me strange, sir, that I said I did not fear the work of devils after what I saw.'

'No. Some are too ready to see the Devil's hand in every piece of ill they do not understand. It was my own first reaction to what I saw, but I think Brother Guy has some other explanation in mind. He is – investigating the body.'

She crossed herself.

'Although equally,' I continued, 'we must not be blind to Satan's workings in the world.'

'I think—' She paused.

'Go on. You may speak freely with me. Sit down, please.'

'Thank you.' She sat, fixing me with her keen blue eyes. They had a watchful quality. I noticed how clear and healthy her skin was.

'I think the Devil works in the world through men's evil, their greed and cruelty and ambition, rather than possessing them and driving them stark mad.'

I nodded. 'I think so too, Alice. I have seen enough of the qualities you mention in the courts. Not just among the accused either. And the people who possessed them were all too sane.' Lord Cromwell's face suddenly appeared in my mind's eye with startling vividness. I blinked.

Alice nodded sadly. 'Such evil is everywhere. Sometimes it seems to me the wish for money and power can turn men into roaring lions, seeking what they might devour.'

'Well put. But where can a young maid have encountered such evil?' I asked gently. 'Here, perhaps?'

'I observe the world, I think upon things.' She shrugged. 'More than is proper in a woman, perhaps.'

'No, no. God allowed reason to women as well as men.'

She smiled wryly. 'You would not find many here to agree with you, sir.'

I took another swig of the potion. I felt it warming and relaxing my tired muscles. 'This is good. Master Poer was telling me you are skilled in the healing arts.'

'Thank you. As I told him, my mother was a wise woman.' Her face darkened a moment. 'Some in the town associate such work with the dark arts, but she merely gathered knowledge. She had it from her mother, who had it from her mother in turn. The apothecary often sought her advice.'

'And you became an apothecary's assistant.'

'Yes. He taught me much. But he died and I came back home.'

'To lose your house.'

She set her lips. 'Yes, the tenancy expired on my mother's death. The landlord demolished the house and enclosed our bit of land for sheep.'

'I am sorry. These enclosures ruin the countryside. It is a matter of concern to Lord Cromwell.'

She looked at me curiously. 'Do you know him? Lord Cromwell?'

I nodded. 'Yes. I have served him a long time, in one way and another.'

She gave me a long, deeply curious look, then dropped her gaze and sat silent, her hands in her lap. Work-roughened hands, but still shapely.

'You came here after your mother died?' I asked her.

She raised her head. 'Yes. Brother Guy is a good man, sir. I – I hope you will not think badly of him for his strange looks, sir. Some do.'

I shook my head. 'I must look deeper than that, if I am to be any good as an investigator. Though I confess I had a shock when I first saw him.'

She gave a sudden laugh, a flash of white even teeth. 'So did I, sir. I thought it was a face carved in wood, come to life. It was weeks before I came to see him as a man like others. He has taught me a great deal.'

'Perhaps one day you will be able to put that knowledge to use yourself. I know in London there are women apothecaries. But they are mostly widows, and doubtless you will marry.'

She shrugged. 'Maybe one day.'

'Mark said you had a swain who died. I am sorry.'

'Yes,' she said slowly. The watchful look was back in her eyes. 'Master Poer seems to have told you much about me.'

'We – well, we need to learn all we can of all who live here, as you must realize.' I gave her what I hoped was a reassuring smile.

She stood up again and walked over to the window. When she turned her shoulders were tensed and she seemed to have come to a decision.

'Sir, if I were to give you some information, would you keep it in confidence? I need my position here—'

'Yes, Alice, you have my word.'

'Brother Edwig's clerks, they said that they had brought all the current account books, at your request.'

'That is so.'

'But they have not brought all, sir. They have not brought the account book Commissioner Singleton had the day he died.'

'How do you know?'

'Because all the books they carried are brown. The one the commissioner was studying had a blue cover.'

'Had it indeed? How do you know this?'

She hesitated. 'You will keep it to yourself that I told you?'

'Yes, I promise. I would like you to trust me, Alice.'

She took a deep breath. 'On the afternoon of Commissioner Singleton's death I had been into town to buy some supplies. On the way back I passed the bursar's young assistant, Brother Athelstan, and the commissioner standing outside the counting-house door.'

'Brother Athelstan?'

'Yes. Commissioner Singleton was holding a large blue book in his hands, shouting at Athelstan. He did not bother to lower his voice as I passed.' She gave a sardonic little smile. 'After all, I am only a woman servant.'

'And he said?'

'"He thought he'd keep this from me, hidden in his drawer?" I remember his words. Brother Athelstan stuttered something about his having no right to ferret about the bursar's private room while he was away, and the commissioner replied he had the right to go everywhere, and the book put a fresh light on the year's accounts.'

'What did Brother Athelstan say to that?'

'Nothing. He was in a great fright, he looked like a dog thrown from a window. Commissioner Singleton said he was going to make a study of the book, then he stalked off. I remember the triumphant look on his face. Brother Athelstan just stood there some moments. Then he saw me. He gave me a glare, then went inside and banged the door shut.'

'And you heard nothing more about this?'

'No, sir. Night was just falling when this happened, and the next I heard the commissioner was dead.'

'Thank you, Alice,' I said. 'That could be very helpful.' I paused, studying her carefully. 'By the way, Master Poer told me you have had some trouble with the prior.'

The bold look came back to her face. 'In my early days here he sought to take advantage of my position. It is not a problem now.'

I nodded. 'You speak straight, Alice, I admire that. Please, if you think of anything that may help my enquiries, come to me. If you need protection, I will give it. I will follow up this missing book, but I will take care not to mention that you have spoken to me.'

'Thank you, sir. And now, with your pardon, I should assist Brother Guy.'

'That is a grim job for a maid.'

She shrugged. 'It is part of my duties, and I am used to dead flesh. My mother used to lay out people who died in the town.'

'You have more stomach than I, Alice.'

'Yes, my life has left me few gentle qualities,' she said with sudden bitterness.

'I did not mean that.' I raised a hand in protest. As I did so my arm brushed against my cup, almost knocking it over. But Alice, who had walked back to the table and stood opposite me, reached swiftly across and grasped it, setting it upright again.

'Thank you. By heaven, you have a quick hand.'

'Brother Guy is forever dropping things in the infirmary. And now, sir, with your leave I must go.'

'Of course. And thank you for telling me about the bursar.' I smiled. 'I know a king's commissioner can be an intimidating figure.'

'No, sir. You are different.' She looked at me seriously a moment, then quickly turned and left the room.

☩

I NURSED MY POTION, which slowly warmed my vitals. The thought that Alice appeared to trust me also sent probing fingers of warmth through me. If I had met her in another context, and if she had not been a servant—

I thought on her last words. How was I 'different'? I supposed what she had seen of Singleton had led her to think all commissioners were hectoring bullies, but had I sensed something more in her words? I could not imagine she felt attracted to me in the way I realized I was to her. I realized too that I had revealed that Mark had repeated all she told him. That might undermine her trust in him; a thought that I was alarmed to realize gave me a twitch of pleasure. I frowned, for jealousy is one of the deadly sins, and turned my mind to what she had said about the account book. That sounded a promising line of enquiry.

After a while Mark reappeared. I was relieved to note, as he opened the door, that the sawing had stopped.

'I have signed for the account books, sir. Eighteen great tomes. There was much grumbling from the bursar's men about how this will disrupt their work.'

'A pox on their work. Did you lock our room behind you?'

'Yes, sir.'

'Did you happen to notice whether any of the books had a blue cover?'

'They were all brown.'

I nodded. 'I think I know why Brother Edwig has been giving young Athelstan a hard time. There was something he did not tell us earlier. We will have another talk with our bursar, this could be important—' I broke off as Brother Guy came in. His face was drawn and pale. Under his arm was a stained apron which he threw into a basket in the corner.

'Commissioner, might we have a private word?'

'Of course.'

I rose and followed him. I feared he would take me to poor Whelplay's body, but to my relief he led me outside. The sun was beginning to set, casting a pink glow over the white herb garden. Brother Guy picked his way among the plants until he came to a large, snow-covered bush.

'I know now what killed poor Simon, and it was not possession by a demon. I also noticed him twisting his body over and waving his hands. But it was nothing to do with you. The spasms are characteristic. And the loss of voice, the visions.'

'Characteristic of what?'

'Poison from the berries of this bush.' He shook the branches, to which a few black dead leaves still clung. '*Belladonna*. The deadly nightshade, as it is called in this country.'

'He was poisoned?'

'Belladonna has a faint but distinctive smell. I have worked with it for years, I know it. It was in poor Simon's guts. And in the dregs of the cup of warm mead by his bed.'

'How was it done? When?'

'This morning, without doubt. The onset of symptoms is rapid. I blame myself, if only Alice or I had stayed with him all the time—' He passed a hand over his brow.

'You could not have known this would happen. Who else spent time alone with him?'

'Brother Gabriel visited him last night late, after you retired, and again this morning. He was most upset, I gave him permission to pray over the boy. And the abbot and bursar came to see him later.'

'Yes. I knew they were coming.'

'And also this morning, when I went in to check on him, I found Prior Mortimus there.'

'The prior?'

'He was standing by the bed, looking down at him, a worried look on his face. I thought he was worried about the consequences of his harsh treatment.' He set his lips. 'Belladonna juice is sweet-tasting, the smell too faint to be noticed in mead.'

'It is used as a remedy for some ailments, is it not?'

'In small doses it relieves constipation, and has other uses. There is some in my infirmary, I often prescribe it. Many of the monks will have some. Its properties are well known.'

I thought a moment. 'Last night Simon began to tell me something. He said Commissioner Singleton's death was not the first. I intended to question him again today when he woke.' I gave him a sharp look. 'Did you or Alice tell anyone what he had said?'

'I did not, and nor would Alice. But he might have rambled deliriously to his other visitors.'

'One of whom decided his mouth must be stopped.'

He bit his lip and nodded heavily.

'Poor child,' I said. 'And all I could think of was that he was mocking me.'

'Things are seldom what they seem.'

'Here least of all. Tell me, Brother, why have you told me this rather than going straight to the abbot?'

He gave me a bleak look. 'Because the abbot was among his visitors. You have authority, Master Shardlake, and I believe you seek the truth, however much I suspect we might disagree on matters of religion.'

I nodded. 'For the moment I instruct you to keep secret what you have told me. I must think carefully how to proceed.' I looked at Brother Guy to see how he would take orders from me, but he only nodded wearily. He looked down at my mud-caked leg.

'Have you had an accident?' he asked.

'I fell in the bog. I managed to get myself out.'

'The ground is very unsafe out there.'

'I think there is no safe ground under my feet anywhere here. Come inside, or we'll catch an ague.' I led the way indoors. 'Strange that my misplaced fear he was mocking me should lead to this discovery.'

'At least now Prior Mortimus cannot say that Simon is surely in hell.'

'Yes. I think that may disappoint him.' Unless he is the killer, I thought, in which case he knows already. I gritted my teeth. If I had not allowed Alice and Brother Guy to dissuade me from talking to Simon last night, not only might I have had his full story, not only might I have been led to the killer, but Simon would still be alive. Now I had two murders to investigate. And if what the poor novice had muttered in his delirium about Singleton not being the first was true, then there were three.

Chapter Fourteen

I HAD HOPED TO GO into Scarnsea that afternoon, but it was now too late. In the last glow of the sunset I trudged again through the precinct to the abbot's house, to talk to Goodhaps. The old cleric was again bibbing alone in his room. I did not tell him that Novice Whelplay had been murdered, only that he had been very ill. Goodhaps seemed uninterested. I asked him what he knew of the account book Singleton had been studying just before his death. Singleton, he said, had told him only that he had prised a new book out of the counting house, which he hoped would be useful. The old man muttered in a surly tone that Robin Singleton kept much to himself, using him only to burrow in books. I left him to his wine.

A cold, keening wind had risen, cutting through me like a blade as I made my way back to the infirmary. As those loud bells pealed out again for Vespers I could not help reflecting that anyone who might have information was at risk: old Goodhaps, or Mark, or me. Whelplay's killing had been carried out with a cold and ruthless hand, and might have escaped detection had I not put Brother Guy in mind of belladonna by mentioning Simon's strange postures and gestures. We might be dealing with a fanatic, but not someone ruled by impulse. What if he was planning to put poison in my dinner plate, or sought to make a gap between my head and shoulders such as he had with Singleton's? I shivered and pulled my coat tighter around my neck.

BOOKS WERE STACKED on the floor of our room. Mark sat staring into the fire. He had not yet lit the candles, but the firelight cast a flickering glow over his troubled face. I sat opposite him; the chance to rest my poor bones by a warm fire was welcome.

'Mark,' I said, 'we have a new mystery.' I told him what Brother Guy had said. 'I have spent my life deciphering secrets, but here they seem to multiply and grow more terrible.' I passed a hand over my brow. 'And I blame myself for that boy's death. If only I had insisted, last night, in pressing him. And there in the infirmary, when he bent his poor body and waved his arms, all I could think of was that he might be mocking me.' I stared bleakly before me, momentarily overcome with guilt.

'You were not to know what had happened, sir,' Mark said hesitantly.

'I was tired, I allowed myself to be pressed to leave him. Lord Cromwell said in London that time was of the essence. Now here we are four days later with no answers and another death.'

Mark stood up and lit candles from the fire. I felt suddenly angry with myself; I should be encouraging him, not giving in to despair, but the novice's death had momentarily overwhelmed me. I hoped his soul had found rest with God; I would have prayed for it had I believed prayers for the dead made any difference.

'Do not give up, sir,' Mark said awkwardly as he set the candles on the table. 'We have this new matter of the bursar to investigate. That may take us forward.'

'He was away when the murder was done. But no,' I forced a smile. 'I shall not give up. Besides, I dare not, this is Lord Cromwell's commission.'

'I took the chance to look over the outhouses while you were in the church. You were right, they are busy places. The stables, the forge, the buttery, all in constant use. I couldn't see anywhere that large items might be hidden.'

'Those side chapels in the church might repay invesigations. And I saw something interesting on the way out to the marsh.' I told him of the yellow gleam at the bottom of the pond. 'That's one place you might use to dispose of evidence.'

'We should investigate then, sir. You see, we have leads. The truth will prevail.'

I laughed hollowly. 'Oh Mark, you have not spent a lifetime around His Majesty's courts to say that. But you are right to encourage me.' I picked at a loose thread on the seat cover. 'I am become melancholy. I have felt my spirits weighing heavily on me for some months but it is worse here. My humours must be out of balance, too much black bile in my organs. Perhaps I should consult Brother Guy.'

'This is no place to cheer one.'

'No. And I confess I fear danger too. I was thinking of it now, in the yard. A footstep behind me, the swish of a sword through the air—' I looked up to where he stood over me. His boyish features were full of concern, and I was conscious of the weight this mission laid on him.

'I know. This place, the silence broken by those bells that make you start like a jack beetle.'

'Well, alertness is a good thing. I am glad you are ready to admit your fear. That is a good manly thing, better than the bravado of youth. And I should be less melancholy. I must pray for fortitude tonight.' I looked at him with sudden curiosity. 'What will you pray for?'

He shrugged. 'I am out of the habit of praying at night.'

'It should not be a mere habit, Mark. But don't look so worried, I am not going to lecture you about prayer.' I heaved myself upright. My back was tired, and sore again. 'Come, we should rouse ourselves, have a look at those account books. Then after supper we will tackle Brother Edwig.'

I lit more candles, and we set the books on the table. As I opened the first one, revealing lined pages filled with numbers and scratchy writing, Mark looked across at me seriously.

'Sir, could Alice be in danger because of what she told you? If

Simon Whelplay was killed because he might divulge a secret, the same could happen to her.'

'I know. The sooner I confront the bursar about this missing book, the better. I promised Alice I would keep her involvement secret.'

'She is a brave woman.'

'And an intriguing one, eh?'

He reddened, then suddenly changed the subject. 'Brother Guy said the novice had four visitors?'

'Yes, and they are also the four senior officers who knew Singleton's purpose here – them and Brother Guy.'

'But it was Brother Guy who told you Simon was poisoned.'

'All the same, I must be wary of taking him entirely into my confidence.' I held up my hand. 'Now, these accounts. You are used to monastic accounts from Augmentations?'

'Of course, I was often set to audit them.'

'Good. Then look through these and tell me if anything strikes you. Any items of expenditure that seem too high, or do not tally. First, though, lock the door. God's death, I am becoming as nervous as old Goodhaps.'

We set to work. It was a dull task. Double-entry accounts, with their endless balances, are harder to follow than simple lists if one is not a figurer by trade, but so far as I could tell there was nothing unusual in the books. The monastery's revenues from its lands and the beer monopoly were substantial; low expenditure on alms and wages was balanced by high spending on food and clothes, especially in the abbot's household. There appeared to be a surplus in hand of some £500, a goodly sum but not unusual, augmented by some recent land sales.

We worked until the bells tolled through the frosty air, announcing dinner. I stood up and paced the room, rubbing my tired eyes. Mark stretched out his arms with a groan.

'It all seems as one would expect. A wealthy house; there is much more money than in the small houses I used to deal with.'

'Yes. There is much gold behind these balances. What could be in this book Singleton had? Perhaps everything is too much in order; maybe these figures are for the auditor and the other book shows the true ones. If the bursar is defrauding the Exchequer that is a serious offence.' I banged my book shut. 'Now come, we had better go and join the holy brethren.' I gave him a serious look. 'And make sure we eat only from the common dish.'

We crossed the cloister yard to the refectory, passing monks who bowed low to us. In doing so one slipped and fell, for many feet had passed across the yard now, turning it into a mass of packed slippery snow. As I passed the fountain I saw the stream of water had frozen in mid air, a long spike of ice protruding from the nozzle like a stalagtite.

✠

SUPPER WAS a sombre meal. Brother Jerome was absent, presumably shut up somewhere on the prior's orders. Abbot Fabian mounted the lectern and made a solemn announcement that Novice Whelplay had died from his ague, and there were shocked exclamations and appeals to God's mercy along the tables. I noticed some venomous looks cast at the prior, especially from the three novices, who sat together at the furthest end of the table. I heard one of the monks, a fat fellow with sad rheumy eyes, mutter a curse on those without charity, glaring all the while at Prior Mortimus, who sat looking ahead with a stern, unbending gaze.

The abbot intoned a long Latin prayer for the departed brother's soul; the responses were fervent. This evening he stayed to dine at the obedentiaries' table, where a great haunch of beef was served with runcible peas. There were subdued attempts at conversation, the abbot saying he had never seen such snow in November. Brother Jude, the pittancer, and Brother Hugh, the fat little chamberlain with the wen on his face I had met in the chapter house, who always seemed to sit together and argue, now disputed whether the statutes obliged the town to clear the road to the monastery of snow, but without much enthusiasm. Brother Edwig alone became animated, talking worriedly about the pipes freezing in the privy and the cost of repairing them when the weather warmed and they burst. Soon, I thought, I will give you something worse to worry you. I was surprised at the strength of my emotion, and chid myself, for it is a bad thing to allow dislike to cloud one's judgement of a suspect.

There was another at table that night under the influence of even stronger emotions. Brother Gabriel barely touched his food. He appeared devastated by the news of Simon's death, lost in a world of his own. I was all the more shocked, then, when he suddenly lifted his head and cast a look at Mark of such intense longing, such burning emotion, that it made me shiver. I was glad Mark was attending to his plate and did not see it.

It was a relief when at last grace was said and everyone filed out. The wind had risen higher, sweeping up little waves of snow and sending them stinging into our faces. I signalled Mark to wait in the doorway as the monks raised their cowls and hurried off into the night.

'Let us tackle the bursar. You have your sword buckled on?'

He nodded.

'Good. Keep your hand on it when I talk to him, remind him of our authority. Now, where is he?'

We waited a few moments more, but Brother Edwig did not emerge. We went back into the dining hall. I could hear the bursar's stuttering tones, and we found him leaning over the monks' table where Brother Athelstan sat, looking sulky. The bursar was stabbing a finger at a paper.

'That balance is not c-correct,' he was saying. 'You have altered the payment for hops.' He waved a receipt angrily, then, seeing us, bowed and gave his insincere smile.

'Commissioner, good evening. I trust my b-books are in order?'

'What books we have. I would speak with you, please.'

'Of course. One moment, I pray.' He turned back to his assistant. 'Athelstan, I see as plain as day you have altered a figure in the left hand column to disguise the fact your figures do not balance.' I noticed that his stutter seemed to vanish when he was angry.

'Only by a groat, Brother Bursar.'

'A groat is a groat. Check every entry till you find it, all two hundred. I will see a true balance or none. Now go.' He waved an arm, and the young monk scuttled past us.

'Pardon me, C-Commissioner, I have to deal with b-blockheads.'

I motioned Mark to guard the door, and he stood, hand on sword. The bursar gave him an uneasy glance.

'Brother Edwig,' I said severely. 'I have to charge you with concealment of a book of account from the king's commissioner, a book with a blue cover which you attempted to hide from Com-missioner Singleton, which you repossessed after his murder and have concealed from me. What do you say?'

He laughed. But many men charged with a true bill of crime will laugh to disconcert their accuser.

'God's death, sir,' I shouted. 'Do you mock me?'

He raised his hands in demurral. 'No sir, I beg pardon, but – you are incorrect, this is a m-misunderstanding. Did the Fewterer girl tell you this? Of course, Brother Athelstan told me that malapert s-saw him arguing with Commissioner Singleton.'

I cursed inwardly. 'How I came by my knowledge is no concern of yours. I will have your answer.'

'Of c-c-course.'

'And do not tumble and spit your words to gain time to think up lies.'

He sighed and clasped his hands together. 'There was a m-misunderstanding with Commissioner Singleton, may God rest him. He asked for our ac-c-c—'

'Account books, yes.'

'—as you did, sir, and I gave them to him as I have to you. B-but, again as I have told you, he often came into the counting house on his own, when it was shut, to see what he could f-find. I do not deny his right, sir, only that it m-made for confusion. On the day before he was killed he came up to Athelstan as he was l-locking the doors, and waved a book at him, as the girl no doubt told you. He had taken it from my inner office.' He spread his hands. 'B-but, sir, it was not an account book. It contained mere jottings, p-projections of future income I made some time ago, as he would have seen as soon as he examined it properly. I can show it to you if you wish.'

'You took it back from the abbot's house after his death, without telling anyone.'

'No, sir, I did not. The abbot's servants found it in his room when they cleared it, s-saw my writing and returned it to me.'

'But when we spoke earlier you said you were unsure which book Commissioner Singleton took.'

'I – I had forgotten. The book is unimportant. I can s-send it to you, sir, you can see for yourself.'

'No. We will come with you now and fetch it.'

He hesitated.

'Well?'

'Of course.'

I motioned Mark to stand aside, and we followed him across the cloister yard, Mark taking up a lamp to light the way. Brother Edwig unlocked the counting house and we climbed the stairs to his private office. He unlocked his desk and pulled a thin blue book from a drawer.

'This is it, sir. See for yourself.'

I looked inside. Indeed there were no neat columns, only scrawled jottings and arithmetical reckonings.

'I will take this for now.'

'B-by all means. B-but may I ask, as this is a private office, if you would come to me before taking any more books? To prevent confusion?'

I ignored the question. 'I see from your other records that the monastery has a large surplus, larger this year than last. Sales of land have brought in fresh capital. Why then is there objection to Brother Gabriel's proposals for repair of the church?'

He looked at me seriously. 'Brother Gabriel would spend everything we have on the r repairs. He would allow all else to f fall down. The abbot *will* give him money for repairs, but we have to beat him down or he will take all. It is a matter of negotiation.'

It was all so plausible. 'Very well,' I said. 'That is all. For now. One thing more. You mentioned Alice Fewterer. The girl is under my special protection, and if any harm befalls her you will find yourself at once under arrest and sent to London for enquiry.' I turned and marched out.

✝

'WAYS OF NEGOTIATION, indeed,' I said as we walked to the infirmary. 'He's as slippery as they come.'

'He could not have killed Singleton, though. He was away. And a fat little hog like that couldn't have struck his head off.'

'He could have killed Simon Whelplay. Perhaps there is more than one of them acting together in this business.'

Back in our room, we studied the account book. It seemed, as the bursar said, to contain nothing more than random calculations and jottings, all in his neat round hand, going back years by the faded look of the ink in the earlier part. I tossed it aside, rubbing my tired eyes.

'Perhaps Commissioner Singleton thought he had found something when he had not?'

'No. I don't think so. From what Alice said his accusation was specific, he said the book shed new light on the year's accounts.' I exclaimed and banged my fist into my palm. 'Where are my wits? What if he has more than one book with a blue cover? This may not be the one!'

'We could go back now, and turn the counting house upside down.'

'No. I am exhausted. Tomorrow. Now let's rest, it will be a busy day. There's Singleton's funeral to get through, then we must go to Scarnsea to see Justice Copynger. I want to talk to Jerome too. And we should investigate the fish pond.'

Mark groaned. 'Truly there is no rest for Lord Cromwell's emissaries. At least we may find ourselves too busy to be frightened.'

'With any luck. And now I am going to bed. Say a prayer for some progress tomorrow.'

✝

WE WOKE early next morning, just as dawn was breaking. I rose and scraped frost from the inside of the window. The rising sun was casting fingers of pink light across the snow. It was a beautiful but sterile scene.

'No sign of a thaw.' I turned to find Mark standing shirtless by the fire, a shoe in his hand, staring around the room with a puzzled expression. He raised a hand.

'What was that? I heard something.'

'I heard nothing.'

'It was like a footstep. I did hear it.' Frowning, Mark threw the door open. There was nobody there.

I sat down on the bed again; my back was stiff and sore that morning. 'You are imagining things. This place is unsettling you. And don't stand there half-bare. The world doesn't want to see your belly, flat as it may be.'

'Sir, I did hear something. I thought it was outside.' He thought a moment, then crossed to the cupboard, which served as a storage space for clothes. He threw open the door, but it contained only dust and mouse-droppings. I looked down at him, envying the play of smooth, symmetrical muscles down his back.

'Only mice,' I said. 'Come on.'

✝

As we sat at breakfast we had a visit from the abbot, ruddy-cheeked and swathed in furs against the cold. He was accompanied by Dr Goodhaps, who cast nervous, rheumy eyes about the infirmary, a dewdrop on the end of his nose.

'I have sad news,' Abbot Fabian began in his pompous way. 'We must postpone the late commissioner's interment.'

'How so?'

'The servants have not been able to dig deep enough. The ground is hard as iron and now they have poor Simon's grave to dig as well in the monks' cemetery. Today will be needed to finish the task. Then we could have both funerals tomorrow.'

'It cannot be helped. Will the funerals be held together?'

He hesitated. 'As Simon was a religious that must be a separate ceremony. That is allowed in the injunctions . . .'

'I have no objection.'

'I wondered, sir, how your enquiries are going. The bursar really needs his books back as soon as possible, I fear—'

'He will have to wait, I am not finished yet. And this morning I am going into town to see the Justice.'

He nodded portentously. 'Good. I am positive, Commissioner, that poor Commissioner Singleton's murderer is to be found in the town, among the smugglers and ill-doers there.'

'When I return I would like to interview Brother Jerome. Where is he? I have not seen his smiling face.'

'In solitude, as a penance for his behaviour. I must warn you, Commissioner, if you talk to him you will only have fresh insults. He is beyond control.'

'I can make allowance for the mad. I will see him when I return from Scarnsea.'

'Your horses may have difficulty getting there. Last night's wind has blown the snow into great drifts. One of our carts has had to turn back, the horses could not manage.'

'Then we will walk.'

'That too may be difficult. I have been trying to tell Dr Goodhaps—'

The old man spoke up. 'Sir, I have come to ask, may I not go home tomorrow, after the funeral? Surely I can be of no more use? If I were to get to the town I could find a place in a coach, or I wouldn't mind staying at an inn till the snow melts.'

I nodded. 'Very well, Master Goodhaps. Though I fear you may have a wait in Scarnsea before this weather changes.'

'I don't mind, sir, thank you!' The old man beamed, nodding his head so that the dewdrop fell on his chin.

'Go back to Cambridge. Say nothing of what has happened here.'

'I want only to forget about it.'

'And now, Mark, we must go. My lord Abbot, while we are in town I would like you to sort out more papers for me. The deeds of conveyance on all land sales for the last five years.'

'All of them? They will have to be fetched—'

'Yes, all of them. I want you to be able to swear you have given me the deeds of every sale—'

'I will arrange it, of course, if you wish.'

'Good.' I got up. 'And now we must be on our way.'

The abbot bowed and left, old Goodhaps scuttling after him.

'That worried him,' I said.

'The land sales?'

'Yes. It strikes me that if there is any fraudulent accounting going on, it would most likely be the concealment of income from land sales. That is the only way they could raise large amounts of capital. Let's see what he comes up with.'

We left the kitchen. As we passed Brother Guy's dispensary we glanced in, and Mark suddenly grasped my arm.

'Look! What's happened to him?'

Brother Guy lay face down on the floor under the big crucifix, arms extended in front of him. Sunlight glinted on his shaven brown pate. For a moment I was alarmed, then I heard the murmur of Latin prayer, soft but fervent. As we went on I reflected again that I must be careful how far I took the Spanish Moor into my confidence. He had confided in me, and was the most agreeable of those I had met here. But the sight of him lying prone, making fervid entreaties of a piece of wood, reminded me that as much as the others he was muzzled in the old heresies and superstitions, enemy of all I stood for.

Chapter Fifteen

OUTSIDE, THE MORNING WAS bitterly cold again under a clear blue sky. During the night the wind had blown big drifts against the walls, leaving parts of the courtyard almost bare of snow. It made a strange sight. We passed once again through the gate. Turning, I saw Bugge the gatekeeper peering out, withdrawing his head when he caught my glance. I blew out my cheeks.

'God's wounds, it's a relief to be away from all those eyes.' I looked up the road, which like the courtyard was a sea of drifts. The whole landscape, even the marsh, was white, broken only by skeletal black trees, clumps of reeds in the marsh and, in the distance, the grey sea. I had obtained another staff from Brother Guy, and took a firm grip on it.

'Thank Heaven for these overshoes,' Mark ventured.

'Yes. The whole country will be a sea of mud when this snow melts.'

'If it ever does.'

We had a long trudge through the drear landscape, and it was an hour before we reached the first streets of Scarnsea. We said little, for we were both still in sombre mood. There was hardly anyone about that day and in the bright sunlight I noticed anew how dilapidated most of the buildings were.

'We need Westgate Street,' I said as we arrived again in the square. At the wharf a small boat was pulled up, an official in a black coat inspecting bales of cloth while a couple of townsmen stood by, stamping their feet against the cold. Out at sea, at the mouth of the channel through the marsh, stood a large ship.

'The customs man,' Mark observed.

'They must be taking cloth over to France.'

We turned into a street of new, well-built houses. On the door of the largest the town's arms were engraved. I knocked, and the well-dressed servant who answered confirmed it was Justice Copynger's house. We were led to wait in a fine drawing room with cushioned wooden chairs and a buffet displaying a great richness of gold plate.

'He does himself well,' Mark observed.

'Indeed.' I crossed to where the portrait of a stern-looking man with fair hair and a spade-shaped beard hung on the wall. 'That's very good. And painted in this room, by the background.'

'He's rich then—' Mark broke off as the door opened to admit the original of the painting, a tall, strongly built man in his forties. He was swathed in a brown robe trimmed with sable fur and had a severe, serious air. He shook my hand firmly.

'Master Shardlake, this is an honour. I am Gilbert Copynger, Justice of the town and Lord Cromwell's most loyal servant. I knew poor Master Singleton; I thank Christ you have been sent. That monastery is a cesspit of corruption and heresy.'

'Nothing is straightforward there, certainly.' I indicated Mark. 'My assistant.'

He nodded briefly. 'Come through to my study. You will take some refreshment? I think the Devil himself has sent this weather. Are you kept warm at the monastery?'

'The monks have fires in every chamber.'

'Oh, I don't doubt that, sir. I don't doubt it at all.'

He led us down the hall to a cosy room with a view of the street, and cleared papers from stools before the fire. 'Let me pour you both some wine. Forgive the disorder, but the paperwork I have from London . . . the minimum wage, the poor laws . . .' he sighed. 'And I am required to provide reports of any treasonable mutterings. Fortunately there are few of those in Scarnsea, but sometimes my informers make them up and I have to investigate words that were never said. At least it means people realize they have to be careful.'

'I know Lord Cromwell sleeps easier knowing there are true men such as yourself in the shires.' Copynger nodded gravely at the compliment. I sipped the wine. 'This is excellent, sir, thank you. Now, time presses. There are matters on which I would welcome information.'

'Anything I can do. Master Singleton's murder was an insult to the king. It cries out for vengeance.'

It should have been a relief to have the company of a fellow reformer, but I confess I did not take to Copynger. Although the Justices were indeed burdened with an ever-greater workload from London on top of their judicial duties, they did well from it. It has ever been the custom for Justices to profit from their functions, and more duties meant more profit even in a poor town, as Copynger's wealth bore witness. To me his ostentation sat ill with his humourless, pious air. But that was the new type of man we were breeding in England then.

'Tell me,' I asked, 'how are the monks regarded in the town?'

'They are loathed for the leeches they are. They do nothing for Scarnsea, they don't come into the town unless they have to and then they are haughty as the Devil. The charity they give is tiny and the poor have to walk to the monastery on dole days to get even that. It leaves the main burden of maintaining the indigent on the ratepayers.'

'They have a beer monopoly, I believe.'

'And charge an extortionate price. Their beer is filthy stuff, hens roost in their brewhouse and drop dung in the brew.'

'Yes, I saw that. It must be vile indeed.'

'And no one else may sell beer.' He spread his arms wide. 'They milk their lands too, for all they can get. Don't let anyone say monks are easy landlords. Things are worse since Brother Edwig took over as bursar; he would skin a flea for the fat on its arse.'

'Yes, I believe he would. Speaking of the monastery's finances, you reported to Lord Cromwell there had been land sales at undervalue.'

He looked crestfallen. 'I fear I have no details. I'd heard rumours, but word got out I'd been making enquiries, and now the big landowners keep their doings from my ears.'

I nodded. 'And who are they?'

'Sir Edward Wentworth is the biggest hereabouts. He's in close with the abbot, for all he's related to the Seymours. They go hunting together. There have been rumours among the tenantry that monastery lands have been sold to him secretly and the abbot's steward now collects rents on Sir Edward's behalf, but I've no way of finding out for certain, it's beyond my authority.' He frowned crossly. 'And the monastery owns land far and wide, even out of the county. I am sorry, Commissioner. If I had more authority . . .'

I thought a moment. 'It may be stretching my brief, but as I have power to investigate all matters involving the monastery I think I could extend that to enquiring about land sales they have made. What if you were to renew your enquiries on that basis? Invoke Lord Cromwell's name?'

He smiled. 'A request in that name would bring them running. I will do what I can.'

'Thank you. It could be important. By the way, I believe Sir Edward is cousin to Brother Jerome, the old Carthusian at the monastery?'

'Yes, Wentworth's an old papist. I hear that the Carthusian speaks open treason. I'd have him hanged from the cloth-hall steeple.'

I thought a moment. 'Tell me, if you did hang Brother Jerome from the steeple, how would the townsfolk react?'

'They'd have a feast day. As I said, the monks are hated. This is a poor town now and the monks make it poorer. The port is so silted up you can hardly get a rowboat through.'

'So I have seen. I hear some have turned to smuggling. According to the monks, they use the marshes behind the monastery to get to the river. Abbot Fabian tells me he has complained, but the town authorities wink at it.'

At once Copynger's face was watchful. 'The abbot will say anything to make trouble. It's a matter of resources, sir. There is but one revenue man and he cannot be out watching the ways through those marshes every night.'

'According to one of the monks there has been activity out there recently. The abbot suggested it may have been smugglers who broke in and killed Singleton.'

'He's trying to divert attention, sir. There is a long history of smuggling here, finished cloth carried through the marsh and shipped to France in fishing boats. But why would one of those people want to kill the king's commissioner? He had no brief to investigate smuggling. Did he?' I noticed a sudden worried look in his eyes.

'No indeed. And neither have I, unless those activities should be relevant to Master Singleton's death. My feeling is the killer came from inside the monastery.'

He looked relieved. 'If landlords were allowed to enclose more land for sheep, that would bring more profit to the town and people would not turn to smuggling. There are too many small farmers doubling as weavers.'

'Apart from any smuggling there may be, is the town loyal? No trouble with extreme sectarians, for example, no witchcraft hereabouts? You know the monastery was desecrated?'

He shook his head. 'Nothing. I'd know, I've five paid informers. A lot of people don't like the new ways, but they keep their heads down. The biggest complaints have been about the abolition of saints' days, but that's only because they were holidays. And I've never heard of practitioners of the black arts hereabouts.'

'No hot gospellers? No one who has read the Bible and seen some mysterious prophecy only he can fulfil?'

'Like those German Anabaptists who would kill the rich and hold all goods in common? They should be burned. But there's none of that here. There was a moonstruck forgemaster's apprentice last year, preaching the Day of Judgement was come, but we set him in the stocks then cleared him out. He's in gaol now, where he belongs. Preaching in English is one thing, but allowing the Bible to blockish servants and peasants will fill England with makebates.'

I raised an eyebrow. 'You are among those who consider only heads of households should be allowed to read the Bible?'

'There is much to be said for that view, sir.'

'Well, the papists would allow it to nobody. But to return to the subject of the monastery, I read there has been a history of ill-doings there. Sinful acts between the monks.'

Copynger snorted with disgust. 'That still goes on, I'm sure. The sacrist, Brother Gabriel, he was one of them and he's still there.'

'Was anyone from the town involved?'

'No. But there are fornicators at that place as well as sodomites. Women servants from Scarnsea have suffered at their filthy hands. No woman under thirty would work there, not since one young girl went missing altogether.'

'Oh?'

'An orphan from the poorhouse who went to work for the infirmarian. Two years ago. She used to come back and visit the town, then suddenly she stopped coming. When enquiries were made Prior Mortimus said she'd stolen some gold cups and run away. Joan Stumpe, the poorhouse keeper, was convinced something had happened to her. But she's an old busybody, and there was no proof.'

'She worked for the infirmarian?' Mark spoke up, a note of anxiety in his voice.

'Yes. The black goblin we call him. You'd think all Englishmen had work, giving a post to a man like that.'

I reflected a moment. 'Might I talk to this Mistress Stumpe?'

'You have to take what she says with a peck of salt. But she should be at the poorhouse now. There's a dole day at the monastery tomorrow, she'll be getting ready for it.'

'Then let us seize the hour,' I said, rising. Copynger called for a servant to fetch our coats.

'Sir,' Mark said to the magistrate as we were waiting. 'There is a young girl working for the infirmarian now, one Alice Fewterer.'

'Oh yes, I remember.'

'I understand she had to get work because the family's land was enclosed for sheep. I know the Justices have oversight of the enclosure laws; I wondered if it was all done legally? Whether something might be done for her?'

Copynger raised his eyebrows. 'I *know* it was done legally, young man, because the land is mine and it was I that enclosed it. The family had an old copyhold that expired on her mother's death. I needed to take down that cottage and put the land to sheep if I was to make any profit at all.'

I gave Mark a warning look. 'I'm sure you did everything properly, sir,' I said soothingly.

'The thing that would profit the people of this town,' Copynger said, a cold eye on Mark, 'would be to close the monastery, throw out the lot of them and pull down those idol-filled buildings. And if the town has an extra burden of poor relief in the shape of a load of unemployed abbey-lubbers, I'm sure Master Cromwell would agree it was right for some monastery lands to be granted to prominent citizens.'

'Speaking of Lord Cromwell, he has stressed the importance of keeping what has happened quiet for now.'

'I've told no one, sir, and none of the monks has been to town.'

'Good. The abbot has been told not to talk of it too. But some of the monastery servants will have contacts in Scarnsea.'

He shook his head. 'Very few. They keep apart, the townspeople like the abbey-lubbers no more than the monks.'

'It will get out eventually though. It's in the nature of things.'

'I am sure you will resolve this soon,' he said. He smiled, his cheeks reddening. 'May I say what an honour it is to meet one who has spoken personally with Lord Cromwell. Tell me, sir, what is he like, in person? They say he is a man of strong manner, for all his humble origins.'

'He is indeed, Justice, a man of strong words and deeds. Ah, here is your servant with our coats.' I cut him off; I was tired of his unctuous fawning.

✝

THE POORHOUSE lay on the fringe of the town, a long low building in much need of repair. On the way we passed a little group of men sweeping snow from the streets under the eye of an overseer. They wore grey smocks with the town's arms sewn on, far too thin for such weather. They bowed to Copynger as we passed.

'Licensed beggars,' the Justice observed. 'The men's warden at the poorhouse is good at putting them to honest labour.'

We entered the building, which was unheated and so damp the plaster had fallen in places from the walls. A group of women sat around the hall sewing or working at spinning wheels, while in one corner a plump, middle-aged matron was sorting through a large pile of odoriferous rags, helped by a group of scrawny children. Copynger went over and spoke to her and she led us to a neat little cubbyhole, where she introduced herself as Joan Stumpe, the children's overseer.

'How may I help you, sirs?' The wrinkled face was kindly, but the brown eyes keen.

'Master Shardlake is currently investigating some matters at the monastery,' Copynger told her. 'He is interested in the fate of young Orphan Stonegarden.'

She sighed. 'Poor Orphan.'

'You knew her?' I asked.

'I brought her up. She was a waif left in the yard of this building nineteen years ago. A newborn baby. Poor Orphan,' she said again.

'What was her name?'

'Orphan *was* her name, sir. It's a common name for foundlings. We never found out who her parents were, so she was given Stonegarden as a surname by the men's warden, as she was found in the yard.'

'I see. And she grew up under your care?'

'I have charge of all the children. A lot die young, but Orphan was strong and she thrived. She helped me round the place, she was always cheerful and willing—' She suddenly looked away.

'Go on, Goodwife,' Copynger said impatiently. 'I have told you before, you are too soft with these children.'

'They often have a brief stay on earth,' she replied spiritedly. 'Why should they not have some enjoyment of it?'

'Better go broken to heaven than in one piece to hell,' Copynger said brutally. 'Most that live end as thieves and beggars. Go on.'

'When Orphan reached sixteen the overseers said she must go out to work. It was a shame, she had a swain in the miller's son and if that had been allowed to develop she'd have been married off.'

'She was pretty, then?'

'Yes, sir. Small with fair hair and a sweet, gentle face. One of the prettiest faces I have ever seen. But the men's overseer has a brother working for the monks; he said the infirmarian needed a helper, so she was sent there.'

'And this was when, Mistress Stumpe?'

'Two years ago. She would come back and visit me on her free days, every Friday without fail. She was as fond of me as I was of her. She didn't like it at the monastery, sir.'

'Why not?'

'She wouldn't say. I teach the children never to criticize their betters, or they'll be done for. But I could see she was frightened.'

'Of what?'

'I don't know. I tried to find out but she wouldn't say. She worked for old Brother Alexander first, and then he died and Brother Guy came. She was afraid of him, with his strange appearance. The thing was she'd stopped seeing Adam, the miller's son. He'd come to see her, but she'd tell me to send him away.' She gave me a sharp look. 'And when that happens it often means a woman's been ill used.'

'Did you ever see any marks, bruises?'

'No, but she seemed lower in spirits each time I saw her. Then one day, six months or so after she started at the monastery, she just didn't turn up one Friday, nor the next.'

'You must have been worried.'

'I was. I decided to go there and find out what I could.' I

nodded. I could imagine her marching stoutly along and banging on Master Bugge's gate.

'They wouldn't let me in at first, but I stood making noise and trouble till they fetched that Prior Mortimus. Scottish barbarian. He stood and told me Orphan had stolen two gold chalices from the church one night and disappeared.'

Copynger inclined his head. 'Perhaps she did, it happens often enough with these children.'

'Not Orphan, sir, she was a good Christian.' Mistress Stumpe turned to me. 'I asked the prior why I hadn't been told, and he said he knew nothing of the girl's contacts in town. He threatened to swear out a warrant against her for theft if I didn't go away. I reported it to Master Copynger, but he said without evidence of ill-doing there was nothing he could do.'

The magistrate shrugged. 'There wasn't. And if the monks had sworn out a warrant against her, that would have been one up for them against the town.'

'What do you think happened to the girl, Mistress Stumpe?'

She looked me in the eye. 'I don't know, sir, but I dread to think.'

I nodded slowly. 'But Justice Copynger is quite right, he could do nothing without evidence.'

'I know that, but I knew Orphan well. It wasn't in her to steal and run away.'

'But if she was desperate . . .'

'Then she'd have come to me rather than risk the rope for stealing. But nothing's been seen or heard of her these eighteen months. Nothing.'

'Very well. Thank you, Goodwife, for your time.' I sighed. Everywhere I turned suspicions remained suspicions; there was nothing I could grasp hold of and tie to Singleton's murder.

She led us back to the hall, where the children picking rags looked up with pale, wizened faces from their tasks. The sickly stench of the old clothes carried clear across the room.

'What are your charges doing?' I asked her.

'Looking through the rags people give for something to wear tomorrow. It's dole day at the monastery. It'll be a hard walk in this weather.'

I nodded. 'Yes, it will. Thank you, Mistress Stumpe.' I turned in the doorway as we left; she was already back with the children, helping them pick through the festering piles.

✝

JUSTICE COPYNGER offered us dinner at his house, but I said we must return to the monastery. We set off, our boots crunching through the snow.

'We will have missed dinner,' Mark said after a while.

'Yes. Let's find an inn.'

We found a respectable enough coaching house behind the square. The landlord ushered us to a table looking out on the wharf and I watched the boat we had seen earlier, laden with bales, being oared carefully through the channel towards the waiting ship.

'God's wounds,' Mark said, 'I'm hungry.'

'Yes, so am I. But we'll keep clear of the beer. Did you know, under the original rule of St Benedict the monks only had one meal a day in the winter – dinner? He made the rule for the Italian climate, but they kept it in England as well to begin with. Imagine standing in prayer for hours a day, in winter, on one meal a day! But of course, as the years passed and the monasteries got wealthier, it became two meals a day, then three, with meat, with wine . . .'

'At least they still pray, I suppose.'

'Yes. And believe their prayers intercede with God for the dead.' I thought of Brother Gabriel and his anguished intensity. 'But they are wrong.'

'I confess it sends my head to spinning, sir, all this theology.'

'It shouldn't, Mark. God gave you a brain. Use it.'

'How is your back today?' he asked, changing the subject. I reflected it was becoming a talent of his.

'Bearable. Better than it was first thing.'

The innkeeper brought us dishes of rabbit pie, and we ate silently for a while.

'What do you think became of that girl?' Mark asked at length.

I shook my head. 'Jesu knows. There are so many threads of enquiry, they merely multiply. I had hoped for more from Copynger. Well, now we know women have been molested at the monastery. By whom? Prior Mortimus, who troubled Alice? Others? As for the girl Orphan, Copynger's right. There's no evidence she *didn't* just run away, and the old woman's fondness for her could be colouring her judgement. There's nothing to *lay hold of*.' I clenched a fist on the empty air.

'What did you think of Justice Copynger?'

'He's a reformer. He will help us where he can.'

'He talks of true religion and how the monks oppress the poor, yet he lives richly while turning people off their land.'

'I don't like him either. But you should not have asked him about Alice's mother. It's not your place. He's our only reliable source of information and I don't want him crossed. We've little enough help. I'd hoped for more information on the land sales, to connect with the bursar's books.'

'It seemed to me the Justice knew more about the smugglers than he said.'

'Of course he did. He's taking bribes. But that's not why we're here. I'm with him on one thing: the murderer comes from within the monastery, not from Scarnsea. The five senior obedentiaries.' I ticked them off on my fingers. 'Abbot Fabian, Prior Mortimus, Edwig, Gabriel and Guy. Any of them is tall and strong enough to have despatched Singleton – except Brother Edwig, who was away. And any of them could have killed the novice. That is, of course, if what Brother Guy told us about deadly nightshade is true.'

'Why would he lie?'

Again I saw in my mind's eye the dead face of Simon Whelplay as we lifted him from the bath. The thought of him being poisoned because I might talk to him kept recurring, turning in my guts like a torsion.

'I don't know,' I replied, 'but I'm taking nothing on trust. They'll all lose heavily if the monastery closes. Where will Brother Guy find employment in the world as a healer, with his strange face? As for the abbot, he's wedded to his status. And I think the other three may all have things to hide. Financial chicanery by Brother Edwig? He could be hiding money away against the risk of the place going, though he'd need the abbot's seal on any land sales.'

'And Prior Mortimus?'

'There's little I'd put past him. As for Brother Gabriel, the old serpent of temptation still visits, I'm sure of that. He's not taken his eyes off you since you came. I can imagine he has his attachments among the monks, even if not to poor Whelplay, but then you come along showing a fine calf, in your good doublet and hose, and he starts dreaming of you out of them.'

Mark pushed his plate away, frowning. 'Must you adumbrate the details, sir?'

'Lawyers must spend their time adumbrating details, however sordid. Gabriel may appear gentle, but he is a tormented man, and tormented men do wild, irrational things. If recent acts of sodomy could be proved against him, he could face the rope. Rough questioning from Singleton could have made him desperate, especially if there are others to protect. And then there is Jerome. I want to see what he has to say. I'm intrigued by his calling Singleton a liar and perjurer.'

Mark did not reply. He was still frowning. 'Oh, wake up,' I said in a burst of irritation. 'Does it matter if the sacrist covets your arse? He's hardly likely to get it.'

There was a flash of anger in his eyes. 'I was not thinking of myself, sir, but Alice. The girl who disappeared was also Brother Guy's assistant.'

'That *had* occurred to me as well.'

He leaned forward. 'Would it not be better, and safer for all, to take the obedentiaries, and Jerome, and arrest them all on suspicion? Take them to London and get what they know out of them?'

'On what evidence? And how question them, the torture? I thought you disapproved of such methods.'

'Of course not. But – stiff questioning?'

'And what if I am wrong, and it is not one of them at all? And how would we keep such a mass arrest secret?'

'But – time and danger press.'

'Do you think I don't know that?' 'I burst out in sudden anger. 'But bullying won't fetch out the truth. Singleton tried that and look where it got him. You untangle a knot with slow teasing, not sharp pulling, and believe me we have here a knot such as I have never seen. But I will unpick it. I will.'

'I am sorry, sir. I did not mean to question . . .'

'Oh, question, Mark,' I said irritably. 'But question sensibly.' My anger had animated me, and I rose and threw some coins on the table.

'Come, let's go. We're wasting the afternoon, and I have a mad old Carthusian waiting.'

Chapter Sixteen

WE SAID LITTLE as we walked back to the monastery, under a sky that was rapidly clouding over again. I was angry with myself for my outburst, but my nerves were frayed and Mark's naivety had irritated me. I had found a new mood of determined resolution, though, and set a sharp pace on the road until I stumbled in a drift and Mark had to steady me, which irritated me further. As we neared the walls of St Donatus, a bitter wind began blowing and it started to snow once more.

I banged unceremoniously on the door of Bugge's gatehouse; he appeared, wiping food from his mouth with a dirty sleeve.

'I wish to see Brother Jerome. At once, please.'

'The prior has custody of him, sir. He's at Sext.' He nodded in the direction of the church, from which a faint chanting was audible.

'Then fetch him out of it!' I replied sharply. The churl went off muttering, and we pulled our coats, already white with snowflakes, round us tightly as we waited. Shortly Bugge reappeared, accompanied by Prior Mortimus, a frown on his red face.

'Ye wish to see Jerome, Commissioner? Has something happened that I should be fetched from church?'

'Only that I have no time to waste. Where is he?'

'After his insults to you, he's kept locked in his cell in the dorter.'

'Then take us to him, please. I wish to question him.'

He led us away to the cloister. 'I dread to think what insults ye'll get, bearding him in his own den. If ye're minded to have him committed for treason, ye'll be doing us all a service.'

'Will I? He's friendless here, then?'

'Pretty well.'

'There's a few friendless people here. Novice Whelplay, for example.'

He looked at me coldly. 'I tried to teach Simon Whelplay a contrite spirit.'

'Better broken to heaven than in one piece to hell?' Mark muttered.

'What?'

'Something a reforming magistrate said to Master Poer and me this morning. By the way, I hear you visited Simon early yesterday.'

He reddened. 'I went to pray over him. I did not want him dead, just cleansed of what possessed him.'

'Even at the price of his life?'

He came to a halt and faced me, a harried look on his face. The weather was getting worse; snowflakes whirled round us as our coats and the prior's habit billowed in the wind.

'I didn't want him dead! It wasn't my doing, he was possessed. Possessed. His death wasn't my fault, I won't be blamed!'

I studied him. Had he gone to pray over the novice yesterday from some sense of guilt? No, I reflected, Prior Mortimus was not one to question the rightness of anything he did. It was strange; his air of brutal certainty reminded me of radical Lutherans I had met. And no doubt he had contrived some intellectual sophistry that allowed him to molest young women without trouble to his conscience.

'It is cold,' I said. 'Lead on.'

He led us without further converse into the dorter, a long, two-storey building facing the cloister. Smoke rose from many chimneys. I had never seen the inside of a monks' dormitory before. I knew from the *Comperta* that the early Benedictines' great communal dormitories had long since been partitioned off into comfortable individual rooms, and so it was here. We passed down a long corridor with many doors. Some were open, and I could see warm fires and comfortable beds. The heat was welcome. Prior Mortimus halted before a closed door.

'Normally, it's locked,' he said, 'to make sure he doesn't go wandering.' He pushed the door open. 'Jerome, the commissioner wishes to see you.'

Brother Jerome's cell was as austere as those I passed had been comfortable. No fire burned in the empty grate, and apart from a crucifix above the bed the whitewashed walls were bare. The old Carthusian sat on the bed dressed only in his nether hose; his skinny torso was twisted and bent around the shoulders, as knotted and crooked as my own but with the marks of injury not deformity. Brother Guy stood bent over him with a cloth, washing a dozen small weals that disfigured his skin. Some were red, others yellow with pus. An ewer of water gave off the sharp smell of lavender.

'Brother Guy,' I said, 'I am sorry to disrupt your ministrations.'

'I am nearly finished. There, Brother, that should ease the infected sores.'

The Carthusian gave me an ugly glare before turning to the infirmarian. 'My clean shirt, please.'

Brother Guy sighed. 'You weaken yourself with this. You could at least soak the hairs to soften them.' He passed him a grey garment of hair cloth, the animal hairs sewn into the fabric on the inner side standing out stiff and black. Brother Jerome slipped it on, then struggled into his white habit. Brother Guy gathered up his ewer, bowed to us and went out. Brother Jerome and the prior looked at each other with mutual distaste.

'Mortifying yourself again, Jerome?'

'For my sins. But I take no pleasure in the mortification of others, Brother Prior, unlike some.'

Prior Mortimus gave him a filthy look, then handed me his key. 'When you've finished, give the key to Bugge,' he said, then turned and left abruptly, closing the door behind him with a snap. I was suddenly conscious that we were now shut in a confined space with a man whose eyes sparked hatred at us from his pale, lined face. I looked round for somewhere to sit, but there was only the bed, so I stood leaning on my staff.

'Are you in pain, crookback?' Jerome asked suddenly.

'A little discomfort. We have had a long walk through the snow.'

'Do you know the saying, to touch a dwarf brings good luck, but to touch a hunchback means ill fortune? You are a mockery of the human form, Commissioner, doubly so for your soul is twisted and cankered like all Cromwell's men.'

Mark stepped forward. 'God's bones, sir, you have a vile tongue.'

I waved him to silence, and stood staring at Jerome.

'Why do you abuse me, Jerome of London? They say you are mad. Are you? Would madness be your defence were I to have your arse hauled off to the Tower for your treasonable talk?'

'I would make no defence, crookback. I would be glad to have the chance to be what I should have been before, a martyr for God's Church. I shit on King Henry's name and his usurpation of the pope's authority.' He laughed bitterly. 'Even Martin Luther disowns King Henry, did you know? He says Junker Heinz will end by making himself God.'

Mark gasped. Those words alone were enough to have Jerome executed.

'Then how you must burn with shame that you took the oath acknowledging the king's supremacy,' I said quietly.

Jerome reached for his crutch and rose painfully from the bed. He tucked the crutch under his arm and began slowly pacing the cell. When he spoke again it was in a quiet, steely tone.

'Yes, crookback. Shame and fear for my eternal soul. Do you know who my family are? Did they tell you that?'

'I know you are related to Queen Jane, God rest her.'

'God will not rest her. She burns in hell for marrying a schismatic king.' He turned and faced me. 'Shall I tell you how I came to be here? Shall I put a case to you, master lawyer?'

'Yes, tell me. I shall sit to listen.' I lowered myself onto the hard bed. Mark remained standing, hand on sword, as Jerome dragged himself slowly up and down the room.

'I left the world of idle show when I was twenty. My late second cousin was not born then, I never met her. I lived over thirty years in peace at the London Charterhouse; a holy place, not like this soft corrupted house. It was a haven, a place devoted to God in the midst of the profane city.'

'Where wearing hair shirts was part of the Rule.'

'To remind us always that flesh is sinful and corrupt. Thomas More lived with us four years. He wore the hair shirt ever after, even under his robes of state when he was lord chancellor. It helped keep him humble, and steadfast unto death when he stood out against the king's marriage.'

'And before, when he was lord chancellor and burning all the heretics he could find. But you were not steadfast, Brother Jerome?'

His back stiffened, and when he turned I expected another outburst. But his voice remained calm.

'When the king said he required an oath from all members of the religious houses acknowledging him as Supreme Head of the Church, only we Carthusians refused, though we knew what that would mean.' His eyes burned into me.

'Yes. All the other houses took the oath, but not you.'

'There were forty of us, and they took us one by one. Prior Houghton first refused the oath and was interrogated by Cromwell himself. Did you know, Commissioner, when Father Houghton told him that St Augustine had placed the authority of the Church above Scripture, Cromwell replied that he cared naught for the Church and Augustine might hold as he pleased?'

'He was right. The authority of Scripture stands above that of any scholar.'

'And the opinion of a tavern keeper's son stands above St Augustine's?' Jerome laughed bitterly. 'When he would not submit, our venerable prior was judged guilty of treason and executed at Tyburn. I was there; I saw his body sliced open by the executioner's knife while he still lived. But it wasn't the usual hanging fair that day, the crowd watched silently as he died.'

I glanced at Mark; he was watching Jerome intently, his face troubled. The Carthusian continued. 'Your master had no better luck with Prior Houghton's successor. Vicar Middlemore and the senior obedentiaries still would not swear, so they too went to Tyburn. This time there were calls against the king from the crowd. Cromwell wasn't going to risk a riot the next time, so he tried all manner of pressure to make the rest of us take the oath. He put his own men in charge of the house, where Prior Houghton's arm, stinking and rotten, was nailed to the gate. They kept us half-starved, mocked our services, tore up our books, insulted us. They picked off trouble-makers one by one. Someone would suddenly be sent off to a more compliant house or just disappear.'

He paused and leaned his good arm on the bed for a moment. I looked up at him.

'I have heard these stories,' I said. 'They are mere tales.'

He ignored me and resumed his pacing. 'After the north rebelled last spring, the king lost patience with us. The remaining brethren were told to swear or be taken to Newgate where they would be left to starve to death. Fifteen swore and lost their souls. Ten went to Newgate, where they were chained in a foul cell and left without food. Some lasted for weeks—' He broke off suddenly. Covering his face with his hands he stood rocking on his heels, weeping silently.

'I have heard such rumours,' Mark whispered. 'Everyone said they were false—'

I waved him to silence. 'Even if that were true, Brother Jerome, you could not have been among them. You were already here.'

He turned his back on me, wiping his face with the sleeve of his habit, and stood looking from the window, leaning heavily on his crutch. Outside, the snow whirled down as though it might bury the world.

'Yes, crookback, I was one of those who had been spirited away. I had watched my superiors taken, I knew how they died, but despite our daily humiliations we brethren succoured each other. We thought we could hold out. I was a fit, strong man then, I prided myself on my fortitude.' He laughed; a cracked hysterical sound.

'The soldiers came for me one morning, and brought me to the

Tower. It was the middle of May last year, Anne Boleyn had been condemned to die and they were building a great scaffold in the grounds. I saw it. And that was when I became truly afraid. As those guards bustled me down into the dungeons, I knew my resolution might fail.

'They took me to a big underground room and bundled me into a chair. In a corner I saw the rack, the hinged table and the ropes, two big guards standing ready to turn the wheels. There were two others in the room, facing me across a desk. One was Kingston, the warden of the Tower. The other, glowering at me most foully, was your master, Cromwell.'

'The vicar general himself? I don't believe you.'

'Let me tell you what he said. "Brother Jerome Wentworth, you are a nuisance. Tell me straight, without cavil, will you swear to the Royal Supremacy?"

'I said I would not. But my heart banged as though it would burst my chest as I sat before that man, his eyes like the fires of hell, for the Devil looks out of them. How can you face him, Commissioner, and not know what he is?'

'Enough of that. Go on.'

'Your master, the great and wise counsellor, nodded at the rack. "We shall see," he said. "In a few weeks' time Jane Seymour will be queen of England. The king would not have her cousin refusing the oath. Nor does he want your name included among those executed for treason. Either would be an *embarrassment*, Brother Jerome. So, you must swear, or you will be made to." Then he nodded at the rack.

'I told him again I would not take the oath, though my voice shook. He studied me a moment and smiled. "I think you will," he said. "Master Kingston, I have little time. Get him lengthened."

'Kingston nodded at the rackmasters and they hauled me to my feet. They slammed me down on the rack, knocking the breath from my body. They bound my hands and feet, stretching my arms above my head.' Jerome's voice lowered to a whisper. 'It was all so quick. Neither of the rackmasters spoke a word.'

'I heard a creak as they turned the wheel, then there was a great tearing pain in my arms like I had never known. It consumed me.' He broke off, gently massaging his torn shoulder, his eyes vacant. In the memory of his agony he seemed to have forgotten our presence. Beside me, Mark shifted uneasily.

'I was screaming. I hadn't realized till I heard the sounds. Then the pulling stopped, I was still in anguish but the tide –' he fluttered a hand up and down – 'the tide had ebbed. I looked up and there Cromwell stood, staring down at me.

'"Swear now, Brother," he said. "You have only a little fortitude, I see. This will go on till you swear. These men are skilled, they will not allow you to die, but your body is already torn and soon it will be so broken you will never be out of pain again. There is no shame in swearing when you have been brought to it by this road."'

'You are lying,' I said to the Carthusian. Again he ignored me.

'I shouted that I would bear the pain, as Christ had on the Cross. He shrugged and nodded at the torturers, who pulled both wheels this time. I felt the muscles of my legs tear and when I felt my thighbone pull from its socket I screamed that I would swear the oath.'

'An oath sworn under duress is surely not binding in law?' Mark said.

'God's blood, be quiet!' I snapped at him. Jerome started a little, recalled to himself, then smiled.

'It was an oath before God, a perjured oath, and I am lost. Are you kind, boy? Then you should not be in the company of this bent-backed heretic.'

I stared at him fixedly. In truth the power of his story had struck me forcefully; but I had to keep the initiative. I stood up, folded my arms and faced him.

'Brother Jerome, I am tired of these insults and of your tales. I came here to discuss the foul murder of Robin Singleton. You called him perjurer and liar, before witnesses. I would like to know why.'

Jerome's mouth worked into something like a snarl.

'Do you know what torture is like, heretic?'

'Do you know what murder is like, monk? And no more words from you, Mark Poer,' I added as he opened his mouth.

'Mark.' Jerome smiled darkly. 'That name again. Why, your bedesman has a look of the other Mark about him.'

'What other Mark? What are you babbling about now?'

'Shall I tell you? You say you want no more tales, but this is a story that will interest you. May I sit down again? I am in pain now.'

'I will have no more treasonable words or insults.'

'No insults, I promise, nor treason. Just the truth.'

I nodded, and he lowered himself back onto the bed with the help of his crutch. He scratched his chest, wincing at a pang from the hair shirt. 'I see that what I told you of my racking discomfited you, lawyer. This will discomfit you more. The other boy called Mark was one Mark Smeaton. You know that name?'

'Of course. The court musician who confessed to adultery with Queen Anne, and died for it.'

'Yes, he confessed.' Jerome nodded. 'For the same reason I swore.'

'How could you know that?'

'I will tell you. When I had taken the oath before Cromwell in that terrible room, the constable told me I would be lodged in the Tower a few days to recover; arrangements were being made through my cousin for me to be taken as a pensioner at Scarnsea. Jane Seymour would be told I had sworn. Lord Cromwell, meanwhile, had lost interest; he was collecting up my sworn oath with the rest of his papers.

'I was taken to a cell deep underground. The guards had to carry me. It was in a dark, damp corridor. They laid me on an old straw mattress on the floor and left. My mind was in such turmoil at what I had done, I was in such pain. The smell of damp from that rotten mattress made me feel sick. Somehow I managed to rise and went over to the door, where there was a barred window. I leaned against it, for there was a breeze of fresher air from the corridor, and prayed for forgiveness for what I had done.

'Then I heard footsteps, and sobbing and crying. More guards appeared and this time they were half-carrying a young man, just the age of your assistant and with another pretty face, though softer, and streaked with tears. He wore the remnants of fine clothes, and his big scared eyes darted wildly round him. He looked at me beseechingly as he was dragged past, then I heard the door of the next cell open.

'"Compose yourself, Master Smeaton," one of the guards said. "You will be here for tonight. It will be quick tomorrow, no pain." He sounded almost sympathetic.' Jerome laughed again, showing grey decayed teeth. The sound made me shiver. His face worked for a moment, then he went on.

'The cell door slammed and the footsteps receded. Then I heard a voice.

'"Father! Father! Are you a priest?"

'"I am a monk of the Charterhouse," I replied. "Are you the musician accused with the queen?"

'He began to sob. "Brother, I did nothing! I am accused of lying with her, but I did nothing."

'"They say you have confessed," I called back.

'"Brother, they took me to Lord Cromwell's house, they said if I did not confess they would tie a cord round my head and tighten it till they put my eyes out!" His voice was frantic, almost a scream. "Lord Cromwell told them to rack me instead, to leave no marks. Father, I am in such pain but I want to live. I am to be killed tomorrow!" He broke down, I heard him sobbing.'

Jerome sat still, his eyes distant.

'The pain in my leg and shoulder worsened, but I had not the strength to move. I hooked my good arm through the bars to support myself and leaned half-insensible against the door, listening to Smeaton's sobs. After a while he grew calmer and called again, his voice shaking.

'"Brother, I signed a false confession. It helped condemn the queen. Will I go to hell?"

'"If it was tortured from you God will not condemn you for that. A false confession is not like an oath before God," I added bitterly.

'"Brother, I am afraid for my soul. I have sinned with women, it has been easy."

'"If you truly repent, the Lord will forgive you."

'"But I don't repent, Brother." He laughed hysterically. "It was always pleasure. I do not want to die and never know pleasure again."

'"You must compose your soul," I urged him. "You must repent truly, or it will be the fire."

'"It will be purgatory anyway." He began sobbing again, but my head was swimming, I was too weak to call out any more, and I crawled back to my stinking mattress. I did not know the time of day; there is no light down there but the torches in the corridor. I slept a while. Twice I was woken when guards brought a visitor to Smeaton's cell.'

Jerome's eyes flickered up to meet mine for a second, then slid away again. 'Both times I heard him crying most piteously. Then later I woke to see the guard pass with a priest, and there was muttering for a long time, though whether Smeaton made proper confession in the end and saved his soul I do not know. I drifted off to sleep again and when I woke again to my pain all was silent. There are no windows down there, but I knew, somehow, that it was morning and he was gone, dead.' His eyes focused on me again. 'Know then that your master tortured a false confession from an innocent man and killed him. He is a man of blood.'

'Have you told anyone else this story?' I asked.

He gave a strange, twisted smile. 'No. I have had no need.'

'What do you mean?'

'It does not matter.'

'No, it does not matter, for I say the whole thing is a tissue of lies.'

He only shrugged.

'Very well. You have led me away from Robin Singleton again. Why did you call him perjurer and traitor?'

Again he gave that strange, savage smile. 'Because he is. He is a tool of that monster Cromwell, as you are. You all perjure yourselves and betray your due allegiance to the pope.'

I took a deep breath. 'Jerome of London, I can think of only one man who could have hated the commissioner, or rather his office, enough to devise a mad plot to kill him, and that is you. Your infirmity would prevent you from doing the deed yourself, but you are a man who would cozen another to do it. I put it to you that you are responsible for his death.'

The Carthusian reached for his crutch again and stood up painfully. He placed his right hand over his heart; it trembled slightly. He looked me in the eye, still smiling, a secret smile that made me shiver.

'Commissioner Singleton was a heretic and a cruel man and I am glad he is dead. May it vex Lord Cromwell. But I swear on my soul, before God and of my own free will, that I had no part in the killing of Robin Singleton, and I also swear I know of no man in this house of weaklings and fools who would have the fierce stomach to do it. There, I have replied to your accusation. And now I am tired, I would sleep.' He lay back on the bed and stretched himself out.

'Very well, Jerome of London. But we shall speak again.' I motioned Mark to the door. Outside, I locked it and we passed back down the corridor, watched from their open doors by the monks, who had now returned from Sext. As we reached the door to the cloister yard it was thrown open and Brother Athelstan hurried in out of the snow that still tumbled down, his habit white. He pulled up short at the sight of me.

'So, Brother. I have found the reason you are in bad odour with Brother Edwig. You left his private room unguarded.'

He shuffled from foot to foot, his straggly beard dripping melted snow onto the rush matting. 'Yes, sir.'

'That information would have been more use than your tales of mutterings in chapter. What happened?'

He looked at me, his eyes afraid. 'I did not think it important, sir. I came in to do some work and found Commissioner Singleton upstairs in Brother Edwig's room, looking at a book. I pleaded with him not to take it, or at least to let me take a record, for I knew Brother Edwig would be angry with me. When he returned and I told him, he said I should have kept an eye on what Commissioner Singleton was doing.'

'So he was angry.'

'Very, sir.' He hung his head.

'Did you know what was in the book he had?'

'No, sir, I only deal with the ledgers in the office. I do not know what books Brother Edwig has upstairs.'

'Why did you not tell me about this?'

He shifted from foot to foot. 'I was afraid, sir. Afraid that if you asked Brother Edwig about it he would know I had spoken. He is a hard man, sir.'

'And you are a fool. Let me advise you, Brother. A good informer must be prepared to give information even at risk to himself. Otherwise he will be mistrusted. Now begone from my sight.'

He vanished down the corridor at a run. Mark and I hunched ourselves into our coats and stepped out into the blizzard. I looked around the white cloister.

'God's nails, was there ever such weather? I wanted to go round to that fish pond, but we can't in this. Come on, back to the infirmary.'

As we trudged back to our room, I noticed Mark's face was thoughtful and sombre. We found Alice in the infirmary kitchen, boiling herbs.

'You look cold, sirs. Can I bring you some warm wine?'

'Thank you, Alice,' I said. 'The warmer the better.'

Back in our room Mark took a cushion and sat before the fire. I lowered myself onto the bed.

'Jerome knows something,' I said quietly. 'He wasn't involved in the killing, or he wouldn't have given his oath, but he knows something. It was in that smile of his.'

'He's so mazed after being tortured I don't think he knows what he means.'

'No. He's consumed with anger and shame, but his wits are there.'

Mark stared into the fire. 'Is it true then, what he said about Mark Smeaton? That Lord Cromwell tortured him into making a false confession?'

'No.' I bit my lip. 'I don't believe it.'

'You would not wish to,' Mark said quietly.

'No! I don't believe Lord Cromwell was there when Jerome was tortured either. That was a lie. I saw him in the days before Anne Boleyn's execution. He was constantly attending the king, he wouldn't have had time to go to the Tower. And he wouldn't have behaved like that; he wouldn't. Jerome invented it.' I realized my fists were clenched tight.

Mark looked at me. 'Sir, was it not obvious to you from his manner that everything Jerome said was true?'

I hesitated. There had been a terrible sincerity about the way the Carthusian spoke. He had been tortured, of course, that was plain to see. But made to swear a false oath by Lord Cromwell himself? I could not believe that of my master, nor the story of his involvement with Mark Smeaton and his torture – alleged torture, I told myself. I ran my hands through my hair.

'There are some men who are skilled in making false words seem true. I remember there was a man I prosecuted once, who pretended to be a licensed goldsmith, he fooled the guild—'

'It's hardly the same, sir—'

'I cannot believe Lord Cromwell would have prepared false evidence against Anne Boleyn. You forget I have known him for years, Mark; he rose to power in the first place because of her reformist sympathies. She was his patron. Why would he help kill her?'

'Because the king wanted it, and Lord Cromwell would do anything to keep his position? That is what they whisper at Augmentations.'

'No,' I said again decisively. 'He is hard, he has to be with the enemies he faces, but no Christian could do such a thing to an innocent man, and believe me, Lord Cromwell is a Christian. You forget how many years I have known him. Were it not for him there would have been no Reform. That cankered monk told us a seditious tale. One you had better not repeat outside this room.'

He gave me a keen, hard look. For the first time, I felt uncomfortable under his gaze. Alice came in with steaming mugs of wine. She passed me one with a smile, then exchanged a look with Mark that seemed to carry a different level of meaning. I felt a stab of jealousy.

'Thank you, Alice,' I said. 'That is very welcome. We have been talking with Brother Jerome and could do with some sustenance.'

'Have you, sir?' She did not seem much interested. 'I have only seen him a few times, limping about. They say he is mad.' She curtsied and left. I turned back to Mark, who sat staring into the fire.

'Sir,' he said hesitantly, 'there is something I wish to tell you.'

'Yes? Go on.'

'When we return to London – if we ever get out of this place – I do not wish to return to Augmentations. I have decided. I cannot bear it.'

'Bear what? What do you mean?'

'The corruption, the greed. All the time we are pestered by people wanting to know which monasteries will be down next. They write pleading letters, they turn up at the door claiming acquaintance with Lord Rich, they promise if they are granted lands they will do loyal service to Rich or Cromwell.'

'*Lord* Cromwell, Mark—'

'And the high officials talk of nothing but which courtier may go to the block next, who will have their posts. I hate it, sir.'

'What has brought this about? Is it what Jerome said? Do you fear ending up somehow like Mark Smeaton?'

He looked at me directly. 'No, sir. I have tried to tell you before how I feel about Augmentations.'

'Mark, hear me. I do not like some of the things that are happening now any more than you. But – it is all to an end. Our goal is a new and purer realm.' I got up and stood above him, spreading my arms wide. 'The monastic lands, for example. You have seen what this place is like, these fat monks steeped in every heresy the pope ever devised, living on the backs of the town, becking and scraping to their images when, given the chance, they would play the filthy person with each other, or young Alice, or you. It's all coming to an end, and so it should. It's a disgrace.'

'Some of them are not bad people. Brother Guy—'

'The institution is rotten. Listen: if Lord Cromwell can get these lands into the king's hands then, yes, some will be given to his supporters. That is the nature of patronage, it is how society works, it is inevitable. But the sums are vast; they will give the king enough money to make him independent of Parliament. Listen, you feel for the plight of the poor, do you not?'

'Yes, sir. It is a disgrace. People like Alice thrown off their lands everywhere, masterless men begging in the streets—'

'Yes. It is a disgrace. Lord Cromwell tried to put a Bill through Parliament last year that would truly succour the poor, set up almshouses for those who could not work and provide great public works for those without labour, building roads and canals. Parliament turned the Bill down because the gentry did not want to pay a tax on income to fund it. But with the wealth of the monasteries in the king's coffers, he won't need Parliament. He can build schools. He can pay to provide an English bible in every church. Imagine it, work for everyone, all the people reading God's word. And that is why Augmentations is vital!'

He smiled sadly. 'You do not think, like Master Copynger, that only householders should be allowed to read the Bible? I have heard Lord Rich believes the same. My father is not a householder, they would not allow him the Bible. Nor am I.'

'You will be one day. But no, I do not agree with Copynger. And Rich is a rogue. Cromwell needs him now, but he will ensure he rises no further. Things will settle down.'

'Will they, sir?'

'They must. They must. You need to think, Mark, you need to pray. I cannot — I cannot cope with doubts, not now. There is too much at stake.'

He turned back to the fire. 'I am sorry to vex you, sir.'

'Then believe what I say.'

My back ached. For a long time we were silent as dusk fell outside and the room slowly darkened. It was not a comfortable quietude. I was glad I had spoken so vigorously to Mark and I believed all I had said about the future I thought we were building. Yet as I sat there Jerome's words came back to me, and his face, and my lawyer's instinct told me that he had not been lying. But if everything he had said was true, then Reform was being built on an edifice of lies and monstrous brutality. And I was part of it all. Lying there, I was horrified. Then a thought came to comfort me. If Jerome was mad he might have come truly to believe in something that was only a fantasy in his head. I had known such things before. I told myself that must be the answer; what was more, I should cease from agonizing over this; I needed rest and a clear head for the morrow. In such ways do men of conscience comfort themselves against their doubts.

Chapter Seventeen

ALL AT ONCE Mark was shaking me awake; I must have fallen asleep lying there.

'Sir, Brother Guy is here.'

The infirmarian stood looking down at me; hastily I got to my feet.

'I have a message, Commissioner. The abbot has the land deeds you requested and some correspondence he wishes to send out. He is on his way.'

'Thank you, Brother.' He looked at me intently, fingering the rope at the waist of his habit with long brown fingers.

'I will shortly be going to the night service for Simon Whelplay. Commissioner, I feel I should tell what I suspect about his poisoning to the abbot.'

I shook my head. 'Not yet. His killer does not know murder is suspected and that may give me an advantage.'

'But how am I to say he died? The abbot will ask.'

'Say you are unsure.'

He passed a hand across his tonsure. When he spoke again his voice was agitated.

'But, sir, knowledge of how he died should guide our prayers. We should be asking the Lord to receive the soul of a slain man, not a sick one. He died without shrift or housel, that alone is a danger to his soul.'

'God sees all. The boy will be admitted to heaven or no as He wills.'

The infirmarian looked set to argue further, but just then the abbot entered. His old servant followed behind, carrying a big leather satchel. Abbot Fabian looked grey and worn, peering at us through tired eyes. Brother Guy bowed to his superior and left us.

'Commissioner, I have brought the deeds of the four land sales made this last year. Also some correspondence – business letters and some personal letters from the monks. You asked to see correspondence before it went out.'

'Thank you. Put the satchel on the table.'

He hesitated, rubbing his hands together nervously. 'May I ask how things went in the town today? Did you make progress? The smugglers—'

'Some progress. My lines of enquiry seem to multiply, my lord Abbot. I also saw Jerome this afternoon.'

'I trust he was not – not—'

'Oh, he insulted me again, naturally. I think he should remain in his cell for the present.'

The abbot coughed. 'I have had a letter myself,' he said hesitantly. 'I have put it with those others; it is from an old friend, a monk at Bisham. He has friends at Lewes Priory. They say terms of surrender are being negotiated with the vicar general.'

I smiled wryly. 'The monks of England have their own communication networks, it was ever so. Well, my lord, I think I may say Scarnsea is not the only house with a mischievous history that Lord Cromwell thinks would be better closed.'

'This is not a mischievous house, sir.' There was a slight tremble in his deep voice. 'Things went well and peacefully until Commissioner Singleton came!' I fixed him with an affronted look. He bit his lip and swallowed and I realized I was looking at a frightened man, near the edge of his reason. I felt his sense of humiliation, his confusion as his world shook and trembled about him.

He raised a hand. 'I am sorry, Master Shardlake, forgive me. This is a difficult time.'

'Nonetheless, my lord, you should mind your words.'

'I apologize again.'

'Very well.'

He collected himself. 'Master Goodhaps has made ready to leave tomorrow morning, sir, after Commissioner Singleton's funeral. The night service will begin in an hour, followed by the vigil. Will you attend?'

'Will there be a vigil over the two bodies together? The commissioner and Simon Whelplay?'

'No, as one was in orders and the other a layman the services will be separate. The brethren will be divided between the two vigils.'

'And will stand over the bodies all night, with blessed candles lit, their purpose to ward off evil spirits?'

He hesitated. 'That is the tradition.'

'A tradition disapproved in the king's Ten Articles of Religion. Candles are allowed for the dead only in remembrance of God's grace. Commissioner Singleton would not have wanted superstitious powers imputed to his funeral candles.'

'I will remind the brethren of the provision.'

'And the rumours from Lewes – keep those to yourself.' I nodded in dismissal and he left. I looked after him thoughtfully.

'I think I have the upper hand there now,' I told Mark. A cold shiver went through me. 'God's wounds, I'm tired.'

'One could pity him,' Mark said.

'You think I was too hard? Remember his pompous manner the day we came? I need to stamp my authority; it may not be pretty, but it is necessary.'

'When will you tell him how the novice died?'

'I want to investigate the fish pond tomorrow, then I'll consider where to go next. We can look through those side chapels as well. Come now, we should study those letters and the deeds. Then we should look in on the vigil for poor Singleton.'

'I have never been to a night service.'

I opened the satchel, and tipped a pile of letters and parchments over the table. 'We should show respect, but I'm not joining in a night's worth of mummery about purgatory. You'll see, it's a strange affair.'

✠

THERE WAS NOTHING to take exception to in the letters; the business missives were routine, purchases of hops for the brewhouse and the like. The few personal letters from the monks to their families mentioned the death of a novice only as the result of an ague in the terrible weather, the same explanation the abbot gave in his formally mellifluous letter to the dead boy's parents. I felt again a stab of guilt over Simon's death.

We looked over the land deeds. The prices seemed to be what one would expect for parcels of farmland and there was no evidence of sales at undervalue to curry political support. I would check with Copynger, but again I had the feeling that great care had been taken to make sure the monastery's affairs were in order, on the surface at least. I ran my hands over the red seal at the bottom of each deed, impressed with the image of St Donatus bringing the dead man to life.

'The abbot himself has to impress the seal on any deed,' I mused.

'Anyone else would be guilty of forgery,' Mark observed.

'Remember we saw the seal on his desk the day we came? It would be safer locked away, but I imagine he likes displaying it there, as a symbol of his authority. "Vanity, vanity, all is vanity."' I stretched out my arms. 'I do not think I will eat in the refectory tonight, I am too tired. You may get something from the infirmarian if you wish. You could bring me some bread and cheese.'

'I will do that.' He left the room, and I sat thinking. Since our argument at the inn there was a new reserve, a distance, in Mark's voice. Sooner or later I would have to raise the matter of his future again. I had an obligation not to let him throw away a career; an obligation not just to Mark but also to his father and mine.

✠

WHEN HE HAD still not returned after ten minutes I began to grow impatient; I was hungrier than I had realized. I heaved myself up and went out to look for him. I saw there was a light coming from the open door of the infirmarian's kitchen and I heard a sound too, soft and indistinct. A woman sobbing.

I pushed the door wide. Alice sat at the table, her head in her hands. Her thick brown hair was in disarray, hiding her face. She was weeping softly, a sad keening noise. She heard me and looked up. Her face was red and blotchy, the strong regularity of her features dissolved. She half-rose, wiping her face on her sleeve, but I motioned her to remain seated.

'No, no, stay, Alice. Pray tell me what ails you so.'

'It is nothing, sir.' She coughed to hide a break in her voice.

'Has someone done something to upset you? Please tell me. Is it Brother Edwig?'

'No, sir.' She gave me a puzzled look. 'Why should it be him?'

I told her of my talk with the bursar, and that he had guessed the source of my information. 'But do not fear, Alice, I told him you are under my personal protection.'

'It is not that, sir. It is just —' she bowed her head — 'I feel alone, sir. I am alone in the world. You cannot know what that is like.'

'I think I can understand. I have not seen my family for years. They live far from London. I have only Master Poer at my house. I know I have a position in the world, but I too can feel alone. Yes, alone.' I smiled at her sadly. 'But have you no family at all? No friends in Scarnsea that you visit?'

She frowned, playing with a loose thread on her sleeve. 'My mother was the last of our family. The Fewterers were not popular in the town, women healers are always a little apart.' Her voice became bitter. 'People come to women like my mother and grandmother for help with their ills, but they do not like the sense of obligation. Once when he was young Justice Copynger came to my grandmother, seeking help for a griping in his guts that would not leave him. She cured him, but he would not so much as acknowledge her in the street afterwards. And it did not stop him taking our cottage when my mother died. I had to sell all our sticks of furniture that I had grown up with, for I had nowhere to put them.'

'I am sorry. Such thefts of land should be stopped.'

'So I do not go into Scarnsea any more. On my rest days I stay here, looking at Brother Guy's books. He helps me try to read them.'

'Well then, you have one friend.'

She nodded. 'Yes, he is a good man.'

'Tell me, Alice, did you ever hear of a girl who worked here before you, a girl named Orphan?'

'I heard she took some gold cups and ran away. I do not blame her.'

I decided to say nothing of Goodwife Stumpe's fears; I did not wish to worry Alice further. I felt an overpowering urge to rise and clasp her to my breast, to ease the ache of loneliness in us both. I fought it down.

'Perhaps you too could leave,' I suggested diffidently. 'You did once, when you went to work for the apothecary in – Esher, was it not?'

'I would leave this place if I could, all the more after what has happened these last ten days. It is full of dusty old men and there is neither love nor warmth in their ceremonies. And I wonder still over what poor Simon meant about warning me.'

'Yes, so do I.' I leaned forward. 'Perhaps I may do something to help. I have contacts in the town, and in London too.' She looked at me curiously. 'I can feel for your position, truly I can, and I would help you. I would not have you –' I felt myself blush – 'put under any – any obligation to me for it, but if you would accept help from an ugly old hunchback I would gladly give it.'

Her look of curiosity deepened. She frowned. 'Why do you call yourself old and ugly, sir?'

I shrugged. 'I am approaching forty, Alice, and I have always been told I am ugly.'

'It is not so, sir,' she said hotly. 'Why only yesterday Brother Guy remarked how your features have a rare combination of refinement and sadness.'

I raised my eyebrows. 'I hope Brother Guy is not of Gabriel's inclination,' I said jokingly.

'No, he is not,' Alice said with sudden heat. 'And you should not insult yourself so, sir. Is there not enough suffering in the world?'

'I am sorry.' I laughed nervously. I was overcome with embarrassment and pleasure at her words. She sat looking at me sadly and despite myself I lifted a hand to reach across and touch hers. Then we both jumped as the church bells began to peal, clashing and echoing through the night. I let my hand fall as we both laughed nervously. The door opened and Mark walked in. Alice at once rose and went to a cupboard; I guessed she did not want him to see her tear-streaked face.

'I am sorry I took so long, sir.' He spoke to me but his eyes were on Alice's back. 'I went to the privy and then stopped in the infirmary hall. Brother Guy is there, the ancient monk is very ill.'

'Brother Francis?' Alice turned quickly. 'Then please excuse me, sirs, I must go to him.' She brushed by us, her footsteps pattering up the corridor. Mark's face was concerned.

'Has she been crying, sir? What ails her?'

I sighed. 'Loneliness, Mark, only loneliness. Now come, those infernal bells are tolling for the vigil.'

✝

As we passed through the infirmary hall, we saw Alice and Brother Guy standing over the old monk's bed. Blind Brother Andrew sat in his chair as usual, cocking his head from side to side to catch the sounds of Alice and Brother Guy's movements. The infirmarian looked up as I approached the bed.

'He is sinking,' he said quietly. 'It seems I must lose another.'

'It is his time.' We all looked round as the blind monk spoke.

'Poor Francis, he has watched nearly a hundred years as the world falls down to its end. He has seen the coming of the Antichrist, as was foretold. Luther, and his agent Cromwell.'

I realized he had no idea I was there. Brother Guy stepped hastily towards him, but I laid a restraining hand on his arm.

'No, Brother, let us hear.'

'Is that a visitor?' the blind monk asked, turning his milky eyes towards me. 'Did you know Brother Francis, sir?'

'No, Brother. I am a – visitor.'

'When he was professed it was still the time of the wars between Lancaster and York. Think of that. He told me there was an old monk at Scarnsea then, as old as Francis is now, who had known monks who were here at the time of the Great Pestilence.' He smiled softly. 'Those must have been great days. Over a hundred brothers here, a clamour of young men seeking the habit. This old man told Brother Fabian that when the Pestilence came half the monks died in a week. They partitioned the refectory, for the survivors could not bear the sight of the empty tables. The whole world was stricken then as it fell a further step towards its close.' He shook his head. 'Now all is vanity and corruption as the end nears. Soon Christ will come and judge all.'

'Quiet, Brother,' Brother Guy murmured anxiously, 'quiet.' I looked across at Alice; she dropped her eyes. I studied the ancient monk; he lay quite unconscious, his wrinkled face calm.

'Come, Mark,' I said quietly. 'Let us go.'

✝

WE MUFFLED ourselves up and went out. The freezing night was still, moonlight glinting on the snow as we crunched along to the church. A subdued glow of candlelight was visible from the windows.

At night the church had quite a different aspect. It seemed like a great cavern, the roof lost in echoing darkness. Pinpoints of light came from candles lit before favoured images round the walls, and there were two larger oases of light, one beyond the rood screen in the choir, the other in a side chapel. I led Mark there, guessing Singleton would have the less exalted setting.

The open coffin stood on a table. Posted round it were nine or ten monks, each holding a large candle. They made a strange sight, those cowled figures in the dark, their sombre faces lit from below. As we approached I saw Brother Athelstan there; he quickly lowered his head. Brother Jude and Brother Hugh shuffled aside to give us room.

Singleton's head had been set upon his neck and a block of wood laid between the head and the coffin's back to hold it in place. His eyes and mouth had been closed and but for the red line round the neck he could have been lying in the repose of natural death. I looked down, then lifted my head hastily at the smell that rose from the body, cutting through the monks' fusty odour. Singleton had been dead over a week and out of the vault he was decomposing fast. I nodded gravely to the monks and withdrew a few paces.

'I am going to bed,' I said to Mark. 'You may stay if you wish.'

He shook his head. 'I will come with you. It is a doleful sight.'

'I would pay my respects to Simon Whelplay. But as laymen I doubt we would be welcome.'

Mark nodded and we turned away. The sound of a Latin psalm came from behind the rood screen where the novice lay. I recognized Psalm 94.

'O Lord God, to whom vengeance belongeth: O God, to whom vengeance belongeth, shew thyself.'

✝

EXHAUSTED THOUGH I was, I slept badly again. My back pained me and I only dozed in fits and starts. Mark too was restless, grunting and mumbling in his dreams. Just as the sky lightened I fell at last into a deep sleep, only to be woken by Mark an hour later. He was already up and dressed.

'Jesu's mercy,' I groaned. 'Is it full day?'

'Aye, sir.' There was still something withdrawn about his tone.

A shaft of pain ran through my hump as I heaved myself up; I could not go on like this.

'No more noises this morning?' I asked. I had not intended to bait him, but it was coming to annoy me the way my words seemed to slide from him like water from a duck.

'As a matter of fact, I did think I heard something a few minutes ago,' he said coldly. 'It's gone now.'

'I have been thinking on what Jerome said yesterday. You know he is mad. It is possible he himself believes the stories he told us, and that that made them sound – credible.'

Mark met my gaze. 'I am not sure he is mad at all, sir. Only in great agony of soul.'

I had hoped Mark would accept my explanation; though I did not realize it then, I needed reassurance.

'Well, one way or the other,' I said sharply, 'what he says had no bearing on Singleton's death. It may even have been smoke to hide something he does know. And now we must press on.'

'Yes, sir.'

By the time I was shaved and dressed Mark had gone down the hall to breakfast. As I approached the kitchen, I heard his voice and Alice's.

'He should not make you labour so,' Mark was saying.

'It makes me strong,' Alice replied in a voice lighter than any I had heard her use. 'I will have arms thick and strong as yours one day.'

'That would be meet for no lady.'

Feeling a pang of jealousy, I coughed and went in. Mark was at table, smiling at Alice as she manoeuvred stone urns into a row. They did indeed look heavy.

'Good morning. Mark, would you take those letters to the abbot's house? Tell him I will keep the deeds for now.'

'Of course.' He left me with Alice, who set bread and cheese on the table. She seemed in better spirits this morning and made no reference to our conversation the night before, asking me only if I fared well that morning. I was a little disappointed at the formality of the question, for her words the evening before had gladdened my heart, although I was glad I had withdrawn my hand; there were enough complications here.

Brother Guy came in. 'Old Brother August needs his pan, Alice.'

'At once.' She curtsied and went out. Outside, the bells began tolling loudly. They seemed to echo round my skull.

'Commissioner Singleton's funeral will be in half an hour.'

'Brother Guy,' I said, suddenly awkward, 'may I consult with you, professionally?'

'Of course. Any assistance I can give.'

'I am having trouble with my back. Since the long ride here it pains me where – where it protrudes.'

'Would you like me to look?'

I took a long, deep breath. I hated the thought of a stranger seeing my deformity, but I had been suffering ever since the journey from London and was starting to become anxious some lasting damage might have been done. 'Very well,' I said, and began to remove my doublet.

Brother Guy went behind me and I felt cool fingers on my back, probing the knotted muscles. He grunted.

'Well?' I asked anxiously.

'Your muscles have gone into a spasm. They are very knotted. But I can see no damage to your spine. With time and rest your back should ease.' He stepped round and studied my face with a cool professional gaze as I dressed again.

'Does your back often give you much pain?'

'Sometimes,' I said shortly. 'But there is little to be done about it.'

'You are under much strain. That never helps.'

I grunted. 'I have not slept well since coming here. But who is to wonder at that?'

His large brown eyes studied my face. 'Were you well before?'

'My dominant humour is melancholy. These last few months I have felt it growing, I fear the balance of my humours is becoming undermined.'

He nodded. 'I think you have an overheated mind, not surprising after what you have witnessed here.'

I was silent a moment. 'I cannot help feeling responsible for that boy's death.' I had not meant to confide in him so, but Brother Guy had a way of drawing one out despite oneself.

'If anyone is responsible it is I. He was poisoned while under my care.'

'Does what has happened here frighten you?' I asked.

He shook his head. 'Who would harm me? I am only an old Moor.' He was silent a moment. 'Come to the infirmary. I have an infusion that may help you. Fennel, hops, one or two other ingredients.'

'Thank you.' I followed him down the hall, and sat on the table while he selected herbs and set water to heat on the fire. I eyed the Spanish cross on the opposite wall, and remembered the day before, seeing him lying prone before it.

'Did you bring that from your homeland?'

'Yes, it has followed me on all my travels.' He measured some herbs from his stock into the water. 'When this is ready take a little, not too much or you will want to sleep away the day.' He paused. 'I am grateful you trust me to prescribe for you.'

'I must trust you as a physician, Brother Guy.' I paused. 'I think you were unhappy with what I said yesterday, regarding the funeral prayers.'

He inclined his head. 'I follow your reasoning. You believe God is indifferent to forms of prayer.'

'I believe salvation comes through God's grace. You do not agree? Come, let us forget my position for a minute and talk freely, as Christian scholars.'

'Only as scholars? I have your word?'

'Yes, you do. God's bones, that mixture stinks.'

'It needs to stew a little.' He folded his arms. 'I understand why the new ways have come to England. There has been much corruption in the Church. But these matters could be dealt with by reform as has been done in Spain. Today thousands of Spanish friars are at work converting the heathens in the Americas, amidst terrible privations.'

'I cannot imagine English friars in that setting.'

'Nor can I. But Spain has shown reform is possible.'

'And has its own Inquisition as a reward from the pope.'

'My fear is the English Church will not be reformed, but destroyed.'

'What will be destroyed, though? What? The power of the papacy, the false doctrine of purgatory?'

'The king's Articles of Religion admit purgatory may exist.'

'That is one reading. I believe purgatory is false. When we die salvation is by God's grace alone. The prayers of those left on earth do not matter a rush.'

He shook his head. 'But then, sir, how should a man strive to be saved?'

'By faith.'

'And charity?'

'If one has faith, charity will follow.'

'Martin Luther holds that salvation is not really by faith at all, God predetermines before a soul is even born whether it will be saved or damned. That seems a cruel doctrine.'

'So Luther interpreted St Paul, yes. I, and many others, say he is wrong.'

'But if every man is allowed his own interpretation of the Bible, will not people bring forth such cruel philosophies everywhere? Shall we not have a Babel, chaos?'

'God will guide us.'

He stood and faced me, his eyes dark with — what? Sadness? Despair? Brother Guy was always a hard man to read.

'Then you would strip away all?'

I nodded. 'Yes, I would. Tell me, Brother, do you believe like old Brother Paul that the world is drifting towards its end, the Day of Judgment?'

'That has been the central doctrine of the Church since time immemorial.'

I leaned forward. 'But must that be? May not the world be transformed, made as God willed it?'

Brother Guy clasped his hands before him. 'The Catholic Church has often been the only light of civilization in this world. Its doctrines and rituals unite man in fellowship with suffering humanity and all the Christian dead. And they urge him to charity: Jesu knows he needs urging. But your doctrine tells each man to find his own individual salvation through prayer and the Bible. Charity and fellowship then are lost.'

I remembered my own childhood, the fat drunken priest telling me I could never take orders. 'The Church showed me little charity in my youth,' I said bitterly. 'I seek God in my heart.'

'Do you find him there?'

'Once he visited it, yes.'

The infirmarian smiled sadly. 'You know, until now a man from Granada, or anywhere in Europe, could go into a church in England and be immediately at home, hear the same Latin services, be comforted. With that international brotherhood taken away, who now will place a halter on the quarrels of princes? What will become of a man like me when he is stranded in a hostile land? Sometimes when I have gone into Scarnsea the children have thrown rubbish at me. What will they throw when the monastery is not there to protect me?'

'You have a poor view of England,' I said.

'A realistic view of fallen mankind. Oh, I see it from your perspective. You reformers are against purgatory, Masses for the dead, relics, exactly those things the monasteries epitomize. So they will go, I realize that.'

'And you would prevent it?' I looked at him keenly.

'How can I? It has been decided. But I fear without the universal church to bind us together, a day will come in this land when even belief in God will be gone. Money alone will be worshipped, and the nation, of course.'

'Should one not be loyal to one's nation, one's king?'

He picked up his potion, said a quick prayer over it, and poured the mixture into a glass bottle. He looked across at me sternly.

'In worshipping their nationhood men worship themselves and scorn others, and that is no healthy thing.'

'You are sore mistaken as to what we want. We seek the Christian commonwealth.'

'I believe you, but I fear I see things falling into a different path.' He handed me the bottle and a spoon. 'That is my opinion as a scholar. There, you should take a measure now.'

I swallowed it with a grimace; it tasted as bitter as it smelt. The slow peal of bells, which had formed the background to our talk, grew louder. The church clock struck eight.

'We should go,' Brother Guy said. 'The service is about to start.'

I put the bottle in my robe and followed him down the corridor. Looking at the fringe of black, woolly hair round the dark crown of his head, I reflected he was right in one respect: if the monasteries were dissolved he would have no safe haven in England any more; even his spicy odour was different from the common stink. He would have to beg a licence to go abroad, to a Spanish or French monastery. And he might not be given one, those countries were our enemies now. If the monastery went down, Brother Guy had more to lose than any of them.

Chapter Eighteen

THE MONKS WERE PROCESSING into the church, led by the abbot. Brother Guy left me to join his brethren. Among a couple of other latecomers I saw Prior Mortimus and Brother Edwig hurrying across the cloister yard from the counting house. I remembered what Goodhaps had said about the two of them running the place. And yet I had seen no signs of friendship between them. The prior moved along at a fast walk, kicking up the snow, the little bursar half-running to keep up. Mark joined me. Old Goodhaps was by his side, casting glances at the sky, which was grey again.

'Good morning, Master Shardlake. Do you think it will snow?' he asked anxiously. 'I want to be on the road once the service is over.'

'The road to Scarnsea is passable. Now come, we shall be late.'

I led the way into the church. The monks had filed past the rood screen into the choir stalls, I could hear them coughing and shuffling. On our side of the screen Singleton's coffin, still open, had been set on some chairs. Some way off another coffin stood surrounded by candles: Simon Whelplay's. The abbot stood by Singleton's coffin; not too near, for as we approached we caught again the smell of decay.

'If you lay mourners would sit with the coffin while the Dirige is offered up,' he said solemnly, 'and afterwards bear the coffin to the churchyard. Prior Mortimus has offered to be the fourth bearer. If, er –' he glanced at my hump – 'you are able to take the weight.'

'I am quite capable,' I said sharply, though I winced at the thought.

'I can't,' Dr Goodhaps piped up. 'I have arthritis in my shoulder, I should be in bed a week—'

'Very well, Dr Goodhaps,' the abbot said wearily. 'I will find a monk to be the fourth bearer.' For the first and last time I exchanged a look of sympathy with Abbot Fabian over the old man's head. Then he bowed and walked behind the screen, and we took our seats behind Singleton's coffin. Goodhaps coughed and buried his nose in a handkerchief.

The service began. That morning, for all I sat behind the stinking coffin of a murdered man, I found myself lulled along by the monks' beautiful, polyphonic chant. The psalms, and the Latin readings from Job, struck a chord.

And thou sayest, how doth God know? Can he judge through the dark cloud? Thick clouds are a covering to him, that he seest not; and he walketh in the circuit of heaven.

Thick clouds indeed, I thought. I am still in a fog here. I shook myself angrily. This would not do, where was my resolution? And then something occurred to me that I had not considered before, though I should have. Mark and Dr Goodhaps sat on either side of me; the old man still with the handkerchief to his nose while Mark stared before him, lost in thought. I nudged him.

'Will Alice be in the infirmary this morning?' I whispered.

'I believe so.'

'Good.' I turned to Goodhaps. 'And I would like you to come there too before you leave.' He gave me a put-upon look.

I turned back to the service. The chanting ebbed and flowed, dying out at last to silence. The monks filed out of the choir and a servant who had been waiting in the church hurried over and took up the coffin lid. I looked for the last time at Singleton's hard face and had a sudden memory of him in court, the fiery words and lively sweeps of the arm, the passion for argument. Then the lid was screwed down and his face was put in darkness for ever. The prior and a squarely built, middle-aged monk appeared and Mark and I bent with them to take the weight of the coffin. As I lifted it I felt something move within. Mark turned to me, his eyes wide.

'His head,' I whispered. 'It's slipped away.'

We bore the coffin from the church, horribly conscious of the head and the piece of wood rolling about inside, the monks following behind in a long procession. On the way out I saw Brother Gabriel standing over Novice Whelplay's coffin, praying fervently. As we passed he looked up at us with blank, despairing eyes.

We walked through the snow, the deadbell tolling in our ears, to the lay churchyard, where a grave had been dug, a brown slash in the white expanse. I glanced at Prior Mortimus beside me; his hard face wore an expression of unaccustomed thoughtfulness.

Servants were waiting with spades; they took the coffin and laid it in the grave. Snowflakes began falling silently in the grey morning, dusting the excavated earth as the final prayers were said and holy water sprinkled over the coffin. As the first clods banged down, the monks turned and processed silently back to the church. As I followed them, the prior fell into step beside me.

'They can't wait to be out of the cold. If they'd had the watches I've had in winter weather—' He shook his head.

'Indeed?' I asked with interest. 'Were you once a soldier?'

'Do I seem that rough to you? No, Master Shardlake, I was once the town constable at Tonbridge. I helped the sheriff arrest wrong-doers, watched for thieves on winter's nights. And in the day I was a schoolmaster. Does that surprise you, that I should be a scholar?'

I inclined my head. 'A little, but only because you cultivate a rough manner.'

'I don't cultivate it, I was born with it.' He smiled sardonically. 'I am from Scotland; we don't have your smooth English ways. We don't have much at all beyond fighting, not in the border country I come from. Life there is a battle, cattle-raiding lords fighting each other and you English.'

'What brought you to England?'

'My parents were killed when I was a boy. Our farm was raided – oh, by another Scots lord, not the English.'

'I am sorry.'

'I was at school at Kelso Abbey then. I wanted to go far away and the fathers paid for me to go to an English school. I owe everything to the Church.' His mocking eyes for once were serious. 'The religious orders stand between the world and bloody chaos, Commissioner.'

Another refugee, I thought, another beneficiary of Brother Guy's international community.

'What made you take orders?'

'I tired of the world, Commissioner, of how people are. Children forever fighting and avoiding lessons unless ye keep them well whipped. The criminals I helped catch, all the stupid greedy men. A dozen more waiting to be caught for every one tried and hanged. Ach, man is a fallen creature, far from grace and harder to keep in order than a pack of dogs. But in a monastery at least God's discipline can be kept.'

'And that is your vocation on earth? To keep men disciplined?'

'Is it not yours? Do ye not also feel outrage for that man's murder? Are ye not here to find and punish his killer?'

'The commissioner's death outraged you?'

He stood and faced me. 'It is a further step to chaos. You think me a hard man, but believe me the Devil's reach is far and even in the Church men like me are needed to keep him at bay. As the king's law seeks to keep order in the secular world.'

'What if the laws of the world and the Church conflict?' I asked. 'As they have in recent years?'

'Then, Master Shardlake, I pray some resolution may be found so Church and prince may work in harmony again, for when they fight they allow the Devil in.'

'Then let the Church not challenge the prince's will. Well, I must return to the infirmary. I will leave you here, you will be returning to the church. For the funeral of poor Novice Whelplay,' I added meaningfully.

He answered my gaze. 'I shall pray for that lad to be admitted to heaven in God's time. Sinner as he was.'

I turned away, peering through the snowflakes to where Goodhaps was tottering along; Mark had given him his arm. I wondered if he would make it to the town, make his escape.

✝

IN THE INFIRMARY HALL Alice was still tending the old dying monk. He was conscious again and she was gently spooning gruel into his mouth. Attending to the ancient her face had a new softness, a gentleness. I asked her to accompany us to the infirmarian's little kitchen. I left them all there while I fetched the book the bursar had given me. They all looked at me expectantly as I held it up.

'According to the bursar, this is the book poor Singleton obtained just before he died. Now, Dr Goodhaps, and Alice Fewterer, I want you both to look at it and say whether you have seen it before. You will notice it has a large stain of red wine on the cover. It occurred to me in church that those who had seen the book should remember that stain.'

Goodhaps reached across and took the account book, turning it over in his hands. 'I remember the commissioner reading a book with a blue cover. It might have been this. I don't know, I don't remember.'

'With your pardon.' Alice leaned across and took the book. She studied the cover, turned it over, then said decisively, 'This is not the book.'

My heart quickened. 'You are sure?'

'The book Brother Edwig handed the commissioner had no stain on it. I would have remarked it; the bursar likes everything so clean and tidy.'

'Would you swear to that in a court of law?'

'I would, sir.' She spoke quietly and seriously.

'So now I can be sure the bursar played me false.' I nodded slowly. 'Very well. Alice, I thank you again. All of you, keep this quiet.'

'I will not be here,' Goodhaps said smugly.

I looked from the window; the snow had stopped. 'Yes, Dr Goodhaps, I think you should be on your way. Mark, perhaps you could aid the doctor on his road to town?'

The old man cheered up. 'Thank you, sir. An arm to lean on would be welcome, and I have my bags at the abbot's house. My horse is here, if it could be returned to London when the weather allows . . .'

'Yes, yes. But, Mark, make as much haste as you can. We have things to do when you return.'

He helped the old man to his feet. 'Goodbye, Commissioner,' Goodhaps said. 'I hope you keep safe in this pestiferous place.' And with that cheerful valediction, he left us. I returned to my room, secreting the book under the bedclothes. I felt pleased. This was progress. I wanted to investigate the church and the pond next, and wondered how long it would take Mark to get to Scarnsea and back; on his own, little over an hour, but with the old man – I chid myself for a soft noddle, but I had not liked to think of Goodhaps stumbling through the drifts with his bags.

I decided to visit the horses; they had not been out for several days. I went back outside and made my way over to the stables. There a stable boy, sweeping up, assured me the animals were in good condition. Indeed both Chancery and Mark's Redshanks looked well, and were pleased to see me after so long inside. I stroked Chancery's long white head.

'Would you be out, old horse?' I said softly. 'Better to be bored in here than adrift in that place outside. There are worse things than standing in a stall.'

The stable boy passed, giving me an odd look.

'Do you not talk to your horses?' I asked him. He muttered something unintelligible and returned to his sweeping.

I said goodbye to the animals and walked slowly back to the

infirmary. In the courtyard I saw that a space had been cleared in the snow. Squares of different sizes had been chalked on the exposed ground and half a dozen monks were playing a game that involved making intricate steps on the throw of a dice. Bugge stood watching, leaning on his spade. At the sight of me the monks paused and made to step aside, but I waved them to continue. I recognized the game from Lichfield, an elaborate combination of hopscotch and dice that was played in all the Benedictine houses.

As I stood watching, Brother Septimus, the fat foolish monk whom Brother Guy had chid for over-eating, limped by, puffing and blowing as he waddled through the snow.

'Come and join us, Septimus,' one of the monks called. The others laughed.

'Oh no – no I couldn't, I would fall.'

'Come, we're playing the easy version. No trouble even for a noddle like you to follow.'

'Oh no–no.'

One of the monks grasped his arm and led him protesting into the middle of the cleared area, the monk already there moving aside. They were all grinning, even Bugge. Almost at once, though, Septimus slipped on a patch of ice and went over, landing on his back with a howl. The other monks roared with laughter.

'Help me up,' Brother Septimus howled.

'He's like a woodlouse on its back! Come, woodlouse, up with you!'

'Give him some snowballs!' one called. 'That'll raise him!'

The monks began throwing snowballs at the poor creature, who between his weight and infirmity found it impossible to rise. He cried out as snowballs burst all over him, twisting and rolling so that he looked more like a stranded tortoise than ever.

'Stop!' he yelled. 'Brothers, I pray you, desist!'

They went on pelting and catcalling. This was no good-natured jest such as I had witnessed the night before. I was considering whether to intervene when a loud voice cut through the noise.

'Brethren! Stop that now!'

The monks dropped their snowballs as the tall figure of Brother Gabriel strode up, frowning angrily.

'Is this Christian brotherhood? You should be ashamed of yourselves! Help him up!' Two of the younger monks hastily aided the puffing, gasping Septimus to his feet.

'To the church! All of you! Prime is in ten minutes!' The sacrist started a little as he noticed me among the watchers. He came over to me as the brothers dispersed.

'I am sorry, Commissioner. Sometimes monks can be like naughty schoolboys.'

'So I see.' I recalled my conversation with Brother Guy. 'No Christian brotherhood in that performance.' I looked at Gabriel anew, realizing he was not a senior official for nothing; he was more than capable of exercising authority and moral force when necessary. Then as I watched the power seemed to drain from his face and it was overcome with sadness.

'It seems a universal rule in this world that people will always look for victims and scapegoats, does it not? Especially at times of difficulty and tension. As I said earlier, sir, even monks are not immune to the Devil's wiles.' He gave a brief bow and followed his brethren into the church.

I resumed my way to the infirmary, passing again through the hall to the inner corridor. I felt hungry and paused at the kitchen to take an apple from the bowl there. As I did so something outside caught my eye. A great splash of scarlet across the white snow. I crossed to the window. Then my legs almost gave way.

Alice was lying face down in the garden, a broken pot at her side. She lay in a lake of blood that even now spread steaming across the snow.

Chapter Nineteen

I GROANED ALOUD and pressed a fist into my mouth. Simon Whelplay had died for talking to me; not Alice too. I rushed outside, praying desperately for a miracle – though I scorned miracles – that the evidence of my eyes might be made false.

She lay sprawled face down, next to the path. There was so much blood over and around her that for a sickening moment I thought her head had been struck off like Singleton's. I forced myself to look closely; she was whole. I stepped over the shards of the pot and knelt beside her. Hesitantly, I touched the pulse in her neck and cried out in relief when I felt it beating strongly. At my touch she stirred, groaning. Her eyes fluttered open, startlingly blue in her bloodstained face.

'Alice! Oh, praise God, you live. He has wrought a miracle!' I reached down and hugged her to me, gasping for joy as I felt her living warmth, the beating of her heart even as the ferrous tang of blood filled my nostrils.

Her arms pushed at my chest. 'Sir, what is this, no—' I released her and she sat up groggily.

'Forgive me, Alice,' I said, covered in confusion. 'It was relief, I thought you dead. But lie still, you are badly hurt. Where are you injured?'

She looked down at her vermilion-stained dress, staring in puzzlement for a moment, then put her hand to her head. Her face softened and, to my amazement, she laughed.

'I am not hurt, sir, only stunned. I slipped in the snow and fell.'

'But—'

'I was carrying a pitcher of blood. You remember, from the monks' bleeding. This is not my gore.'

'Oh!' I leaned against the infirmary wall, almost giddy with relief.

'We were going to pour it over the garden. We have been keeping it warm, but Brother Guy said to wait till the snow is gone. I was taking it to the storehouse.'

'Yes. Yes, I see.' I laughed ruefully. 'I have made a fool of myself.' I looked down at my blood-spattered doublet. 'And ruined my clothes.'

'They will clean, sir.'

'I am sorry I — ah — seized you as I did. I meant no harm.'

'I see that, sir,' she said awkwardly. 'I am sorry I frightened you so. I have never slipped before, but these paths through the snow are turning to ice. Thank you for your care.' She bowed her head. I saw that her body was held compressed in on itself, and realized with a pang of disappointment that my embrace had been unwelcome.

'Come in,' I said. 'You should go indoors, lie down a while after your fall. Do you feel giddy?'

'No, I am all right.' She did not take my proffered arm. 'I think we should both change.' She stood up, dripping with bloody snow, and I followed her inside. She went to the kitchen and I returned to my room. I changed into the other set of garments I had brought, leaving my bloodied clothes on the floor. I sat on the bed to await Mark's return. I could have gone to Alice and asked her to arrange for my clothes to be cleaned, but I felt an embarrassed reluctance.

I seemed to wait a long time. I heard the dead bell tolling again in the distance; now Simon Whelplay's funeral was over and he too was being laid in the earth. I cursed myself for not letting Goodhaps make his way to town alone. I wanted to go to the fish pond, and then I had plans for dealing with Brother Edwig.

I heard voices. I frowned and opened the door. Murmurs from the kitchen, Mark's and Alice's tones. I strode down the hallway.

Alice's dress lay on a scrubbing board where she had been washing it. She was dressed only in her white undershift, and she and

Mark were clasped in each other's arms. But they were not laughing, her face against his neck was full of sadness and Mark's too was serious, as though he were comforting rather than embracing her. They saw me and jumped apart, startled. I saw the movement of full, firm breasts under her shift, the hard nipples pressing against the material. I looked away.

'Mark Poer,' I said sharply, 'I asked you to hurry. We have work.'

He blushed. 'I am sorry, sir – I—'

'And you, Alice, is that what you call modesty?'

'I have only one clean dress, sir.' Her tone was defiant. 'This is the only place I can wash it.'

'Then you should have locked the door against intruders. Mark, come.' I inclined my head and he followed me back up the passage.

In our room I stood facing him. 'I told you not to dally there. You have obviously had more converse with her than I thought!'

'We have talked whenever we could these last few days.' He faced me boldly. 'I knew you would not approve. I cannot help my heart.'

'Nor could you with the queen's lady. Is this to have the same end?'

He reddened. 'This is clean different,' he burst out. 'My feelings for Mistress Fewterer are noble! I feel for her as for no woman before. You can scoff, but it is true. We have done nothing sinful, no more than hold and kiss as you saw. She was upset after falling in the snow.'

'*Mistress* Fewterer? You forget that Alice is no mistress, she is a servant.'

'That did not stop you embracing her when she fell in the snow. I have seen you looking at her, sir. You admire her too!' He took a step towards me, his face suddenly angry. 'You are *jealous*!'

'God's death!' I shouted. 'I have been too soft with you. I should cast you out now, to take your busy cock back to Lichfield and see if you can find a place as a ploughman!'

He said nothing. I forced myself to speak calmly.

'So, you think me a poor cripple full of jealousy. Yes, Alice is a fine girl, I won't deny that. But we have serious business here. What would Lord Cromwell think of you taking time out to dally with the servants, eh?'

'There is more to life than Lord Cromwell,' he muttered.

'Is there? Would you like to tell him that? And that's not all. What would you do, take Alice back to London? You say you do not want to go back to Augmentations, but is a servant's status all you seek?'

'No.' He hesitated, casting his eyes down.

'Well?'

'I thought perhaps you might let me be your assistant, sir, your clerk. I have helped you in your work, you have said I am good at it—'

'A clerk?' I repeated incredulously. 'A lawyer's jobbing clerk? Is that the reach of your ambition?'

'It is a bad time to ask, I know,' he said sulkily.

'God's blood, any time would be bad for that request! You would shame me before your father and shame yourself too, for lack of honest ambition. No, Mark, I will not have you as a clerk.'

He spoke with sudden heat. 'For one who is always talking of the welfare of the poor and building a Christian commonwealth, you have a lean view of common people!'

'There must be degrees in society. Not all are of the same degree and God never ordained otherwise.'

'The abbot would agree with you there. So would Justice Copynger.'

'God's death, you go too far!' I shouted. He faced me in silence, retreating behind that infuriating, impassive mask of his. I waved a finger at him.

'Listen to me. I have gained a measure of Brother Guy's confidence. He told me what happened to Simon Whelplay. Do you

235

think he would have acted similarly if he, rather than I, had come upon a scene like that just now? When that girl is under his protection? Well?'

Still he did not reply.

'There must be no more dalliance with Alice. Do you understand? No more. And I urge you to think very carefully on your future.'

'Yes, sir,' he muttered coldly. I could have struck his expressionless face.

'Get your coat. We are going to investigate that pond. We can look round the chapels on the way back.'

'It is like hunting for a needle in a haystack,' Mark said sullenly. 'The things could be buried.'

'It will only take an hour or so. Come on. And you had better prepare your flesh for the touch of cold water,' I added maliciously. 'It will be a lot colder than the arms of that girl.'

✝

WE MADE OUR WAY in silence. I was burning with anger; anger at Mark's thoughtlessness and insolence, but also at myself, for what he had said about my jealousy was true. To see him holding Alice, when she had shrunk from me, had burned me to the heart. I glanced sideways at him. First with Jerome, now with Alice. How could this obstinate, self-indulgent boy always leave me feeling in the wrong?

As we passed the church the monks were going in once more in double file. Simon was buried now in the monks' churchyard, but evidently there was to be a further service for him, though there had been none for Singleton. I reflected bitterly that Simon would have been grateful for a tenth of the attributes and opportunities God had lavished on Mark. The last of the brothers filed in, the door banged shut, and we walked on past the outhouses to the lay cemetery.

Mark stopped suddenly. 'Look there,' he said. 'That is strange.' He pointed to Singleton's grave, its brown earth standing out against the snow. The fresh snowfall had covered everything around with a further dusting, but not the grave.

We crossed to it and I exclaimed with disgust. The grave was covered with a viscous liquid, glittering in the weak sun. I bent down, touched it carefully and lifted my finger to my nose. Then I snorted angrily.

'Soap! Someone's coated the grave with soap. To prevent the grass growing. It has melted the snow.'

'But why?'

'Haven't you heard the story that grass will not grow on the graves of the sinful? There was a woman hanged for infanticide when I was a boy. Her husband's family would steal out and coat the grave with soap so nothing would grow, like this. It's a vicious piece of mischief.'

'Who has done it?'

'How should I know?' I snapped. 'God's passion, I'll have Abbot Fabian bring the lot of them out here to clean it under my supervision – no, under yours, it'll be a bigger humiliation to do it under you.' I turned away furiously.

We trudged on, traversing the graveyard and then the orchard, now almost a foot deep in snow. Watery sunlight was reflected from the stream and the ice-covered circle of the fish pond.

I pushed my way through the frozen rushes. The ice was thicker now, a light covering of snow round the edges. But by bending down and squinting hard I could still discern something gleaming faintly near the middle of the pond.

'Mark, see that pile of loose stones, under where the wall is patched. Fetch a big one and break the ice.'

He sighed, but at a stern look from me went off and fetched a great lump of limestone. I stood back as he raised the boulder above his head and flung it into the centre of the pond. There was a tremendous crash, satisfying somehow, though I flinched as a spout of water and shards of ice flew into the air. I left the water to settle, then carefully approached the edge, got down on hands and knees again and peered in. Disturbed fish milled about frantically.

'Now – yes, just there, do you see it? A gleam of yellow?'

'I think so,' Mark agreed. 'Yes, there's something. Shall I try fishing for it? If I take your staff and you hold my other arm, by stretching I might reach it.'

I shook my head. 'No. I want you to go in for it.'

His face fell. 'The water is near frozen.'

'Singleton's killer may have thrown his bloody clothes in there too. Go on, it can't be more than two or three feet deep. You'll live.'

For a moment I thought he would refuse, but he set his lips and bent to remove his coat, his overshoes and finally his boots. Those expensive leather shoes would be no better for a soaking. He stood a moment shivering on the bank, his solid bare legs and feet nearly as white as the snow. Then he took a deep breath and waded in, shouting aloud at the shock of the cold water.

I had expected it to reach his thighs, but he had taken no more than a couple of steps before, with a cry, he sank to his chest. Great bubbles of stinking gas belched up around him, smelling so vile I took an involuntary step back. He stood there gasping as the foul air dissipated.

'There's a foot of mud – ugh—' he gasped.

'Yes,' I said. 'Of course. The silt from the stream will fall to the bottom. Can you see anything? Can you reach?'

He gave me a withering look, then with a groan he bent down, his arm disappearing under the water. He scrabbled about. 'Yes – something – it's sharp—' his arm reappeared. He was holding a great sword, its handle gilded with gold. My heart leaped as he threw it on the bank.

'Well done!' I breathed. 'Now – again – is there anything more?'

He bent again, his whole shoulder disappearing under the surface and sending slow ripples towards the icy rim.

'Jesu, it's cold. Wait – yes – there is something – it's soft – cloth I think.'

'The killer's clothes!' I breathed.

He rose, pulling, and then overbalanced with a shout, falling right under the surface as another figure shot up out of the water. I gaped at the sight of a human form, dressed in a sodden robe. Its upper body seemed to hang in the air a moment, hair swirling round its head, then it splashed down into the reeds.

Mark's head rose again. He howled with shock and fear, flapping for the shore. Hauling himself onto the bank, he collapsed onto the snow, his yells turning to gasps and his eyes bulging, as mine were, at the sight of the figure in the reeds. A woman's body, grey and rotten and draped in the rags of a servant's dress. The eye sockets were empty; a lipless mouth was drawn back over grey clenched teeth. Rats-tails of hair dripped onto its face.

Mark got shakily to his feet. He crossed himself, over and over, praying. '*Deus salve nos, deus salve nos, mater Christi salve nos...*'

'It's all right,' I said gently, all my anger gone. 'It's all right.' I put a hand on his shoulder; he was shaking like a leaf. 'She must have been lying under the silt. Gases built up and you disturbed them. You're safe, the poor creature can do us no harm.' But my own voice broke as I looked at the terrible thing lying there.

'Come, you'll catch an ague. Put on your boots.' He did so, the action seeming to calm him a little.

I saw that something else had risen to the surface and lay floating there; a large black piece of cloth, bloated with gas. I reached over with my staff, dreading a second body, but it was only an empty monk's habit. I hauled it in and set it on the bank. I could see dark patches that could have been the marks of congealed blood. I suddenly remembered the fat carp we had eaten on our first night and shuddered.

Mark was still staring at the body in horror. 'Who is it?' he stuttered.

I took a deep breath. 'My guess is those are the remains of Orphan Stonegarden.' I looked at the dreadful head, grey skin stretched over a skull. '"A sweet gentle face," Goodwife Stumpe said. "One of the prettiest I have ever seen." So this is what Simon Whelplay meant about warning a woman of danger. He knew.'

'So now we have three deaths.'

'I pray God it's the last.' I forced myself to pick up the monk's robe. I turned it over and paused at the sight of a little harp sewn into the fabric. I had seen it before; it was the sacrist's badge of office. My mouth fell open with amazement.

'It's Brother Gabriel's,' I gasped.

Chapter Twenty

I TOLD MARK TO RUN and fetch the abbot, as fast as he could to warm his blood. I watched him plough away through the snow, then turned back to the pond. Bubbles were still rising from the silt, churning the surface. I wondered if the relic was down there, and perhaps the chalices the poor girl was supposed to have stolen.

I made myself approach the cadaver. There was a thin silver chain round its neck and after a moment's hesitation I bent and took it, snapping the links easily between my fingers. There was a tiny medallion on the end, with the crude figure of a man bearing a load on his back. I pocketed it and took up the sword. It was an expensive weapon, a gentleman's sword. A maker's mark was stamped into the blade: *JS.1507*, above the effigy of a square building with four pointed towers.

I went and sat down on the pile of rubble by the wall. I was stiff with shock as I sat staring at the bundle among the reeds. Between that and the cold my fingers and toes soon became numb and I got up, waving my arms and stamping my feet to restore the circulation.

I walked up and down, the snow creaking under my boots, pondering what these discoveries meant. I began to see a pattern, facts slotted into place in my head. After a while I heard voices from the orchard, and saw Mark hurrying back, accompanied by two black-habited figures, the abbot and the prior. Prior Mortimus carried a large blanket. Abbot Fabian's face was aghast as he came to a halt and stared at the thing on the bank. He crossed himself and muttered a prayer. The prior went over to the body, his face contorted with disgust. His eyes went to the sword, which I had placed on the bank.

'Was the woman killed with that?' he breathed.

'I do not think so. The body was preserved under the silt; I think it had been there a long time. But I believe this is the sword that killed Singleton. This pond has been used as a hiding place more than once.'

'Whose corpse is it?' There was a note of panic in the abbot's voice.

I gave him a level stare. 'I have been told a former assistant of the infirmarian disappeared two years ago. A girl called Orphan Stonegarden.'

The prior looked at the body again. 'No,' I heard him mutter. There was anger in his voice and sorrow too, disbelief. 'But – she ran away,' he said. 'She was a thief . . .'

We looked round at the sound of more people approaching. Four servants, carrying a stretcher between them. The abbot nodded to Prior Mortimus, and he threw the blanket over the body. The abbot leaned towards me.

'There is a great hue and cry at the monastery. People saw Master Poer come running to my house; he told me you had found a body and I asked the servants to bring a stretcher to carry it back. But – please – may we keep it covered, just say someone drowned in the pond for now, not that it is a woman—'

'For the present,' I agreed. I hid the sword in the soaked habit as the servants approached. They hung back, crossing themselves. 'Mark, help them,' I said. I noticed that under his coat he had exchanged his wet clothes for a blue servant's shirt. He helped them lay the blanket-covered form on the stretcher and lifted it; it seemed light as paper.

'Take the stretcher to the infirmary,' I said. We formed a procession behind the servants. I glanced at Prior Mortimus once or twice and he looked away. Discoloured water dripped from the body, staining the snow.

A CROWD HAD GATHERED, monks and servants buzzing around in the orchard like a swarm of bees. The prior called to them angrily to go about their business and they dissipated with many backward glances at the blanket-covered stretcher. Brother Guy approached us.

'Who is it? They say someone drowned in the pond.'

I turned to the bearers. 'Take the corpse to the infirmary for Brother Guy to examine. Mark, go with him. And take this, put it in our room.' I handed him the soaked habit. 'Careful of the sword,' I murmured. 'It is sharp.'

'I should tell the brethren something,' the prior said.

'Only that a body has been found in the pond. Now, my lord Abbot, I would talk with you.' I nodded towards his house.

✠

AGAIN HE FACED me across his desk, still covered with papers and with the abbey seal resting on its lump of red wax. His face seemed to have aged a decade in a few days, the confident glow in his cheeks replaced by grey, exhausted fear.

I laid the sword on his desk. He looked at it with distaste. I placed the little silver chain beside it, and pointed at it. 'Do you recognize that, my lord?'

He bent and looked at it. 'No, I have never seen it. Was it on — on—'

'The body. Yes. And the sword?'

He shook his head. 'We have no swords here.'

'I won't ask if you recognize that body as Orphan Stonegarden, it is beyond recognizing. I will have to see if Goodwife Stumpe recognizes the pendant.'

He looked at me with horror. 'The poorhouse overseer? Does she have to be involved? She has no love for us.'

I shrugged. 'And she will have less if it transpires her ward was murdered and thrown in your fish pond. She told me the girl was unhappy working here. What can you tell me about that?'

For answer he buried his head in his hands. I thought he would begin sobbing, but after a moment he lifted his face.

'It is not good to have young girls working in monastic houses. There I agree with Lord Cromwell. But Brother Alexander was infirmarian then, he was getting old and needed help. The girl was sent and he wanted to take her on.'

'Perhaps he liked her looks. I hear she was comely.'

He coughed. 'Not Brother Alexander. In fact I thought it safer than having a boy to assist him. That was in the days before the visitation, when – er—'

'I see. When a boy might have to watch his arse. But Brother Guy was infirmarian by the time she disappeared?'

'Yes. Brother Alexander was named in the bishop's visitation. It broke him, he died of a seizure soon after. Then Brother Guy came.'

'So who was it that bothered the girl? I believe somebody did.'

He shook his head. 'Commissioner, it is a temptation to have a pretty girl around the cloister. Women tempt men, as Adam tempted Eve. Monks are only human—'

'From what I have heard she did no tempting, but was harried and pestered. I ask again, what do you know?'

His shoulders sagged. 'There were complaints from Brother Alexander. A young monk called Brother Luke, who works in the laundry, was said to have – molested her.'

'You mean he took her forcibly?'

'No, no, no. It did not go so far. I spoke to Brother Luke, forbade him her presence. He troubled her again and I told him if he did not stop I would make him leave.'

'And others? Obedientiaries, perhaps?'

He looked at me with scared eyes. 'There were complaints against Brother Edwig and Prior Mortimus. They had – had made lewd suggestions, Brother Edwig persistently. Again I – I warned them.'

'Brother Edwig?'

'Yes.'

'And your warnings had effect?'

'I am the abbot, sir,' he said with a touch of his old pomposity. He hesitated. 'Could it not be the girl drowned herself, if she was – in despair?'

'The story was she stole two gold chalices and fled.'

'So we thought when they vanished from the church at the time she went. But – could she not have repented of what she had done, thrown them in the pond and drowned herself?'

'I want the pond drained, but even if those chalices are found it proves nothing. Her killer could have taken them and tossed them in after her, to throw enquiry off the scent. This matter must be fully investigated, my lord. It may need the involvement of the civil authority. Justice Copynger.'

He bowed his head and sat in silence for some moments.

'It's all over, isn't it?' he said suddenly, his voice muffled.

'What do you mean?'

'Our life here. The monastic life in England. I have been deluding myself, haven't I? Legalities will not save us. Even if Commissioner Singleton's killer should turn out to be from the town.'

I did not answer him.

He took a paper from his desk, his hand trembling slightly. 'Earlier I looked again at the draft Instrument of Surrender Commissioner Singleton gave me.' He quoted: ' "We do profoundly consider that the manner and trade of living which we and others of our pretensed religion have practised and used many days, doth most principally consist in dumb ceremonies and in certain constitutions of Roman and other foreign potentates." I thought at first Lord Cromwell wanted our lands and wealth, that passage was merely a bonus for the reformers.' He looked up at me. 'But after what I have heard from Lewes – it's a standard clause, isn't it? All the houses *are* to come down. And after this Scarnsea is finished.'

'Three people have died most horribly,' I said, 'yet you seem concerned only with your own survival.'

He looked puzzled. 'Three? No, sir, only two. One, if the girl killed herself—'

'Brother Guy believes Simon Whelplay was poisoned.'

He frowned. 'Then he should have told me. As abbot.'

'I asked him to keep it to himself for the time being.'

He stared at me. When he spoke again it was almost a whisper.

'You should have seen this house just five years ago, before the king's divorce. Everything ordered and secure. Prayer and devotion, the summer timetable then the winter, unchanging, centuries old. The Benedictines have given me such a life as I could never have had in the world; a ship's chandler's son raised to abbot.' He gave a sad flicker of a smile. 'It's not just myself I mourn for, Commissioner; it's the tradition, the life. Already these last two years order has started to break down. We all used to have the same beliefs, think the same way, but already the reforms have brought discord, disagreement. And now murder. Dissolution,' he whispered. 'Dissolution.' I saw two great tears take form in the corners of his eyes. 'I will sign the Instrument of Surrender,' he said quietly. 'I have no alternative, have I?'

I shook my head slowly.

'I will get the pension Commissioner Singleton promised?'

'Yes, my lord, you will get your pension. I wondered when we would come to that.'

'First, though, I will have to obtain the formal agreement of the brethren. I hold everything in trust for them, you see.'

'Do not do so quite yet. But when I give the word, tell them.'

He nodded dumbly, lowering his head again to hide his tears. I looked at him. The prize Singleton had sought so earnestly had fallen into my lap, the murders had broken the abbot. And now I thought I knew who the murderer was, who had killed them all.

✝

I FOUND BROTHER GUY in his dispensary. Mark sat on a stool beside him, still in his servant's clothes. The infirmarian was cleaning knives in a bowl of water, stained brownish-green. The cadaver lay on the table, covered with the blanket, for which I was grateful.

Mark's face was pale, and even the infirmarian's dark features had an underlying pallor, as though there were ashes under his skin.

'I have been examining the body,' he said quietly. 'I cannot be sure, but from her height and build I think it is the girl Orphan. And the hair was fair. But I can tell you how she died. Her neck was broken.' He lowered the blanket, exposing that dreadful head. He rotated it slowly; it swung loose, the vertebrae dislocated. I fought down nausea.

'Murdered then.'

'She couldn't have done that going into the pond. Master Poer says the bottom is thick silt.'

I nodded. 'Thank you, Brother. Mark, those other things we found, are they in our room? We have a call to make. Have you a change of clothes?'

'Yes, sir.'

'Go and put them on. You shouldn't be going around dressed as a servant.'

Mark left us and I took his stool. The infirmarian bowed his head.

'First Simon Whelplay poisoned under my nose, and now it seems this poor girl who used to be my assistant murdered too. And I thought her a thief.'

'How long was she with you?'

'Not long, a few months. She was hard-working enough, but I found her withdrawn, a little surly. I believe she trusted Brother Alexander, but no one else. I was preoccupied with putting the infirmary in order; he had left it in a poor state. I took less notice of her than I should.'

'Did she say anything about unwanted attentions from the monks?'

He frowned. 'No. But one day I came in and found her struggling with one of the brethren, in the corridor outside her door. She had the room Alice occupies now, at the end of the corridor. He was trying to embrace her, making lewd remarks.'

'Who was it?'

'Brother Luke, the launderer's assistant. I sent him away and complained to the abbot, though Orphan did not want trouble made. Abbot Fabian said he would speak to Luke. He told me it was not the first time. After that Orphan seemed more friendly, though she still spoke little. Then, not long after, she vanished.'

'No one else troubled her that you know of?'

'Not that I saw. But, as I say, she did not confide in me.' He smiled sadly. 'I don't think she ever became used to my strange colouring. Not surprising, I suppose, for a girl from a small town.'

'And afterwards Alice came.'

'Yes, and I resolved to win her trust from the beginning. That, at least, I believe I have done.'

'You are treating Brother Jerome. What would you say is the state of his mind?'

He looked at me carefully. 'As well as a man can be who, for good or ill, devoted his life to demanding ideals and a harsh way of life, and then was tortured into a betrayal of them. His mind is sore troubled, but he is not mad, if that is what you mean.'

'Well, it seems madness to me further to weaken a wasted body by wearing a hair shirt. Tell me, does he ever talk of his time in the Tower?'

'No. Never. But he was grievously racked. That I can swear to.'

'He told me about that. More too, but I think it was just tales to vex me.' Brother Guy did not respond. I stood up and as I did so a spasm ran through my back. I winced, grasping the table.

'What is the matter?'

I took deep breaths. 'I twisted something as I rose. I will suffer for days now.' I gave him a bitter smile. 'You and I both know what it is like to have people stare at us as oddities, eh, Brother? But at least your appearance is a natural phenomenon, it does not cause you pain. And there is a land where it is normal.'

✝

MARK HAD CHANGED into his spare shirt and doublet and was sitting on my bed. His face looked drawn.

'Are you all right?' I asked gruffly.

He nodded. 'Yes, sir. That poor creature—'

'I know. I am sorry you were put through that. It was a fearful shock. I had no idea—'

'No. Nobody could have known—'

'Mark, we need to put our – differences – aside. We have one aim in common, I think. To find the cruel murderer at large in this place.'

He stared at me. 'Of course, sir. How could you ever doubt that?'

'I don't, I don't. Listen, I have been thinking. The only reason Gabriel's habit could have been thrown in the pond was because it was soaked in blood. The murderer wore it to kill Singleton, then threw it in there with the sword.'

'Yes. But – Brother Gabriel, the killer?' He shook his head.

'Why not? Why shouldn't he be? I thought you despised him as a pederast?'

'I do.' He thought a moment. 'But – I cannot see him as a murderer. He seems a man of – strong affections, if you can call them that, but not one who would willingly do harm. Or be bold enough to strike.'

'Oh, he can be bold enough when he wants. And he has very strong affections. Violently strong. And where there are violent affections there may perhaps be violent hatreds too.'

He shook his head. 'I cannot see it. Please believe me, sir, I am not being awkward, but I cannot see Brother Gabriel as a killer.'

'I have felt sorry for the man, even liked him. But we can't decide these things on the basis of emotion. We need cold logic. How can we know whether someone is capable of murder or not after a few days' acquaintance? Especially in this place, where all our senses are heightened and distorted by danger?'

'I still can't see it, sir. He seems so – soft-natured.'

'We might as well accuse Brother Edwig on the basis that he is a despicable creature, more like an animated calculus than a man. He is full of deceits too, and lusts as well, apparently. But that doesn't allow us to say he is a murderer.'

'He was away when Singleton was killed.'

'And Gabriel wasn't. And I can see a chain of motive for Gabriel. No, we must put emotion aside.'

'As you would have me do with Alice.'

'This is not the time to discuss that. Now, will you come with me to confront Gabriel?'

'Of course. I do want this killer caught too, sir.'

'Good. Then buckle on your sword again. Leave that other sword here, but bring the habit. Wring it out in the bowl first. Let us put these matters to the test.'

Chapter Twenty-one

MY HEART WAS POUNDING as we went back outside, but my head was clear. It was well past midday now, and the sun hung low in a hazy sky; one of those great red winter suns that you can look straight into, as though all the fire were leached out of it. And, in that cold, so it felt.

Brother Gabriel was in the church. He sat in the nave with the old monk I had seen copying in the library, examining a great pile of ancient volumes. They looked up at our approach, Gabriel's eyes flickering uneasily between Mark and me.

'More ancient books, Brother?' I asked.

'These are our service books, sir, with the musical notations. No one prints them, we have to copy them when they fade.'

I picked one up. The pages were parchment; Latin words were marked phonetically and interspersed with red musical notation, different psalms and prayers for each day of the calendar, the ink faded at the edges from long years of handling. I dropped it on a bench.

'I have some questions, Brother.' I turned to the old monk. 'Perhaps you could leave us?' He nodded and scuttled away.

'Is something amiss?' the sacrist asked. There was a tremor in his voice.

'You have not heard, then? About the body found in the fish pond?'

His eyes opened wide. 'I have been engaged, I have just come from fetching Brother Stephen from the library. A body?'

'We believe it to be a girl who disappeared two years ago. One Orphan Stonegarden.'

His mouth dropped open. He half-rose, then sat again.

'Her neck was broken. It appears she was killed and thrown in the pond. There was a sword there too; we think the one that killed Commissioner Singleton. And this.' I nodded to Mark, who passed me the habit. I waved the badge under the sacrist's nose. 'Your robe, Brother Gabriel.'

He sat there gaping.

'The badge is yours?'

'Yes, yes it is. That — it must be the robe that was stolen.'

'Stolen?'

'Two weeks ago I sent a habit to the launderer and it never came back. I enquired, but it was never found. The servants steal habits now and then; our winter robes are good wool. Please, sir, you cannot think—'

I leaned over him. 'Gabriel of Ashford, I put it to you that you killed Commissioner Singleton. He knew of your past, and discovered some recent felony you could have been tried and executed for. So you killed him.'

'No.' He shook his head. 'No!'

'You hid the sword and your bloodied robe in the pond, which you knew to be a safe hiding place as you had used it before to hide that girl's body. Why kill Singleton in such a dramatic way, Brother Gabriel? And why did you kill the girl? Was it jealousy because Brother Alexander befriended her? Your fellow sodomite? And Novice Whelplay too, your other friend. He knew what had become of her, didn't he? But he wouldn't betray you. Not until the end, when he started talking in his illness, so you poisoned him. Since then you have seemed racked with pain, as one in an agony of conscience. It all fits, Brother.'

He stood up and faced me, gripping the back of his chair while he took a couple of long breaths. Mark's hand strayed to his sword.

'You are the king's commissioner,' he said, his voice shaking, 'but you harangue like a cheap lawyer. I have killed nobody.' He began to shout. 'Nobody! A sinner I am, but I have broken none of the king's laws these two years! You may enquire of every soul here, and in the town too if you wish, and you will find nothing! Nothing!' His voice echoed round the church.

'Calm yourself, Brother,' I said in measured tones. 'And answer me civilly.'

'Brother Alexander was neither my friend nor my enemy; he was a foolish, lazy old man. As for poor Simon,' he gave a sigh that was almost a groan, 'yes, he befriended the girl in his first days as a novice, I think they both felt lost and threatened here. I told him he should not be mixing with servants; that it would do him no good. He said she had told him she was being pestered—'

'By whom?'

'He would not say, she had sworn him to silence. It could have been one of half a dozen monks. I said he should not become involved in such things; he should get the girl to tell Brother Guy. He had just been made infirmarian after Alexander died. Of shame,' he added bitterly.

'And then she disappeared.'

A spasm twisted his face. 'Like everyone else I thought she had run away.' He looked at me bleakly, then went on in a new voice, cold and calm. 'Well, Commissioner, I see you have created a theory that gives you a solution. So perhaps now someone will be paid to give false testimony and send me to the gallows. Such things are done these days. I know what happened to Sir Thomas More.'

'No, Brother Gabriel, there will be no false witnesses. I will uncover the evidence I need.' I stepped closer to him. 'Be warned. You are under the gravest suspicion.'

'I am innocent.'

I looked into his face a moment, then stepped back. 'I will not have you arrested now, but for the present you will not leave the monastery precincts. If you attempt to leave that *will* be taken as an admission of guilt. You understand?'

'I will not leave.'

'Be available to speak to me whenever I require. Come, Mark.'

I got up and strode away, leaving Brother Gabriel amidst his pile of books. Outside the church I struck the stone doorway with my hand.

'I thought I had him.'

'Do you still think him guilty?'

'I don't know. I thought if I confronted him and he was guilty he'd collapse. But,' I shook my head, 'he's hiding something, I know it. He called me a haranguing lawyer and perhaps I am, but if twenty years about the courts have taught me anything it's when a man is concealing things. Come.'

'Where now?'

'The laundry. We can check his story and see this Luke at the same time.'

✝

THE LAUNDRY was housed in a large outhouse next to the buttery. Steam issued from ventilator grilles, and I had seen servants going in and out of there with baskets of clothes. I unlatched the heavy wooden door and stepped inside. Mark closed it behind him.

Within it was warm and very dim. At first I could see only a big stone-flagged chamber with baskets and buckets dotted around. Then Mark said, 'Jesu,' and I saw them.

The chamber was full of dogs, a dozen of the great lurchers that had been roaming the yard on our first day, before the snow came. The room stank of their piss. They all rose slowly to their feet and two stepped forward growling, hackles raised and lips flickering back over yellow teeth. Mark slowly unsheathed his sword, and I grasped my staff hard.

I could hear noises behind an inner door and thought of shouting, but I had been brought up on a farm and knew that would only startle the dogs and make them spring. I gritted my teeth; we would not come out of this unmarked. I gripped Mark's arm with my free hand. I had led him to the horror in the pond; and now to this.

There was a creak and we spun round as the inner door opened and Brother Hugh appeared, a bowl of offal in his plump hands. At the sight of us his mouth dropped open. We stared at him desperately, and he collected himself and called to the dogs.

'Brutus, Augustus! Here! Now!' He tossed chunks of offal onto the flags. The dogs looked between him and us, then one by one slunk over to the food. The leader stood growling for a few seconds more, but finally turned and joined the others. I took a shuddering breath. Brother Hugh waved at us urgently.

'Inside, sir, I pray you. Now, while they're eating.'

Circling round the slobbering animals, we followed him to the inner room. He closed the door and latched it. We found ourselves in the steam-filled laundry room. Supervised by two monks, servants were labouring over cauldrons of clothes boiling over fires, or squeezing habits and undershirts out in presses. They looked at us curiously as we took off our heavy coats. I had started to sweat profusely and so had Mark. He gripped the edge of a table and took deep breaths; he was pale and I feared he would faint, but after a moment his colour returned. My own legs were unsteady as I turned to Brother Hugh, who stood bobbing agitatedly, wringing his hands.

'Oh sirs, my lord Commissioner, thank Jesu I came when I did.' He bowed at Our Lord's name, as did the others.

'We are grateful to you, Brother. But those dogs should not be there, they could kill someone.'

'But, sir, they know everyone; by your leave it was only seeing strangers. The abbot said to keep them here while the snow lasted.'

I wiped the sweat from my brow. 'Very well, Brother Chamberlain. You have charge of the laundry?'

'I do. How can I help you? The abbot said we are to assist however we can. I heard someone has drowned in the pond.' His red-rimmed eyes were full of curiosity.

'The prior will be making an announcement about that. I have come with an enquiry for you, sir. Have you a table?'

He led us to a corner, away from the others. I signalled Mark to lay out Brother Gabriel's habit and pointed to the badge.

'Brother Gabriel reported he had a habit disappear a couple of weeks ago. Do you remember?'

I confess I hoped for a denial, but he nodded promptly. 'Yes, sir. We hunted up and down for it. The bursar gets angry if things go missing, that's why I keep a book.' He disappeared into the steam, returning with a ledger. 'See, sir, there is the entry for it coming in, and that is the note of it being reported lost.' I studied the date. Three days before Singleton was killed.

'Where was it found, my lord?' he asked.

'Never mind that. Who could have had the opportunity to steal it?'

'In the day we're always here working, sir. The laundry's locked at night, but—'

'Well?'

'Keys have been lost. My assistant can be – well, a bit careless, shall I say.' He smiled nervously, running his hand over the wen on his face. 'Brother Luke, over here!'

Mark and I exchanged glances as a tall, powerfully built monk in his late twenties came over to us. He had red hair, heavy features and a surly expression.

'Yes, Brother?'

'You have lost two sets of keys since you've been with me, haven't you, Luke?'

'They slip out yer pocket,' he said sullenly.

'They do if you are careless,' I agreed. 'When was the last time you lost a key?'

'In the summer it was.'

'And before that? How long have you worked in the laundry?'

'Four years, sir. The other time was a couple of years ago.'

'Thank you, Brother Hugh. I would have a word with Brother Luke in private. Where can we go?'

Brother Luke's eyes swivelled anxiously as the chamberlain, looking disappointed, led us to an anteroom where clothes were drying. I faced the young monk sternly.

'Do you know what has been found in the fish pond?'

'They say a dead body, sir.'

'A woman's body, that we think is a girl called Orphan. We have been told that you used to trouble her.'

His eyes widened with terror, then suddenly he was on his knees on the floor, grasping the hem of my robe with thick red fingers.

'I didn't do it, sir. I sported with her only, nothing more! And I wasn't the only one! She was a wanton, she tempted me!'

'Let me go! Look at me!'

He looked up, still kneeling, his eyes wide. I leant forward.

'I want the truth. On your life. Did she tempt you, or did you trouble her?'

'She – she was a woman, sir. The very sight of her was temptation! Her image filled my mind, I was always thinking of her. Satan placed her in my path to tempt me, but I have confessed. I have made confession!'

'I don't give a rush for your confession. You pestered her even after the abbot warned you off, didn't you? Brother Guy had to complain a second time!'

'But I did nothing after that! The abbot said he'd make me leave! By Jesu's blood, I left her alone after that! By his holy blood!'

'The abbot didn't place the matter in the hands of the prior?'

'No, the prior—'

'Well? Well, boy, what?'

'He – he had been guilty of the same thing, and the bursar too.'

'Yes. Any others? Who was it made the girl's life such a misery towards the end?'

'I don't know, sir. I swear, I swear, I never went near the infirmary after the abbot's warning. By Our Lady—'

'Our Lady!' I snorted. 'I doubt even *she* would be safe from the likes of you were she to return to earth. Get out, begone!'

I glared after him as he scrambled up and fled back into the laundry.

'You scared him to the marrow,' Mark said with a sardonic grin.

'It's easy with cowardly churls like that. The prior and the bursar, eh? Look, there's a door, we can get out that way and avoid those dogs.'

We stepped back into the courtyard. The confrontation with the dogs came back to my mind. I felt drained and it was my turn to lean against the wall for a moment. A babble of noise made me look round.

'God's death, what's going on now?'

People had stopped to watch a procession that was making its way towards the gates. Two monks held up a statue of St Donatus in his Roman robes, hands folded in front of him and wearing a pious expression. The tall thin figure of Brother Jude the pittancer followed, carrying a leathern bag. Finally came Bursar Edwig himself, a winter coat over his habit and gloves on his hands. They approached the space under the gatehouse, where Bugge stood ready to open the gates.

'The dole day,' Mark said.

✝

BY THE TIME we reached the gate, Bugge had opened it. A crowd outside stood looking at the statue, which the two servants had elevated to their shoulders. Brother Jude raised his bag and called to them.

'Behold! The image of our patron, most holy and sainted Donatus, martyr to the heathen! In the name of his great goodness this charity is given. Pray to him for remittance of your sins!'

We shouldered our way through the onlookers. There were forty or fifty adults crowded round in the snow, old widows and beggars and cripples, some wearing little more than rags and blue-faced with cold. A separate group of whey-faced children was gathered round the plump figure of Mistress Stumpe. The smell from the crowd, even on this cold day, was dreadful. The sea of wretches, who had trudged the mile from the town, bowed and crossed themselves at the monk's words. He stopped abruptly as I appeared at his side.

'What are you doing?' I snapped.

'Just – just distributing the doles, sir—'

'You are asking those poor souls to worship that piece of wood.'

Brother Edwig scuttled forward. 'Only in r-remembrance of the saint's g-goodness, Commissioner.'

'He called on them to pray to the statue! I heard him! Take it away, now!'

The monks lowered the statue and hastily bore it off. Brother Jude, thoroughly shaken, signalled for the baskets to be brought forward. Some of the townspeople were grinning openly.

The almoner called out again in a flustered voice. 'Come forward for your dole and meats.'

'No shoving now,' Bugge shouted as, one by one, the destitute approached. Each was given a tiny silver farthing, the smallest coin of the realm, and something from the baskets. There were apples, loaves of bread, thinly sliced bacon.

Brother Edwig was at my side. 'We m-meant no harm with the s-saint, sir. It is an old ceremony, we forgot its implications. We will am-mend it.'

'You had better.'

'W-we give charity every month. It's in our f-founding charter. The m-meat, these p-people wouldn't see any otherwise.'

'With all your income I would have thought you could spare more funds than this.'

Brother Edwig's face darkened with sudden anger. 'And Lord Cromwell would have all our money, for his cronies! Is that charity?' He bit off the words without a trace of a stutter, then turned and walked quickly away. The crowd looked at me curiously as the monks went on handing out scraps, and the pittancer's bag chinked, slowly emptying.

I sighed. My anger at the spectacle had got the better of me, now everyone would know there was a king's commissioner here. I felt utterly exhausted after my outburst, but crossed over to where Mistress Stumpe stood by the roadside with the children, waiting for the adults to finish. She curtsied.

'Good morning, sir.'

'A moment, Mistress, if you would. Over here.'

We walked a little way from the children. She eyed me curiously.

'I want you to look at this, tell me if you recognize it.' My back to the crowd, I produced the silver chain I had taken from the corpse's neck. She grabbed at it with an exclamation.

'The St Christopher! I gave it to Orphan when she came here! Sir, have you found her—?' She broke off at my expression.

'I am sorry, Mistress,' I said gently. 'It was found on a body pulled from the fish pond this morning.'

I had expected tears, but the old woman only clenched her hands into fists.

'How did she die?'

'Her neck was broken. I am sorry.'

'Have you found who did it? Who was it?' Her voice broke, became a thin screech. The children looked round anxiously.

'Not here, madam. Please. This is not to be told abroad yet. I will find who did it, I swear to you.'

'Revenge her, in God's name revenge her.' Goodwife Stumpe's voice faltered, and then she did begin to cry, softly. I took her gently by the shoulder.

'Say nothing yet. I will send word by Justice Copynger. Look, the adults are finished. Try to compose yourself.'

The last of the adult doles had been given, and a line of people was already heading back along the road to town, ragged black figures like crows against the stark white snow. Goodwife Stumpe nodded to me quickly, took a deep breath and led the children over. I went back through the gate to where Mark stood waiting. I feared she might break down again, but the overseer's voice was steady as she encouraged the children to step forward. Brother Edwig had disappeared.

Chapter Twenty-two

I ENTERED THE DARK CHURCH quietly, closing the big door carefully behind me. Beyond the rood screen candles were flickering, and I could hear the monks' voices chanting a psalm. The evening service of Vespers was in progress.

After leaving Mistress Stumpe I had told Mark to go to the abbot and order him to ensure Brother Gabriel did not leave, and to arrange for the cleaning of Singleton's grave. I wanted the pond, too, drained on the morrow. Mark had been reluctant to give orders to Abbot Fabian, but I told him if he was to make his way in the world he would have to get used to dealing with those of high station. He went off without further comment, his manner stiff-backed again.

I had stayed in our room; I needed time alone to think. I sat before the fire as darkness began falling outside. Exhausted as I was, it was hard not to fall asleep before the warmth of the crackling logs. I stood up and splashed water over my face.

The launderer's confirmation that Gabriel's robe had been stolen was a grievous disappointment, for I had thought to have our man. I was still certain he was holding something back. Mark's words came back to mind and surely they were true: Gabriel had nothing about him of the brutal savage our murderer must be. Savage, I thought; where had I had heard that term before? I remembered; it was how Goodwife Stumpe had described Prior Mortimus.

The bells began their clangour; the monks would be in service now for an hour. At least, I reflected, that would provide an opportunity to do what Singleton had done, and I myself should have done earlier: investigate the counting house while Brother Edwig was out of the way. Despite my exhaustion and the weight of anxiety upon me, I realized I felt better in myself, less sluggish of mind somehow. I took another dose of Brother Guy's potion.

I made my way quietly down the dim nave, invisible to those chanting behind the rood screen. I put my eye to one of the ornamented gaps in the stone, fashioned to give lay people in the congregation a tantalizing glimpse of the mystery of the Mass being performed on the other side.

Brother Gabriel was conducting, apparently absorbed in the music. I could not but admire the skill with which he led the monks in the chanting of the psalm, their voices rising and falling in harmony as their eyes moved between his directing hands and the service books on their lecterns. The abbot was present, his face sombre in the candlelight. I remembered his last despairing whisper: 'Dissolution.' Looking over the monks I saw Guy and, to my surprise, Jerome next to him, his white Carthusian habit standing out in contrast to the Benedictine black. They must be letting him out for services. As I watched, Brother Guy leaned over and turned a page for the crippled Carthusian. He smiled, and Brother Jerome nodded with thanks. It struck me that the infirmarian, with his austerity and devotion, might be one of the few at Scarnsea of whom Jerome might approve. Were they friends after all? They had not seemed so when I had come upon Guy dressing Jerome's wounds. My eye turned to Prior Mortimus, and I saw he was not chanting, but staring fixedly before him. I remembered he had been horrified, and angered too, at the sight of the girl's body. Brother Edwig, in contrast, was singing lustily, standing between Brother Athelstan and his other assistant, the old man.

'Which of them?' I whispered under my breath. 'Which of them? God, guide my poor brain.' I felt no answering inspiration. Sometimes in those desperate days it seemed God did not hear my prayers. 'Please let there be no more deaths,' I prayed, then silently rose and left the church.

✝

THE CLOISTER YARD was deserted as I inserted the key marked 'Treasury' into the lock of the counting house. The damp chill of the interior made me shiver and I gathered my coat around me. All was as before; the desks, the ledger-lined walls, the chest against the far wall. A candle had been left burning on a table and I took it over to the chest. Selecting another key, I opened it.

The interior was divided into racks filled with bags, each with the denominations of the coins they contained and the totals entered on tags. I took out those containing gold coins; angels, half-angels and nobles. Opening a couple at random, I counted out the coins, checking the marked total. Everything tallied, and the amount recorded in the chest agreed with what the accounts had shown. I closed it. As big a sum here as in any counting house in England, and secure enough, for a monastery was harder to get into and rob than a merchant's strongroom.

I took up the candle and opened the door to the staircase. I paused at the top. The counting house was a little higher than the other buildings and in daylight the window gave a view across the cloister to the fish pond and, beyond that, the marsh. I wondered whether the hand of the Penitent Thief lay down there in the pond; I would know on the morrow.

I unlocked the door to the bursar's private sanctum. Setting the candle on his desk, I began by glancing at some of the ledgers stacked round the walls of the windowless, claustrophobic room; they were routine accounts, going back years. The desk was tidy, papers and quills set out with geometric straightness. Brother Edwig seemed a man obsessed with order and precision.

The desk had two deep drawers. I tried key after key until I found one that would unlock them. The first contained a couple of Latin books, which I lifted out: Thomas Aquinas's *Summa Contra Gentiles* and *Summa Theologica*. I looked at them with distaste; so Brother Edwig had a taste for the old discredited scholasticism of the Italian saint. As though one could prove God's existence by logic, when only faith would answer; but I could imagine Aquinas's desiccated syllogisms appealing to that arid mind.

I replaced the books and unlocked the other drawer. Within was a stack of ledgers laid on top of each other. I smiled grimly; all had blue covers. 'Thank you, Alice,' I breathed. Three or four were like the one he had given me, filled with rough notes and calculations going back several years. One had a wine stain on the cover, but to my disappointment it contained only more jottings. I pulled out the last one, which was also stained. He must have been drinking wine one day, and spilled the flagon. That would have annoyed him, having his pristine books so marked.

The last book contained records of land sales going back over the last five years. My heart began to pound and my body felt suddenly charged with excitement. I laid it on the desk and brought the candle close with a hand that trembled slightly, coughing as the wick smoked. Details of the parcels sold, the buyers, the prices and the dates the documents were sealed. I looked at the most recent. According to the book there had been four large sales in the last year which had not been recorded in the monastery's account books. They totalled nearly a thousand pounds, an enormous sum. One of them, the largest, was to Jerome's relative. I blew out my cheeks. This must be the book Singleton had seen.

I thought a moment, then took a paper and quill from the desk and rapidly copied the entries down. Copynger could be set to confirm these sales had actually taken place. I would have no more of tales of notes and projections; this time I would present Brother Edwig with evidence he could not wriggle away from.

I replaced the books and paced the room slowly, reflecting. Had the bursar and the abbot too, as he had custody of the monastery seal, been engaged in fraud? Surely they must know that if the monastery was surrendered and the Augmentations officials came in, they would be found out. Or could Edwig have gained access to the seal and used it without the abbot's knowledge? It would be easy enough. And where was the money? The proceeds of these sales constituted another half-chestful of gold. I stood looking at the backs of the old ledgers that lined the walls, wondering.

Something caught my eye. The candle flame was flickering. I realized there was a draught behind me; the door had been opened. I turned slowly. Brother Edwig stood in the doorway, staring at me. He cast a quick glance at his desk, which I was glad I had relocked. Then he pressed his palms together and spoke.

'I had n-no idea anyone was here, Commissioner. You startled me.'

'I am surprised you did not call out.'

'I w-was too astonished.'

'I am allowed all access. I decided to have a look at some of these ledgers you have round the walls. I had just begun.' Had he seen me at his desk? No, or I would have felt the draught before.

'I fear those are only old accounts.'

'So I see.'

'I am g-glad to see you, sir,' he said, giving his quick mirthless smile. 'I wanted to ap-pologize for my outburst this morning. I was upset by the ceremony's interruption. I beg you will take no note of w-words spoken in thoughtless heat.'

I replaced the ledger, inclining my head. 'I know many think as you do, even if they do not say it. But you are wrong. Such moneys as go to the Exchequer will be used by the king to benefit the commonwealth.'

'Will they, sir?'

'You think not?'

'In these days when all men are consumed by greed? Is it not said covetousness was never more attacked nor more seductive? His friends will pressure the king for largesse. And who can hold the k-king to account?'

'God. He has placed the welfare of his people in the king's hands.'

'But kings have other p-priorities,' Brother Edwig said. 'Pray do not misunderstand me, I do not criticize King Henry.'

'That would be unwise.'

'I mean k-kings in general. I know how they throw money to the winds. I have seen for myself how it is wasted on armies, for example.'

There was an animated light in his eyes that I had never seen before, an eagerness to talk that made him appear at once more human.

'Have you?' I encouraged him. 'How is that, Brother?'

'My father was an army paymaster, sir. I spent my childhood as a camp-follower while I learned his trade. I was with King Henry's army in the war against France twenty years ago.'

'When the Spanish king deceived him, promising support and then abandoning him?'

He nodded. 'And all done for the sake of g-glory and conquest. I saw the armies rampaging through France, I s-spent my childhood looking at dead soldiers laid out in rows in camp, sir, their bodies going green, prisoners hanged at the g-gate. I was at the siege of Therouanne.'

'Warfare is a terrible thing,' I agreed. 'For all that many say it is noble.'

He nodded vigorously. 'And always the priests moved among the wounded, giving unction, trying to mend what man had torn as-s-sunder. I decided then to become a monk, put my f-figuring skills at the service of the Church.' He smiled again and this time it was a smile with life in it, a wry smile. 'People say I am mean, do they not?'

I shrugged.

'To me, every groat that goes to the Ch-Church is won for God from the sinful world. Can you understand that? It goes to support prayer and charity. But for what we give them the p-poor would have nothing. We *have* to give alms, because of our faith.'

'And for kings it is a choice, one they may choose not to make?'

'Just so. And the payment we receive for Masses for the dead, sir. It is good in God's eyes, it helps the dead in purgatory and brings merit for the giver.'

'Purgatory again. You believe in it?'

He nodded vigorously. 'It is a real place, sir, we disregard it at the peril of many pains to come. And does it not make sense, that God weighs up our merits and sins and casts us in the balance as I balance my accounts?'

'So God is a great figurer?'

He nodded. 'The greatest of all. Purgatory is real; it lies beneath our feet as we stand. Have you not heard of the great volcanoes in Italy, where purgatory's fires spew out on the land?'

'Do you fear it?'

He nodded slowly. 'I believe we should all fear it.' He paused, collecting himself and eyeing me carefully. 'Forgive me, but the Ten Articles do not deny purgatory.'

'No indeed. What you have said is permissible. And interesting. But were you not also implying just now that the king might not act responsibly in his headship of the Church?'

'I told you, sir, I s-spoke only of kings in general, and I said the Church, not the pope. With respect, m-my views are not heretical.'

'All right. Tell me, with your background in the army, would you know how to use a sword?'

'Such as killed the commissioner?'

I raised my eyebrows.

'I guessed that was how it was done when I heard how the body looked on my return from the estates. I saw enough men beheaded when I was young. But I forswore that world as soon as I reached manhood. I had seen more than enough blood by then.'

'The life of a monk has its drawbacks though, does it not? The vow of celibacy, for example, that must be hard.'

His composure faltered. 'W-what do you mean?'

'As well as the death of the commissioner I now have to investigate the death of a young girl.' I told him whose body was found in the pond. 'Your name was given, among others, as one who had behaved improperly towards her.'

He sat down at the desk, bowing his head so I could not see his face. 'Celibacy is hard,' he said quietly. 'D-do not think I relish the urges that come over me, as some do. I hate these d-devilish passions. They tear down the edifice of a holy life it takes such labour to build. Yes, sir, I w-wanted the girl. It is as w-well I am a timid man: each time she gave me harsh words I went away. But I would come back. She seemed to tempt me just as the lust for glory tempts men to war.'

'*She* tempted *you*?'

'She could not do otherwise. She was a woman, and what are women on earth for if not to tempt men?' He took a deep breath. 'D-did she kill herself?'

'No. Her neck was broken.'

He shook his head. 'Sh-she should n-never have been allowed here. Women are the D-Devil's instruments.'

'Brother Edwig,' I said quietly. 'You may call yourself timid, but I think perhaps you are the hardest man here. And now I will leave you, you will have figuring to do.'

✠

I STOOD OUTSIDE on the landing, collecting my thoughts. I had been certain Gabriel was the murderer and had killed in hot passion. But if the book I had found was the same one Singleton had uncovered then Brother Edwig had a clear motive for my predecessor's death. Yet Singleton had been killed in a passion, and I could see no passion in the bursar save for figuring and money, though a fraud he almost certainly was. And he had not been at Scarnsea that night.

As I turned to the stairs, a light on the marsh caught my attention. I made out two yellow flickers, far out on the mire they seemed. I remembered reflecting there would be half a chestful of gold in those land sales, and that Brother Edwig had come upon me the day I went out on the marsh. And if one wanted to move gold, who better to turn to than professional smugglers? I caught my breath and hurried back to the infirmary.

✠

ALICE WAS SEATED in the prior's kitchen, cutting the roots from some herb. She looked at me with sharp hostility for a second, then forced her features into a smile.

'Preparing one of Brother Guy's potions?'

'Yes, sir.'

'Is Master Mark returned?'

'In your room, sir.'

The hostility in her aloof courtesy saddened me. Mark, then, had told her what I had said to him.

'I have been at the counting house. I saw lights out on the marsh from an upper window. I wondered whether the smugglers may be busy again.'

'I do not know, sir.'

'You told Master Mark you would show us the trackways.'

'Yes, sir.' Her voice was wary.

'I would be interested to see them. I wonder if you would take me tomorrow.'

She hesitated. 'I have duties for Brother Guy, sir.'

'If I were to speak to him?'

'As you instruct.'

'And — there are one or two matters I would like to talk to you about, Alice. I would be your friend, you know.'

She looked away. 'If Brother Guy says I should accompany you, then of course I will.'

'Then I will ask him,' I replied in a tone as cold as hers. I felt hurt and angry as I went along the corridor to our room, where Mark stood looking gloomily out of the window.

'I have asked Alice to show me the paths through the marsh,' I said without preliminary. 'I saw lights there just now. I see from her manner you have told her what I said about leaving her alone.'

'I have told her you think it unseemly that we associate.'

I took off my coat and flung myself into the chair. 'So it is,' I said. 'Have you given the abbot my orders?'

'Commissioner Singleton's grave will be cleaned tomorrow and then the pond drained.'

'I would like you there. I will go out on the marsh with Alice alone. And before you say something you might regret, I have asked her to do this because I think those smugglers may matter to our

enquiry after all. And then I am going to the town, to see Copynger.'
I told him what I had found in Brother Edwig's office.

'I wish I were among ordinary people again,' he said, avoiding
my eye. 'Everywhere you turn here you seem to find a rogue or a
thief.'

'Have you thought any more on what we said, about what you
will do when we return to London?'

'No, sir.' He shrugged. 'There are rogues and thieves aplenty there
too.'

'Then perhaps you should live in the trees, among the birds, so
that you are not soiled by contact with the world,' I said curtly. 'And
now I will take some more of Brother Guy's good potion and sleep
till dinner. This has been as long and hard a day as any I have
known.'

Chapter Twenty-three

SUPPER IN THE REFECTORY that night was a subdued affair. The abbot called on everyone to observe silence during the meal, enjoining them to pray for the soul of what he called the unknown person whose body had been found in the pond. The monks wore strained, worried expressions and I caught many fearful, anxious looks cast at me. It was as though the sense of dissolution the abbot had mentioned was already starting to pervade the entire monastery.

Mark and I walked back to the infirmary in silence; we were both exhausted, but also I sensed once again the distance that had come on Mark since I forbade him to court Alice. When we regained our room I threw myself down on my cushioned chair, while Mark put some more logs on the fire. I had told him of my encounter with Brother Edwig. My head was still abuzz with it.

'If I set Copynger about his enquiries tomorrow morning we should have an answer the day after. If even one of those land sales is confirmed, we have Edwig for fraud. And it gives him a clear motive for murder.'

Mark sat down on a pile of cushions opposite, his face alive with interest. Whatever our quarrels, he was as eager as I to catch our murderer. I wanted to test my thoughts against his wits, and also it was cheering to hear him talk enthusiastically again.

'We always come back, sir, to the fact he was away. Away when Singleton found the book and away when, the same night, he was murdered.'

'I know. Only Athelstan knew and he said he told no one else.'

'Could Athelstan be the killer?'

'Him strike off a man's head, a commissioner? No. Remember how frightened he was when he approached me to offer himself as an informer. He hasn't the courage to defy a mouse.'

'Is that not an emotional reaction to his personality?' There was a note of sarcasm in Mark's voice.

'All right. Perhaps I was carried away with the logical edifice I had built when I accused Gabriel. Yet it all seemed to fit so well. But yes, of course we must take our judgement of men's characters into account and Athelstan's is palpably weak.'

'And why should he care if Brother Edwig goes to the gallows, or even if the monastery goes down? He is hardly devout.'

'And how could he have come by that sword? I wish I could trace its history; in London I could probably discover the maker through his mark. The swordsmiths' guild would know. But we're trapped down here by this snow.'

'Sir, what if Singleton told someone else what he had found in the counting house and they decided to kill him? The abbot, perhaps. His seal would be on those deeds.'

'Yes. A seal he leaves lying on his desk, where anybody could use it while he was away.'

'Prior Mortimus, then? He's brutal enough for murder, surely? And isn't it said that he and Brother Edwig run the place?'

'Those two in a fraud together? I wonder. I must get that answer from Copynger.' I sighed. 'How long is it since we set out from London? A week? It seems a lifetime.'

'Just six days.'

'I wish I had time to go back. But even sending a message would take days in this snow. Pox on it, is it going to go on for ever?'

'It seems so.'

✝

SHORTLY AFTER Mark got into his little wheeled cot and pulled it back under my bed. I sat on, staring into the banked-up fire. Through windows already frosting again with ice I heard the bells ring out for

Compline. Whatever happened, whatever nightmares unfolded, the services still went on.

I thought of Lord Cromwell, waiting in London for my reply. I must try to send a message soon, even if it were only to say I had no answers and two more murders to solve. I could imagine his angry face, his oaths, his wondering again about my loyalty. But if Copynger confirmed the land sales I could have Brother Edwig arrested for fraud. I had a vision of myself interrogating him in Scarnsea gaol, manacled in some dark hole, and found the thought gave me pleasure. That disturbed me and I reflected how dislike of a man and the prospect of power over him led the mind into unpleasant paths. Guilt stole over me and I began thinking once more about Mark and Alice. How pure were my motives there? All I had said to Mark about the difference in their degree, and his obligation to his family to succeed, was true. Yet I knew the worm of jealousy stirred in me. The sight of them embracing in the kitchen came back to me and I clenched my eyes shut as another vision stirred in the corner of my mind's eye, of Alice embracing me instead of him. All the time I could hear Mark's breathing, which had deepened into sleep.

I prayed that God might lead my actions into a true and just path; a path such as Christ might have followed. Then I must have slept for the next thing I knew I had started awake and was staring at a dead fire. Hours must have passed; my back ached and I was chilled to the bone. I rose painfully from the chair, undressed and climbed wearily into bed.

✝

I FELL AT ONCE into a deep sleep and woke next morning more rested than for a week past. Brother Guy's prescription was doing me good. After breakfast I wrote a letter to Justice Copynger and gave it to Mark.

'Take this into Scarnsea now. Ask Copynger if he can get a reply to me by tomorrow.'

'I thought you wished to see him yourself.'

'I want to go out on the marsh while the weather holds.' I looked up at the sky, which was dark with clouds again. 'Tell the abbot the cleaning of Singleton's grave can be done when you return. Are arrangements in place to drain the pond?'

'They have a sump they can drain the stream into. Apparently they clear out the silt every ten years or so.'

'When was it last done?'

'Three years ago.'

'So that body would have lain undisturbed for many years yet. And yet not for ever.'

'Maybe the murderer needed to get rid of it quickly.'

'Yes. And then it would be hard to get out again.'

'No need to go to the church now.'

'No, let's get the pond drained first. You will have a busy day,' I added in an effort at cheerfulness. But that very effort seemed to make him close in on himself again. 'Yes, sir,' he said quietly and left the room.

I read more routine correspondence which the abbot's servant brought, then went in search of Alice. I felt a mixture of nervousness and excitement, like a boy, at the thought of seeing her. Brother Guy told me she was hanging herbs in the drying house and would be free shortly, so I went into the courtyard to see how the weather was faring. The clouds were high and I hoped we might escape more snow. I shivered at the endless cold.

My attention was drawn by raised voices. By the gatehouse I saw two figures struggling, one dressed in black and the other in white. I hurried over. Jerome was in the grasp of Prior Mortimus, who had him in a firm grip. He was trying to seize a paper Jerome held tightly in one hand. Despite his disabilities, the Carthusian was putting up a fierce struggle. Nearby Bugge was holding a squirming small boy by the collar.

'Give me that, ye whoreson!' the prior growled. Jerome tried to stuff the paper in his mouth, but the prior hooked a foot beneath his good leg and he toppled over, landing on his back in the snow. Prior

Mortimus reached down, tore the paper from his hand and stood breathing heavily.

'What is this tumult?' I demanded.

Before the prior could answer, Jerome hauled himself up on his elbow and spat at him, a gobbet of spittle landing on his habit. He exclaimed in disgust and launched a sudden kick at the Carthusian's ribs. The old man fell back with a yell to lie shrieking in the churned-up snow. Prior Mortimus held up a letter.

'See, Commissioner, I caught him trying to smuggle this out!'

I took it and read the superscription. 'It's addressed to Sir Thomas Seymour!'

'Is he not one of the king's council?'

'He is, and the late queen's brother.' With a glance at Jerome, who lay glaring up at us like a wild beast, I tore it open. A chill ran down my spine as I read. It addressed Seymour as cousin, referred to his imprisonment in a corrupt house where a king's commissioner had been murdered, and said there was a story he should know, of ill deeds by Lord Cromwell. He then went on to repeat the story of his encounter in prison with Mark Smeaton, and the musician's torture by Cromwell.

I am now confined here by another of Cromwell's commissioners, a grim-faced hunchback. I tell you this story now in the hope you may use it against Cromwell, that tool of the Antichrist. The people hate him and will hate him more when this is known.

I crumpled the paper in my hand. 'How did he get out?'

'He disappeared after Prime and I came looking for him. Meanwhile our good Bugge was visited by this boy from the poorhouse, saying he had come to fetch a message from one of the monks. Bugge was suspicious and wouldn't let him in.' The gate-keeper nodded in satisfaction, grinding his knuckles into the urchin's collar. He had ceased his struggles and was staring in astonished terror at Jerome lying on the snow.

'Who sent you here?' I asked him.

'A servant brought a note, sir,' he answered tremulously, 'asking me to take a letter for the London post.'

'I found this on him,' Bugge said. He opened his free hand, which held a gold ring.

'Yours?' I asked Jerome. He turned his head away.

'Which servant, boy? Answer, you are in serious trouble.'

'Mister Grindstaff, sir, from the kitchen. The ring was to pay me and the post coach.'

'Grindstaff!' the prior snorted. 'He takes Jerome his food, he's always been against the changes. I'll put him out on the road tonight – unless you'd take harsher measures, Commissioner?'

I shook my head. 'Make sure Jerome is kept locked in his cell all the time. You should not have let him out for services – see what has come of it!' I turned to Bugge. 'Let the boy go.'

Bugge hauled the urchin to the gate and shoved him out on the road with a cuff.

'Get up, you,' Prior Mortimus snapped at Jerome.

He tried to struggle up, but fell back. 'I can't, you unchristian churl.'

'Help him,' I ordered Bugge. 'Lock him in his cell.' The gatekeeper hauled Jerome to his feet and led him roughly away.

'Cromwell has many enemies!' Jerome shouted at me over his shoulder. 'His just end will come!'

I turned to the prior. 'Have you an office we can go to?'

He led me through the inner cloister to a room with a warm fire. A jug of wine stood on a paper-strewn desk and he poured us each a cup.

'Is this the first time Jerome has disappeared after a service?'

'Yes. He is always watched.'

'Is there any chance he could have sent another letter out before today?'

'Not since he was confined, the day you came. But before – yes.'

I nodded, biting a fingernail. 'He must be guarded closely from now on. This letter is a serious matter. It should be reported to Lord Cromwell at once.'

He gave me a calculating look. 'Would ye perhaps tell Lord Cromwell that a monk loyal to the king stopped the letter going?'

'We'll see.' I looked at him coldly. 'There was another matter I wanted to discuss with you. Orphan Stonegarden.'

He nodded slowly. 'Aye, I'd heard questions were being asked.'

'Well? Your name has been mentioned.'

He shrugged. 'Even old celibates get lusty. She was a fine-looking girl. I tried to get her to romp with me, I'll not deny it.'

'You who are charged with keeping discipline in this house, and told me yesterday that discipline is all that keeps the world from chaos?'

He stirred uneasily in his chair. 'A tumble with a warm girl's a different matter from unnatural passions that rot the relations monks should have with each other,' he said sharply. 'I'm not perfect, nobody is except the saints and not all of them.'

'Some would say, Prior Mortimus, those words make you a hypocrite.'

'Oh come, Commissioner, aren't all men hypocrites? I wished the girl no harm. She rejected me quickly enough, and that old pederast Alexander reported me to the abbot. I felt sorry for her afterwards,' he added in a quieter voice, 'drifting about the place like a wraith. I never talked to her again, though.'

'Did anyone take her by force, that you know of? Goodwife Stumpe believes someone did.'

'No.' His face darkened. 'I wouldn't have stood for that.' He let out a long breath. 'It was bad, seeing her yesterday. I knew her at once.'

'So did Goodwife Stumpe.' I folded my arms. 'Brother Prior, your fine feelings amaze me. I can hardly believe this is the same man I saw kick a cripple not half an hour ago.'

'A man's place in the world is hard, a monk's most of all. He has obligations set by God, and fierce temptations to resist. Women – they're different, they deserve a peaceful life if they behave. Orphan was a good girl, not like that malapert Guy has working for him now.'

'She too had an approach from you, I hear.'

He was silent a moment. 'I wasn't fierce with her, y'know. Orphan. When she turned me away I didn't press her.'

'But others did. Brother Luke.' I paused. 'Brother Edwig.'

'Aye. Brother Alexander reported them too – though his own greater sins were to find him out,' he added maliciously. 'The abbot dealt with Brother Luke and told Brother Edwig to leave her be. And me as well. He doesn't often give me orders but he did then.'

'They tell me, you know, that you and Brother Edwig run this place.'

'Someone has to, Abbot Fabian's always been more interested in hunting with the local gentry. We see to the dull things that keep the monastery going.'

I wondered whether to mention the monastery's financial affairs, or land sales in general, to see how he reacted. But no, I should not warn any of them till I had evidence to hand.

'I never believed she'd stolen those cups and run away, you know,' he said quietly.

'You told Goodwife Stumpe she had.'

'It was how it looked, and it was the line Abbot Fabian told us to take – he bestirred himself over that. I hope ye find who put her in there,' he added grimly. 'When ye do I wouldn't mind five minutes alone with them myself.'

I stared at his face, full of righteous anger. 'I imagine you would enjoy that,' I said coldly. 'And now you must excuse me, I am late for an appointment.'

✝

ALICE WAS WAITING in the infirmary kitchen, a pair of stout overshoes on her feet and an old wool coat beside her. 'You need something warmer than that,' I said. 'It will be cold out there.'

'It will suffice,' she said, wrapping it round her. 'It was my mother's and it warmed her for thirty winters.'

We set out for the gate in the rear wall, following the path Mark and I had taken the day before. I was disconcerted to realize she was a good inch taller than me. Most men are, because of my bent back, but usually I can look women in the eye. I pondered on what it was that had attracted both Mark and me to Alice, for she was no conventional beauty, demure and pale. But simpering blonde maids had never attracted me; it was the spark of one strong spirit meeting another I had always yearned for. My heart lurched anew at the realization.

We passed Singleton's grave, still stark brown against the whiteness. Alice was as distant and uncommunicative as Mark had been. It made me angry to be confronted with this silent insolence again, and I wondered whether it was a tactic they had agreed between them, or whether it came to each naturally. But then the ways of expressing discontent to those in power are limited.

As we ploughed through the orchard, where today a flock of starveling crows sat cawing in the trees, I tried to make conversation. I asked how she had come to pass her childhood playing around the marsh.

'Two little boys lived in the cottage next to ours. Brothers, Noel and James. We used to play together. Their family had been fishermen for generations; they knew all the paths through the marsh, all the landmarks that keep you on firm ground. Their father was a smuggler as well as a fisherman. They're all dead now, their ship was lost in a great storm five years ago.'

'I am sorry.'

'It's what fishermen have to expect.' She turned to me, a spark of animation entering her voice. 'If folk do take treated cloth to France and bring back wine, it's only because they're poor.'

'I have no interest in prosecuting anybody, Alice. I merely wonder whether some moneys that may be unaccounted for, and perhaps the lost relic, could be taken out that way.'

We arrived opposite the fish pond. A little way off some servants, supervised by a monk, were working by a little lock gate in the stream, and I saw the water level in the pond had already fallen.

'Brother Guy told me about that poor girl,' Alice said, wrapping her coat around her more tightly. 'He said she did my work before I came.'

'Yes, she did. But the poor creature had no friends apart from Simon Whelplay. You have people who will guard you.' I saw anxiety in her eyes and smiled reassuringly. 'Come, there is the gate. I have a key.'

We went through, and again I stood looking over the white expanse of the marsh, the river in the distance and the little knoll with the ruined buildings halfway between.

'I nearly fell in the first time I came out here,' I observed. 'Are you sure there is a safe way? I don't see how you can descry landmarks when everything is covered in snow.'

She pointed. 'See those banks of tall reeds? It's a question of finding the right ones, and keeping them at the right distance from you. It's not all marsh, there are firmer patches, and the patterns of the reeds are their signposts.' She stepped from the path and tested the ground. 'There will be a frozen crust in places; you have to take care not to step through.'

'I know. That is what I did last time.' I hesitated on the bank and smiled nervously. 'You have the life of a king's commissioner in your hands.'

'I will take care, sir.' She walked back and forth along the path a few times, judging where we should cross and then, bidding me walk exactly in her footprints, stepped down onto the marsh.

✠

SHE LED THE WAY slowly and steadily, pausing often to take bearings. I admit my heart pounded at first; I looked back, conscious of our growing distance from the monastery wall, the impossibility of help if one fell in. But Alice seemed confident. Sometimes when I stepped in her tracks the ground was firm, at others oily black water seeped in to fill the depressions. Our progress seemed slow and I was surprised when, looking up, I saw we were almost at the knoll, the ruins of tumbled stone only fifty yards away. Alice stopped.

'We need to go up on the knoll, then another path leads down to the river. It is more dangerous on that side, though.'

'Well, let us get to the knoll at least.'

A few moments later we stepped up onto firm ground. The knoll was only a few feet above the level of the bog, but from there I had a clear view both back to the monastery and down to the river, still and grey. The sea was visible in the distance and a cutting breeze gave the air a salty tang.

'So smugglers would take their contraband this way?'

'Yes, sir. A few years ago the revenue men from Rye chased some smugglers out there, but they lost their way. Two men went down in seconds, vanished without trace.' I followed her gaze out over the white expanse and shivered, then looked around the knoll. It was smaller than I had expected, the ruined buildings little more than heaps of stone. One, though roofless, was more complete than the rest and I saw the remains of a fire, a bare patch in the snow covered with ashes.

'People have been here very recently,' I said, turning over the ashes. I poked around the site with my staff, half hoping to find the relic or a chest of gold hidden away, but there was nothing. Alice stood watching me silently.

I went back to her and stood looking around. 'The first monks must have had a harsh life. I wonder why they came here; for security perhaps.'

'They say the marsh has risen gradually as the river mouth has silted up. Perhaps it wasn't marsh then, just a point near the river.' She did not sound much interested.

'This scene would make an arresting painting. I paint, you know, when I have time.'

'I have only seen the paintings on the glass in the church. The colours are pretty, but the figures always seem unreal somehow.'

I nodded. 'That's because they're not in proportion and there's no sense of distance, perspective. But painters now try to show things as they are, to show reality.'

'Do they, sir?' Her voice was still cool, distant. I cleared the snow from a patch of ancient wall and sat down.

'Alice, I would like to talk with you. About Master Mark.'

Her look at me was bleak.

'I know he has formed an attachment to you, and I believe it is an honourable one.'

At once she became animated. 'Then why, sir, do you forbid him to see me?'

'Mark's father is the steward of my father's farmlands. Not that my father is rich, but I have been lucky to make my way, through the law, into the service of Lord Cromwell himself.' I thought to impress her, but her expression did not change.

'My father gave his word to Mark's that I would try to advance the boy in London. I have done that; not alone, his own good mind and fair manner have played their part.' I coughed delicately. 'Unfortunately there was some trouble. He had to leave his post—'

'I know about the lady-in-waiting, sir. He has told me all.'

'Oh. Has he? Then don't you see, Alice, he has a last chance with this mission to return to favour. If he takes it he could advance himself further, have a secure and wealthy future, but he will have to find a wife of rank. Alice, you are a fine girl. If you were a London merchant's daughter, it would be another matter. Why, if that were so, you might find me as a suitor as well as Mark.' I had not meant to say that, but it came in a sudden rush of feeling. She frowned, her face uncomprehending. Had she not realized? I took a deep breath. 'In any event, if Mark is to advance, he cannot go wooing a servant. It is hard, but it is how society works.'

'Then society is wicked,' she said with sudden cold anger. 'I have thought so for a long time.'

I stood up. 'It is the world God has made for us, for weal or woe we must live in it. Would you hold Mark back, prevent his advancement? If you encourage him, that is what will happen.'

'I would do nothing to hinder him,' she said hotly. 'I would do nothing against his wishes.'

'But he may wish for something that would hinder him.'

'It is for him to say. Though, if we are not to speak, he can say nothing.'

'Would you spoil his chances? Really?'

She studied me closely, so closely I felt uneasy as I never had in my life under a woman's look. At length she gave a heavy sigh. 'Sometimes it seems all those I love are to be taken from me. But perhaps that is a servant's lot,' she added bitterly.

'Mark said you had a swain, a woodsman who died in an accident.'

'If he had not I would be secure in Scarnsea, for landlords do nothing but cut down woods these days. Instead I am in this place.' Tears appeared in the corners of her eyes and angrily she wiped them aside. I would fain have held her to me and comforted her, but I knew it was not my arms she wanted.

'I am sorry. It is in the world's nature that often we lose those we love. Alice, it may be the monastery has little future now. What if I were to try and find a post for you in the town, through Justice Copynger? I may be seeing him tomorrow. You should not be here, where these terrible things are happening.'

She wiped her eyes and gave me a strange look, full of feeling. 'Yes, I have learned here the depths of violence in mankind. It is a frightening thing.' I see that look before me now as I write, and shiver at the memory of what was to come.

'Let me help you away from it.'

'Perhaps, sir, though it will be hard to pay that man respect.'

'I understand. But, I must say again, it is the way of the world.'

'I am afraid here now. Even Mark is fearful.'

'Yes. And so am I.'

'Sir, Brother Guy said some other things were found in the pond as well as the girl's body. May I ask what they were?'

'Only a robe, which seems not to hold the clue I hoped for, and a sword. I am having the pond drained to see what else may be there.'

'A sword?'

'Yes. I believe the one that killed Commissioner Singleton. It had a maker's mark that should make it possible to trace, but I would need to go to London to follow that up.'

'Don't go, sir, please,' she said with sudden feeling. 'Don't leave us. Sir, I beg forgiveness if I have been impertinent with you, but please do not go. It is only your presence here that ensures my protection.'

'I think you exaggerate my powers,' I said gloomily. 'I could not save Simon Whelplay. But I do not see how I could get there in this snow without taking a week upon the road, and I do not have that amount of time.'

Her face filled with relief. I ventured to lean over and pat her arm. 'It touches me that you have such faith in me.'

She withdrew her arm, but smiled. 'Perhaps you have too little faith in yourself, sir. Perhaps in other circumstances, without Mark—' She left the sentence unfinished, lowering her head demurely. I confess my heart was thudding. We stood on the knoll in silence for a moment.

'I think we should go back now,' I said, 'rather than try to reach the river. I am expecting a message from the Justice. And, Alice, I will do something for you, I promise. And — thank you for your words.'

'And you for your help.' She smiled quickly, then turned and led the way back down to the bog. The return journey was easier; we had only to step in the footprints made earlier. Following behind her, I gazed at the back of her neck, and once I nearly reached out and touched it. I reflected that it was not just monks who made fools of themselves and could easily turn into hypocrites.

An awkwardness had descended on me, and we said little on the way back. But at least it felt a warmer silence than on the way out. At the infirmary hall Alice left me, saying she had duties to attend to. Brother Guy was dressing the fat monk's leg. He looked up.

'You have returned? You look cold.'

'I am. Alice was very helpful, I am grateful for her assistance.'

'How is your sleep?'

'Much improved, thanks to your good potion. Have you seen Mark?'

'I passed him a few moments ago. He went into your room. Take the potion a few more days,' he called after me as I left the hall, trying to decide whether to tell Mark of my talk with Alice. I reached our room and opened the door.

'Mark, I have been out—' I broke off, staring round. The room was empty. And then came a voice, from the empty air it seemed.

'Sir! Help me!'

Chapter Twenty-four

'**H**ELP!' There was an edge of panic in Mark's muffled voice, which to my confused mind seemed to issue from empty space. Then I saw the cupboard had been pulled out a little. Peering behind, I saw a door in the panelled wall. With difficulty, I dragged the cupboard out.

'Mark! Are you in there?'

'I'm shut in! Open it, sir! Quick, he may come back!'

I twisted the handle, which was old and rusty. There was a click and the door opened, letting out a draught of dank air. Mark shot from the darkness, dusty and dishevelled. I stared into the blackness a moment, then back at him.

'God's flesh, what has happened? Who may come back?'

He took deep whooping breaths. 'I closed the door behind me when I went in, then found it couldn't be opened from inside. I was trapped. There's a spyhole there; someone *was* spying on us earlier. I saw you come through it and called out.'

'Tell me what happened, from the beginning.' At least, I thought, he had been shocked out of his sulk. He sat down on the bed.

'After you left, I spoke to Prior Mortimus about clearing the pond. They are draining it now.'

'Yes, I saw that.'

'I came back here to fetch my overshoes. While I was putting them on I heard sounds again.' He looked at me boldly. 'I knew I was right.'

'Your ears are sharper than your wits to shut yourself up like that. Go on.'

'It always seemed to come from the cupboard. I thought to pull it out to see what lay behind and found that door. I went inside with a candle. There is a passageway and I was going to find where it led. I closed the door lest someone come in, but as I pulled it shut the draught blew out the candle and left me in darkness. I put my shoulder to the door, but it wouldn't budge.' He reddened. 'It unmanned me. I hadn't my sword. But without the candle I could see a pinpoint of light — there's a spyhole there, cut in the panelling.' He pointed to a tiny hole in the wall. I stood up and inspected it: from the inner side it looked like a nail hole.

'How long were you shut up?'

'Not long. By God's mercy you were only a few minutes. Did you go on the marsh?'

'Yes. There have been smugglers out there — we found a fire. I had a talk with Alice, we will speak of it later.' I lit two candles from the fire and passed him one. 'Well, shall we try this passage again?'

He took a deep breath. 'Yes, sir.'

I locked the door of our room against intruders, then we squeezed behind the cupboard and opened the door. Within lay a dark, narrow corridor.

'Brother Guy said there was a connecting passage from the infirmary to the kitchen,' I said, remembering. 'Closed off at the time of the Great Pestilence.'

'This has been used much more recently.'

'Yes.' Within I could see a pinpoint of light where the spyhole had been cut through the wooden panelling. 'This gives a clear view of the room. It looks recently cut.'

'Brother Guy chose our room for us.'

'Yes. Where anyone could spy on us, overhear us.' I turned to the door. It had the type of latch that can be opened from the outside only. 'Let us make safe this time.' I pushed it almost shut, but inserted my handkerchief into the gap to prevent it closing on us.

We made our way up the passage. It was narrow, running parallel with the wall of the infirmary building. One side was formed by the wood panelling of the infirmary rooms, the other by the stone of the claustral buildings. The remnants of rusty torch brackets lined the damp walls. It was evidently long disused – it stank of damp and strange bulbous mushrooms grew in corners. After a short distance the passage took a right angle, then opened into a chamber. We stepped in and cast our light around.

We were in a prison cell, square and windowless. Ancient leg-irons were fastened to the wall, and a heap of mouldy cloth and wood in one corner indicated the remains of a bed. I cast my light over the walls. Words were scratched all over the stone. I read one deeply indented row of letters. *Frater Petrus tristissimus. Anno 1339.* 'Brother Peter the most sad. I wonder what he did.'

'There's a way out,' Mark said, crossing to a heavy wooden door. I bent to the keyhole. There was no light from the other side. I put my ear to the door, but could hear nothing.

Slowly I turned the handle. The door opened quietly inwards and I saw the hinges had been greased. We came out behind another cupboard, which had been pushed just far enough from the wall to let a man squeeze through. We went out and found ourselves in a stone-flagged corridor. A little way off was a door, half-open. I heard a murmur of voices, plates clinking.

'It's the kitchen passage,' I breathed. 'Back inside, quick, before someone sees us.'

I squeezed in again after Mark, and bent to close the door, coughing a little in the damp air. Suddenly a hand was clamped over my mouth, and I froze as another pressed on my hump. The candles were extinguished. Then Mark whispered in my ear.

'Quiet, sir. Someone's coming!'

I nodded, and he lowered his hands. I could hear nothing; he had indeed the ears of a bat. A moment later the glow of a candle appeared round the corner and a figure followed; robed and cowled, staring into the prison room from a gaunt, dark face. Brother Guy's candle picked out our figures in the corner and he started.

'Jesu save us, what are you doing here?'

I stepped forward. 'We might ask you the same question, Brother. How did you get in here? We locked our door.'

'And I unlocked it. I had a message the pond was emptied and came to call you, but there was no reply. For all I knew you'd both dropped dead, so I let myself in with my key and saw that open door.'

'Master Poer has heard someone behind the wall several times, and this morning he found the door. We have been spied on, Brother Guy. You gave us a room with a hidden passage behind. Why? And why did you not tell me there was an open way from the infirmary to the kitchens?' My voice was harsh. I had begun to see Brother Guy as something like a friend in that place. I cursed myself for allowing myself to become close to a man who, when all was said and done, was still a suspect.

His face set. The candlelight flickered strangely over his long nose and narrow dark features. 'I had forgotten that door was in your room. Sir, this passage hasn't been in use for nearly two hundred years.'

'It was used this morning! And you gave us the one room where a spyhole could be cut in the wall!'

'It is not the only room,' he said calmly. His gaze was level, the candle held in a steady hand. 'Did you not see? This passage runs behind the panelling of the infirmary wall, behind all the rooms on that corridor.'

'But there is a spyhole only behind ours. Are visitors normally put in our room?'

'Those who do not stay with the abbot. Usually messengers, or officials from our estates come to discuss business.'

I waved my hand around the dank little cell. 'And what in God's name is this horrible place?'

He sighed. 'This is the old monks' prison. Most houses have them; in years gone by abbots used to imprison brethren who had sinned grievously. In canon law they still have the power, though it's never used.'

'No, not in these soft times.'

'Prior Mortimus asked a few months ago whether the old cell still existed; he was talking of bringing it back into use for punishment. I told him so far as I knew it did. I haven't been here since an old servant showed it to me when I took over as infirmarian. I thought the door was sealed off.'

'Well, it wasn't. So Prior Mortimus asked about it, did he?'

'He did.' His voice hardened. 'I would have thought you would have approved, the vicar general seems to want our life to be hard and cruel as can be.'

I let a moment's silence fall between us. 'Be careful what you say before witnesses, Brother.'

'Yes. It is a world full of new marvels, where the king of England will hang a man for speaking words.' He made an effort to collect himself. 'I am sorry. But Master Shardlake, for all that yesterday we had a scholarly discussion about the new ways, there is a weight of fear and anxiety on everyone here. I only want to live in peace, Commissioner. We all do.'

'Not all, Brother. Someone could have come through this passage to the kitchen to kill Commissioner Singleton. It means they would not have needed a key to get to the kitchen. Yes, of course — that makes the kitchen the ideal place for someone to arrange to meet him, lie in wait and murder him.'

'Alice and I were up all that night tending old Brother James. No one could have come past us without being seen.'

I took his candle and held it up to his face. 'But you could have done it, Brother.'

'I swear by Our Lord's holy blood I did not,' he said passionately. 'I am a physician, my oath is to preserve life, not take it.'

'Who else knew of the passage? You said the prior spoke of it. When?'

He put a hand to his brow. 'He raised it at an obedientiaries' meeting. I was there, the abbot, Prior Mortimus, Brother Edwig and Brother Gabriel. Brother Jude the pittancer was there too and Brother

Hugh the chamberlain. Prior Mortimus was talking as usual of how discipline needed to be stronger. He said he'd heard tell of an old monk's cell somewhere behind the infirmary. He was half-joking, I think.'

'Who else in the monastery might know of it?'

'New novices are told there is an old cell hidden in the precinct, to scare them, but I don't think anyone quite knew where it was. And I had forgotten till you mentioned it the day you came. I told you, I thought it locked up for years!'

'So people knew it existed. What about your friend, Brother Jerome?'

He spread his hands. 'What do you mean? He is not my friend.'

'I saw you helping him yesterday with his book, in service.'

Brother Guy shook his head. 'He is a brother in Christ, and a poor cripple. Has it come to such a pass that to aid a cripple turn the pages of his book becomes the basis of accusations? I had not thought you such a man, Master Shardlake.'

'I seek a murderer, Brother,' I said curtly. 'All the obedentiaries are under my watch, including you. So, anyone at that meeting could have had his memory stirred and decided to go ferreting for this passage.'

'I suppose so.'

I looked round the dank cell again. 'Let us go. This place makes my bones ache.'

We returned up the passage in silence. Brother Guy went out first, and I bent to retrieve my handkerchief. As I did so I saw something glimmering faintly in the candlelight. I scraped the stone flag carefully with a fingernail.

'What's that?' Mark asked.

I held my finger close. 'God's death, so that's what he was about,' I whispered. 'Yes, of course, the library.'

'What is it?'

'Later.' I wiped my hand carefully on my robe. 'Come on, my bones will freeze before I get to sit by a fire today.'

When we regained our room I dismissed Brother Guy, then stood warming my hands at the grate.

'God's nails, that place was cold.'

'It surprised me to hear Brother Guy speak against the vicar general.'

'He spoke against the king's *policy*, but he would have had to speak against his headship of the Church to commit treason. In the heat of the moment he just said what they all think.' I blew out my cheeks. 'No, I found a trail in there, but it leads to someone else.'

'To whom?'

I looked at him, pleased his sulks seemed to be forgotten.

'Later. Come, we must go to the pond before they start emptying it themselves. We need to see if anything else is in there.' We left the room, my mind racing.

✝

WE RETRACED our way through the orchard, to where a little crowd of servants stood by the fish pond, holding long poles. Prior Mortimus was with them. He turned to us.

'The stream's been diverted, Commissioner, and the water drained out. But we'll have to let it through again soon or it'll flood the land by the sump.'

I nodded. The pond was now a deep empty bowl, shards of ice embedded in the thick greyish-brown silt at the bottom. I called over to the servants.

'A shilling for the man who finds anything in there!'

Two servants came forward and hesitantly climbed down into the silt, probing with their poles. At length one of them called out and held something up. Two gold chalices.

'Orphan was supposed to have taken those,' the prior breathed.

I had hoped we might find the relic, but another ten minutes of searching revealed nothing beyond an old sandal. The servants climbed out again, and the man who had found the chalices passed them to me. I gave him his shilling and turned to find the prior looking at them.

'They're the ones, no doubt.' He let out a long breath. 'Commissioner, remember, if you find the man who killed that poor girl, give me some time alone with him.' He turned and walked off. I raised an eyebrow at Mark.

'Does he really feel for her death?' he asked.

'There is no end to the strange depths of the human heart. Come, we must go to the church.'

Chapter Twenty-five

MY LEGS WERE TIRED and my back hurt as yet again we plodded back to the monastery. I envied Mark as he ploughed on energetically, sturdy legs kicking up the snow. When we reached the courtyard I stopped to catch my breath.

'The trail in that room leads us back to Brother Gabriel. It seems he was concealing things after all. Let us go and find him. We'll look for him in the church first. When I talk to him I want you to stand just out of earshot. Don't ask, there is a reason.'

'As you wish, sir.' I could tell he was annoyed by my secrecy, but it was part of the plan I had made. I had been surprised by what I had found in that passage, but I could not help a feeling of satisfaction that my earlier suspicions of Gabriel had not, after all, been groundless. Truly the human heart holds strange and unaccountable depths.

The day was still cloudy and the church interior was dim as we walked down the nave. There was no susurration of prayers from the side chapels; it must have been the monks' recreation time. I made out the figure of Brother Gabriel halfway down the nave. He was supervising a servant polishing a large metal plaque set into the wall.

'The verdigris is coming off.' His deep voice echoed around as we approached. 'Guy's formula works.'

'Brother Gabriel,' I said, 'I fear I am always sending away your servants. But I must talk with you again.'

He sighed and bade the man depart. I read the Latin engraved into the plaque above the figure of a monk lying on a bier.

'So the first abbot is buried there in the wall?'

'Yes. That metalwork is exceptional.' He glanced at Mark, who stood a little way off as I had bid him, then turned back to me. 'Unfortunately it is a copper alloy, but Brother Guy came up with a formula for cleaning it.' He spoke rapidly, his manner nervous.

'You have a busy life, Brother, responsible for the church music and the decoration too.' I looked up at the railed walkway, the statue of Donatus with the tools lying beside it and the workmen's basket secured by its cat's cradle of ropes to the walkway and the bell tower. 'No progress with the works, I see. Are you still negotiating with Brother Edwig?'

'Yes. But surely you have not come to discuss that?' Irritation crept into his voice.

'No, Brother. Yesterday I put a case to you, a lawyer's accusation, you said. An accusation of murder. You said I was building a false picture.'

'Yes, I did. I am no murderer.'

'One thing, though, we haranguing lawyers develop is an instinct as to when people are holding things back. We are seldom wrong.'

He said nothing, eyeing me intently.

'Let me put another case to you, a set of suppositions shall we say, and you can correct me as we proceed if I err. Is that fair?'

'I do not know what trick this is.'

'No trick, I promise. Let me start with a meeting of the obedentiaries a few months ago. Prior Mortimus mentioned the old monks' cell and a passage leading from the infirmary to the kitchen quarters.'

'Yes — yes, I remember it.' He was breathing a little faster now, blinking more often.

'It was never followed up, but I think it rang a bell in your mind. I think you went to the library, where you knew all the old plans of the monastery could be found. I saw them when you showed me the library; I remember then you seemed anxious I should not see them. I think you found the passage, Brother; I think you went in there and bored a spyhole into what is now our room. The kitchener said you had been lurking round the kitchen, where I now know the entrance to the passage is.'

He licked dry lips.

'You do not contradict me, Brother.'

'I – I know nothing of this.'

'No? Mark has heard noises some mornings, and I scoffed at him, saying it was mice. Today, though, he explored our room and found the door and the spyhole. I wondered who had been in there, I even suspected the infirmarian, but then I found something on the floor, under the spyhole. Something that glistened. And I realized that the man who had been looking in at us had not been out to spy. He had a different purpose.'

Brother Gabriel let out a groan that seemed to issue from the depths of his being. He sagged like a puppet with its strings cut.

'You have a love of young men, Brother Gabriel. It must have come to consume you utterly if you would go to such lengths to watch Mark Poer dressing in the morning.'

He swayed and I thought he would fall. He put a hand against the wall to steady himself. His face when he looked at me was first deathly pale, then it reddened with a burning flush.

'It is true,' he whispered. 'Jesu forgive me.'

'God's death, that must have made a strange journey, through that dolorous old cell with your cock swelling in the dark.'

'Please – please.' He raised a hand. 'Don't tell him, don't tell the boy.'

I took a step closer. 'Then tell me all you have been concealing. That passage is a secret way into the kitchen, where my predecessor was murdered.'

'I never wanted to be like this,' he hissed with sudden passion. 'Male beauty has obsessed me so long, since I first saw the image of St Sebastian in our church. My mind fixed on it as those of other boys did on St Agatha's breasts on her statue. But they could turn to matrimony. I was left alone with – this. I came here to escape the temptation.'

'To a monastery?' I asked incredulously.

'Yes.' He laughed, a desolate sound. 'Healthy young men do not become monks these days, or few of them. Mostly it is poor creatures like Simon, who cannot cope with life in the world. I had no lust for Simon, let alone old Alexander. I have sinned with other men but few times these past years, and never since the visitation. With prayer, with work, I have achieved control. But then visitors come, reeves from our lands in the shire, messengers, and I sometimes see – I see a beautiful boy who sets me afire, then I scarce know what I do.'

'And usually visitors are lodged in our room.'

He bowed his head. 'When the prior mentioned the passage I wondered if it might lead behind the visitors' room. You are right, I looked at the plans. God help me, I cut the spyhole to see them in their nakedness.' He looked over at Mark again, this time with a trapped, angry expression. 'Then you came, with *him*. I had to see him, he is so fine, he is like the culmination of – of my quest. For the ideal.' He started to speak quickly, almost gabbling. 'I would go into the passage when I guessed you would be rising. God forgive me, I was there yesterday, and on the day poor Simon was buried. I went again this morning, I could not resist. Oh, what have I become? Can a man be more humiliated before God?' He clenched his fist and raised it to his mouth, biting his hand till a bead of blood appeared.

It occurred to me he would have watched me dressing too, seen the bent back from which Mark always tactfully averted his gaze. It was not a pleasant thought.

I leaned forward. 'Listen to me, Brother. I have told Mark nothing yet. But you will tell me all you know about the deaths here, you will tell me what you have been holding back.'

He took his hand from his mouth and stared at me in puzzlement. 'But Commissioner, there is nothing else to tell. My shame was my secret. Everything else I told you was true, I know nothing of these terrible deeds. I was not spying. The only reason I used that passage was to – to watch the young men who came.' He drew a shuddering breath. 'I only wanted to look.'

'And you are concealing nothing else?'

'Nothing, I swear. If I could do anything to help you solve these terrible crimes, by Jesu I would.'

He crouched against the wall, shamed almost beyond bearing. I felt a wave of anger that I had, once again, followed a trail that led to a dead end. I shook my head, expelling my breath angrily.

'God's death, Brother Gabriel, you have led me a dance. I had thought you the killer.'

'Sir, I know you would have the monastery down. But I beg you, do not use what I have done. Do not let my sins cause the end of Scarnsea.'

'God's blood, you exaggerate these sins of yours. Such solitary vice is not even enough to justify prosecuting you. If this house closes, it will be for other reasons. I only wonder sorrowfully that a man should waste his life on such a strange idolatry. You are as silly a creature as any under heaven.'

He closed his eyes in shame, then looked up and I saw his lips move in prayer. Then his mouth fell open and his eyes, still looking upward, seemed to bulge from his head. Puzzled, I edged closer. So quickly I had no time to move, he turned and, with a shout, launched himself at me with arms outflung.

What happened next is etched into my mind so vividly my hand trembles as I write. He shoved me violently in the chest. I fell over backwards, landing on the stone with an impact that knocked all the breath from me. For a moment I thought he had gone mad and would kill me. I looked up and for a second I saw him standing there, his eyes wild. Then something else appeared, descending from above in a rush of air, a great figure of stone that landed where I had been standing a moment before, smashing Gabriel to the earth. I can hear it now, the great ringing crash of the stone hitting the floor mingling with the dreadful crunching of Gabriel's bones.

✠

I RAISED MYSELF on my elbows and lay there stupidly, mouth open, staring at the painted statue of St Donatus, now shattered into pieces on top of the sacrist, whose arm stuck out underneath as a lake of blood spread out across the floor. The statue's head had broken off and lay at my feet, staring at me with an expression of pious sorrow, painted tears white under the eyes.

Then I heard Mark's voice, a yell such as I had never heard.

'Get away from the wall!'

I looked up. The plinth the statue had stood on was teetering on the edge of the walkway, fifty feet above. I could just make out a cowled figure behind it. I scrabbled away just before it hit the ground where I had lain. Mark grabbed me and helped me up, his face deathly pale.

'Up there!' he cried. I followed his gaze. A dim figure was heading away along the walkway, towards the presbytery.

'He saved me.' I stared at the wreckage of the sacrist's limbs under the stone, the lake of blood. 'He saved me!'

'Sir,' Mark whispered urgently. 'We have him. He's on the walkway. The only way down is the stairs either side of the rood screen.'

I collected my scattered wits, and looked at the stone staircases at either side of the screen. 'Yes, you're right. Did you see who it was?'

'No. Just a figure in a habit, with the cowl up. He's gone towards the top of the church. If we go up the stairs, one on each side, we can cut him off. We'll have him, there's no other way down. Can you do it, sir?'

'Yes. Help me up.'

Mark helped me to my feet. He drew his sword and I grasped my staff, taking deep breaths to try and calm my pounding heart. 'We'll go parallel and keep each other in sight.'

He nodded and ran quickly to the right-hand staircase. Averting my eyes from Gabriel's body, I took the left.

I mounted slowly. My heart was thumping so hard it made my

throat pulse, and white flashes danced before my eyes. I took off my heavy coat and laid it on the stairs. The cold chilled my bones but I had greater freedom of movement as I crept upwards.

The stairs led onto the narrow platform running round the interior. It was of iron mesh and, looking down, I could see far below the candles winking before the altar and the saints' shrines, the heap of stone and the great scarlet pool of Gabriel's blood. The platform was no more than three feet wide and only an iron rail separated me from the drop. Just ahead the mason's tools lay in an untidy heap beside the ropes, secured to the workmen's basket hanging out over the gap by rivets driven into the walls. I peered along the platform, cursing the poor light. All the windows were underneath the walkway and it was no more than twilit up there. I could not see far ahead, but there was someone ahead; there must be. I carefully manoeuvred my way along, bending to get under the ropes.

Just ahead the platform was level with the top of the rood screen. It ran from one side of the nave to the other, seven feet wide with, on the top, the statues at which I had previously peered from ground level. From there they had appeared quite small, but now, glancing at the dim figures through the gloom, I saw they were life-sized.

Cautiously, carefully gripping the rail, I moved down the platform past the screen. The rail creaked with every few steps and once I felt it wobble under my hand. I told myself that the mason and his men clattered along safely whenever they worked up here, but could not help wondering whether the blocks crashing over might have weakened it.

Across the church I made out Mark moving slowly along in parallel. He raised his sword and I waved my staff in acknowledgement. Between us, now, we must have the killer trapped. I gripped the staff hard. My legs had begun trembling and I cursed at them to be still.

I moved steadily on, staring ahead into the gloom. Nothing. No sound. As I approached the top of the church the walkway bent round in a half-circle, and a few moments later Mark and I were staring at each other, standing fifty feet apart at either end of the presbytery. And between us nothing, nobody. He looked at me incredulously.

'He came this way, I saw him,' he called.

'Then where is he? There's nobody this end of the church. You must have been mistaken, he must have headed down the other way, towards the door.' I stared back the way I had come, past the rood screen to where the end of the walkway was lost in the darkness.

'I'd swear on my life he came this way, I'd swear it.'

'All right.' I took a deep breath. 'Keep calm. If he's down the other end of the church we still have him. No one has gone down the stairs, we would have heard. We'll go back to the other end.'

'Perhaps we should go down. One of us could fetch help.'

'No, it's hard to keep an eye on both staircases at once, in a place this size he could slip away if he gets down.'

We took a parallel course once more, back the way we had come. My eyes were sore from peering intently ahead. As I passed the rood screen with its statues, something nagged at my mind. I was well past before it came to me: there had been the usual three statues: St John the Baptist, Our Lord and the Virgin. But there was a fourth as well.

Even as I paused and turned something whistled through the air and struck the wall beside me. A dagger clattered onto the walkway at my feet as I turned, realizing that what I had taken for the middle statue was in fact a living man in Benedictine habit. Even now a dim figure was clambering over the railing onto the walkway. I turned and ran towards him, but my foot caught in the mesh of the walkway and I fell forward onto the railing. For a second my head and shoulders hung out over the nave and I stared terrified over the drop, then I managed to haul myself upright. The figure had gone. I heard footsteps clattering down the stairs.

'Mark!' I called. 'This side! He's escaping!'

Mark was some distance ahead and by the time he had run back to the top of the stairs on the far side the monk had descended. I heard footsteps pattering away; he ran beside the wall on my side, making it impossible to see him. I ran down the stairs and arrived at the bottom just as Mark appeared opposite. In the distance the church door slammed shut.

'He was standing on the rood screen, with the statues!' I shouted. 'Did you see who it was? He was gone in a flash.'

'No, sir, he was down on the stairs by the time I reached you.' He stared up at the screen. 'He must have climbed out on the screen as we were going up the stairs. God's wounds, he must have courage to stand up there with no rail or support.'

'Hoping reformers would instinctively avert their eyes from statuary. He's got away.' I looked at the dagger I had picked up from the walkway. A sharp, unornamented weapon of steel. No clue there. I banged my fist on the wall, sending a wave of pain shooting up my arm.

'But, sir, what about Gabriel? Did you not think him the killer after all? What did you find in the hidden passage?'

I hesitated. 'I was mistaken, completely mistaken. He had no secrets. And now someone else has died because of me. Despite my prayers,' I added, looking angrily up at the roof for a moment. 'But I swear he shall be the last.'

Chapter Twenty-six

I HAD ORDERED the four surviving senior obedientiaries to the church. Abbot Fabian, Prior Mortimus, Brother Edwig and Brother Guy stood with Mark and me in the nave as servants hauled lumps of stone from Gabriel's body. Strangely, I found I could bear the terrible sight, a shocked, numbed feeling had descended on me. I watched the obedientiaries' reactions: Brother Guy and Prior Mortimus stood impassive, Brother Edwig wrinkled his face with distaste, Abbot Fabian turned away and vomited into the aisle.

I ordered them to accompany me to Gabriel's little office, where stacks of books for copying sat on the floor, and the broken statue of the Virgin still leaned mournfully against the wall. I asked them where the monks had been an hour before, when the stone fell.

'All over the precinct,' Prior Mortimus replied. 'It's recreation hour. Not many would be out in this weather, most would be in their cells.'

'Jerome? Is he safe?'

'Locked in his cell since yesterday.'

'And you four. Where were you?'

Brother Guy said he had been studying alone in his dispensary; Prior Mortimus had been in his office, again alone. Brother Edwig told me his two assistants would verify he had been in the counting house, while Abbot Fabian had been giving his steward instructions. I sat looking at them; even those with alibis could not be trusted, those who served them could be persuaded or threatened to lie. The same would be true of any alibis the monks gave each other. I could question every single servant and monk in the place, but how long would that take and where would it get me? I suddenly felt helpless.

'So Gabriel saved you?' Prior Mortimus broke the silence.

'Yes, he did.'

'Why?' he asked. 'With respect, sir, why should he give his life for you?'

'Perhaps it is not so surprising. I think he had been led to believe his own life was of little worth.' I stared hard at the prior.

'Then I hope his act is helping him now at his judgement. He had many sins to weigh in the balance.'

'Perhaps not such great matters in God's eyes.'

There was a hesitant knock at the door, and the frightened face of a monk appeared.

'Pray pardon, there is a letter for the commissioner from Justice Copynger. The messenger says it is urgent.'

'Very well. Gentlemen, stay here for now. Mark, come with me.'

✝

As we marched down the church we saw Gabriel's body had been removed; two of the servants were washing the flags; steam rose from the hot water as they swabbed away the blood. When we opened the door a sea of faces looked at us, monks and servants, all murmuring anxiously. Grey clouds of breath issued from fifty mouths. I saw Brother Athelstan, his eyes alight with curiosity, and Brother Septimus staring round in bewildered anxiety, wringing his hands. At the sight of us, Brother Jude called on the crowd to clear a way. We strode through them, led by the monk who had fetched us. At the gatehouse Bugge stood holding a letter, his sharp little eyes full of curiosity.

'The messenger said it was most urgent, Commissioner, I hope you'll forgive the interruption. Is it true Brother Gabriel's been killed in an accident in the church?'

'No, Master Bugge, it was no accident. He died saving my life from a murderer.' I took the letter and walked away, halting in the centre of the courtyard. I felt safer away from high walls just then.

'That'll be all over the precinct in an hour,' Mark said.

'Good. The time for secrecy is over.' I broke the seal and read the single sheet. I bit my lip anxiously.

'Copynger has begun his enquiries. He's ordered Sir Edward and another local landowner named in that book to attend him. Messages have come back saying they're cut off on their estates because of the snow, but if a messenger can get in they can get out, so he's sent for them again. This smacks of delaying tactics. These people have things to hide.'

'You could confront Brother Edwig now.'

'I don't want that slippery eel saying it was all just exercises and projections. I want to confront him with hard evidence. But I won't have it by tomorrow, or the day after – not at this rate.' I folded the letter. 'Mark, who could have known we were going to the church this morning? I told you by the pond. Remember I said we must go to the church.'

'Prior Mortimus was there, but he was walking away.'

'Perhaps he has sharp ears, like yours. The point is, no one else knew we were going. Assuming, that is, that someone did go up there to lie in wait for me.'

He thought. 'But how would anyone know you would come to rest just under those blocks of stone?'

'You're right. Oh God, I cannot think straight.' I kneaded my brow with my fingers. 'All right. What if our killer was up on that walkway for a different reason? What if he just took the opportunity to rid the world of me when I paused where I did?'

'But why would anyone go up there? There aren't even any works going on.'

'Who would know most about the works now Gabriel is dead?'

'Prior Mortimus is in charge of the daily running of the house.'

'I think I will talk to him.' I paused, folding the letter away. 'But first, Mark, there is something I must tell you.'

'Yes, sir.'

I looked at him seriously. 'That letter you took to Copynger about the land sales. I asked him also to find out if there were any boats going to London. It would take a week to cross the Weald in these snows, but after that letter of Jerome's I need to see Cromwell. It occurred to me there might be a boat going and there is; one is leaving on the afternoon tide with a cargo of hops. It should arrive in London in two days, returning the day after. If we're lucky with the weather I'll be away four days. I mustn't miss the chance. And I want you to stay here.'

'But should you leave now?'

I paced up and down. 'I have to take this opportunity. Remember, the king doesn't know what's been going on here. If Jerome got any other letters out and the king saw them, Cromwell could be in trouble. I don't want to go, but I must. And there's something else. Remember that sword?'

'The one in the pond?'

'It had a maker's mark. Swords like that are made to order. If I can find the maker, I should be able to find whom he made it for. And it's the only lead I have now.'

'Except to question Brother Edwig when we have evidence about the land sales.'

'Yes. You know, I cannot see Brother Edwig working with an accomplice. He seems too self-contained.'

Mark hesitated. 'Brother Guy could have killed Singleton. He's stringy, but looks fit enough, and he's tall.'

'He could, but why him particularly?'

'The hidden passage, sir. He could so easily have slipped away that night and gained access to the kitchen. He wouldn't have needed a key.'

I kneaded my brow again. 'Any of them could have done it. The evidence all points in different ways. I need more; I pray I find it in London. But I need a presence here; I want you to move into the abbot's house. Check the letters, keep an eye on what's happening.'

He gave me a sharp look. 'You want me away from Alice.'

'I want you safe away from the precincts, like old Dr Goodhaps. You can take his room, it's a finely appointed place for someone of your age to sit in state.' I sighed. 'And yes, I would prefer you away from Alice. I have spoken to her, I have told her that involvement with you could damage your prospects.'

'You had no right, sir,' he said with sudden vehemence. 'I have the right to decide my own path.'

'No, Mark, you do not. You have obligations, to your family and to your own future. I order you to move to the abbot's house.'

I saw ice in the wide blue eyes that had captivated poor Gabriel. 'I have seen you look lustfully after her yourself,' he said, and there was contempt in his voice.

'*I* control myself.'

He looked me up and down. 'You have no choice.'

I set my teeth. 'I should kick your arse out on the road for that. I wish I did not need you here while I am away, but I do. Well, are you going to do as I say?'

'I shall do all I can to help you catch the man who has killed these people. He should be hanged. But I make no promise for what I do afterwards, though you disown me utterly.' He took a deep breath. 'I am minded to ask Alice Fewterer for her hand.'

'Then I may have to disown you,' I replied quietly. 'By God's flesh I would not, but I cannot ask Lord Cromwell to take back a man married to a servant girl. That would be impossible.'

He did not answer. I knew in my heart that if it came to the worst, even after what he had said, I would take him as a clerk; find him and Alice a room in London. But I would not make it easy for him. I met his gaze with a look as steely as his own.

'Pack a bag for me,' I ordered curtly. 'And saddle Chancery. I think the road is clear enough to ride to town. I will see the prior

now, then leave for London.' I walked away; I would have wished
for his company in tackling Prior Mortimus, but after what had
passed we were better apart.

✠

THE OBEDENTIARIES were still in Gabriel's office, as dejected a
group as I had ever seen. It struck me how disconnected they were
from each other; the abbot in his increasingly fragile haughtiness,
Guy's lonely austerity, the prior and the bursar the ones who kept the
place functioning and yet, I sensed again, not friends. So much for
spiritual brotherhood.

'You should know, Brothers, I am going to London. I need to
report to Lord Cromwell. I will be back in about five days and Mark
Poer is to deputize till I return.'

'How can ye get there and back in five days?' Prior Mortimus
asked. 'They say these snows reach to Bristol.'

'I am taking a boat.'

'What have you to discuss with Lord Cromwell?' Abbot Fabian
asked nervously.

'Private matters. Now, I have let it be known how Brother
Gabriel died. And I have decided Orphan Stonegarden's body should
be delivered to Goodwife Stumpe for burial. Please arrange it.'

'But then the town will know she died here.' The abbot frowned,
as though he was finding it hard to puzzle things out.

'Yes. Matters have gone too far now for secrecy about that.'

He raised his head and looked at me with a touch of his old
haughty manner.

'I must protest, Master Shardlake. Surely such a matter, affecting
everybody here, should have been discussed with me first, as abbot.'

'Those days are done, my lord,' I said shortly. 'Now you may all
go, except Prior Mortimus.'

They passed out, the abbot giving me a vacant, puzzled look as
he went. I folded my arms and faced the prior. I dragged reserves of
mental energy from somewhere, I know not where.

'I have been considering, Brother, who knew I was coming to the church. You were there, by the pond, when I told my assistant.'

He laughed incredulously. 'I had left you.'

I studied him, but could see only angry puzzlement. 'Yes, you had. Then the person who pushed the stone was not lying in wait for me at all, but had another purpose. Who could have had reason to go up there?'

'Nobody, not till the works are agreed upon.'

'I would like you to accompany me back to the walkway to take another look.' I had remembered the missing relic, the gold that must be concealed somewhere if I was right about the land sales. Could they be hidden somewhere up there, was that why the killer had been on the walkway?

'As ye like, Commissioner.'

I led the way to the stairs and mounted again. My heart pounded as we came out on the walkway. Down below the servants were still cleaning, squeezing reddened mops into pails of water. This is what a man comes to. I was overcome with sudden nausea and clutched at the rail.

'Are you all right?' Prior Mortimus stood a couple of paces off. It suddenly occurred to me that if he should choose to seize me, he was stronger than I: I should have brought Mark.

I waved him away. 'Yes. Let us proceed.'

I looked at the little heap of tools where the blocks of stone had been, the workmen's basket suspended from its cradle of ropes.

'How long is it since any work was done here?'

'The ropes and basket went up two months ago, so the workmen could get to the statue, which was in a perilous state, remove it and examine the crack. That basket suspended from the wall and the tower by moveable ropes is an ingenious arrangement; the mason devised it. They'd hardly begun when Brother Edwig ordered the work stopped; he was right, Gabriel shouldn't have started before the programme was approved. Then he dragged his heels to show Gabriel who was in charge.'

I looked at the mesh of ropes. 'A dangerous task.'

He shrugged. 'Scaffolding would be safer, but can you imagine the bursar approving the cost?'

'You do not like Brother Edwig,' I ventured casually.

'He's like a fat wee ferret, hunting out pennies wherever he can.'

'Does he consult you much about the monastery finances?' I watched him carefully, but his shrug was casual.

'He consults no one but my lord Abbot, though he wastes my time and everyone else's making them account for every last farthing.'

'I see.' I turned away and looked up at the bell tower. 'How do you reach the bells?'

'There's another staircase leading up from the ground floor. I can take ye up if ye wish. I doubt the works will be continued now. Gabriel's lost that one by getting himself killed.'

I raised my eyebrows. 'Prior Mortimus, how is it that you were moved by the death of a servant girl, yet show no sorrow for the death of a brother you must have worked with many years?'

'I said before, a monk's obligations in this life are clear different from a mere woman's.' He gave me a steely look. 'One of those obligations is not to be a pervert.'

'I am glad you are not a judge in King's Bench, Brother Prior.'

✠

HE TOOK ME BACK down the stairs to the nave and through another door, to where a long spiral staircase led up to roof level. It was a long climb and I was breathless by the time we came out on a narrow wooden passageway leading to another door. An unglazed window gave a dizzying view out over the precinct and beyond, white fields and the forest in one direction and the grey sea in the other. It must have been the highest point for miles. A freezing wind whined mournfully, ruffling our hair.

'It's through here.' The prior led me through the door into a bare, wood-floored chamber where thick bell ropes hung to the floor.

Looking up, I could see the dim outlines of the huge bells above. In the centre of the room, railed off, was a large circular hole. I looked over the rails and had another view of the church floor; we were so high now the men below seemed like ants. I could see the basket hanging twenty feet underneath, the outlines of tools and buckets visible inside it under a large cloth. The ropes led up through the hole into the room, where they were secured to more enormous rivets driven into the walls.

'But for the hole the sound of the bells would deafen those working the bell ropes,' the prior observed. 'They have to plug their ears as it is.'

'I can imagine; they almost deafen one at ground level.' I noticed a flight of wooden steps. 'Do those lead to the bell tower itself?'

'Yes, they're used by the servants who go up to clean and maintain them.'

'Let us go up. After you.'

The stairs led to another room, where a rail surrounded the bells themselves. They were indeed enormous, each larger than a man and fixed to the roof with huge rings. Nothing was hidden up here either. I went over to the bells, taking care not to go too close to the edge, for the railing was low. The nearest bell was covered with ornate metalwork and had a large plaque fixed to it, inscribed in a strange language.

'*Arrancado de la barriga del infiel, año 1059*,' I read aloud.

'Taken from the belly of the infidel,' Prior Mortimus said. I started; I had not realized he was so close.

'Commissioner,' he said, 'I would ask you something. You saw the abbot earlier?'

'Yes.'

'He's a broken man. He's not fit for the office any more. When it comes to a replacement, Lord Cromwell will want a hard man who'll be loyal to him. I know he's been promoting supporters in the monasteries.' He looked at me meaningfully.

I shook my head in surprise. 'Prior Mortimus, do you really think this house will be allowed to continue? After what has happened here?'

He looked taken back. 'But surely – our life here – it can't really end. There's no law to make us surrender. I know people say the monasteries will come down, but that can't be allowed, surely.' He shook his head. 'Surely not.' He took another step closer, pressing me back against the railing, his foul body odour rancid in my nostrils. My heart began thumping wildly.

'Prior Mortimus,' I said. 'Please stand away.'

He stared at me and then stepped back.

'Commissioner,' he said intently, 'I could save this house.'

'The future of the monastery is something I must discuss only with Lord Cromwell.' My mouth was dry, for a terrible moment I had thought he was about to push me over. 'I have seen all I need. There is nothing hidden here. Let us go down now.'

We descended in silence. I was never so glad to stand on firm ground again.

'Will ye be leaving now?' the prior asked.

'Yes. But Mark Poer carries my authority while I am away.'

'When ye talk to Lord Cromwell, will ye mention what I said, sir? Please. I could be his man.'

'I have many things to tell him,' I said shortly. 'And now, I must go.'

I turned and walked quickly away to the infirmary. The shock of Gabriel's death had suddenly caught up with me; my head spun and my legs threatened to give way as I walked though the infirmary hall to our room. Mark was not there, but a pannier had been made up containing my papers, some food and a change of shirt. I pushed it aside and sat on the bed, letting myself give way to a trembling that shook me from head to toe. I found myself suddenly weeping uncontrollably, and I gave way to it. I wept for Gabriel, for Orphan, for Simon, even for Singleton. And for my own terror.

I was feeling calmer, washing my face in the water bowl, when there was a knock at the door. I hoped it might be Mark come to say farewell, but it was Alice, looking curiously at my flushed face.

'Sir, the servant has brought your horse round. It is time to leave for town if you are to catch your boat.'

'Thank you.' I took my pannier and rose to my feet. She stood before me.

'Sir, I wish you would not go.'

'Alice, I must. In London I may find some answers that can end this horror.'

'The sword?'

'Yes, the sword.' I took a deep breath. 'While I am away, don't go out if you can help it, stay here.'

She did not reply. I hurried past her, for fear that if I hesitated a moment longer I might say something I would regret. Her look as I passed was unfathomable. At the front door the stable boy stood with Chancery, who waved his white tail and whinnied as he saw me. I stroked his flank, glad for at least one being that greeted me with affection. I mounted with my usual difficulty and headed for the gate, which Bugge held open. I stopped and looked back over the white courtyard for a long moment, I know not for what. Then I turned, nodded to Bugge and led Chancery out onto the Scarnsea road.

Chapter Twenty-seven

THE JOURNEY TO LONDON was uneventful. There was a favourable wind and the little cargo boat, a two-masted crayer, followed a strong tide up the Channel. It was even colder out at sea and we travelled over leaden waves under a grey sky. I kept to the little cabin, only venturing out when the tang of hops became too strong. The boatman was a sullen creature of few words, aided by a scrawny youth; both rebuffed my attempts to draw them into conversation about life in Scarnsea. I suspected the boatman was a papist because once when I came on deck I found him mumbling over a rosary, which he quickly pocketed when he saw me.

We were two nights at sea and I slept well, wrapped in blankets and my coat. Brother Guy's potion had made a real difference, but also away from the monastery I realized how oppressive that life of constant fear and turmoil had been. I reflected how in that atmosphere it was no wonder Mark and I had quarrelled; perhaps we could yet repair things when all this was over. I thought of Mark, no doubt establishing himself now in the abbot's house. I was sure he would ignore my instructions about Alice; his words had implied as much. I guessed she would tell him that I had revealed my own feelings for her, out on the marsh, and felt a hot flush of embarrassment. I worried for their safety, too, but told myself that if Mark kept to the abbot's house, no doubt with visits to the infirmary, and if Alice went quietly about her duties, surely nobody would have any motive to harm them.

✝

WE ARRIVED AT Billingsgate in the afternoon of the third day, after a short wait at the mouth of the Thames for the tide to turn. The banks of the estuary were covered with snow, though I fancied not so thickly as at Scarnsea. Standing on the deck, I made out a slushy growth of ice on the far bank. Following my glance the boatman addressed me almost for the first time on our journey.

'I fancy the Thames may freeze again, like last winter.'

'You may be right.'

'I remember last year, sir, when the king and the court rode across the frozen Thames. Did you see it?'

'No, I was in court. I am a lawyer.'

I remembered Mark's description of it, though. He had been working in Augmentations when word came that the king was to ride across the ice from Whitehall to the Christmas celebrations at Greenwich Palace, with all the court, and he wanted the Westminster clerks to follow too. It was all political, of course; a truce had been called with the northern rebels and their leader, Robert Aske, was in London to parley with the king under a safe conduct. The king wanted to provide a spectacle to show Londoners that rebellion would not interfere with his celebrations. Mark never tired of telling how all the clerks were sent out with their papers to the riverside, forcing their reluctant horses onto the ice.

His own horse nearly threw him as the king himself rode past, a massive figure on a huge warhorse, Queen Jane on her palfrey tiny at his side, and behind them all the ladies and gentlemen of the court, then the household servants. Finally Mark and the other clerks and officials joined the end of the great train that went hallooing and shouting across the ice, horses and carts slipping and slithering, watched from their windows by half London. The clerks were there only to contribute to the spectacle; they were sent back across London Bridge again that night, clutching their papers and ledgers. I remember discussing it with Mark months later, after Aske's arrest for treason.

'They say he is to be hanged alive in chains at York,' Mark had said.

'He was a rebel against the king.'

'But he was given safe conduct; why, he was entertained at court for Christmas.'

'"*Circa regna tonat.*"' I quoted Wyatt's lines at him. 'Around thrones the thunder rolls.'

The boat lurched; the tide was turning. The boatman steered into the middle of the river and soon the great spire of St Paul's, and the huddle of ten thousand white-covered roofs, came into view.

✠

I HAD LEFT Chancery stabled in Scarnsea and when I disembarked I walked home as the sun began to set. The sword from the pond knocked uncomfortably at my leg; I had put it in Mark's scabbard, which was too small for it, and I was unused to wearing a weapon.

This time it was a relief to be back in the London throng; just one more anonymous gentleman, instead of the focus of all that fear and hate. The sight of my house uplifted my sore heart, as did the welcome I had from Joan. My return was unexpected and she had only a poor fowl, an old boiled crone, for my supper, but I was happy to sit again at my own table. Afterwards I went to bed, for I had only one full day in London and much to do.

✠

I LEFT THE HOUSE early, before the winter sunrise, on an old ambling nag we kept. Cromwell's office at Westminster was already a hive of candlelit activity by the time I arrived. I told Chief Clerk Grey I needed an urgent appointment. He pursed his lips and glanced towards Cromwell's sanctum.

'He has the Duke of Norfolk with him.'

I raised my eyebrows. The duke was the leader of the anti-reformist faction at court, Cromwell's arch-enemy and a haughty aristocrat; I marvelled at him deigning to visit him at his office.

'Nonetheless, it is urgent. If you could take a message, saying I need to see him today.'

The clerk eyed me curiously. 'Are you well, Master Shardlake? You look very tired.'

'I am well enough. But I do need to see Lord Cromwell. Tell him I will wait on him whenever he wishes.'

Grey knew I would not interrupt his master without reason. He knocked nervously at the door and went in, reappearing a few minutes later to tell me Lord Cromwell would see me at eleven at his house in Stepney. I would have liked to have gone over to the courts, to see what news there was among the lawyers and soothe myself with familiar scenes, but other matters needed attention. I adjusted the sword and rode away through the pink icy dawn to the Tower of London.

✝

I HAD ORIGINALLY thought of visiting the swordmakers' guild, but all the guilds lived among mountains of paper whose contents they guarded with jealous secrecy and it could take all day to prise information from them. I had met the Tower armourer, a man named Oldknoll, at a function some months before, and remembered that he was said to know more about weaponry than anyone in England. He was, too, Cromwell's man. My letter of appointment as commissioner gained me entrance to the Tower, and I found myself passing through the gate under the looming mass of London Wall. I crossed the bridge over the frozen moat into the great fortress, the bulk of the White Tower dwarfing the lesser buildings around it. I never liked the Tower; I always thought of those who had come across that moat and never left alive.

The lions in the Royal Menagerie were howling and roaring for their breakfasts and I watched as a pair of wardens in their scarlet and gold coats scurried across the snow-covered Tower Green bearing great pails of offal for them. I shivered, remembering my encounter with the dogs. Leaving the nag in the stables, I climbed the steps to the White Tower. Inside the Great Hall soldiers and officials milled about, and I saw two guards leading a crazed-looking old man in a torn shirt roughly towards the steps leading down to the dungeons. I showed my commission to a sergeant, who led me to Oldknoll's room.

The armourer was a gruff, hard-faced soldier. He looked up from a sheaf of paper he was studying gloomily, and bade me sit.

'God's wounds, Master Shardlake, the paperwork we have these days. I hope you have not brought me more.'

'No, Master Oldknoll, I have come to pick your brains if I may. I am on a mission for Lord Cromwell.'

He gave me his attention. 'Then I will do all I can to aid you. You seem under strain, sir, if I may say so.'

'Yes, everyone is saying so. And they are right. I need to know who made this.' I unsheathed the sword, handing it to him carefully. He bent to study the maker's mark, gave me a startled glance, then looked more closely.

'Where did you get this?'

'In a monastery fish pond.'

He crossed to the door and closed it carefully, before laying the sword on the desk.

'You know who made it?' I asked.

'Oh yes.'

'Is he alive?'

Oldkoll shook his head. 'Dead these eighteen months.'

'I need to know everything you can tell me about that sword. What those letters and symbols signify, to start with.'

He took a deep breath. 'You see the little castle stamped there? That indicates the maker was trained at Toledo in Spain.'

My eyes widened. 'So the owner would be a Spaniard?'

He shook his head. 'Not necessarily. Many foreigners go to learn weaponry at Toledo.'

'Including Englishmen?'

'Until the religious changes. Englishmen are not welcome in Spain now. But before, yes. Those who have studied at Toledo usually take the Moorish fortress, the Alcazar, as their mark on the sword they submit on applying to the guild for admission. That is what this man did. Those are his initials.'

'JS.'

'Yes.' He gave me a long look. 'John Smeaton.'

'God's flesh! A relative of Mark Smeaton, Queen Anne's lover?'

'His father. I knew him slightly. This sword would be the one he made to gain entry to the guild. Fifteen hundred and seven, that would be about the right date.'

'I did not know Smeaton's father was a sword-maker.'

'He started out as one. A good one, too. But he had an accident some years ago, lost parts of two fingers. He didn't have the strength in his hand afterwards for sword-making, so he turned to carpentry. He had a small works over at Whitechapel.'

'And he is dead?'

'He had a seizure two days after his son's execution. I remember it being spoken of, he had no one to leave the business to. I think it was closed down.'

'But he must have had relatives. This sword is valuable; it would have been part of his estate.'

'Aye, it would.'

I took a deep breath. 'So Singleton's death was connected with Mark Smeaton. Of course, Jerome knew that somehow. That's why he told me the story.'

'I don't follow you, sir.'

'I must find out who this sword passed to after John Smeaton died.'

'You could go to his house. He lived above his shop like most craftsmen. The new owners would have bought it from the executors.'

'Thank you, Master Oldknoll, you have been a great help.' I took the sword and buckled it on. 'I must go, I am due at Lord Cromwell's house.'

'I am glad to have assisted. And Master Shardlake, if you are going to see Lord Cromwell—'

I raised my eyebrows. It was always the same, if people knew you were visiting Cromwell there would be some favour to ask.

'It's only — if you get the chance, could you ask him if he could send me less paperwork? Every night this week I've had to sit up making returns on the weaponry, and I know they have the information already.'

I smiled. 'I will see what I can do. It is the temper of the times, though; it is hard to go against the tide.'

'This tide of paper will end by drowning us,' he said sorrowfully.

✝

LORD CROMWELL'S house in Stepney was an imposing red-brick mansion he had had built a few years before. It housed not just his wife and son but a dozen young sons of clients, whom he had taken into his household for their education. I had visited it before; the house was like a miniature court with its servants and teachers, clerks and constant visitors. As I approached I saw a crowd of ragged people waiting outside. An old blind man, shoeless in the snow, stood with his hand out, calling, 'Alms, alms by your mercy.' I had heard that Cromwell got his servants to distribute doles from the side gate in an effort to gain popularity among the London poor. It was a scene uncomfortably reminiscent of the monastery dole day.

I stabled my horse and was led indoors by Blitheman the steward, an amiable fellow. Lord Cromwell would be a little late, he said, and offered me some wine.

'That would be welcome.'

'Tell me, sir, would you care to see Lord Cromwell's leopard? He likes it to be shown to visitors. It's in a cage at the back.'

'I heard he had recently acquired such a beast. Thank you.'

Blitheman led me through the busy house to a yard at the back. I had never seen a leopard, though I had heard of those fabulous spotted creatures, which could run faster than the wind. He led me out, smiling proprietorially. My nostrils were assailed with a great stink, and I found myself looking through the bars of a metal cage perhaps twenty feet square. The stone floor was dotted with gobbets of meat, and a great cat prowled up and down. Its fur was golden with black spots, and everything in its lean, muscled frame spoke of savage power. As we entered the yard it turned and snarled, showing huge yellow fangs.

'A fearsome beast,' I said.

'Fifteen pounds it cost my lord.'

The leopard sat down and stared at us, occasionally lifting its lips in a snarl.

'What is its name?' I asked.

'Oh, it has no name, it would not be godly to give a Christian's name to such a monster.'

'Poor creature, it must be cold.'

A boy in livery appeared at the door and muttered to Blitheman.

'Lord Cromwell is returned,' Blitheman said. 'Come, he is in his study.' With a last glance at the snarling leopard, I followed him inside. I reflected that my master, too, had a savage reputation and wondered whether he was sending a deliberate message by possessing such a creature.

✝

LORD CROMWELL'S study was a smaller version of his Westminster office, packed with paper-strewn tables. Normally it was gloomy, but today the sunlight reflected from the snow in the garden sent a penetrating white light across the heavy creases and folds of his face as he sat behind his desk. His look at me when I was shown in was hostile, his mouth set tight and his chin projecting angrily. He did not bid me sit.

'I had expected to hear from you sooner,' he said coldly. 'Nine days. And the business isn't settled yet, I can tell by your look.' He noticed my sword. 'God's blood, do you wear a weapon in my presence?'

'No, my lord,' I said, hastily unbuckling it. 'It is a piece of evidence, I had to bring it.' I laid it on a table where an illustrated copy of the English Bible lay open at a picture of Sodom and Gomorrah consumed by flames. I told him all that had happened: the deaths of Simon and Gabriel and the discovery of Orphan Stonegarden's body, the abbot's offer of surrender, my suspicions about the land sales, and finally Jerome's letter, which I passed to him. Except when he was reading it he glared at me throughout with that unblinking gaze of his. When I had finished he let out a snort.

'God's holy wounds, it's a chaos worse than Bedlam. I hope when you get back that boy of yours is still alive,' he added brutally. 'I've spent time cozening Rich into taking him back; it'd better not be wasted.'

'I thought I should report to you, my lord. Especially when I found that letter.'

He grunted. 'They should have reminded me that the Carthusian was there, Grey will hear about that. Brother Jerome will be dealt with. But I'm not concerned with letters to Edward Seymour. All the Seymour family look to my favour now the queen's dead.' He leaned forward. 'But these deaths unsolved do worry me. They must not come out now, I don't want my other negotiations upset. Lewes Priory is about to surrender.'

'They are giving in?'

'I had word yesterday; the surrender will be signed this week. That's what I was seeing Norfolk about, we're going to divide their lands between us. The king's agreed in principle.'

'It must be a goodly parcel.'

'It is. Their Sussex estates will go to me and those in Norfolk to the duke. The prospect of lands soon brings old enemies to the negotiating table.' He gave a bark of laughter. 'I'm going to set my son Gregory up in the abbot's fine house, make a landowner of him.' He paused and the steely look returned. 'You seek to distract me, Matthew, put me in a better mood.'

'No, sir. I know this has gone slowly but it is the hardest and most dangerous puzzle I have known—'

'What's the importance of that sword?'

I told him of its discovery and my talk with Oldknoll earlier. He furrowed his brows. 'Mark Smeaton. I didn't think he was one to cause trouble from beyond the grave.' Lord Cromwell came round his desk and picked up the sword. 'It's a fine weapon all right, I wish I'd had it when I was soldiering in Italy in my youth.'

'There must be a connection between the killings and Smeaton.'

'I can see one,' he said. 'A connection to Singleton's death, anyway. Revenge.'

He thought a moment, then turned and gave me a hard look. 'This is not to be repeated to anyone.'

'On my honour.'

He put down the sword and began pacing up and down, hands folded behind him. His black robe billowed around his knees.

'When the king turned against Anne Boleyn last year, I had to act quickly. I'd been associated with her from the beginning, and the papist faction would have worked my fall with hers; the king was starting to listen to them. So it had to be me that rid the king of her. Do you see?'

'Yes. Yes, I see.'

'I persuaded him she was adulterous and that meant she could be executed for treason, without her religion coming into it. But there would have to be evidence and a public trial.'

I stood looking at him silently.

'I took some of my most trusted men and assigned to each a friend of hers whom I had chosen – Norris, Weston, Brereton, her brother Rochford – and Smeaton. Their task was to get either a confession, or something that could be made to look like evidence that they had lain with her. Singleton was the man I assigned to deal with Mark Smeaton.'

'He made up a case against him?'

'Smeaton looked to be the easiest one to force into a confession; he was just a boy. So it proved, he confessed to adultery after a session on the Tower rack. The same one I used on that Carthusian, who must indeed have met him because all he reported Smeaton saying was true.' His tone as he went on was reflective, matter of fact.

'And one of the visitors the Carthusian saw coming to the cell that night would have been Singleton himself. I sent him to make sure that in his speech from the scaffold – there's a tradition that should be done away with – the boy did not retract his confession. He was reminded that, if he said anything amiss, his father would suffer.'

I stared at my lord. 'So what people said was true? Queen Anne and those accused with her were innocent?'

He turned to me. The harsh light caught his face and seemed to leach his eyes of expression as he frowned at me.

'Of course they were innocent. No one may say so, but the whole world knows it, the juries at the trial knew. Even the king half-knew though he couldn't admit it to himself and irk his fine conscience. God's death, Matthew, you're innocent for a lawyer. You've the innocence of a reformist believer without the fire. Better to have the fire without the innocence, like me.'

'I believed the charges were true. So many times I have said so.'

'Best to do what most people did on that subject and keep a closed mouth.'

'Perhaps I did know, deep down,' I said quietly. 'In some part of me God has not reached.'

Cromwell looked at me impatiently, irritation in his face.

'So Singleton was killed for revenge,' I said at length. 'Someone killed him in the same manner Anne Boleyn was executed. But who?' A thought came to me. 'Who was Smeaton's second visitor? Jerome mentioned the priest come to shrive him and two others.'

'I'll have Singleton's case papers looked out, see what they say about Smeaton's family. I'll have them at your house within two hours. Meanwhile go to old Smeaton's place, that's a good notion. You return to Scarnsea tomorrow?'

'Yes, the boat leaves before dawn.'

'If you find anything before you go, send the information to me. And Matthew—'

'Yes, my lord.'

He had moved out of the sunlight, the fierce anger and power were back in his eyes. 'Make sure you find the murderer. I have kept this from the king too long. When I tell him I must have the killer's name to give him. And get the abbot's seal on that surrender. I suppose at least there you've achieved something.'

'Yes, my lord.' I hesitated. 'When the house surrenders, what will happen to it?'

He smiled grimly. 'Same as with them all. The abbot and the monks will get their pensions. The servants will have to shift for themselves and serve them right, greedy lubbers. As for the buildings, I'll tell you what I have planned for Lewes. I'm sending a demolition engineer down there; I'm going to have him raze the church and claustral buildings to the ground. And when all the monastery lands are in the king's hands and we rent them out, I'm going to put a clause in every lease saying the tenant must take down any monastic buildings. Even if they just take the lead off the roofs and let the locals take the stone for building, it'll be the same result. No trace left of their centuries of mummery, just a few bare ruins to remind people of the king's power.'

'There are some fine buildings.'

'A gentleman can't live in a church,' Cromwell said impatiently. His eyes narrowed. 'You're not turning papist on me are you, Matthew Shardlake?'

'Never,' I said.

'Then go. And don't fail me this time. Remember, I have it in my power to build up a lawyer's business, but I can also ruin it.' He gave me his bull-like glare again.

'I will not fail, my lord.'

I picked up the sword and left.

Chapter Twenty-eight

I LEFT WESTMINSTER with my mind in a whirl. I went over the names of everyone at the monastery, trying to find a possible link with the Smeaton family. Could John Smeaton have met Brother Guy in Spain thirty years ago? If he were an apprentice, then he and the sacrist would have been of an age.

All the time I was turning these matters over, in my heart there was a dull, leaden feeling. I had believed Thomas Cromwell incapable of the unchristian acts attributed to him over Anne Boleyn's fall. And now he had casually admitted they were true. And it was not Cromwell who had gulled me into false belief; I had done that for myself.

The horse had been picking its way slowly over the icy ruts in the road, but halfway down Fleet Street it stopped and tossed its head anxiously. A little way ahead a crowd had gathered, blocking the road. Looking over their heads I saw two of the constable's men struggling with a young apprentice. He was resisting fiercely, shouting out at his captors.

'You are the forces of Babylon, you seize God's chosen children! The righteous will prevail, the mighty shall be pulled down!'

The guards pinioned his arms behind his back and hauled him away, still kicking. Some of the crowd yelled catcalls after him, others shouted support.

'Be steadfast, brother! The Lord's chosen will triumph!'

I heard another rider at my elbow, and turned to see the sardonic features of Pepper, the fellow lawyer I had encountered the day I undertook the mission to Scarnsea.

'Ho, Shardlake!' he called amiably. 'So they've taken another hot gospeller. An Anabaptist by the sound of him. They'd have all our property, you know!'

'Is there a round-up of unlicensed preachers? I've been out of London again.'

'There's talk of Anabaptists in London, the king's ordered all suspects to be taken. He'll burn a few and just as well. They're more dangerous than the papists.'

'There is safety nowhere these days.'

'Cromwell's taken the opportunity to have a general round-up. Cutpurses, fraudsters, unlicensed preachers, they've all been lurking in their dog-holes in this fearsome weather and he's rooting them out. Not before time. D'you remember that old woman with the talking bird we saw?'

'Aye. It seems an age ago.'

'It turned out you were right; the bird just repeats words it's taught. They've brought in a couple of boatloads of the creatures and they're the talk of the City, everyone with a town house wants one. The old woman's been charged with fraud, she'll probably be whipped at the cart's tail. But where have you been, keeping by your fire in this cold?'

'No, Pepper, I have been out in the country, Lord Cromwell's business again.'

'I hear he's looking for a new bride for the king already,' he said, fishing for gossip. 'There's talk of a marriage among the German princes, Hesse or Cleves. That'd tie us to the Lutherans.'

'I have heard nothing. As I say, I have been away on Lord Cromwell's business.'

He looked at me enviously. 'He keeps you busy. D'you think he might have work to spare for me?'

I smiled wryly. 'Yes, Pepper, probably he would.'

✝

AT HOME I LOOKED over the correspondence I had been too weary to do more than glance at the night before. There were letters about

C. J. SANSOM

cases I was handling; people were becoming anxious for replies on several matters. There was also a letter from my father. The harvest had been poor that year, the farm would show little profit and he was thinking of running more land for sheep. He hoped my business was prospering and that Mark was doing well at Augmentations – I had said nothing of his disgrace. He added that it was said in the country more monasteries would come down. Mark's father said that would be good, it would mean more work for Mark.

I put the letter down and sat staring gloomily into the fire. I thought of Mark Smeaton on the rack under torture, guilty of no crime. And Jerome on the same rack. No wonder he hated the office I embodied. So all he had said was true. He must have known of the link between Singleton and Mark Smeaton, or why tell me the story? Yet he had sworn no one in the monastery had killed Singleton. I tried to remember his exact words, but I was too tired. My thoughts were interrupted by a knock at the door, and Joan came in.

'A letter has just come, sir. From Lord Cromwell.'

'Thank you, Joan.' I took the thick letter from her and turned it over in my hands. It was marked 'Most secret'.

'Sir,' she said hesitantly. 'May I ask you something?'

'Of course.' I smiled at her; her plump face was anxious.

'I have wondered, sir, is all well with you? You appear troubled. And Master Mark, is he safe down there on the coast?'

'I hope so,' I said. 'I do not know about his future, though, he does not want to return to Augmentations.'

She nodded. 'That does not surprise me.'

'Doesn't it, Joan? It did me.'

'I could see he was unhappy there. I have heard it is a wicked place full of greedy men, if you will forgive me.'

'Perhaps it is. But there are so many such places. If we were to avoid them all and just sit by our fires, we should all be beggars, should we not?'

She shook her head. 'Master Mark is different, sir.'

'Why different? Come, Joan, he has beguiled you as he does all women.'

'No, sir,' she said, stung. 'He has not. Perhaps I see him more clearly than you. He has as gentle a nature as I have ever seen under that amiable surface, injustice pains him. I have wondered whether in a way he sought his disgrace with that girl, to get away from Westminster. He has strong ideals, sir, sometimes I think he has too many to survive in this harsh world.'

I smiled sadly. 'And I thought I was the one with high ideals. "And the veil was lifted from mine eyes."'

'Pardon, sir?'

'Nothing, Joan. Do not worry. I must read this.'

'Of course, I beg pardon.'

'No need. And, Joan – I thank you for your care.'

☦

I TURNED TO the letter with a sigh. It contained notes made by Singleton and letters to Cromwell about his progress with Mark Smeaton. They made it clear a coldly calculated plan had been set to trap the young musician with perjured evidence and kill him. Alleging the queen had bedded with someone of such humble origins would be particularly shocking to the public, Singleton said, so it was important to have him in the net. He referred to Smeaton mockingly as a silly creature, a lamb to be led to the slaughter. At Cromwell's house they had smashed his lute against the wall before his eyes and left him naked in a cellar all night, but it had taken torture to make him swear a false confession. I prayed he was safe in heaven.

There was a memorandum from Singleton about the boy's family. His mother was dead and there was only his father; no other male relatives at all. John Smeaton had an older sister out in the country somewhere, but there had been a quarrel and he had not seen her for years. Singleton told Cromwell the lack of relatives with connections would make it easier to deal with the boy as they liked, without questions raised.

I put the letter carefully back in its envelope. I recalled Singleton's funeral, the sight of the coffin lid shutting on his face, and I confess now I was glad. I called for the horse to be brought round; it was time to set out for Whitechapel. I was glad to get into my coat and step out of doors again, with a goal to follow. It released me from the whirling chaos in my mind.

Chapter Twenty-nine

IT WAS A LONG RIDE out to Whitechapel, well beyond London Wall; a fast-growing area, filled with the wattle-and-daub hovels of the poor. Thin smoke from a hundred fires rose into the still air. Here the bitter weather was more than just a serious inconvenience; looking at the pinched, hungry faces I reflected that for some here this would be one hardship too many. Such wells as they had must have frozen, for I saw many women carrying pails of water up from the river. I had changed into my clothes of cheapest cloth, for gentlemen were not always safe out here.

The street where Smeaton had had his forge was one of the better ones, housing several workshops. Singleton's papers said he had lived in a two-storey building next to a smithy and I found it readily enough. It was no longer a carpenter's; the shutter covering the shop-front had been nailed down and painted over. I tied the nag to a post and rapped on the flimsy wooden door.

It was opened by a poorly dressed young man with untidy black hair framing a pale, hollow-cheeked face. He asked what I wanted without much interest, but when I said I was a commissioner from Lord Cromwell's office he shrank away, shaking his head.

'We've done nothing, sir. There's nothing here to interest Lord Cromwell.'

'You are not accused of anything,' I said mildly. 'I have some enquiries, that is all. About the last owner of this place, John Smeaton. There will be a reward for those who help me.'

He still looked dubious, but invited me inside. 'Excuse my home, sir,' he muttered, 'but I've no work.'

In truth it was a sorry chamber he led me into. It had obviously been a workshop in the recent past, for it consisted only of one long, low room, the brick walls blackened with years of soot. A carpenter's bench now served as a table. It was cold; the fire consisted of a few stony coals that gave off as much smoke as heat. Apart from the bench there was no furniture save a few battered chairs and straw mattresses on the floors. Around the poor fire three thin children sat huddled together with their mother, who nursed a coughing baby in her lap. They all looked up at me with sullen, indifferent expressions. The room was dim, the only light coming from a small rear window now the old shopfront was nailed up. The place smelt strongly of smoke and urine, and the whole scene filled me with a chill sadness.

'Have you been here long?' I asked the man.

'Eighteen months, since the old owner died. The man who bought it lets us this room. There's another family in the living quarters upstairs. The landlord's Master Placid, sir, he lives in the Strand.'

'You know who the old owner's son was?'

'Yes, sir. Mark Smeaton, that lay with the great whore.'

'I presume Smeaton's heirs sold it to Master Placid. Do you know who they were?'

'The heir was an old woman. When we moved in there was a pile of Master Smeaton's belongings, some clothes and a silver cup and a sword—'

'A sword?'

'Yes, sir. They were in a pile over there.' He pointed to a corner. 'Master Placid's man told us John Smeaton's sister would be coming to collect them. We were not to touch them or we'd be out.'

'Nor did we, sir,' added the woman by the fire. Her child coughed harshly and she hugged it to her. 'Quiet, Fear-God.'

I fought to suppress my excitement. 'The old woman? Did she come?'

'Yes sir, a few weeks later. She was from the country somewhere, she seemed nervous in the city. Her lawyer brought her.'

'Do you remember her name,' I asked eagerly, 'or what part of the country she came from? Might it have been a place called Scarnsea?'

He shook his head. 'I'm sorry, sir, I only remember she was from the country somewhere. A little fat woman, past fifty, with grey hair. She only said a few words. They picked up the bundle and the sword and left.'

'Do you remember the lawyer's name?'

'No, sir. He helped her with the sword. I remember her saying she wished she had a son she could give it to.'

'Very well. I would like you to look at my sword — no, don't be alarmed, I'm only taking it out to show you — and tell me if this might be the one the woman took.' I laid it out on the bench. The man peered at it and his wife came over, still hugging the child.

'That looks like it,' she said. She eyed me narrowly. 'We did take it out of its scabbard, sir, but only to have a look, we didn't do anything with it. But I recognize that gold-coloured handle, and those marks on the hilt.'

'We said it was a fine piece,' the man added. 'Didn't we, Elizabeth?'

I sheathed the weapon. 'Thank you both, your information has been helpful. I am sorry your child is ill.' I reached out to touch the baby, but the woman raised her hand.

'Don't stroke her, sir, she's alive with nits. She won't stop coughing. It's the cold, we've lost one already. Quiet, Fear-God.'

'She has an unusual name.'

'Our vicar is strong for Reform, sir, he's named them all. He said it would help us in the world now, to have children with such names. Here, children, stand up.' The other three stood on rickety legs, revealing bloated wormy stomachs, and their father pointed to them in turn. 'Zealous, Perseverance, Duty.'

I nodded. 'They shall each have sixpence, and here are three shillings for your help.' I counted out the contents of my purse. The children grabbed the coins eagerly; the father and mother looked as if they could not believe their good fortune. Overcome with sudden emotion, I turned and left them quickly, mounted the horse and rode away.

✠

THE PITIFUL SCENE at the house haunted me, so it was a relief to turn my thoughts back to what I had discovered. It made no sense. The person who had inherited the sword, the only person with a family motive for vengeance, an old woman? There were no women over fifty at the monastery, apart from a couple of old serving women, tall thin old crones who did not answer the young man's description. The only person who did that I had encountered in my time at Scarnsea was Goodwife Stumpe. And no short old woman could have dealt that blow. But Singleton's papers had been definite there were no male relatives. I shook my head.

I realized that in my preoccupation I had let the horse wander and it was heading down towards the river. I did not feel like going home yet and let the nag take the lead. I sniffed the air. Was it my imagination, or was it, at last, getting warmer?

I passed an encampment on a snowy piece of waste ground, where a group of workless men had made a camp. Presumably they had lighted here in the hope of finding casual labour at the docks; they had built a lean-to from pieces of driftwood and sacking and sat huddled round a fire. They gave me unfriendly looks as I passed, and a thin yellow cur ran from the camp and barked at the nag. She tossed her head and neighed, and one of the men called the dog to heel. I rode away quickly, patting the horse until she calmed.

We were down at the riverside; ships were drawn up and men were busy unloading. One or two were as dark as Brother Guy. I brought the nag to a halt. Directly ahead a great ocean-going carrack was drawn up at the quay, its square prow ornamented with an obscenely grinning naked mermaid. Men were hauling crates and boxes from the hold; I wondered from what far reach of the round globe it had come. Looking up at the great masts and the mesh of rigging I was surprised to see mist curling round the crow's nest. Wreaths of fog, I now saw, were floating up the river and I could feel distinctly warmer air.

The nag was showing signs of anxiety again and I turned and headed slowly back towards the City, through a street of store-houses. Then I paused. An extraordinary babel of noise was coming from one of the wooden buildings; screeches and yells and a host of voices in strange tongues. It was bizarre, hearing those unearthly sounds in the misty air. Overcome with curiosity, I tied the nag to a post and went across to the warehouse, from which a sharp smell issued.

The open door showed a dreadful sight. The warehouse was full of birds, in three great iron cages each as tall as a man. They were birds such as the old woman had had, which Pepper had reminded me of. There were hundreds of them, of all sizes and innumerable colours: red and green, golden and blue and yellow. They were in the most miserable state: all had had their wings cut, some right to the bone and badly done too, so that the mutilated ends were covered with raw sores; many were diseased, with half their feathers gone, scabs on their bodies and eyes surrounded with pus. For every one that clung with its claws to the sides of the cages another lay dead on the floor among great heaps of powdery droppings. The worst thing was their shrieking; some of the poor birds simply made harsh piteous cries as though appealing for an end to their suffering, but others cried out over and again in a variety of tongues; I heard words in Latin, in English, in languages I did not understand. Two of them, clinging upside down to the bars, shrieked at each other, one calling out 'A fair wind', over and again, while the other answered '*Maria, mater dolorosa*' in the accent of a Devon man.

I stood, transfixed by the horrible scene, until I was interrupted by a rough hand on my shoulder. I turned to find a sailor dressed in a greasy jerkin eyeing me suspiciously.

'What business have you here?' he asked sharply. 'If ye've come to trade ye should go to Master Fold's rooms.'

'No – no, I was passing, I heard the noise and wondered what it was.'

He grinned. 'The Tower of Babel, eh, sir? Voices possessed by the spirit and speaking in tongues? Nay, just more of these birds the gentry all want now for playthings.'

'They are in a most pitiful state.'

'There's plenty more where they came from. Some always die on the voyage. More will die from the cold, they're weak brutes. Pretty though, ain't they?'

'Where did you get them?'

'The isle of Madeira. There's a Portuguese merchant there, he's realized there's a market in Europe for them. You should see some of the things he buys and sells, sir; why he ships boatloads of black Negroes from Africa as slaves for the Brazil colonists.' He laughed, showing gold-capped teeth.

I felt a desperate urge to escape from the chill, fetid air of the warehouse. I excused myself and rode away. The harsh cries of the birds, their unearthly simulacra of human speech, followed me down the muddy street.

✝

I RODE BACK under the City wall into a London suddenly grey and foggy, full of the sound of water dripping from melting icicles on the house eaves. I halted the nag outside a church. I normally attended church at least once a week, but had not been to a service for over ten days. I was in need of spiritual comfort; I dismounted and went inside.

It was one of those rich City churches attended by merchants. Many London merchants were reformers now and there were no candles. The figures of saints on the rood screen had been painted over and replaced by a biblical verse:

The Lord knoweth how to deliver the godly out of temptations, and to reserve the unjust unto the day of judgement to be punished.

The church was empty. I stepped behind the rood screen. The altar had been stripped of its decorations, the paten and chalice standing on an unadorned table. A copy of the new Bible was chained to the lectern. I sat down in a pew, reassured by these familiar surroundings, a total contrast to Scarnsea.

But not all the accoutrements of the old ways had gone. From where I sat I could see a cadaver tomb of the last century. There were two stone biers, one above the other. On the top one was the effigy of a rich merchant in his fine robes, plump and bearded. On the lower tier lay the effigy of a desiccated cadaver in the rags of the same clothes, and the motto: 'So I am now; so I once was: as I am now; so shall ye be.'

Looking at the stone cadaver I had a sudden vision of Orphan's decomposed body rising from the water, then of the diseased rickety children at Smeaton's house. I had a sudden sick feeling that our revolution would do no more than change starveling children's names from those of the saints to Fear-God and Zealous. I thought of Cromwell's casual mention of creating faked evidence to hound innocent people to death, and of Mark's talk of the greedy suitors come to Augmentations for grants of monastic lands. This new world was no Christian commonwealth; it never would be. It was in truth no better than the old, no less ruled by power and vanity. I remembered the gaudy, hobbled birds shrieking mindlessly at each other and it seemed to me like an image of the king's court itself, where papists and reformers fluttered and gabbled, struggling for power. And in my wilful blindness I had refused to see what was before my eyes. How men fear the chaos of the world, I thought, and the yawning eternity hereafter. So we build patterns to explain its terrible mysteries and reassure ourselves we are safe in this world and beyond.

And then I realized that blinkered thinking of another sort had blinded me to the truth of what had happened at Scarnsea. I had bound myself to a web of assumptions about how the world worked, but remove one of those and it was as though a mirror of clear glass were substituted for a distorting one. My jaw dropped open. I realized who had killed Singleton and why and, that step taken, all fell into place. And I realized I had little time. For a few moments more I sat with my mouth open, breathing heavily. Then I roused myself and rode as fast as the nag would go, back to the place where, if I was right, the last piece of the puzzle lay: the Tower.

✝

IT WAS DARK by the time I rode over the moat again, and Tower Green was lit by flaming torches. I almost ran into the Great Hall and made my way again to Master Oldknoll's office. He was still there, carefully transferring information from one paper to another.

'Master Shardlake! I trust you've had a profitable day. More than mine, at least.'

'I must speak urgently to the gaoler in charge of the dungeons. Can you take me straight there? I've no time to wander round trying to find him.'

He read the importance of the matter from my face. 'I'll take you now.' He picked up a great bunch of keys and led me off, taking a torch from a passing soldier. As we passed through the Great Hall he asked if I had ever been to the dungeons before.

'Never, I'm glad to say.'

'They are grim places. And I've never known them busier.'

'Yes. I wonder what we are coming to.'

'A country full of godless crime, that's what. Papists and mad gospellers. We should hang them all.'

He led me down a narrow spiral staircase. The air became sharp with damp. There was green slime on the walls, fat beads of water running down it like sweat. We were below the level of the river now.

At the bottom was an iron gate, through which I saw a torchlit underground chamber where a little group of men stood round a paper-strewn table. A guard in Tower livery came over to us and Oldknoll addressed him through the bars.

'I have one of the vicar general's commissioners here, he needs to see Chief Gaoler Hodges at once.'

The guard opened the gate. 'Over there, sir. He's very busy; we've taken in a load of Anabaptist suspects today.' He led us over to the table, where a tall thin man stood checking papers with another guard. On both sides of the chamber there were heavy wooden doors with barred windows, from one of which a loud voice issued, calling out verses from the Bible.

'Behold I am against them saith the Lord of Hosts, and I will burn the chariots and the sword shall devour thy young lions . . .'

The gaoler raised his head. 'Shut your mouth! Do you want a whipping?' The voice subsided and he turned to me, bowing. 'Your pardon, sir, I am trying to sort the delations for all these new prisoners. Some of them are to go before Lord Cromwell for interrogation tomorrow, I don't want to send him the wrong ones.'

'I need information about a prisoner who was here eighteen months ago,' I said. 'Do you remember Mark Smeaton?'

He raised his eyebrows. 'I'm not likely to forget that time, sir. The queen of England in the Tower.' He paused, remembering. 'Yes, Smeaton was down here the night before his execution. We had instructions to separate him from the other prisoners, he was to have some visitors.'

I nodded. 'Yes, Robin Singleton came to make sure he was keeping to his confession. And there were other visitors. Would they be recorded?'

The gaoler exchanged a look with Oldknoll and laughed. 'Oh yes, sir. Everything's recorded nowadays, isn't it, Thomas?'

'At least twice.'

The gaoler sent one of his men off, and a few minutes later he returned with a heavy log book. The gaoler opened it.

'May 1536, the sixteenth.' He ran his finger down the page. 'Yes, Smeaton was in the cell that mayhemmer's in.' He nodded at the door from which the declamations had issued; silent now, only darkness visible through the bars.

'His visitors?' I asked impatiently, coming to peer over his shoulder. He shrank away a little as he bent once more to his book. Perhaps a hunchback had once brought him bad luck.

'See, there's Singleton, brought in at six. Another, marked "relative" at seven and then "priest" at eight. That's the Tower priest, Brother Martin, come to confess him before his execution. A pox on that Fletcher, I've told him always to put in the names.'

I ran my finger down the page, looking at the other prisoners' names. 'Jerome Wentworth called Jerome of London, monk of the London Charterhouse. Yes, he's here too. But I need to know about that relative, Master Hodges, most urgently. Who is this Fletcher, one of your guards?'

'Aye, and he doesn't like the paperwork. His writing's not good.'

'Is he on duty?'

'No, sir, he's had leave for his father's funeral up in Essex. He won't be back till tomorrow afternoon.'

'He comes on duty then?'

'At one.'

I bit my finger. 'I will be at sea by then. Give me paper and a pen.'

I quickly scribbled two notes and handed them to Hodges.

'This one asks Fletcher to tell me all he remembers of that visitor, everything. You will impress on him that the information is vital, and if he can't write the answer get someone else to. When he's done, I want the answer taken at once to Lord Cromwell's office with this other letter. It asks him to provide his fastest rider, to bring Fletcher's answer to me down at Scarnsea. The roads will be hell itself if this snow's melting, but a good man might be able to reach me by the time my boat gets in.'

'I'll take it to Lord Cromwell myself, Master Shardlake,' Oldknoll said. 'I'll be glad to get out in the air.'

'I'm sorry about Fletcher,' Hodges said. 'Only there's so much paperwork now, sometimes it doesn't get done properly.'

'Just make sure I have that answer, Master Hodges.'

I turned away, and Oldknoll led me out of the dungeons. As we mounted the stairs we heard the man in Smeaton's cell shouting again: a litany of garbled quotations from the Bible, cut off with a sharp crack and a yell.

Chapter Thirty

I WAS LUCKY WITH THE winds on the return journey; once out at sea the mist faded and the boat was driven down the Channel by a light south-east wind. The temperature had risen several degrees; after the biting cold of the last week it felt almost warm. The boatman had a cargo of finished cloth and iron tools to bring back, and was in a more cheerful mood.

As we approached land on the evening of the second day, I saw the coastline, wreathed in light mist. My heart quickened; we were nearly there. I had spent much time on the voyage thinking; what I did next depended on whether the messenger from London had arrived. And it was time for another talk with Jerome. Now a thought I had tried to suppress these last couple of days came to the front of my mind: were Mark and Alice still safe?

The mist made it hard to see as we navigated the channel through the marsh to Scarnsea wharf. The boatman asked diffidently if I could take a pole and push the boat from the banks if we came too close and I agreed. Once or twice it almost stuck in the thick, glutinous mud through which little rivulets of melting snow were running. I was glad when at last we reached the wharf. The boatman helped me onto dry land with thanks for my help, and perhaps ended by thinking less badly of at least one reforming heretic.

✝

I MADE MY WAY at once to Copynger's house. He was just sitting down to supper with his wife and children and invited me to join his board, but I said I must get back. He led me to his comfortable study.

'Have there been any more happenings out at the monastery?' I asked as soon as the door was shut.

'No, sir.'

'Everyone is safe?'

'So far as I know. I have news of those land sales, though.' He reached into his desk, producing a parchment deed of conveyance. I studied the ornate calligraphy, the clear impression of the monastery seal in red wax at the foot. The deed conveyed a large parcel of arable land on the other side of the Downs to Sir Edward Wentworth for a hundred pounds.

'That's a cheap price,' Copynger said. 'It's a goodly parcel.'

'None of this was entered in the official books I saw.'

'Then you have the rogues, sir.' He smiled happily. 'In the end I went to Sir Edward's house myself, and took the constable with me. That scared him, it reminded him I've powers of arrest, for all his haughtiness. He gave up the deed in half an hour, started whining he'd bought it all in good faith.'

'Who did he negotiate with at the monastery?'

'His steward dealt with the bursar, I believe. You know Edwig has control of everything to do with money there.'

'But the abbot would have had to seal the deed. Or someone would.'

'Yes. And, sir, it was part of the arrangement that the sale be kept secret for a while, the tenants would remit the rents to the monastery's steward as usual and he'd pass them on to Sir Edward.'

'Secret conveyances are not illegal in themselves. Hiding the transaction from the king's auditors is, though.' I rolled up the parchment and put it in my satchel. 'You have done well. I am grateful. Keep on with your enquiries and say nothing for now.'

'I ordered Wentworth to keep my visit secret, on pain of trouble from Lord Cromwell's office. He'll say nothing.'

'Good. I will act soon, I await some information from London first.'

He coughed. 'While you are here, sir, Goodwife Stumpe has been asking for you. I told her you should be back this afternoon and she parked herself in my kitchen after lunch. She won't move till she's seen you.'

'Very well, I can give her a few minutes. By the way, what forces have you at your command here?'

'My constable and his assistant, and my three informers. But there are good reformist men in the town I could muster if needed.' He eyed me narrowly. 'Are you expecting trouble?'

'I hope not. But I expect to make arrests very soon. Perhaps you could make sure your men are available. And that the town gaol is ready.'

He nodded, smiling. 'I'll be happy to see some monkish prisoners there. And, sir,' he gave me a meaningful look, 'when this business is over, will you commend me to Lord Cromwell for my assistance? I have a son who is almost old enough to go up to London.'

I smiled wryly. 'I fear a recommendation from me would carry little weight just now.'

'Oh.' He looked disappointed.

'And now, if I could see the goodwife?'

'You don't mind seeing her in the kitchen? I don't want her dirty shoes on this matting.'

He led me to the kitchen, where the overseer sat nursing a jug of ale. Copynger shooed out a couple of curious kitchenmaids, and left me with her.

The old woman came straight to the point. 'I am sorry to take your time, sir, but I had a favour to ask. We buried Orphan two days ago in the churchyard.'

'I am glad her poor body is at rest.'

'I paid the mortuary fee myself, but I've no money for a headstone. I could see, sir, you felt for what was done to her, and I wondered — it is a shilling, sir, for a cheap gravestone.'

'And for an expensive one?'

'Two, sir. I can arrange for you to be sent a receipt.'

I counted out two shillings. 'This mission is setting me up as a dole-giver,' I said ruefully, 'but she should have a good headstone. I won't pay for Masses, though.'

She snorted. 'Orphan needs no Masses, I spit on Masses for the dead. She is safe with God.'

'You speak like a reformer, Goodwife.'

'I am, sir, and proud.'

'By the way,' I added casually, 'have you ever visited London?'

She gave me a puzzled look. 'No, sir. I went as far as Winchelsea once.'

'No relatives in London?'

'All my people live around here.'

I nodded. 'That's what I thought. Don't worry, Goodwife.' I sent her away and said a quick farewell to Copynger, who was markedly less effusive now he knew I was not in Cromwell's favour. I collected Chancery from the ostler and rode the misty path back to the monastery.

✝

I FELT IT growing warmer still as I made my way slowly in the dark, Chancery stepping carefully for the pathway was slick with melting snow. All around I heard the drip and gurgle of meltwater running into the marsh. After a while I dismounted and led the horse along: the idea of Chancery's wandering into that mire in the dark was not pleasant. At length the monastery wall and the lights of Bugge's gatehouse loomed through the mist. The keeper came quickly to my knock, carrying a torch.

'You're back, sir. That's a dangerous ride out there tonight.'

'I needed to make haste.' I led Chancery through the gate. 'Has a rider brought a message for me, Bugge?'

'No, sir, there's been nothing.'

'Pox on it. I'm expecting a man from London. If he comes, you're to find me at once. Day or night.'

'Yes, sir. I'll do that.'

'And till I give further word no one, and I mean no one, is to leave the monastery precincts. Do you understand? If anyone wants to go out, you are to send for me.'

He looked at me curiously. 'If you order it, Commissioner.'

'I do.' I took a deep breath. 'What has been happening these last few days, Bugge? Is everyone safe? Master Mark?'

'Yes, sir. He's up at the abbot's house.' He looked at me keenly, his eyes glinting in the torchlight. 'But there's others been on the move.'

'What d'you mean? Don't speak in riddles, man.'

'Brother Jerome. He got out of his room yesterday. He's disappeared.'

'You mean he's run off?'

Bugge laughed maliciously. 'That one couldn't run far, and he's not been through my gate. No, he's hiding in the precinct somewhere. The prior'll soon root him out.'

'God's death, he was to be kept safe!' I gritted my teeth. Now I could not question him about Mark Smeaton's visitor; everything depended on the messenger.

'I know, sir, but nothing's being done properly any more. The servant in charge of him forgot to lock his door. You see, sir, everyone's frightened, Brother Gabriel being killed was the last straw. And there's talk the place is to be shut down.'

'Is there?'

'Well, it follows, sir, doesn't it? With these killings, and the talk of more monasteries being taken by the king? What do you say, sir?'

'God's flesh, Bugge, do you think I'm going to discuss matters of policy with you?'

He looked chastened. 'I'm sorry, sir. I meant no impertinence. But—' He paused.

'Well?'

'The talk is that if the monasteries go down the monks will get pensions but the servants will be put out on the road. Only I'm nearly sixty, sir, I've no family and no trade but this. And there's no work in Scarnsea.'

'I can't help what gossip-mongers say, Bugge,' I replied more gently. 'Now, is your assistant here?'

'David, sir? Yes.'

'Then get him to stable Chancery for me, would you? I am going to the abbot's house.'

I watched as the boy led Chancery across the yard, stepping carefully through the slush. I remembered my talk with Cromwell. Bugge and all the others would be out, cast on the parish if there was no work. I remembered the day I had gone to the poorhouse, the licensed beggars clearing the snow. Little as I liked Bugge it was not pleasant to think of him at such work, his beloved scraps of authority gone. It would kill him in six months.

I started round at a movement and clutched John Smeaton's sword. A figure was just visible through the mist, standing against the wall.

'Who's there?' I called sharply.

Brother Guy stepped forward, his hood raised over his dark face. 'Master Shardlake,' he said in his lisping accent. 'So you are back?'

'What are you doing, Brother, standing there in the dark?'

'I wanted some air. I have spent the day with old Brother Paul. He died an hour ago.' He crossed himself.

'I am sorry.'

'His time had come. At the end he seemed back in his childhood. He spoke of your civil wars last century, York and Lancaster. He saw old King Henry VI led drooling through the streets of London at his restoration.'

'We have a strong king now.'

'No one could doubt that.'

'I hear Jerome has escaped.'

'Yes, his keeper left his door unlocked. But they will find him, even in a place so large as this. He's in no condition to hide out. Poor man, he is weaker than he seems, a night out will do him no good.'

'He is mad. He could be dangerous.'

'The servants have no mind on their duties now. The brothers too, they're all worrying what will become of them.'

'Is Alice safe?'

'Yes, quite safe. She and I have been working hard. Now the weather is breaking everyone is coming down with fevers. It is those foul misty humours from the marsh.'

'Tell me, Brother, were you ever in Toledo?'

He shrugged. 'When I was little our family moved from town to town. We did not reach safety in France till I was twelve. Yes, I remember we were in Toledo for a while. I remember a great castle, the sound of iron being beaten in what seemed a thousand workshops.'

'Did you ever meet an Englishman there?'

'An Englishman? I don't remember. Not that it would have been unusual in those days, there were many Englishmen in Spain then. There are none now, of course.'

'No, Spain has become our enemy.' I stepped closer and looked deep into his brown eyes, but they were unfathomable. I hitched up my coat. 'I must leave you now, Brother.'

'Will you want your room at the infirmary?'

'We shall see. But have it warmed. Goodnight.'

I left him and walked off towards the abbot's house. Passing the outbuildings I cast nervous glances into the shadows, looking for the white glimmer of a Carthusian robe. What, now, did Jerome mean to do?

THE OLD SERVANT answered my knock. He told me Abbot Fabian was at home, in conference with the prior, and Master Mark was in his room. He led me upstairs to Goodhaps's old chamber, empty now of bottles and the smell of the unwashed old man. Mark was working at the table, where a pile of letters lay spread out. I noticed his hair was growing long; he would have to visit the barber in London if he was to be fashionable again.

His greeting was brief, his eyes cold and watchful. I had little doubt he had probably spent as much as he could of the last few days with Alice.

'Looking over the abbot's correspondence?'

'Yes, sir. It all seems routine.' He eyed me carefully. 'How did things go in London? Did you find out about the sword?'

'Some clues. I have made some more enquiries and await a messenger from London. At least Lord Cromwell seems unworried about letters from Jerome reaching the Seymours. But I hear he has escaped.'

'The prior has been searching up and down with some of the younger monks. I helped yesterday for a while, but we found no trace. The prior is sore angry.'

'I can imagine. And what of these rumours the monasteries are going down?'

'Apparently a man from Lewes was at the inn saying the great priory has surrendered.'

'Cromwell said that was about to happen. He's probably sending agents round the country to spread the news, to put the other houses in fear. But rumours flying around are the last thing I want now. I'll have to try and reassure the abbot, get him to believe there's a chance Scarnsea can stay open, just for now.' The coldness in Mark's look intensified; he did not like the lie. I remembered Joan's words about him being too idealistic for this world.

'I have had a letter from home,' I told him. 'The harvest was poor, I'm afraid. Your father says he hopes the monasteries will go down, that'll bring more work to Augmentations.' Mark did not reply, only met my eyes with a chill, unhappy gaze.

'I'm going down to the abbot,' I told him. 'Stay here for now.'

✝

ABBOT FABIAN sat facing the prior across his desk. They looked as though they had been there some time. Abbot Fabian's face was more haggard than ever; Prior Mortimus's face was red, a mask of anger. They both rose to their feet at my entrance.

'Master Shardlake, sir, welcome back,' the abbot said. 'Was your journey successful?'

'Insofar as Lord Cromwell is unconcerned about any correspondence Jerome may have sent. But I hear the rogue has escaped.'

'I've turned the place upside down looking for the old bastard,' Prior Mortimus said. 'I don't know what hole he's got into, but he can't have got over the wall or past Bugge. He's here somewhere.'

'With what purpose in mind, I wonder.'

The abbot shook his head. 'That is what we have been debating, sir. Maybe he awaits an opportunity to escape. Brother Guy believes in his state of health he will not last long in the cold, without food.'

'Or maybe he awaits the chance to do someone a mischief. Me, for example.'

'I pray not,' the abbot said.

'I have told Bugge no one is to leave the precinct without my permission for the next day or so. See the brothers are told.'

'Why, sir?'

'A precaution. Now, I hear there are rumours from Lewes and everyone is saying Scarnsea will go down next.'

'You as much as told me so yourself,' the abbot said with a sigh.

I inclined my head. 'From my talks with Lord Cromwell, I gather nothing is certain now. I may have been hasty.' I felt a stab of guilt, lying to them. But it was necessary. There was one I did not wish scared into precipitate action.

Abbot Fabian's face lit up and a spark of hope crept into the prior's eyes.

'Then we won't be put down?' the abbot asked. 'There is hope?'

'Let us say talk of dissolution is premature and should be discouraged.'

The abbot leaned forward eagerly. 'Perhaps I should address the monks at supper. It is due in a half-hour. I could say that — that there are no plans to close us down?'

'That would be a good idea.'

'Ye'd better prepare something,' the prior said.

'Yes, of course.' The abbot reached for quill and paper. My eyes were drawn to the monastery seal, still at his elbow.

'Tell me, my lord, do you normally keep the door of this room unlocked?'

He looked up, surprised. 'Yes.'

'Is that wise? Could not someone come in here, unseen, and put the monastery seal on any document they chose?'

He stared at me blankly. 'But there are always servants in attendance. No one is allowed just to walk in.'

'No one?'

'No one but the obedentiaries.'

'Of course. Very well, I will leave you. Until supper.'

☩

ONCE AGAIN I watched the monks filing into the refectory. I remembered my first night there; Simon Whelplay in his pointed cap standing by the window, shivering as the snow fell outside. Tonight through that window I could see water dripping from shrinking icicles, black patches in the melting snow where ruts were turning into tiny streams.

The monks seemed withdrawn, hunched into their habits as they took their places at the tables. Anxious, hostile glances were cast to where I stood by the abbot's side at the great carved lectern. As Mark passed me to take his place at the top table I grasped his arm.

'The abbot's going to make a speech saying Scarnsea will not be taken by the king,' I whispered. 'It's important. There is a bird here I do not want startled out of its bush; not yet.'

'I am tired of this,' he muttered. He shrugged off my arm and took his seat. My cheeks flushed at his open rudeness. Abbot Fabian shuffled his notes and then, a new glow in his rubicund cheeks, told the brethren the rumours that all the monasteries were to come down were wrong. Lord Cromwell himself had said there were no plans to seek Scarnsea's surrender at present, despite the cruel murders, which were still under investigation. He added that no one was to leave the precincts.

Reactions among the monks varied. Some, especially the older ones, sighed and smiled with relief. Others looked more doubtful. I glanced along the obedentiaries' table. The junior obedentiaries, Brother Jude and Brother Hugh, looked relieved and I saw hope in Prior Mortimus's face. Brother Guy, though, shook his head slightly and Brother Edwig only frowned.

The servants brought in our dinners: thick vegetable soup, followed by mutton stew with herbs. I watched carefully to see that I was served from the common bowl and no one could interfere with the dishes as they were passed down the table. As we began eating, Prior Mortimus, who had already helped himself to two glasses of wine, turned to the abbot.

'Now we are safe, my lord, we should get on with the appointment of the new sacrist.'

'Fie, Mortimus, poor Gabriel was only buried three days ago.'

'But we must proceed. Someone will need to negotiate with the bursar over the church repairs, eh, Brother Edwig?' He tipped his silver cup at the bursar, who still wore a frowning look.

'S-so long as someone more reasonable than G-Gabriel is appointed, who understands we can't afford a big p-programme.'

Prior Mortimus turned to me. 'When it comes to money our bursar is the closest man in England. Though I never understood why you were so against scaffolding being used for the repairs, Edwig. Ye can't carry out a proper programme using ropes and pulleys.'

The bursar reddened at being made the centre of attention.

'All r-r-right. I accept you'll have to have scaffolding up there to do the w-works.'

The abbot laughed. 'Why, Brother, you argued that point with Gabriel for months. Even when he said men could get killed you would not move. What has come over you?'

'It was a m-m-matter of negotiation.' The bursar looked down, scowling into his plate. The prior took another glass of the strong wine and turned a flushed face to me.

'Ye'll not have heard the story of Edwig and the blood sausages, Commissioner.' He spoke loudly, and there were titters from the monks at the long table. The bursar's downcast face went puce.

'Come now, Mortimus,' the abbot said indulgently. 'Charity between brethren.'

'But this is a story of charity! Two years ago, the dole day came round and we'd no meat to give the poor at the gate. We'd have had to slaughter a pig to get some, and Brother Edwig wouldn't have it. Brother Guy had just come then. He'd bled some monks and started keeping the blood to manure his garden. The tale is Edwig there suggested we take some and mix it with flour to make blood puddings to give at the dole; the poor would never know it wasn't pig's blood. All to save the cost of a pig!' He laughed uproariously.

'That tale is untrue,' Brother Guy said. 'I have told people so many times.'

I looked at Brother Edwig. He had stopped eating and sat hunched over his plate, gripping his spoon tight. Suddenly he threw it down with a clatter and rose to his feet, dark eyes ablaze in his red face.

'Fools!' he shouted. 'Blasphemous fools! The only blood that should matter to you is the blood of Our Saviour, Jesus Christ, which we drink at every Mass when the wine is transformed! That blood which is all that holds the world together!' He clenched his plump fists, his face working with emotion, the stammer gone.

'Fools, there will be no more Masses. Why do you clutch at straws? How can you believe these lies about Scarnsea remaining safe when you hear what is happening all over the land? Fools! Fools! The king will destroy you all!' He banged his fists on the table, then turned and marched out of the refectory. He slammed the door, leaving a dead silence.

I took a deep breath. 'Prior Mortimus, I call that treason. Please take some servants and have Brother Edwig placed in custody.'

The prior looked aghast. 'But sir, he said nothing against the king's supremacy.'

Mark leaned across urgently. 'Surely, sir, those words weren't treason?'

'Do as I command.' I stared at Abbot Fabian.

'Do it, Mortimus, for mercy's sake.'

The prior set his lips, but rose from the table and marched out. I sat a moment bowed in thought, aware of every eye in the place upon me, then rose to follow, gesturing Mark to stay behind. I reached the refectory doorway in time to see the prior leading a group of torch-bearing servants out of the kitchen, towards the counting house.

A hand was suddenly laid on my arm. I whirled round; it was Bugge, his face intent.

'Sir, the messenger has come.'

'What?'

'The rider from London, he's here. I've never seen a man so covered in mud.'

I stood a moment, watching as Prior Mortimus banged on the counting-house door. I could not decide whether to follow him in or go to the messenger. I felt my head swim, saw little motes dancing in front of my eyes. I took a deep breath, and turned to Bugge, who was eyeing me curiously.

'Come,' I said, and led the way back to the gatehouse.

Chapter Thirty-one

THE MESSENGER SAT hugging the fire in Bugge's lodge. Despite the mud that caked him from head to foot I recognized a young man I had seen delivering letters at Cromwell's office. The vicar general would already know what the gaoler had said.

He stood up, a little shakily for I could see he was exhausted, and bowed.

'Master Shardlake?'

I nodded, too tense to speak.

'I am to hand this to you personally.' He handed me a paper bearing the Tower seal. I turned my back to him and Bugge, broke the seal and read the three lines within. It was as I had thought. I forced my features into composure as I turned to face Bugge, who was staring at me intently. The messenger had slumped back beside the fire.

'Master gatekeeper,' I said, 'this man has ridden far. See he has a room with a good fire for the night and victuals if he wants them.' I turned to the messenger. 'What is your name?'

'Hanfold, sir.'

'There may be a message to take back tomorrow morning. Goodnight. You have done well to ride so fast.'

I left the gatehouse, crumpling the paper in my pocket, and walked rapidly back across the outer court. I knew what I had to do now and my heart had never been heavier.

I stopped. Something. A shadow of movement in the corner of my vision. I turned so quickly I almost overbalanced in the slush. It had been by the blacksmith's lean-to, I was sure, but I could see nothing now.

'Who is there?' I called out sharply.

There was no reply, no sound but the steady drip of water as the snow melted from the roofs. The mist was growing thicker. It curled around the buildings, blurring their outlines and making haloes round the dim yellow glow from the windows. My ears alert for any sound, I went on to the infirmary.

Brother Paul's bed lay stripped, the blind monk sitting in his chair beside it with bowed head. The fat monk lay asleep. There was nobody else in the hall. Brother Guy's dispensary was empty too; all the monks must still be at the refectory. Edwig's arrest would have caused a mighty stir.

☩

I WENT DOWN the corridor, past my old room, to where I knew Alice's room was located. There was a strip of candlelight under her door. I knocked and opened it.

She sat on a truckle bed in the little windowless room, stuffing clothes into a big leather pannier. When she looked up at me there was fear in those large blue eyes. Her strong square face seemed to sag with it. I felt a desperate sorrow.

'You are going on a journey?' I was surprised at how normal my voice sounded, I had half-expected a croak.

She said nothing, just sat there with her hands on the straps of the pannier.

'Well, Alice?' Now my voice did tremble. 'Alice Fewterer, whose mother's maiden name was Smeaton?'

Her face flushed, but still she did not speak.

'Oh Alice, I would give my right hand for this not to be true.' I took a deep breath. 'Alice Fewterer, I must arrest you in the king's name for the foul murder of his commissioner, Robin Singleton.'

Then she spoke, her voice shaking with emotion. 'No murder. I did him justice. Justice.'

'To you it must seem so. I am right then, Mark Smeaton was your cousin?'

She looked up at me. Her eyes narrowed, as though she was calculating something. Then she spoke in clear tones of quiet ferocity such as I hope never to hear again from the mouth of a woman.

'More than my cousin. We were lovers.'

'What?'

'His father, my mother's brother, left to seek his fortune in London when he was a boy. My mother never forgave him for leaving the family, but when the man I was to marry died I went to London to claim kin, for all she tried to stop me. There was no work here.'

'And they took you in?'

'John Smeaton and his wife were good people. Good people. They welcomed me into their house and helped me to a position with a London apothecary. That was four years ago, Mark was already a court musician then. Thank God my aunt died from the sweating sickness, at least she was spared what happened.' Tears appeared in her eyes, but she wiped them away and raised her eyes to my face. Again there was something calculating in them, something I could not fathom.

'But you must know all this, *Commissioner* –' I have never heard such contempt put into a single word – 'or why are you here?'

'I knew nothing for certain till half an hour ago. The sword led me to John Smeaton – no wonder you pleaded with me not to go to London that day by the fish pond – but for a while I could go no further. I was puzzled when the records said John Smeaton left no male relatives, and his estate went to an old woman – your mother?'

'Yes.'

'I have turned over the name of everyone in this house, wondering who could have had the skill and strength to behead a man, and in London I was no further forward. Then I thought, what if John Smeaton had another *female* relative? All this time I had assumed a man committed the crime, but then I saw there was no reason why a strong young woman could not have done it. And that led me to you,' I concluded sadly. 'The message I have just had confirmed that a young woman visited Mark Smeaton in his cell the night before he died, and the description is of you.' I looked at her and shook my head. 'It was a grievous sin for a woman to do such a thing.'

Again her voice was level, though dripping with bitterness. 'Was it? Was it worse than what he did?' I marvelled at her control, her steeliness.

'I know what was done to Mark Smeaton,' I said. 'Jerome told me some, the rest I learned in London.'

'Jerome? What has he to do with it?'

'Jerome was in the cell next to your cousin the night you visited him. When he came here he must have recognized you. Singleton as well; that was why he called him liar and perjurer. And, of course, when he swore to me he knew of no *man* here who could have done such a thing, it was a piece of his twisted mockery. He guessed it was you.'

'He said nothing to me.' She shook her head. 'He should have done, so few know what truly happened. The evil of what you people did.'

'I did not know the truth about Mark Smeaton, Alice, nor the queen, when I came here. You are right. It was a wicked, cruel thing.'

Hope appeared in her eyes. 'Then let me go, sir. All the time you have been here you have puzzled me, you are not a brute like Singleton and Cromwell's other men. I have only done justice. Please, let me go.'

I shook my head. 'I can't. What you did was still murder. I have to take you into custody.'

She looked at me pleadingly. 'Sir, if you knew it all. Please listen to me.'

I should have guessed she wanted to keep me there, but I did not interrupt. This was the explanation of Singleton's death I had been seeking for so long.

'Mark Smeaton came to visit his parents as often as he could. He had gone from Cardinal Wolsey's choir to Anne Boleyn's household, become her musician. Poor Mark, he was ashamed of his origins, but he still visited his parents. If his head was turned by the splendour of the court that was no wonder. It seduced him as you would have it seduce Mark Poer.'

'That will never happen. You must know that by now.'

'Mark took me to see the outside of the great palaces, Greenwich and Whitehall, but he would never let me in, even after we became lovers. He said we could only meet in secret. I was content. And then one day I came home from my work at the apothecary's to find Robin Singleton at my widowed uncle's home with a troop of soldiers, shouting at him, trying to make him say his son had spoken of lying with the queen. When I understood what had happened I ran at Singleton and struck him and the soldiers had to haul me off.' She frowned. 'That was when I first knew what anger lay within me. They cast me out, and I do not think John Smeaton told them of my relationship with Mark, or that I was his cousin, or they would have come after me too, to bully me into silence.

'My poor uncle died two days after Mark. I attended the trial, I could see how the jury looked afraid – there was never any doubt about the verdict. I tried to visit Mark in the Tower, but they would not let me see him until a gaoler took pity on me the night before he died. He lay in chains in that awful place, in the rags of his fine clothes.'

'I know. Jerome told me.'

'When Mark was arrested Singleton said if he confessed to sleeping with the queen he would be reprieved by the king's mercy. He told me that when he was first arrested he had a crazy notion that as he had done no wrong the law would protect him!' She gave a harsh laugh. 'England's law is a rack in a cellar! They racked him till his whole world was nothing but a scream. So he confessed, and they gave him two weeks' life as a cripple while he was tried, then they cut his head off. I saw it, I was in the crowd. I promised him my face would be the last thing he saw.' She shook her head. 'There was so much blood. A stream of it shooting through the air. Always there is so much blood.'

'Yes. There is.' I remembered Jerome saying Smeaton had confessed to lying with many women: Alice's picture of him was idealized, but I could not tell her that.

'And then Singleton appeared here,' I said.

'Can you imagine now how I felt that day when I came across the monastery courtyard and saw him arguing with the bursar's assistant? I had heard there was a commissioner come to visit the abbot, but I had not known it would be him—'

'And you decided to kill him?'

'I had dreamed of killing that evil man so many times. I simply knew it was what I must do. There had to be justice.'

'Often in this world there is not.'

Her face became cold and set. 'This time there was.'

'He hadn't recognized you?'

She laughed. 'No. He saw a servant girl carrying a sack, if he noticed me at all. I had been here over a year then, helping Brother Guy. The London apothecary had dismissed me because I was a relative of the Smeatons. I came back to my mother's. She had a lawyer's letter and went to London to fetch my uncle's poor possessions. And then she died – she had a seizure like my uncle – and Copynger evicted me. So I came here.'

'Didn't the townspeople know of your connection to the Smeatons?'

'It was thirty years since my uncle left and my mother's name changed when she married. The name was forgotten, and I was not likely to remind anyone. I said I had been away working in Esher for an apothecary who died.'

'You kept the sword.'

'For sentiment. Of a winter's evening my uncle used to show us some of the moves swordsmen make. I learned a little about balance, steps, angles of force. When I saw Singleton I knew I would use it.'

'By God, madam, you have a fearsome courage.'

'It was easy. I had no keys to the kitchen, but I remembered the story of that old passage.'

'And found it.'

'By looking through all the rooms, yes. Then I wrote an anonymous note to Singleton saying I was an informer, and would meet him in the kitchen in the small hours. I told him I was someone who had a great secret to reveal to him.' She smiled then, a smile that made me shiver.

'And he would have thought it was from a monk.'

The smile faded. 'I knew there would be blood, so I went to the laundry and stole a habit. I had found a key to the laundry in the table drawer in my room when I came here.'

'The key Brother Luke dropped when he was grappling with Orphan Stonegarden. She must have kept it.'

'That poor girl. Better you should look for her killer than Singleton's.' She stared at me fixedly. 'I put on the habit, took the sword, and went through the passage to the kitchen. Brother Guy and I were tending one of the old monks; I said I needed to rest for an hour. It was so easy. I stood behind the cupboard in the kitchen and the moment he stepped past me I struck him.' She smiled, a smile of terrible fulfilment. 'I had sharpened the sword, and his head was off with a stroke.'

'Just like Queen Anne Boleyn's.'

'Just like Mark's.' Her expression changed, she frowned. 'So much blood. I hoped his blood would wash away my anger, but it has not. I still see my cousin's face in dreams.'

Then her eyes lit up and she gave a great sigh of relief as a hand grasped my wrist from behind and pulled my arm behind my back, sending my dagger clattering to the floor. Another wrapped itself round my neck. Looking down I saw a knife held to my throat.

'Jerome?' I croaked.

'No, sir,' Mark's voice answered. 'Do not cry out.' The knife pressed into my flesh. 'Go and sit on that bed. Move slowly.'

I tottered across the room and crumpled upon the truckle bed. Alice stood up and went to Mark's side, putting her arm round him.

'I thought you would never come. I have kept him talking.'

Mark closed the door, and then stood balanced on the balls of his feet, his dagger a foot from my throat; in a moment he could pitch forward and slit my gizzard. His face was not cold now, but full of determination. I looked at him. 'It was you in the courtyard just now? You followed me?'

'Yes. Who else knows, sir?' Still he called me sir. I almost laughed.

'The messenger was one of Lord Cromwell's servants. Cromwell will know its contents by now. So, you know what she has done?'

'She told me when we first lay together the day you left for London. I told her you were clever, I saw you drawing closer and we made preparations to leave tonight. If you had arrived a few hours later you would have found us escaped. I wish you had.'

'There is no escape now. Not in England.'

'We shall not be in England. A boat is waiting out on the river to take us to France.'

'The smugglers?'

'Yes,' Alice said in matter-of-fact tones. 'I lied to you. My childhood friends never drowned and they remain my friends. There is a French ship waiting out at sea, it is picking up a cargo from the monastery tomorrow night, but they are sending a boat in to collect us tonight.'

I started. 'From the monastery? Do you know from whom, or what it is?'

'I do not care. We will wait on the ship till tomorrow, then sail for France.'

'Mark, do you know what this cargo is?'

'No.' He bit his lip. 'I am sorry, sir, only Alice and our escape matter to me now.'

'They have no love of English reformers in France.'

He looked at me with pity. 'I am no reformer. I never have been. Least of all after what I have learned of how Cromwell works.'

'You are a traitor,' I told him. 'False to your king and false to me who treated you as a son.'

He looked at me pityingly. 'I am no son to you, sir. I have never agreed with your religion. You would have realized that if you had ever really listened to what I said instead of treating me as a sounding board for your own opinions.'

I groaned. 'I have not deserved this of you. Nor you, Alice.'

'Who knows what anyone deserves?' Mark said with sudden wildness. 'There is no justice or order in this world, as you would see if you were not so blind. After what Alice has told me, I know that for certain. I go with Alice, I decided that four days ago.' And yet as he spoke I saw his face waver, I saw shame and that the affection he had had for me was not quite gone.

'Have you become a papist, then? I am not as blind as you think, Mark, I sometimes wondered what you truly believed. What then do you think of this woman's desecration of a church? That was you, Alice, wasn't it? You laid that slain cock on the altar after you had killed Singleton, to confuse the trail?'

'Yes,' she said, 'I did. But if you think Mark or I are papists you are wrong. You are both the same, reformers and papists, you fashion beliefs which you force the people to follow on pain of death, while you struggle for power and lands and money, which are all any of you truly want.'

'That is not what I want.'

'Perhaps not. You have a kind heart and I did not enjoy lying to you. But when it comes to what is happening in England now you are as blind as a newborn kitten.' Pity mingled with anger in her voice. 'You should see things through the eyes of common people, but your kind never will. Do you think I would care for any Church after what I have seen of it all? I felt more sorrow at having to kill that cock than at what I did at the altar.'

'And what now?' I asked. 'Is this my death?'

Mark swallowed. 'I would not do that. Not unless you make me.' He turned to Alice. 'We can tie him up and gag him, put him in your cupboard. They'll be looking for him, but they won't think of looking here. When will Brother Guy find you are missing?'

'I told him I was going to bed early. He won't notice I'm gone till I don't appear in the dispensary at seven. By then we will be at sea.'

I struggled to collect my thoughts. 'Mark, please listen to me. You are forgetting Brother Gabriel, Simon Whelplay, Orphan Stonegarden.'

'I had nothing to do with their deaths!' Alice said hotly.

'I know. I had considered whether there might be two killers working in league, but I never thought of two separate killers. Mark, think of what you have seen. Orphan Stonegarden pulled from the fish pond, Gabriel crushed like an insect, Simon driven mad by poison. You have helped me, you have been with me. Would you let the killer loose?'

'We were going to leave you a note, tell you Alice killed Singleton.'

'Please listen to me. Brother Edwig. Is he taken?'

Mark shook his head. 'No. I followed you to the refectory door and heard Bugge say there was a message. Then I followed you to the gatehouse and saw you go back to the infirmary. But Prior Mortimus came up to me and said Brother Edwig was not in his counting house, nor in his cell. He seems to have fled. That is why I took so much time, Alice.'

'He must not escape,' I said urgently. 'He has sold lands, I believe without the abbot's knowledge, he has a thousand pounds hidden somewhere. That boat, it's for his escape. Of course, he has been buying time until it arrived. That was why he killed Novice Whelplay, because he feared he would tell me about Orphan Stonegarden and I might have him arrested.'

He lowered his dagger, his expression astonished. I had his attention now.

'It was Brother Edwig who killed her?'

'Yes! Then he tried to kill me in the church. In the snow it would be days or weeks before anyone came from London to replace me and by that time he would be away. You will be sharing that boat with a murderer.'

'Are you sure of this?' Mark asked.

'Yes. I built a false pattern around Brother Gabriel, but this is the truth. What you tell me about the boat seals matters. Edwig is a great murderer and thief. In all conscience you cannot let him escape.'

For a second I saw him waver. 'You are certain Brother Edwig killed the girl?' Alice asked.

'Certain. It had to be one of the obedentiaries who visited Simon Whelplay. Prior Mortimus and Edwig had a history of troubling women; Mortimus bothered you, but Brother Edwig did not – because he feared he might lose control of himself as he had done with Orphan.'

Mark bit his lip. 'Alice, we cannot allow him to go free.'

She looked at me desperately. 'They'll hang me, or more likely burn me. They'll accuse me of witchcraft because I killed that cock.'

'Listen,' Mark said. 'When we reach the boat we can tell them not to wait, leave tonight. Then he won't get away with his pestiferous gold. They won't want to wait on a murderer.'

'Yes,' she said eagerly. 'We can do that.'

'He will still be at large,' I said.

Mark took a deep breath. 'Then you must catch him, sir. I am sorry.'

'We must go now,' Alice said urgently. 'The tide will be turning.'

'There is time. It is eight by the abbey clock, half an hour to full tide. We still have time to get across the marsh.'

'Across the marsh?' I said, unbelieving.

'Yes,' Alice said, 'by the path I showed you. The boat is waiting in the estuary.'

'But you can't!' I said. 'Have you not seen the weather? The snow is almost melted, the marsh will be naught but liquid mud. I came in through the channel this afternoon, I saw what it was like and it'll be worse now. Meltwater is pouring off the Downs. And there's a heavy mist coming down. You'll never make it! You must believe me!'

'I know the paths well,' she said. 'I can find my way.' But she looked uncertain.

'Mark, in God's name believe me, you will go to your deaths!'

He took a deep breath. 'She knows the way. And does not death wait for us here?'

I took a deep breath. 'Let her escape. Let her go now and take her chance where she will. I will say nothing of your involvement, I swear. God's death, I'm telling you I'll be an accomplice after the fact, I'll put my own life at risk for you both! But don't go out on the marsh!'

Alice looked at him desperately. 'Mark, don't leave me. I can get us through.'

'I tell you, you can't! You haven't seen what it's like out there!'

He looked between us, his face an agony of indecision. I see it now, and think, how young he was, how young to have to decide his fate and hers in an instant. His face set hard and my heart sank.

'We must bind you now, sir. I will try not to hurt you. Alice, where is your nightshift?'

She took the garment from under her pillow, and Mark cut it into long strips with his dagger.

'Lie on your front, sir.'

'Mark, for pity's sake—'

He grasped my shoulder and twisted me over. He bound my arms fast behind me, then my legs, before rolling me over again.

'Mark, don't go out there—'

They were the last words I ever said to him, for then he stuffed a great rag of the shift into my mouth, nearly choking me. Alice threw open the door of the little cupboard and they bundled me inside. Mark paused, looking down at me.

'Wait a moment. His back troubles him.'

Alice watched impatiently as he took the pillow from the bed and wedged it behind me, supporting my back as I lay crouched in the cupboard. 'I am sorry,' he whispered. Then he turned and shut the door, leaving me in darkness. A moment later I heard the outer door close gently.

I wanted to vomit, but I knew if I did I would surely choke. I leaned back against the pillow, taking deep breaths through my nose. Alice had said Brother Guy would not look for her until she failed to appear in the dispensary at seven. I had eleven hours to wait.

Chapter Thirty-two

Twice during that long, cold night I thought I heard distant shouts; people would be looking for Mark and me, and for Edwig as well. Somehow I must have slept, for I had a dream of Jerome's face looking down at me as I lay tied, cackling maniacally, then woke with a start to the thick darkness of the cupboard and the bonds chafing at my wrists.

I had been awake some hours when at last I heard footsteps in the room outside. I summoned up enough energy to kick my heels on the door and a moment later it opened. I winced and blinked at the sudden daylight as Brother Guy looked down at me, his mouth an 'O' of astonishment. Irrelevantly I thought he had done well to keep a full set of teeth to middle age.

He untied my bonds and helped me to my feet, telling me to move slowly lest I injure my stiff back with sudden movement. He led me to my room, where I was glad to sit before a fire, for I was frozen. I told him what had happened, and when he learned Alice had been Singleton's murderer he sat down on the bed with a groan.

'I remember telling her of that passage when she first came. I was trying to make conversation; she seemed so lost and alone. And to think I gave her the care of my patients.'

'I think it was only Singleton who was ever in danger from her. Brother Guy, tell me, is Edwig still at large?'

'Yes, he has vanished as completely as Jerome. But he might have escaped. Bugge left his lodge unattended last night when the hue and cry broke. Or he could have got out at the back, by the marsh. But I did not understand why you were so keen to have him arrested. You have heard worse words than his since you have been here.'

'He killed Gabriel, and Simon, and I believe the girl Orphan as well. And he has stolen a fortune in gold.'

Guy sat stunned, then put his head in his hands. 'Dear Jesu, what has this house become that it has nourished two murderers?'

'Alice would not have been a murderess but for the times we live in. And Edwig would never have got away with this fraud had things been more stable. You might as well ask what a country England has become. And I have been a part of it.'

He looked up. 'Abbot Fabian collapsed last night. After you ordered Brother Edwig arrested. He seems unable to do anything or talk to anyone; he just sits in his room staring into space.'

I sighed. 'He was never capable of dealing with this. Brother Edwig took his seal and used it on the deeds when he sold those lands. He swore the buyers to secrecy and they must have assumed the abbot knew.' I heaved myself up. 'Brother Guy, you must help me. I need to go to the back of the monastery. I need to see whether Alice and Mark could have got away.'

He doubted I was fit for such a journey, but I insisted and he helped me to my feet. I took my staff and we went outside. The monastery lay under a cloudy sky, the air mild and muggy. Its appearance had changed utterly. Everywhere in the courtyard lay little pools of water and piles of dirty slush that only yesterday had been mounds of snow.

People going to and fro stopped and stared as I limped by. Prior Mortimus hurried over. 'Commissioner! We thought ye dead like Singleton. Where is your assistant?'

Again I told the story as a shocked audience of monks and servants surrounded us. I ordered Prior Mortimus to send for Copynger; if Edwig had escaped, the country must be roused to find him.

I do not know how I made it through the orchard. I would not have done without Brother Guy's support for my back was an agony after that night in the cupboard and I felt faint. At last, though, we reached the rear wall. I unlocked the gate and passed through.

I found myself staring at a lake half a mile wide. The whole marsh was covered in water, the river distinguishable only as a ribbon of rapidly flowing current in the centre of an expanse that reached almost to our feet. It was shallow, no more than a foot covering the mud for everywhere reeds poked through, waving in the light breeze, but the soft ground beneath must have been saturated.

'Look!' Brother Guy pointed down at two pairs of footprints, a larger and a slightly smaller one, imprinted in the mud by the gate. They led down the bank, into the water.

'By Jesu,' he said. 'They went in there.'

'They can't have gone a hundred yards,' I breathed. 'In that mist, in the dark, in all that water.'

'What is that? Over there?' Brother Guy pointed to something floating, some way out.

'It's a lamp! One of those little candleholders from the infirmary. They must have been carrying it. Oh God.' I grabbed at the infirmarian for support, for my senses failed at the thought of Mark and Alice losing their footing and falling, lying now somewhere under that flooded morass. Brother Guy lowered me to the bank and I sat taking deep breaths until my senses cleared. I looked up again to see the infirmarian praying quietly in Latin, hands clasped in front of him, his eyes fixed on the lamp drifting gently over the face of the waters.

✝

BROTHER GUY helped me back to the infirmary. There he insisted I rest and eat, sitting me down in his kitchen and serving me himself. Food and drink revived my body, though my heart lay dead within me like a stone. I kept seeing pictures of Mark in my head; laughingly exchanging jests on the road; arguing with me in our room; holding Alice in the kitchen. At the end it was him I mourned most.

'There were only two sets of footprints going out through that gate,' Brother Guy said at length. 'It does not seem Edwig went that way.'

'Not him,' I answered bitterly. 'He'd have been out through the gate when Bugge's back was turned.' I clenched my fists. 'But I'll hunt him down if it takes me the rest of my days.'

There was a knock at the door and Prior Mortimus appeared, his face grim.

'Have you sent to Copynger?' I asked.

'Yes, he should be here soon. But Commissioner, we've found—'

'Edwig?'

'No. Jerome. He's in the church. You should come and see.'

'You're not able,' Brother Guy said, but I shook off his hand and grabbed my staff. I followed the prior to the church, where a crowd had gathered outside. The pittancer stood guard on the door, keeping them out. The prior shouldered through the crowd and we went inside.

Water was dripping somewhere; the only other sound was a faint weeping, a keening. I followed Prior Mortimus down the great empty nave with its candlelit niches, our footsteps echoing, until we came to the niche where the Thief's hand had stood. The heap of crutches and braces that had lain at the base of the plinth were scattered across the floor. I saw now that the block was hollow, there was a space underneath large enough to hold a man. Inside, sitting crouched over and holding something, was Jerome. His white habit was torn and filthy and a great stink rose from him as he sat, weeping piteously.

'I found him half an hour ago,' the prior said. 'He'd crawled under there and pulled the crutches back in front to hide himself. I was looking round the church and I remembered that space under there.'

'What has he got? Is it—?'

The prior nodded. 'The relic. The hand of the Penitent Thief.'

I knelt before Jerome, wincing as pain shot through my joints.

I could see he held a big square box, encrusted with jewels that sparkled in the candlelight. A dark shape was dimly visible inside.

'Brother,' I said gently, 'was it you that took the relic?'

For the first time since I had met him, Jerome's voice was quiet. 'Yes. It is so dear to us, to the Church. It has cured so many people.'

'So you took it in the confusion after Singleton was killed.'

'I hid it under here to save it, to save it.' He clutched it tighter. 'I know what Cromwell will do, he will destroy this holy thing which God gave as a sign of his forgiveness. When they locked me up I knew you might find it, I had to protect it. Now it is lost, lost. I cannot resist any more, I am so tired,' he concluded in a sad, matter-of-fact voice. He shook his head and stared before him, his eyes blank.

Prior Mortimus reached in and took his shoulder. 'Come, Jerome, it's all over. Leave it and come away with me.' To my surprise the Carthusian made no demur. He climbed painfully out of the niche, pulling his crutch after him, and kissed the casket before depositing it carefully on the floor.

'I'll take him back to his cell,' the prior said.

I nodded. 'Yes, do that.'

✝

JEROME DID NOT look at me, or the relic, again, but allowed Prior Mortimus to lead him down the nave in a painful shuffle. I watched him go. If Jerome had told me he had seen Alice visit Mark Smeaton the day I questioned him, instead of playing games, I could have arrested her there and then and with Singleton's killing solved I might have uncovered Edwig sooner. Then Mark would not have died, nor Gabriel. Yet somehow I did not feel anger towards him; all emotion seemed to have been leached out of me.

I knelt and peered at the relic where it lay on the floor. The casket was of richly decorated gold, the stones set in it the largest emeralds I had ever seen. Through the glass I made out a hand, skewered by the wrist to a piece of ancient black wood with a broad-headed nail, lying on a cushion of purple velvet. It was a brown, mummified thing, but discernibly a hand; I could even make out what looked like calluses on the fingers. Could it truly be the hand of the thief who had died with Christ, accepted him on the Cross? I touched the glass, with a second's mad hope that the pains I felt in every joint might vanish, my hump disappear and my back become whole and normal like poor Mark's that I had so envied. But there was nothing, only the sound of my fingernail tapping the glass.

And then I saw a tiny flash of bright gold from the corner of my eye, descending through the air. Something hit the tiled floor a couple of feet away with a tinkle. It spun and came to rest. I stared at it. It was a gold coin, a noble, King Henry's head staring up at me from the floor.

I looked upward. I was standing under the bell tower, above was the tangle of ropes and pulleys that had been the subject of the jests against Edwig at supper. But something was different. The workmen's basket was not there. It had been pulled up into the bell tower.

'He's up there!' I breathed. So that was where he had hidden the gold, in that basket. I should have looked more carefully at what lay under the cover when I had seen it before, the time I went to the bell tower with Mortimus. It was a clever hiding place. So that was why he had stopped the repair work.

I had been fearful when I climbed the winding stairs to the bell tower with Prior Mortimus, but this time I felt nothing but savage, determined fury as I struggled upwards, ignoring the screams of protest from every limb. Emotion had not been drained from me after all, it merely slept. Now an anger such as I had never known before impelled me on. I reached the tower where the bell ropes were. The basket was there, lying empty on its side, a couple more gold coins on the floor. There was no one in the room. I stared at the steps giving access to the bells themselves. More gold coins had been spilled there. I realized anyone here must have heard me climbing up; had he retreated to the bell room?

I climbed the steps carefully, holding my staff before me. I turned the handle of the door and quickly stepped back, using my staff to thrust it open. It was just as well I did, for a figure shot out and swung an unlit wooden torch at the space where I would have been standing. The improvised club jarred harmlessly on my staff and I caught a glimpse of the bursar's face, red and furious, his eyes wide and staring as I had never seen them.

'You are discovered, Brother Edwig,' I called. 'I know about your boat to France! I arrest you in the king's name for theft and murder!'

He darted back inside and I heard his feet pattering away across the boards, accompanied by a metallic chinking sound that puzzled me.

'It's over,' I called. 'There's no other way out of there.' I climbed the last steps and looked in, trying to get a glimpse of him, but from this angle I could see only the floorboards and the great bells beyond the rail. More coins lay scattered around the floor.

I realized this was an impasse; he could not get past me, but I was trapped too. If I were to retreat down the spiral staircase I would be vulnerable to an attack from above and the man I had once taken for a penny-pinching clerk was clearly capable of anything. I advanced into the room, swinging my staff ahead of me.

He was at the other end, behind the bells. He stepped out as I entered and I saw he had two big leather panniers tied together with a thick rope round his neck. The chink of metal sounded from them as he moved. He was breathing hard, brandishing the club in his right hand, the knuckles standing out white and hard.

'What was the plan, Brother?' I called out. 'Take the money from the sales and flee to a new life in France?' I advanced a step, trying to distract him, but he was watchful as a cat and swung the torch threateningly.

'N-no!' He stood there and bawled out the word like a child falsely accused. 'No! This is my fee to enter heaven!'

'What?'

'She refused me and refused me and then the Devil filled my soul with anger and I killed her! Do you know how easy it is to kill someone, Commissioner?' He laughed wildly. 'I saw too much killing as a child, it opened the door to the Devil, always he fills my mind with dreams of b-blood!'

His fat face was scarlet and the veins stood out on his neck as he screamed at me. He had lost control; if I could surprise him, get close enough to ring the bells—

'You'll find it hard to persuade a jury of that,' I called out.

'Pox on your juries!' His stammer vanished as his voice rose to a shout. 'The pope, who is God's vicar on earth, allows the purchase of redemption from sins! I told you, God figures our souls in heaven, the credit balance and the debit! And I will make him such a gift he will take me to his right hand! I am taking almost a thousand pounds to the Church in France, a thousand pounds from the hands of your heretic king. This is a great work in the eyes of God!' He eyed me furiously. 'You will not stop me!'

'Will it buy you forgiveness for Simon and Gabriel too?'

He pointed the torch at me. 'Whelplay guessed what I had done to the girl and would have told you. He had to die, I had to complete my work! And you should have died instead of Gabriel, you crow, God will hold *you* to account for that!'

'You madman!' I shouted. 'I will see you in the Bedlam, displayed as a warning of what perverted religion can do!'

Then he grasped his club in both hands and ran at me with an eldritch scream. The heavy panniers slowed him or he would have had me, but I managed to dodge aside. He whirled round and swung again. I raised my staff, but he knocked it from my hand with the torch. As it clattered to the floor, I realized he had got himself between me and the door. He advanced slowly, swinging the torch, and I backed up against the low railing separating me from the bells and the great drop below. He was cooler again now; I saw those wicked black eyes calculating the distance between us and the height of the rail. 'Where is your boy?' he asked with an evil grin. 'Not here to protect you today?' Then he flew at me and landed a clout on my arm as I lifted it to defend myself. He pushed me hard in the chest and I fell back, over the low railing.

I still relive that fall in dreams, the sensation of twisting as I fell, my hands grasping at empty air. Always I hear Brother Edwig's triumphant shout in my ears. Then my arms slapped against the side of a bell and instinctively I threw my arms round it, clutching at the metal surface, grinding my fingernails into the ornate design on the surface. It stopped my fall, but my hands were slick with sweat and I felt myself slipping down.

Then my foot hit something and I came to rest. I flattened myself against the bell and managed, just, to link my fingers together around it. Glancing quickly down I saw my foot had come to rest on the plaque on the old Spanish bell. I clung on desperately.

Then I felt the bell start to move. My weight was causing it to swing outwards. It hit the neighbouring bell and a deafening clang echoed through the bell tower as the juddering impact threatened to dislodge me. The bell swung back, with me clinging on like a limpet, and I had a glimpse of Edwig taking off his pannier and bending to the floor to pick up the coins he had dropped, all the while glancing malevolently at me. He knew I could only hold on for moments more. Far below I heard faint voices echoing up; the crowd outside must have run in at the unexpected peal of the bell. I dared not look down. The bell swung back and hit its neighbour again; this time it set the whole lot clanging with a noise I thought would burst my ears and now as the bell vibrated with the impact I felt my hands slipping apart.

Then I did the most desperate thing I have ever done in my life. I only made the attempt because I knew the alternative was certain death. In a single movement I let my hands fall apart, twisted in the air and used my foot against the plaque as leverage to hurl myself outwards, towards the rail, commending my soul to God in what I knew was probably my final thought on earth.

I hit the rail with my midriff, knocking the breath from my body.

It shook with the impact as my frantic hands grasped the inner side and I hauled myself over, how I do not know. Then I was lying on the floor in a heap, my back and arms an agony, as across the room Edwig knelt clutching a handful of coins, staring at me in angry bafflement as the clangour of the bells rang and sang in our ears, the vibration now shaking the very floorboards.

He was up in an instant, grabbing for his panniers and running for the door. I threw myself at him, clutching for his eyes. He thrust me off, but was thrown off balance by the weight of the bags. He staggered and came up against the rail as I had done a minute before. As he did so he dropped his leather bags. They fell over the edge, and with a cry he leaned over and snatched at the rope holding them together. He caught hold, but the movement overbalanced him. For a moment he lay spreadeagled across the rails and I believe that if he had let go the gold he might have saved himself, but he held on. The bags' weight tipped him forward and he fell over head first, bouncing off the side of a bell and disappearing from view with a scream of terrified anger, as though in his last moment he knew he faced his Maker before he had made his great gift. I ran to the parapet and saw him still falling, his habit billowing out around him as he spun to earth in the middle of a great shower of coins from the panniers. The crowd fled in panic as he hit the ground in an explosion of blood and gold.

I leaned over the rail, panting and sweating, watching as the crowd slowly crept in again. Some looked down at the bursar's remains, others peered up to where I stood. To my disgust I saw monks and servants get down on hands and knees and begin scrabbling on the floor, grabbing up handfuls of coins.

Epilogue

As I entered the monastery courtyard I saw the great bells had been taken from the church tower and now sat waiting to be melted down. They were in pieces, huge shards of ornamented metal piled in a heap. They would have been cut from the rings holding them to the roof and left to drop to the floor of the church. That would have made a mighty noise.

A little way off, next to a large mound of charcoal, a brick furnace had been erected. It was swallowing lead; a gang of men on the church roof were throwing down chunks and strips of it. More of the auditors' men, waiting below, fetched the lead and fed it into the fire.

Cromwell had been right; the crop of surrenders he had obtained early in the winter had persuaded the other monastic houses that resistance was hopeless and every day now came news of another monastery dissolved. Soon none would be left. All over England abbots were retiring on fat pensions, while the brethren went to take up secular parishes or retire on their own, thinner, stipends. There were tales of much chaos; at the inn in Scarnsea, where I was staying, I heard that when the monks left the monastery three months before, half a dozen who were too old or sick to move any further had taken rooms there and refused to leave when their money ran out; the constable and his men had had to put them on the road. They had included the fat monk with the ulcerated leg, and poor, stupid Septimus.

When King Henry learned of the events at St Donatus he had ordered that it be razed to the ground. Portinari, Cromwell's Italian engineer, who even now was demolishing Lewes Priory, was coming on to Scarnsea afterwards to take down the buildings. I had heard he was very skilled; at Lewes he had managed to undermine the foundations so the whole church came tumbling down at one go in great clouds of dust; they said in Scarnsea it had been a wonderful and terrible sight, and looked forward to seeing the spectacle repeated.

It had been a hard winter, and Portinari had been unable to get his men and equipment down to the Channel coast before spring came. They would be at Scarnsea in a week, but first the Augmenta- tions officers had arrived to take away everything of value, down to the lead from the roof and the brass from the bells. It was an Augmentations man who met me at the gatehouse and checked my commission; Bugge and the other servants were long gone.

I had been surprised when Cromwell sent a letter ordering me to Scarnsea to supervise the process. I had heard little from him since making a brief visit to Westminster to discuss my report in December. He told me then that he had endured an uncomfortable half-hour with the king when Henry learned that mayhem and murder at a religious house had been kept from him for weeks, and that his new commissioner's assistant had absconded with the old commissioner's killer. Perhaps the king had boxed his chief minister's ears, as I had heard he was wont to do; at all events Cromwell's manner had been brusque and he dismissed me without thanks. His favour, I had taken it, was withdrawn.

Although I still held the formal title of commissioner I was not needed, the Augmentations officers were more than capable of carry- ing out the work, and I wondered whether Cromwell had thought to make me revisit the scene of those terrible experiences as a punish- ment for that uncomfortable half-hour of his. It would have been characteristic.

Justice Copynger, now the king's tenant of the former monastery lands, stood a little way off with another man, looking over plans. I approached him, passing a couple of Augmentations officers carrying armfuls of books from the library and heaping them up in the courtyard, ready for burning.

Copynger grasped my hand. 'Commissioner, how are you? We have better weather now than when you were last here.'

'Indeed. Spring is almost come, though that is a cold wind from the sea. How do you find the abbot's house?'

'I have settled in most happily. Abbot Fabian kept it in good repair. When the monastery is down I will have a fine view over the Channel.' He waved towards the monks' cemetery, where men were busy digging up the headstones. 'See, over there I am making a paddock for my horses; I bought the monks' whole stable at a good price.'

'I hope you have not put Augmentations men to that work, Sir Gilbert,' I said with a smile. Copynger had been ennobled at Christmas, touched on the shoulder by a sword held by the king himself; Cromwell needed loyal men in the shires more than ever now.

'No, no, those are my men, paid by me.' He gave me a haughty look. 'I was sorry you did not wish to stay with me while you are here.'

'This place has unhappy memories. I am better in the town, I hope you will understand.'

'Very well, sir, very well.' He nodded condescendingly. 'But you will dine with me later, I hope. I would like to show you the plans my surveyor here has drawn up; we are going to turn some of the monastery outhouses into sheep pens once the main buildings are down. That will be a spectacle, eh? Only a few days now.'

'It will indeed. If you will excuse me for now.' I bowed and left him, wrapping my coat around me against the wind.

I went through the door to the claustral buildings. Inside, the cloister walk was dirty and muddy from the passage of many booted feet. The auditor from Augmentations had set himself up in state in the refectory, where his men brought him a constant stream of plate and gilded statues, gold crosses and tapestries, copes and albs and even the monks' bedding – everything that might have value in the auction to be held in two days' time.

Master William Glench sat in a refectory stripped of its furnishings but filled with boxes and chests, his back to a roaring fire, discussing an entry in his great ledger with a scrivener. He was a tall, thin man with spectacles and a fussy manner; a whole raft of such people had been taken on at Augmentations over the winter. I introduced myself and Glench rose and bowed, after carefully marking the place in his book.

'You seem to have everything well organized,' I said.

He nodded portentously. 'Everything, sir, down to the very pots and pans in the kitchens.' His manner reminded me momentarily of Edwig; I suppressed a shudder.

'I see they are preparing to burn the books. Is that necessary? Might they not have some value?'

He shook his head firmly. 'No, sir. All the books are to be destroyed; they are instruments of papist worship. There's not one in honest English.'

I turned and opened a chest at random. It was full of ornamentation from the church. I lifted out a finely carved gold chalice. It was one of those Edwig had thrown into the fish pond after Orphan's body, to make people think her a runaway thief. I turned it over in my hands.

'Those are not to be sold,' Glench said. 'All the gold and silver is to go to the Tower mint for melting down. Sir Gilbert tried to buy some pieces. He says the ornamentation is fine and so it may be, but they're all baubles of papist ceremony. He should know better.'

'Yes,' I said, 'he should.' I put the chalice back.

Two men carried in a big wicker basket and the scrivener began unloading habits onto the table. 'These should have been cleaned,' the scrivener said crossly. 'They'd fetch more.'

I could sense Glench's impatience to be back at work. 'I will leave you,' I said. 'Make sure not to forget anything,' I added, taking a moment's pleasure in his affronted stare.

I crossed the cloister to the church, keeping a careful eye on the men scrambling over the roof; already fallen tiles lay dotted round the cloister square. Inside the church, light still streamed through the ornate stained-glass windows, still created a kaleidoscope of warm colours on the floor of the nave. But the walls and side chapels were bare now. The sound of hammering and voices echoed down from the roof. At the head of the nave the floor was broken, a mass of shattered tiles. It was the spot where Edwig had fallen and also where the bells would have landed when they had been cut from the roof. I looked up into the yawning empty space of the bell tower, remembering.

Going round the rood screen, I saw the lecterns and even the great organ had been removed. I shook my head and turned to leave.

Then I saw a cowled figure sitting in a corner of the choir stall, facing away from me. For a moment I felt a thrill of superstitious dread as I imagined Gabriel returned to mourn the ruin of his life's work. The figure turned and I almost cried out, for at first I could see no face under the hood, but then I made out the gaunt brown features of Brother Guy. He rose and bowed.

'Brother infirmarian,' I said, 'for a moment I thought you were a ghost.'

He smiled sadly. 'In a way I am.'

I approached and sat down, motioning him to join me. 'I am glad to see you,' he said. 'I wanted to thank you for my pension, Master Shardlake. I imagine it was you who saw I was given an increased allowance.'

'You *were* elected abbot, after all, when Abbot Fabian was declared incapable. You are entitled to a larger allowance, even if you only held the post a few weeks.'

'Prior Mortimus was not pleased when the brethren elected me over him. He has gone back to schoolmastering, you know, in Devon.'

'May God have mercy on his charges.'

'I wondered whether it was right to take the larger sum, when the brethren have to live on five pounds a year. But they would have been given no more had I refused. And with my face I will not have an easy time of it in the world. I think I will keep my monastic name of Guy of Malton rather than revert to my worldly surname of Elakbar – I am allowed to do that, even if "Brother" is forbidden?'

'Of course.'

'Do not look shamefaced, my friend – you are my friend, I think?'

I nodded. 'Yes, I am. Believe me, being sent back here now is no pleasure to me, I have no more wish to be a commissioner.' I shivered. 'It is cold.'

Guy nodded. 'Yes. I have sat here too long. I have been thinking of the monks who sat in these stalls every day for four hundred years, chanting and praying. The venal, the lazy, the devoted, those who were all those things. But –' he pointed up at the clanging, clattering roof – 'it is hard to concentrate.'

As we looked upwards there came a loud hammer blow and a shower of dust. Lumps of plaster fell to the floor with a crash and suddenly daylight streamed in from a hole, a shaft of sunlight spearing to the floor. 'We're through, bullies,' a voice echoed from above. 'Careful there!'

Guy made a strange sound, somewhere between a sigh and a groan. I touched his arm. 'We should go. More plaster will be coming down.'

Outside in the courtyard his face was bleak but composed. Copynger nodded coldly to him as we began walking away towards the abbot's house.

'When the monks left at the end of November Sir Gilbert asked me to stay on,' Guy told me. 'He'd been put in charge of minding the place till Portinari could get here and he asked me to help. The fish pond flooded badly in January, you know; I was able to help him drain it.'

'It must have been hard, living alone here with everyone gone.'

'Not really, not until the Augmentations men came this week and started clearing the place. Somehow it felt, over the winter, as though the house was only waiting for the monks to come back.' He winced as a great chunk of lead crashed to the ground behind us.

'You hoped for a reprieve?'

He shrugged. 'One always hopes. Besides, I had nowhere to go. I have been waiting all this time to hear if I am to be allowed a permit to leave for France.'

'I might be able to help with that, if there is delay.'

He shook his head. 'No. I heard a week ago. I have been refused. There is talk of a new alliance between France and Spain against England, I believe. I had better see if I can exchange this habit for a doublet and hose. It will be strange after all these years. And grow my hair!' He lowered his hood and ran his hand over his bald crown. I saw the fringe of black hair was tinged with white now.

'What will you do?'

'I want to leave in the next few days. I could not bear to be here when they demolish the buildings. The whole town is coming; they are making a fair of it. How they must have hated us.' He sighed. 'I may go to London, where exotic faces are not so rare.'

'You could perhaps become a physician there? You have a degree from Louvain, after all.'

'But would the College of Physicians let me in? Or even the Guild of Apothecaries? A mud-coloured ex-monk?' He raised an eyebrow and smiled sadly.

'I have a client who is a physician. I could plead your cause.'

He hesitated, then smiled. 'Thank you. I would be grateful.'

'And I could help you find accommodation. I will give you my address before you leave. Call on me. Will you?'

'Might not associating with me be risky?'

'I will not work for Cromwell again. I will go back to private practice, live quietly, perhaps paint.'

'Be careful, Matthew.' He glanced over his shoulder. 'I am not sure it is wise even for you to be seen having an amicable talk with me, under Sir Gilbert's eyes.'

'Rot Copynger. I know enough never to do anything that breaks the law. And though I may not be the reformer I was, I am not turned papist either.'

'That does not protect people in these days.'

'Perhaps not. But if no one is safe, which indeed they are not, at least I can be unsafe minding my own business at home.'

We reached the abbot's house, now Copynger's. A gardener was carefully tending the roses, spreading horse dung round the bushes.

'Has Copynger rented much land?' I asked.

'A lot, yes, and at a low rent.'

'He has been lucky.'

'And you have no reward?'

'No. I got Cromwell his murderer, and his stolen gold, and this place surrendered; but not quickly enough.' I paused, remembering those who had died. 'No indeed, not quickly enough.'

'You did all any man could.'

'Perhaps. You know, I often think I might have seen to the depths of what Edwig was had I not disliked him so much, and therefore tried doubly hard to be fair, and certain. Even now I find it hard to realize that that man, so precise and orderly, was so wild and deranged underneath. I wonder if he used that order, that obsession with figures and money, as a way to keep himself under control. I wonder if he feared his dreams of blood.'

'I pray so.'

'But that obsession with figures only fed his madness in the end.' I sighed. 'Uncovering complicated truths is never easy.'

Guy nodded. 'It takes patience, courage, effort. If the truth is what you wish to find.'

'You know Jerome is dead?'

'No. I have had no news since he was taken away last November.'

'Cromwell had him put in Newgate gaol. Where his brethren were starved to death. He died soon after.'

'May God rest his tortured soul.' Brother Guy paused, looking at me hesitantly. 'Do you know what became of the hand of the Penitent Thief? They took it at the same time as Jerome.'

'No. I imagine the precious stones were taken out and the reliquary melted down. The hand itself will probably have been burned by now.'

'It *was* the Thief's hand, you know. The evidence is very strong.'

'Do you still think it could work miracles?'

He did not answer and we walked on in silence for a moment, into the monks' cemetery, where the men were lifting the stones. I saw that in the lay churchyard the family vaults had been broken up into piles of rubble.

'Tell me,' I said at length. 'What has become of Abbot Fabian? I know he was not allowed an abbot's pension as he did not sign the surrender.'

Guy shook his head sadly. 'His sister has taken him in. She is a seamstress in the town. He is no better. Some days he talks of going hunting or visiting with the local landowners and she has to prevent him setting off in the poor clothes that are all he has now, on their old nag. I have prescribed him some medicines, but they do no good. His wits are gone.'

'"How are the mighty fallen",' I quoted.

I realized that unconsciously I had been leading us towards the orchard; the rear wall of the monastery was visible ahead. I paused, a churning feeling in my stomach.

'Shall we go back?' Guy asked gently.

'No. Let us go on.'

We walked to the gate that led to the marsh. I had a set of keys and opened it. We passed through and stood looking out over the bleak landscape. The November flood had long since drained away and the marsh lay brown and silent, clumps of reeds waving quietly in the breeze, their image reflected in stagnant pools. The river was at full tide; seabirds bobbed on the waters, feathers ruffled by the wind from the sea.

I spoke quietly. 'They come to me in dreams, Mark and Alice. I see them struggling in the water, sinking down, crying for help. I wake up screaming sometimes.' My voice broke. 'In different ways I loved them both.'

Brother Guy looked at me for a long moment, then reached into his habit. He passed me a folded paper, much creased.

'I have thought hard about whether to show this to you. I wondered if it might hurt you less not to see.'

'What is it?'

'It appeared on the desk in my dispensary a month ago. I came in from my duties and there it was. I think a smuggler bribed one of Copynger's men to leave it for me. It is from her, but written by him.'

I opened the letter and read, in Mark Poer's clear round hand:

Brother Guy,

I have asked Mark to write this for me as his lettering is better than mine. I send it by a man of the town who comes sometimes to France, it is better you know not who.

I pray you to forgive me for writing to you. Mark and I are safe in France, I will not say where. I do not know how we came through the mire that night, once Mark fell in and I had to haul him out, but we reached the boat.

We were married last month. Mark knows some French and improves so fast, we hope he may obtain a clerkly post in this little town. We are happy, and I begin to feel a peace I have not known since my cousin died, though whether the world will allow us rest in these times I do not know.

There is no reason, sir, why you should care for any of this, but I wished you to know it was a bitter thing for me to have to deceive you, who protected me and taught me so much. I regret it, though I do not regret I killed that man; he deserved to die if ever a man did. I do not know where you will go in the world, but I beg Our Lord, Jesus Christ to watch over and protect you, sir.

Alice Poer.

The twenty-fifth day of January, 1538

I folded the letter and stood looking out over the estuary.

'They do not mention me at all.'

'It was from her to me. They were not to know I would see you again.'

'So they are alive and safe, pox on them. Perhaps now my dreams will stop. May I tell Mark's father? He was sore grieved. Just that I have secret word he is alive?'

'Of course.'

'She is right, there is nowhere safe in the world now, no thing certain. Sometimes I think of Brother Edwig and his madness, how he thought he could buy God's forgiveness for those murders with two panniers of stolen gold. Perhaps we are all a little mad. The Bible says God made man in his image but I think we make and remake him, in whatever image happens to suit our shifting needs. I wonder if he knows or cares. All is dissolving, Brother Guy, all is dissolution.'

We stood silent, watching the seabirds bobbing on the river, while behind us echoed the distant sound of crashing lead.

HISTORICAL NOTE

The dissolution of the English monasteries in 1536–40 was masterminded throughout by Thomas Cromwell as vice regent and vicar general. After conducting a survey of the monasteries, during which much damaging material was collected, Cromwell introduced an Act of Parliament dissolving the smaller monasteries in 1536. However, when his agents began carrying it into effect the result was 'The Pilgrimage of Grace', a massive armed rebellion in the north of England. Henry VIII and Cromwell put it down by tricking the leaders into negotiations until they had time to build up an army to destroy them.

The assault on the larger monasteries came a year later with pressure, as described in the story, being placed on vulnerable larger houses to surrender voluntarily. The intimidation into surrender of Lewes Priory in November 1537 was crucial and over the next three years, one by one, all the monasteries surrendered to the king. By 1540 there were none left; the buildings were left to decay, the lead stripped from the roof by the Augmentations men. The monks were pensioned off. If they resisted, as a few did, they were dealt with savagely. The average abbot and monastery official was undoubtedly more frightened of the commissioners, who were indeed brutal men, than the monks of Scarnsea are of Shardlake. But then Scarnsea is not an average monastery, and nor is Shardlake an average commissioner.

It is generally accepted that the accusations of multiple adultery against Queen Anne Boleyn were fabricated by Cromwell for Henry VIII, who had tired of her. Mark Smeaton was the only one of her alleged lovers to confess, probably on the rack. His father was a carpenter; I have invented his previous occupation as a swordsmith.

The English Reformation remains controversial. The view of older historians, that the Catholic Church was so decayed that some sort of radical reformation was necessary if not inevitable, has recently been challenged by a number of writers, notably C. Haigh, *English Reformations* (Oxford University Press, 1993), and E. Duffy, *The Stripping of the Altars* (Yale University Press, 1992), who paint a picture of a thriving, popular Church. I think Duffy especially over-romanticizes medieval Catholic life; it is interesting that these scholars hardly mention the Dissolution, the last major study of which was by David Knowles in the 1950s, *The Religious Orders in England: The Tudor Age* (Cambridge University Press, 1959). In this exceptional work Professor Knowles, who was himself a Catholic monk, acknowledges that the easy living prevailing in most of the larger monasteries was a scandal. While deploring their forcible extinction, Professor Knowles considers that they had become so remote from their founding ideals that they did not deserve to survive in their existing form.

Nobody really knows what the English people as a whole thought of the Reformation. There was a strong Protestant movement in London and parts of the south-east; the north and the West Country remained strongly Catholic. But the country in between, where most people lived, is still largely *terra incognita*. My own view is that the bulk of the common people probably saw the successive changes imposed from above in the same way as Mark and Alice; just that, changes ordered from above by the ruling classes, who told them what to do and how to think, as they always had. There were so many changes – first to an increasingly radical Protestantism, then back to Catholicism under Mary Tudor and back again to Protestantism under Elizabeth I – that people can hardly have failed to become cynical. They kept quiet, for of course nobody was interested in what they thought, and while Elizabeth may not have wished to make windows into men's souls, her predecessors did, with fire and axe.

Those who benefited most from the Reformation were the 'new men', the emerging capitalist and bureaucratic classes, men of property without birth. I think there were many Copyngers in mid-Tudor England; the Reformation was about a changing class structure as much as anything. That is an unfashionable view nowadays; it is naughty to mention class when discussing history. But fashions have changed, and will again.

**C. J. Sansom's fifth Matthew Shardlake mystery
is available from Penguin Books**

Read on for the first chapter of . . .

THE #1 INTERNATIONAL BESTSELLER

C. J.
SANSOM

author of *Dissolution* and *Revelation*

Heartstone

*A Matthew
Shardlake*
Tudor
Mystery

"[A] knock-your-socks-off novel."
—Patrick Anderson, *The Washington Post*

Chapter One

THE CHURCHYARD was peaceful in the summer afternoon. Twigs and branches lay strewn across the gravel path, torn from the trees by the gales which had swept the country in that stormy June of 1545. In London we had escaped lightly, only a few chimneypots gone, but the winds had wreaked havoc in the north. People spoke of hailstones there as large as fists, with the shapes of faces on them. But tales become more dramatic as they spread, as any lawyer knows.

I had been in my chambers in Lincoln's Inn all morning, working through some new briefs for cases in the Court of Requests. They would not be heard until the autumn now; the Trinity law term had ended early by order of the King, in view of the threat of invasion.

In recent months I had found myself becoming restless with my paperwork. With a few exceptions the same cases came up again and again in Requests: landlords wanting to turn tenant farmers off their lands to pasture sheep for the profitable wool trade, or for the same reason trying to appropriate the village commons on which the poor depended. Worthy cases, but always the same. And as I worked, my eyes kept drifting to the letter delivered by a messenger from Hampton Court. It lay on the corner of my desk, a white rectangle with a lump of red sealing wax glinting in the centre. The letter worried me, all the more for its lack of detail. Eventually, unable to keep my thoughts from wandering, I decided to go for a walk.

When I left chambers I saw a flower seller, a young woman, had got past the Lincoln's Inn gatekeeper. She stood in a corner of

Gatehouse Court, in a grey dress with a dirty apron, her face framed by a white coif, holding out posies to the passing barristers. As I went by she called out that she was a widow, her husband dead in the war. I saw she had wallflowers in her basket; they reminded me I had not visited my poor housekeeper's grave for nearly a month, for wallflowers had been Joan's favourite. I asked for a bunch, and she held them out to me with a work-roughened hand. I passed her a halfpenny; she curtsied and thanked me graciously, though her eyes were cold. I walked on, under the Great Gate and up newly paved Chancery Lane to the little church at the top.

As I walked I chided myself for my discontent, reminding myself that many of my colleagues envied my position as counsel at the Court of Requests, and that I also had the occasional lucrative case put my way by the Queen's solicitor. But, as the many thoughtful and worried faces I passed in the street reminded me, the times were enough to make any man's mind unquiet. They said the French had gathered thirty thousand men in their Channel ports, ready to invade England in a great fleet of warships, some even with stables on board for horses. No one knew where they might land, and throughout the country men were being mustered and sent to defend the coasts. Every vessel in the King's fleet had put to sea, and large merchant ships were being impounded and made ready for war. The King had levied unprecedented taxes to pay for his invasion of France the previous year. It had been a complete failure and since last winter an English army had been besieged in Boulogne. And now the war might be coming to us.

I passed into the churchyard. However much one lacks piety, the atmosphere in a graveyard encourages quiet reflection. I knelt and laid the flowers on Joan's grave. She had run my little household near twenty years; when she first came to me she had been a widow of forty and I a callow, recently qualified barrister. A widow with no family, she had devoted her life to looking after my needs; quiet, efficient, kindly. She had caught influenza in the spring and been dead in a week. I missed her deeply, all the more because I realized how all these years I had taken her devoted care for granted. The contrast with the wretch I now had for a steward was bitter.

I stood up with a sigh, my knees cracking. Visiting the grave had quieted me, but stirred those melancholy humours to which I was naturally prey. I walked on among the headstones, for there were others I had known who lay buried here. I paused before a fine marble stone:

ROGER ELLIARD
BARRISTER OF LINCOLN'S INN
BELOVED HUSBAND AND FATHER
1502–1543

I remembered a conversation Roger and I had had, shortly before his death two years before, and smiled sadly. We had talked of how the King had wasted the riches he had gained from the monasteries, spending them on palaces and display, doing nothing to replace the limited help the monks had given the poor. I laid a hand on the stone and said quietly, 'Ah, Roger, if you could see what he has brought us to now.' An old woman arranging flowers on a grave nearby looked round at me, an anxious frown on her wrinkled face at the sight of a hunchbacked lawyer talking to the dead. I moved away.

A little way off stood another headstone, one which, like Joan's, I had had set in that place, with but a short inscription;

GILES WRENNE
BARRISTER OF YORK
1467–1541

That headstone I did not touch, nor did I address the old man who lay beneath, but I remembered how Giles had died and realized that indeed I was inviting a black mood to descend on me.

Then a sudden blaring noise startled me almost out of my wits. The old woman stood and stared around her, wide-eyed. I guessed what must be happening. I walked over to the wall separating the churchyard from Lincoln's Inn Fields and opened the wooden gate. I stepped through, and looked at the scene beyond.

✝

LINCOLN'S INN FIELDS was an empty, open space of heathland, where law students hunted rabbits on the grassy hill of Coney Garth. Normally on a Tuesday afternoon there would have been only a few people passing to and fro. Today, though, a crowd was gathered, watching as fifty young men, many in shirts and jerkins but some in the blue robes of apprentices, stood in five untidy rows. Some looked sulky, some apprehensive, some eager. Most carried the warbows that men of military age were required to own by law for the practice of archery, though many disobeyed the rule, preferring the bowling greens or the dice and cards that were illegal now for those without gentleman status. The warbows were two yards long, taller than their owners for the most part. Some men, though, carried smaller bows, a few of inferior elm rather than yew. Nearly all wore leather bracers on one arm, finger guards on the hand of the other. Their bows were strung ready for use.

The men were being shepherded into rows of ten by a middle-aged soldier with a square face, a short black beard and a sternly disapproving expression. He was resplendent in the uniform of the London Trained Bands, a white doublet with sleeves and upper hose slashed to reveal the red lining beneath, and a round, polished helmet.

Over two hundred yards away stood the butts, turfed earthen mounds six feet high. Here men eligible for service were supposed to practise every Sunday. Squinting, I made out a straw dummy, dressed in tatters of clothing, fixed there, a battered helmet on its head and a crude French fleur-de-lys painted on the front. I realized this was another View of Arms, that more city men were having their skills tested to select those who would be sent to the armies converging on the coast or to the King's ships. I was glad that, as a hunchback of forty-three, I was exempt from military service.

A plump little man on a fine grey mare watched the men shuffling into place. The horse, draped in City of London livery, wore a metal face plate with holes for its eyes that made its head resemble a skull. The rider wore half-armour, his arms and upper body encased in polished steel, a peacock feather in his wide black cap stirring in the breeze. I recognized Edmund Carver, one of the city's senior aldermen; I had won a case for him in court two years before. He looked uneasy in his armour, shifting awkwardly on his horse. He was a decent enough fellow, from the Mercers' Guild, whose main interest I remembered as fine dining. Beside him stood two more soldiers in Trained Bands uniform, one holding a long brass trumpet and the other a halberd. Nearby a clerk in a black doublet stood, a portable desk with a sheaf of papers set on it slung round his neck.

The soldier with the halberd laid down his weapon and picked up half a dozen leather arrowbags. He ran along the front row of recruits, spilling out a line of arrows on the ground. The soldier in charge was still casting sharp, appraising eyes over the men. I guessed he was a professional officer, such as I had encountered on the King's Great Progress to York four years before. He was probably working with the Trained Bands now, a corps of volunteer soldiers set up in London a few years ago who practised soldiers' craft at week's end.

He spoke to the men, in a loud, carrying voice. 'England needs men to serve in her hour of greatest peril! The French stand ready to invade, to rain down fire and destruction on our women and children. But we remember Agincourt!' He paused dramatically: Carver shouted, 'Ay!', followed by the recruits.

The officer continued. 'We know from Agincourt that one Englishman is worth three Frenchmen, and we shall send our legendary archers to meet them! Those chosen today will get a coat, and thruppence a day!' His tone hardened. 'Now we shall see which of you lads have been practising weekly as the law requires, and which have not. Those who have not – ' he paused for dramatic effect – 'may find themselves levied instead to be pikemen, to face the French at close quarters! So don't think a weak performance will save you from going to war.' He ran his eye over the men, who shuffled and looked uneasy. There was something heavy and angry in the officer's dark-bearded face.

'Now,' he called, 'when the trumpet sounds again, each man will shoot six arrows at the target, as fast as you can, starting with the left of the front row. We've prepared a dummy specially for you, so you can pretend it's a Frenchy come to ravish your mothers, if you have mothers!'

I glanced at the watching crowd. There were excited urchins and some older folk of the poorer sort, but also several anxious-looking young women, maybe wives or sweethearts of the men called here.

The soldier with the trumpet raised it to his lips and blew again. The first man, a thickset, handsome young fellow in a leather jerkin, stepped forward confidently with his warbow. He picked up an arrow and nocked it to the bow. Then in a quick, fluid movement he leaned back, straightened, and sent the arrow flying in a great arc across the wide space. It thudded into the fleur-de-lys on the scarecrow with a force that made it judder like a living thing. In no more than a minute he had strung and loosed five more arrows, all of which hit the dummy. There was a ragged cheer from the children. He smiled and flexed his broad shoulders.

'Not bad!' the officer called grudgingly. 'Go and get your name registered!' The new recruit walked over to the clerk, waving his warbow at the crowd.

A tall, loose-limbed young fellow in a white shirt, who looked barely twenty, was next. He had only an elm bow, and an anxious look. I noticed he wore neither bracer nor finger guard. The officer looked at him grimly as he pushed a hank of untidy blond hair from his eyes, then bent, took an arrow, and fitted it to the string. He pulled the bow back with obvious effort and loosed. The arrow fell well short, thudding into the grass. Pulling the bow had set him off-balance and he nearly fell, hopping on one leg for a moment and making the children laugh.

The second arrow went wide, embedding itself in the side of the butts, and the young man cried out, doubling over with pain and holding one hand with the other. Blood trickled between his fingers. The officer gave him a grim look. 'Haven't been practising, have you? Can't even loose an arrow properly. You're going to the pikemen, you are! A tall fellow like you will be useful in close combat.' The lad looked frightened. 'Come on,' the officer shouted, 'you've four more arrows still to loose. Never mind your hand. This crowd look like they could do with a laugh.'

I turned away. I had myself once been humiliated in front of a crowd and it was not something I relished seeing others endure.

♱

BACK IN Gatehouse Court the flower seller was gone. I went into chambers, where my young clerk Skelly was copying out some orders in the outer office. He was bent closely over his desk, peering carefully at the document through his glasses.

'There is a View of Arms over at Lincoln's Inn Fields,' I told him.

He looked up. 'I've heard the Trained Bands have to find a thousand men for the south coast,' he said in his quiet voice. 'Do you think the French are really going to invade, sir?'

'I don't know, Skelly.' I smiled reassuringly. 'But you won't be called. You've a wife and three children, and you need your glasses to see.'

'So I hope and pray, sir.'

'I am sure.' But these days one never knew.

'Is Barak not back from Westminster?' I asked, glancing over at my assistant's vacant desk. I had sent him to the Requests Office to lodge some depositions.

'No, sir.'

I frowned. 'I hope Tamasin is all right.'

Skelly smiled. 'I'm sure it is only a delay getting a wherry on the river, sir. You know how busy it is with supply boats.'

'Perhaps. Tell Barak to come and see me when he returns. I must go back to my papers.' I went through to my office, little doubting Skelly thought me over-anxious. But Barak and his wife Tamasin were dear friends. Tamasin was expecting a baby in two months, and her first child had been born dead. I dropped into my chair with a sigh and picked up the particulars of a claim I had been reading earlier. My eyes wandered again to the letter on the corner of the desk. I made myself look away, but soon my thoughts returned to the View of Arms: I thought of invasion, of those young men ripped apart and slaughtered in battle.

I looked out of the window, then smiled and shook my head as I saw the tall, skinny figure of my old enemy, Stephen Bealknap, walking across the sunlit court. He had acquired a stoop now, and in his black barrister's robe and white coif he looked like a huge magpie, seeking worms on the ground.

Bealknap suddenly straightened and stared ahead, and I saw Barak walking across the court towards him, his leather bag slung over one shoulder. I noticed my assistant's stomach bulged now against his green doublet. His face was acquiring a little plumpness too that softened his features and made him look younger. Bealknap turned and walked rapidly away towards the chapel. That strange, miserly man had, two years ago, got himself indebted to me for a small amount. Normally bold as brass, Bealknap, for whom it was a point of pride never to part with money, would turn and hasten away if ever he saw me. It was a standing joke at Lincoln's Inn. Evidently he was avoiding Barak now too. My assistant paused and grinned broadly at Bealknap's back as he scuttled away. I felt relieved; obviously nothing had happened to Tamasin.

A few minutes later he joined me in my office. 'All well with the depositions?' I asked.

'Yes, but it was hard to get a boat from Westminster stairs. The river's packed with cogs taking supplies to the armies, the wherries had to pull in to the bank to make way. One of the big warships was down by the Tower, too. I think they sailed it up from Deptford so the people could see it. But I didn't hear any cheering from the banks.'

'People are used to them now. It was different when the *Mary Rose* and the *Great Harry* sailed out; hundreds lined the banks to cheer.' I waved at the stool in front of my desk. 'Come, sit down. How is Tamasin today?'

He sat and smiled wryly. 'Grumpy. Feeling the heat, and her feet are swollen.'

'Still sure the child's a girl?'

'Ay. She consulted some wise woman touting for business in Cheapside yesterday, who told her what she wanted to hear, of course.'

'And you are still as sure the child's a boy?'

'I am.' He shook his head. 'Tammy insists on carrying on as usual. I tell her ladies of good class take to their chambers eight weeks before the birth. I thought that might give her pause but it didn't.'

'Is it eight weeks now?'

'So Guy says. He's coming to visit her tomorrow. Still, she has Goodwife Marris to look after her. Tammy was glad to see me go to work. She says I fuss.'

I smiled. I knew Barak and Tamasin were happy now. After the death of their first child there had been a bad time, and Tamasin had left him. But he had won her back with a steady, loving persistence I would once not have thought him capable of. I had helped them find a little house nearby, and a capable servant in Joan's friend Goodwife Marris, who had worked as a wet nurse and was used to children.

I nodded at the window. 'I saw Bealknap turn to avoid you.'

He laughed. 'He's started doing that lately. He fears I'm going to ask him for that three pounds he owes you. Stupid arsehole.' His eyes glinted wickedly. 'You should ask him for four, seeing how the value of money's fallen.'

'You know, I sometimes wonder if friend Bealknap is quite sane. Two years now he has made a fool and mock of himself by avoiding me, and now you too.'

'And all the while he gets richer. They say he sold some of that gold he has to the Mint for the recoinage, and that he is lending more out to people looking for money to pay the taxes, now that lending at interest has been made legal.'

'There are some at Lincoln's Inn who have needed to do that to pay the Benevolence. Thank God I had enough gold. Yet the way Bealknap behaves does not show a balanced mind.'

Barak gave me a penetrating look. 'You've become too ready to see madness in people. It's because you give so much time to Ellen Fettiplace. Have you answered her latest message?'

I made an impatient gesture. 'Let's not go over that again. I have, and I will go to the Bedlam tomorrow.'

'Bedlamite she may be, but she plays you like a fisherman pulling on a line.' Barak looked at me seriously. 'You know why.'

I changed the subject. 'I went for a walk earlier. There was a View of Arms in Lincoln's Inn Fields. The officer was threatening to make pikemen of those who hadn't been practising their archery.'

Barak answered contemptuously, 'They know as well as anyone that only those who like archery practise it regularly, for all the laws the King makes. It's hard work and you've got to keep at it to be any good.' He gave me a serious look. 'It's no good making laws too unpopular to be enforced. Lord Cromwell knew that, he knew where to draw the line.'

'They're enforcing this. I've never seen anything like it before. And yesterday I saw the constables sweeping the streets for the beggars and vagabonds the King's ordered to be sent to row on the galleasses. Have you heard the latest word – that French troops have landed in Scotland and the Scots are ready to fall on us too?'

'The latest word,' Barak repeated scoffingly. 'Who sets these stories running about the French and Scots about to invade? The King's officials, that's who. Maybe to stop the people rebelling like they did in '36. Against the taxes and the debasement of the currency. Here, look at this.' His hand went to his purse. He took out a little silver coin and smacked it down on the desk. I picked it up. The King's fat jowly face stared up at me.

'One of the new shilling coins,' Barak said. 'A testoon.'

'I haven't seen one before.'

'Tamasin went shopping with Goodwife Marris yesterday in Cheapside. There's plenty there. Look at its dull colour. The silver's so adulterated with copper they'll only give eightpence worth of goods for it. Prices for bread and meat are going through the roof. Not that there is much bread, with so much being requisitioned for the army.' Barak's brown eyes flashed angrily. 'And where's the extra silver gone? To repay those German bankers who lent the King money for the war.'

'You really think there may be no French invasion fleet at all?'

'Maybe. I don't know.' He hesitated, then said suddenly, 'I think they're trying to get me for the army.'

'What?' I sat bolt upright.

'The constable was going round all the houses in the ward last Friday with some soldier, registering all men of military age. I told them I'd a wife and a child on the way. The soldier said I looked a fit man. I flipped my fingers at him and told him to piss off. Trouble is Tamasin told me he came back yesterday. She saw him through the window and didn't answer the door.'

I sighed. 'Your over-confidence will be the end of you one day.'

'That's what Tamasin says. But they're not taking married man with children. Or at least, not many.'

'The powers that be are serious. I think there is going to be an invasion attempt, or why recruit all these thousands of soldiers? You should take care.'

Barak looked mutinous. 'None of this would be happening if the King hadn't invaded France last year. Forty thousand men sent over the Channel, and what happened? We were sent running back with our tails between our legs, except for the poor sods besieged in Boulogne. Everyone says we should cut our losses, abandon Boulogne and make peace, but the King won't. Not our Harry.'

'I know. I agree.'

'Remember last autumn, the soldiers back from France lying in rags, plague-ridden, on all the roads to the city?' His face set hard. 'Well, that won't happen to me.'

I looked at my assistant. There had been a time when Barak might have seen war as an adventure. But not now. 'What did this soldier look like?'

'Big fellow your age with a black beard, done up in a London Trained Bands uniform. Looked as if he'd seen service.'

'He was in charge of the View of Arms. I'd guess a professional officer. No man to cross, I'd say.'

'Well, if he's viewing all the mustered men, hopefully he'll be too busy to bother any more with me.'

'I hope so. If he does return, you must come to me.'

'Thank you,' he said quietly.

I reached for the letter on the corner of my desk. 'In return, I'd like your view on this.' I handed it to him.

'Not *another* message from Ellen?'

'Look at the seal. It's one you've seen before.'

He looked up. 'The Queen's. Is it from Master Warner? Another case?'

'Read it.' I hesitated. 'It worries me.'

Barak unfolded the letter, and read aloud.

'I would welcome your personal counsel on a case, a private matter. I invite you to attend me here at Hampton Court, at three o'clock tomorrow afternoon.'

'It's signed—'

'I know. Catherine the Queen, not lawyer Warner.'

Barak read it again. 'It's short enough. But she says it's a case. No sign it's anything political.'

'But it must be something that affects her closely for her to write herself. I can't help remembering last year when the Queen sent Warner to represent that relative of her servant who was accused of heresy.'

'She promised she would keep you out of things like that. And she's one who keeps her promises.'

I nodded. More than two years before, when Queen Catherine

Parr was still Lady Latimer, I had saved her life. She had promised both to be my patron and never to involve me in matters of politics.

'How long is it since you saw her?' Barak asked.

'Not since the spring. She granted me an audience at Whitehall to thank me for sorting out that tangled case about her Midland properties. Then she sent me her book of prayers last month. You remember, I showed you. *Prayers and Meditations*.'

He pulled a face. 'Gloomy stuff.'

I smiled sadly. 'Yes, it was. I had not realized how much sadness there was in her. She put in a personal note saying she hoped it would turn my mind to God.'

'She'd never put you in harm's way. It'll be another land case, you'll see.'

I smiled gratefully. Barak had known the underside of the political world from his earliest days, and I valued his reassurance.

'The Queen and Ellen Fettiplace in one day!' he said jokingly. 'You will have a busy day.'

'Yes.' I took the letter back. Remembering the last time I had visited Hampton Court, the thought of presenting myself there again set a knot of fear twisting in my stomach.

MORE FROM C. J. SANSOM IN
THE MATTHEW SHARDLAKE SERIES

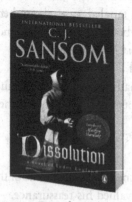

Dissolution
ISBN 978-0-14-200430-2

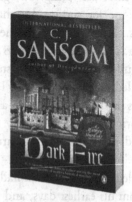

Dark Fire
ISBN 978-0-14-303643-2

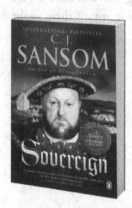

Sovereign
ISBN 978-0-14-311317-1

Revelation
ISBN 978-0-14-311624-0

Heartstone
ISBN 978-0-14-312065-0

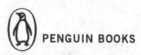

PENGUIN BOOKS